THE SERPENT'S TOOTH

MICHELLE PAVER

BANTAM PRESS

LONDON • TORONTO • SYDNEY • AUCKLAND • JOHANNESBURG

TRANSWORLD PUBLISHERS
61–63 Uxbridge Road, London W5 5SA
a division of The Random House Group Ltd

RANDOM HOUSE AUSTRALIA (PTY) LTD
20 Alfred Street, Milsons Point, Sydney,
New South Wales 2061, Australia

RANDOM HOUSE NEW ZEALAND LTD
18 Poland Road, Glenfield, Auckland 10, New Zealand

RANDOM HOUSE SOUTH AFRICA (PTY) LTD
Endulini, 5a Jubilee Road, Parktown 2193, South Africa

Published 2005 by Bantam Press
a division of Transworld Publishers

A catalogue record for this book is available from the British Library.
ISBN 0593 05394X

Typeset in 12/14pt Bembo by
Falcon Oast Graphic Art Ltd.

Printed in Great Britain by
Mackays of Chatham plc, Chatham, Kent

1 3 5 7 9 10 8 6 4 2

Papers used by Transworld Publishers are natural, recyclable products made from wood grown in sustainable forests. The manufacturing processes conform to the environmental regulations of the country of origin.

THE SERPENT'S TOOTH

PART ONE

CHAPTER ONE

Eden Estate, Jamaica, 1912

Belle had never wanted anything so much as the black onyx inkstand. Lyndon Traherne said she'd never win it because she was only a girl, but he was wrong. She would take first prize from right under his nose, and present the inkstand to Papa, and together they would place it on his desk, where it belonged.

Papa absolutely deserved the best. He was always working on the estate – at the boiling-house or in the cane-pieces – but however late he got home he always came in to kiss her goodnight. She would pretend to be asleep, and wait for the scratch of his whiskers, and his smell of horses and burnt sugar. And whenever she had the nightmare she would pad across to his study, and he would give her a thimbleful of rum and water and a puff at his cigar. Then she'd curl up on the Turkey rug beneath the oil painting of the big house in Scotland, and ask him impossible questions about robins and snow.

So the first prize in the Historical Society Juvenile Fancy Dress Ball *had* to be hers. Her costume had to be the best in Trelawny. Best on the Northside. Best in Jamaica.

To create a sense of drama, she announced that she'd be going as a fairy, when in fact she intended to make a surprise entrance as the Devil. She'd worked it all out. Saved her pocket money, and secretly bought a remnant of crimson sari silk at Falmouth market. She had every detail clear in her mind: the horns, the tail, the flickering flames of Hell. It would be *perfection*.

The day before the party found her furious and tearful amid a storm of botched fragments and crumpled fencing-wire horns.

Her mother came in, and gave her a long, steady look. 'Why didn't you ask me for help?' she said quietly.

'Because I wanted to do it myself!'

Her mother bit her lip and studied the remains. She looked tired, her dark hair coming down from her chignon in wisps. This was the first time she had hosted the Juvenile Ball, and she wanted it to be a success. But their house at Eden wasn't really big enough, so they'd had to move the furniture off the verandah, and erect an awning in the garden. She'd been working for days. And the twins were colicky, which didn't help.

Belle felt a pang of guilt at giving her this added trouble. 'It doesn't matter,' she muttered, aiming a kick at a nearby horn. 'It's my fault for choosing the Devil. I'll just go as a wretched fairy.'

Her mother stooped and picked up a scrap of sari silk. 'You always punish yourself.'

Belle thrust out her lower lip. 'Well, because I deserve it.'

'No you don't. We can use my old dressing gown. The one Papa bought in Kingston that was a mistake? And these can be flames.' She picked up the sari silk. 'A nice, fiery ruff to hide that new bosom you're so embarrassed about.'

Belle's face burned. She'd been worrying about that.

'But you'll have to help,' said her mother. 'You do the horns, the tail, and the hooves.'

'*Hooves?*' said Belle.

'Well, of course. All devils have hooves.'

Somehow, it was finished in time – and it was magnificent. Layer on layer of spangled scarlet flames. Plump red felt horns fixed to an Alice band. Cunning little hooves of crimson satin which fitted over her button boots like demonic spats. And best of all, a three-pronged tail that would be perfect for spiking air-balls, and Lyndon Traherne's pride.

Then, on the morning of the party, disaster struck. Belle got her monthly cramps – what her mother called her *petit ami*.

An odd name for bleeding and stomach ache and appalling embarrassment.

She told her parents that she had a headache, and sneaked a Dover's powder from the bath-house cupboard. She didn't want *anyone* to know. She hated the idea of growing up.

'But you're nearly fourteen,' her mother would say when she was trying to persuade Belle into grown-up combinations, or gently mooting the notion of school in England.

'Thirteen and five months,' Belle would snap back. 'That's nowhere near fourteen.' But even thirteen sounded too old.

She lay curled on her bed, watching the tree-ferns dip and sway against the louvres, and listening to the slap of the servants' slippers and the *chup-chup-zi* of the sugarquits under the eaves.

She felt sore and churned up inside. And that wasn't the worst of it. Ever since she'd started getting the cramps, she'd developed a terrible compulsion: an irresistible urge to picture every man she saw without any clothes. It didn't matter who it was. Old Braverly the cook. Her dashing uncle Ben. Even *Papa*.

And she knew very well *what* to imagine, because last year she'd seen a group of field hands cooling off at the swimming-hole by the Arethusa Road. At the time, they'd looked so happy that she'd simply envied them their freedom. But a few months later, when the cramps started to come, the memory had returned to haunt her. It was awful. Shameful. There must be something wrong with her.

She slept away the morning, and felt a little better, and got dressed and went to the party.

She didn't win.

Everyone agreed that hers was by far the best costume. Better than Dodo Cornwallis's genial, large-footed fairy; better than Sissy Irving's slyly pretty little Pierrot; better even than Lyndon Traherne's steeplechase jockey, in genuine racing silks made specially for him, with real spurs and soft boots of Italian kid.

But it was Lyndon who won.

'Because,' said old Mrs Pitcaithley, the senior judge, 'boys can be jockeys, but girls can't be devils.'

Her mother shot Belle an anxious look, but she was too proud to let her feelings show. She put on a smile and gave Mrs Pitcaithley a regal nod, while in her head she was taking aim with Papa's rifle, and blowing a great hole in Lyndon's narrow, silk-clad chest.

He didn't *need* the inkstand. His papa was the richest man in Trelawny. Lyndon could buy ten inkstands out of his pocket money. He'd probably just lose this one on the steamer when he went back to school.

For her mother's sake, Belle sat through tea under the awning with the other children. She even managed a square of sweet-potato pie with coconut syrup. Then, when the Reverend Prewitt was setting up the magic lantern display, she fled.

She took the path by the river, into the airless green tunnel of the giant bamboo, until she reached her special place under the duppy tree.

Her heart was thudding with rage. She peeled back her stocking and scratched a tick-bite on her knee until it bled. Snatched a handful of ginger lilies and crushed them, breathing in the sharp spicy scent to make her eyes sting. *Why* had she chosen the Devil? If she'd picked any other costume she would have won, and Papa would have got his inkstand. It was all her fault.

Mosquitoes whined in her ears, but she let them bite. The rasp of the crickets was deafening. She welcomed it. Distantly, she could hear the murmur of the party. She ground her teeth. She didn't belong back there. She didn't know the rules.

Girls can't be devils. Why hadn't she known that?

'Because you're *stupid*,' she said aloud. Raising her head, she glared at the spreading branches of the duppy tree.

It was only a young one – not nearly as tall or frightening as the ancient silk-cotton on Overlook Hill – but it was hers, and she felt safe in the folds of its buttressed trunk, with the purple-flowered thunbergia and the white star jasmine festooning its branches, and the big green cotton-cutter beetles patrolling its trunk. A little of the rage lifted from her and floated away.

She ran her hand over the rough bark – and something snagged her skin, making her wince.

It was the head of a nail that had been hammered into the trunk. Someone must have been casting spells again. Perhaps one of the McFarlanes, mother or daughter, paid by a smallholder to catch a person's shadow, or set a love-charm.

The nail had drawn blood. Belle scowled at it. Then she ground her palm onto the rusty iron, to hurt herself some more. That'll teach you, she told herself. You chose the wrong costume, and because of that Papa lost his inkstand—

'Oh, I say,' said a voice behind her. 'Don't hurt yourself. Please.'

She spun round. Blinked in astonishment.

It was Lyndon's father, Mr Traherne. He didn't often attend Historical Society gatherings, but he'd come to Eden as a favour to her mother, whom he'd always admired.

'How d'you do, Mr Traherne,' Belle said politely. She wondered how much he'd heard, and felt herself redden.

He inclined his head in a courtly nod, and went on smoking his cigar. He was sitting on the bench which Papa had built for her last birthday. Belle hadn't spotted him before, because they'd been on opposite sides of the trunk.

'Is this your sanctum?' he asked. 'If so, I apologize for trespassing.'

Awkwardly, she shook her head.

'Bad luck about the prize,' he added, and, to her surprise, he sounded as if he meant it. 'You looked . . . cast down when they awarded it to Lyndon.'

She was embarrassed, but flattered that he'd noticed. And she liked it that he talked to her as if she were a grown-up.

With her heel she dug at the ground, and her red cloven hoof sank into the softness of rotten leaves. 'It's just . . .' she began, 'I didn't know that girls can't be devils.'

Mr Traherne chuckled. 'Oh yes they can!'

She wasn't sure what he meant.

He asked if his cigar smoke troubled her, and she told him no, and that sometimes Papa let her try one of his.

'Well, I shan't let you try one of mine,' he said with a smile. 'It's far too strong. It would make you unwell.'

She wondered if he meant that Papa's cigars were weak by

11

comparison – then told herself not to be such a muff. He was only making conversation. 'When I was little,' she volunteered, 'I wanted to be a boy, you know.'

He raised an eyebrow. 'Did you really?'

She nodded. 'I made everyone call me Bill, and refused to wear frocks or play with dolls. It was after my brother died, and I thought . . . well, that I ought to be a boy. To make up for it to Papa.'

He took that with an understanding nod.

Pressing her lips together, she perched on the end of the bench, arranging her tail carefully beside her.

He offered her his handkerchief to bind up her hand, and she said thank you. In silence they sat side by side, but without any awkwardness, and Belle watched him blowing smoke rings across the river. It was April, and the rains were weeks away, so the Martha Brae was a slow, sludgy olive green that smelt a little off. But Belle was used to it, and Mr Traherne didn't seem to mind.

She cast him a shy glance. He was very old, at least sixty, and acknowledged by everyone to be the most powerful man on the Northside. But she'd never really noticed him before. It was a relief that he was so old. She'd found that with old men she didn't imagine what they were like naked. She simply couldn't.

She reflected that she liked his face. He had strong, almost Roman features, with silver hair and a white moustache, and slightly bulging light blue eyes.

Yes, she thought, a Roman senator. She pictured him walking nobly in the Forum, making laws.

'You know,' he remarked with a curl of his red lips, 'when my son went up to accept the prize, you didn't merely look cast down. For a moment, you looked as if you wanted to kill him.'

She opened her mouth to protest, then shut it again. 'I'd never have carried it out,' she mumbled.

He laughed. 'No attempt to deny it! I like that. You seem rather to enjoy breaking rules.'

Did she? She'd never thought about that before.

'Oh, don't worry,' he said gently. 'All girls like breaking rules. It's in their nature.'

12

Belle frowned. 'What about boys?'

Again he laughed. 'Oh, they *make* the rules.'

That didn't seem at all fair, but she thought it might be rude to say so.

Suddenly Mr Traherne got to his feet. 'Oh, do look, there's a yellowsnake!'

'Ooh, where? Where?'

He gestured with his cigar, then put his hand on her shoulder to shift her a little to the right. 'Other side of the river, under the heliconia – d'you see?'

'. . . Oh, yes! I just caught the tail!' She was elated. It's good luck to see a yellowsnake, and she hadn't seen one since the year before last, when her uncle had taken her shooting in the Cockpits.

That had been such a wonderful day. It was just after the twins were born, and she'd been feeling a bit left out, when suddenly her uncle had swept in from Fever Hill, and taken her off riding for the day. They'd taken a packed lunch, and ridden all over the hills, and she'd felt proud to see him sit his horse so well, for Ben Kelly was the best rider in Trelawny, better even than Papa. They'd yelled insults at the john crows till they were weak with laughter, and he'd taught her to jump.

She was thinking of that when she felt Mr Traherne's hand move slowly down from her shoulder, under the neck of her frock, and onto her breast.

He didn't say anything. Neither did she. She froze. Couldn't look at him. Couldn't breathe.

Keep perfectly still, she told herself. Stare straight ahead. Pretend you haven't noticed. This is a mistake. His hand has slipped by mistake, and he doesn't know it yet. If you stay perfectly still, he'll realize, and take it away. And then we can pretend that it never happened.

She stared straight ahead of her at the great, curved scarlet flowers of the heliconia on the other side of the river.

But they're not flowers at all, she thought in horror. They're claws. Blood-red claws for tearing flesh.

A choking smell of rottenness rose from the green water. She felt sick. She swayed. The heavy hand held her back, pressing painfully into her breast.

This is a mistake, she told herself over and over.

She tried to take refuge in the thought; to make it push away what was happening. Mistake, mistake, mistake.

It was stifling inside the bamboo tunnel. The crickets were deafening. The bitter smell of his cigar caught at her throat.

A burst of laughter from the party made her jump.

Slowly he withdrew his hand. 'I wonder,' he said calmly, 'if we were to wait here very quietly, should we see it again? The yellow-snake. What do you think?'

She clasped her hands in front of her to stop them shaking. She tried to say something, but her tongue wouldn't come unstuck from the roof of her mouth.

From the corner of her eye she saw him toss his cigar in the river. Then he withdrew a silver case from his jacket pocket and opened it, and chose another. 'You know,' he went on in the same easy, conversational tone, 'poor old Lyndon must seem the most awful muff to you, but in fact he's rather an admirer of yours.'

She tried to swallow. What was he talking about? What did he mean?

He sighed. 'I suppose I oughtn't to have told you that. Poor little Lyndon. He'd be mortified if he ever found out.'

She watched him light his cigar. The way he narrowed his eyes against the smoke, and tossed his match into the river. She watched its sure, steady arc.

'You shall have to be very kind,' he went on, 'and promise me that you'll keep it a secret. Will you do that for me?'

There was a silence.

At last she raised her eyes to his face.

He was looking down at her, smiling as he waited for her to reply. His face looked just as it had before: the light blue eyes crinkled and genial. Until you noticed the pupils, which were blank and black as a goat's.

But it *must* have been a mistake, she told herself. He simply didn't realize—

'So what do you say, hm? Are you going to be a good girl, and keep our secret?'

She looked up into his eyes, and slowly nodded.

'That's my clever girl. Now. Let's go and see if they've left us any tea.'

CHAPTER TWO

'Oh, *do* say you'll come,' pleaded Dodo Cornwallis. 'The Palairets throw wizard bathing parties, and everyone will be there.'

'That's why I'm not going,' said Belle.

Dodo cast her an anxious look. 'Because of Lyndon Traherne?'

Belle hesitated. 'Sort of.'

Dodo gave a sympathetic nod. 'Rotten luck about the prize.'

'Mm,' said Belle. 'Rotten.'

Dodo got up and moved to the balustrade. 'I do wish you'd change your mind.'

She looked so disappointed that Belle almost relented. 'It's just that I don't feel like swimming,' she said.

'I understand,' Dodo said quickly. 'And I can quite see why you'd rather stay here. It's so glorious.'

Belle put aside the photograph album and went to join her new friend. She tried to see the garden through the eyes of a girl from England on her first holiday in the tropics. But she couldn't. It didn't look glorious at all.

From where they stood, the double curve of dusty white steps descended into a tangle of tree-ferns, plumbago and ginger lilies, round a hard brown lawn that sloped down to the Martha Brae. Across the river, the Eden Road cut a red slash through the cane-pieces, on its way to Falmouth and the sea. The sun was punishingly hot. The grass was dying before one's eyes.

What's glorious about this? thought Belle.

And yet she adored Eden. And she hated feeling like this. But she couldn't help it. It was two weeks since the Juvenile Ball, and everything felt different. What was wrong with her?

This was her home. She'd been born in this airy, ramshackle old Georgian great house. She'd taken her first steps on this wide verandah, and chased hummingbirds and tried to eat a centipede. But now she felt cut off from it all. Separate. Alone.

Be sensible, she told herself for the hundredth time. Mr Traherne didn't know what he was *doing*. He can't have done. It wouldn't make sense.

She watched the twins toddle round the side of the house and onto the lawn in determined pursuit of Scout, the big bull mastiff. Douglas caught up first, and administered a smack to the huge, wrinkled black head. Scout took it patiently, panting and swinging his tail. Lachlan caught up with Douglas, grabbed the back of his sailor suit, and pulled. Both toddlers tumbled backwards into the grass, and began to howl. Poppy, their nurse, looked on calmly, biting back a smile. Scout attempted to nose Lachlan back onto his feet.

Belle stared at her little brothers and tried to feel something for them, but she could not. She didn't even feel related to them any more.

And she had lied to Dodo. She adored swimming, and longed to go to the Palairets' bathing party at Salt River. But she couldn't risk it. Every time she pictured seeing Mr Traherne again, her stomach turned over.

And yet – she couldn't stop thinking about him. He had been so *nice*. Talking to her as if she were a grown-up. Using long words and assuming that she'd understand. Listening to her. How could he have made such an appalling mistake?

'Is this your papa when he was younger?' said Dodo behind her. She was back on the sofa with the photograph album on her knees.

Reluctantly, Belle went to sit beside her. The photograph album had been her idea. How else did one entertain a girl who was scared of praying mantises, and played with dolls? You could hardly take her into the hills to shoot john crows.

'"Captain Cameron Anthony Lawe,"' read Dodo, following Belle's mother's careful copperplate with her finger. '"Suakin, 1882." I didn't know your papa was ever a soldier.' Dodo's own father was a lieutenant-colonel in Bengal. 'Why did he leave the service?'

'I don't know exactly,' said Belle. 'He was in the Sudan and something awful happened. But it wasn't really his fault.'

'Gosh,' said Dodo. She studied the photograph with placid envy. 'He's awfully dashing. My pater's just fat and bald. At least, he was when I last saw him, and I don't suppose he's got any better.' She turned another page. 'This is your uncle, isn't it? I recognize him from that polo match.' She sighed. 'He's an absolute dream.'

Belle frowned. She didn't like to think of her father or her uncle as being good-looking. They were simply Papa and Ben.

'Sissy Irving says your uncle used to be a *groom*,' said Dodo in disbelief. 'She says he worked for Mr Traherne, and they had a falling-out and he left. But that can't be right, can it?'

Belle bit her lip. 'Actually it is.'

Dodo's blue eyes widened in awe. 'Gosh,' she said again. 'But he's rich now, isn't he? I mean, that new house they're building – I saw it when we went past their estate. How did he get all his money?'

'I don't really know,' said Belle.

Dodo turned another page. 'You're so lucky. Your people are absolutely ripping. An aunt who's so clever that she sits on hospital committees, and a beautiful mamma who does photography. Compared to that, mine are so *dull*.'

'No they're not.'

'Yes they are. *My* aunt just breeds beastly foxhounds. She prefers them to people. My little sister's too small to be any fun, and my brothers are *horrid*. They gave me my nickname. Dodo, because of my beastly big nose.'

'I think you're lovely,' said Belle with feeling.

Dodo blinked. 'Gosh. Thanks.'

Belle meant it. She envied Dodo her mouse-brown hair and colourless eyebrows, and her long, narrow face. Dodo was so English and well-bred. Compared to her, Belle felt dark and coarse.

She glanced at the album in Dodo's lap. It was open at a photograph which her mother had taken. It showed Belle's aunt and uncle sitting side by side, smiling slightly as if at some shared joke. Ben's colouring was dark, because his family came from Ireland, but Aunt Sophie had light brown hair and mischievous hazel eyes, and a wilful mouth. She looked nothing like Belle's mother, her older sister.

Belle had never really noticed that before, but now it struck her forcibly. Aunt Sophie was fair and English-looking, and so was Papa, and so were the twins. Only she and Mamma were dark.

Outsiders, she thought with a flash of resentment.

She watched Dodo turning the pages. Dodo with her boarding-school expressions and her odd combination of humility and assurance. Dodo who always knew without even thinking precisely what was 'done' and what wasn't 'quite-quite'.

Mr Traherne would never have touched Dodo like that.

Belle glanced down at the album. With an unpleasant jolt she saw that her uncle had his hand on Aunt Sophie's shoulder, just as Mr Traherne had had on hers.

Her heart began to pound. She flicked forward to her favourite picture of her parents, standing on the steps with Scout at their feet. Papa had his arm about Mamma and his hand on her shoulder. Why hadn't she noticed that before?

Suddenly she was back in the airless green tunnel of the giant bamboo, and Mr Traherne's hand was heavy on her shoulder. It slid down. It pressed hard against her breast—

No, she told herself. Papa isn't like that. Neither is Ben.

'Who's this?' asked Dodo, making her jump.

Dodo had turned back a few pages and was staring at an old albumen print of a group of young people at a party. The print was foxed and mildewed, but one could just make out a young man in a white suit, gazing down at a dark-haired girl. She was staring straight at the camera, and her face was very handsome in a strong, unsmiling way.

'Who is she?' said Dodo. 'The caption just says "Boxing Day Masquerade, Fever Hill, 1866".'

Belle frowned. 'That's my grandmother. Mamma's mother.' She swallowed. 'Her name was Rose Durrant.'

'She's absolutely lovely. Do you know, I think you take after her a bit.'

'No I don't,' Belle said quickly.

'But you do. The same eyebrows, very marked, and sort of arched. And that Spanish-looking colouring, the dark eyes and hair. Oh, and I've just noticed, they're in fancy dress! That's why she's wearing a mantilla.' She grinned. 'Now we know where you get your talent for dressing up.'

Belle licked her lips. She didn't want to take after her grandmother. It seemed like the worst kind of omen.

'What was she like?' asked Dodo.

Belle shook her head. 'She died ages ago. Long before I was born.'

Dodo waited for her to go on, and looked disappointed when she didn't.

Belle said, 'There usedn't to be any photographs of her at all, except for a small one of Aunt Sophie's that Mrs Herapath gave her. Then last year after Great-Aunt Clemmie died, Mamma found this one.'

Dodo nodded encouragingly.

'We don't really talk about her,' floundered Belle. 'I think she was – well, a bit wicked.'

Dodo's eyes grew round. 'Wicked? How?'

Belle began to feel hot. 'I don't exactly know. I think she ran away with someone. When they were both married to other people.'

'*Gosh*. An adulteress! How absolutely ripping!'

Belle took the album and closed it and put her hands on top. She didn't think it was ripping at all.

The trouble with the Durrants, she'd once heard someone say, *is that they always went too far.*

At the time, Belle had thought that rather dashing. After all, it was a Durrant who'd built Eden, carving it out of the virgin forest at the very edge of the Cockpit country. Now she just found it unnerving.

You seem to enjoy breaking rules, Mr Traherne had said.

Did she? Was that why he'd touched her? Because he could tell that she was an outsider – that there was something wrong with her?

Dodo was watching her anxiously. 'I say, I didn't mean to be nosy. It's just that I admire you so much. You're so different from anyone I've ever met.'

'But I'm not,' cried Belle. 'I'm not different at all!'

Dodo blinked. Belle could see her casting about for something to say that would make things better.

Dodo reached over and touched her arm. 'Do change your mind and come to Salt River.'

'No. No, I can't.'

Dodo bit her lip. 'You're not different at all, you know. And you can't possibly want to stay here on your own, when you could be having a ripping time with us at the seaside.'

Belle hesitated.

Dodo pounced. 'Oh, do come, *do*! It'll be *such* fun! And I bet you *anything* that the beastly Trahernes won't even turn up!'

CHAPTER THREE

'I had no idea,' said Mr Traherne as they walked along the beach, 'that you went in for photography.'

'Oh, Belle's frightfully good,' said Dodo.

'No I'm not,' said Belle.

'Such modesty,' said Mr Traherne.

Belle did not reply.

Everything is *fine*, she told herself, clutching her box Brownie like a shield. Dodo is here, and you've got a nice safe job to do, and we're out in plain sight, taking a walk by the sea. Everything is fine.

The Palairets had a houseful of relatives over from Scotland, and the beach below the big, ugly house on the Montego Bay road was reassuringly noisy. Children in bathing costumes threw themselves off the diving platform. Grown-ups drank tea at little tables under the wild almond trees. Belle could see Mr Traherne's wife in her Bath chair, chatting to her widowed daughter, Mrs Clyne. Surely her presence made everything all right?

'I'm off for another dip,' said Dodo. She was pink with excitement, and Belle guessed that she'd only run over to them because she felt guilty about the unexpected arrival of the Trahernes.

'Don't go,' said Belle.

Dodo flashed her a grin. 'I'll be back soon! I just wish you could come in too. You're such a *muff* for forgetting your costume!'

Belle gave her a tight smile. 'Forgetting' her bathing costume had turned out to be the most awful mistake. She hadn't wanted to be seen in it after what had happened with Mr Traherne; so instead she'd 'forgotten' it at home, and simply taken off her shoes and stockings for a paddle.

To begin with she'd felt quite grown up, helping to watch the little ones in the shallows. Then in disbelief she'd seen the Trahernes' huge, sleek, mustard-coloured motor car pulling up beneath the willow trees.

Shortly afterwards, old Mrs Palairet had asked if she would mind taking a few snaps for 'everyone's' albums, and Belle had been flattered, until Mr Traherne had offered to hold her sun-umbrella.

'Go on, dear,' Mrs Palairet had said. 'What do you say?'

Belle had had no choice but to murmur an obedient 'thank you'.

Now, with a sinking feeling, she watched Dodo racing off for the diving platform like a lanky red setter puppy.

Mr Traherne turned and started slowly up the beach. As he was holding the sun-umbrella and taking the shade with him, Belle followed.

He remarked on the weather in an easy, conversational tone, and she agreed that it was uncommonly hot for the time of year. He didn't say anything more. In his other hand he held an ivory-headed cane, and he seemed content to walk along and tap little pockmarks in the sand.

Belle began fractionally to relax. After all, he was keeping his distance, and there were lots of people about. Lyndon was not a hundred yards behind them, teaching Dodo's little sister to play croquet. A clutch of nurses, coachmen and grooms was having a gossip by the carriages. Aunt Sophie had just splashed into the shallows to rescue Mrs Clyne's howling toddler, who was scared of water.

'I was sorry that your mamma could not be here,' said Mr Traherne in his steady old-gentleman voice.

'I'm afraid,' said Belle, 'that Mamma is indisposed.'

Actually, she wasn't sure about that at all.

'I think I shall be indisposed,' Mamma had announced briskly to Papa at luncheon. 'Sophie's going to Salt River anyway, so I'll ask her to take the girls along too.'

Papa had met her eyes and bitten back a smile. 'You poor darling,' he'd said, sounding amused. 'Shall I come back early, and read to you?'

Mamma had folded her napkin carefully on her lap. 'Yes, why don't you do that?'

The glance that passed between them was laced with humour and excitement and something else, just beneath the surface, that Belle didn't recognize. It made her feel left out.

'Have you done many portrait photographs?' said Mr Traherne, making her jump.

'No,' she said bluntly.

He raised his eyebrows in displeasure, and they walked on in silence. Belle felt herself reddening. She'd offended him. How rude of her simply to say 'no'.

About forty feet ahead of them, a young couple was standing beneath a wild almond tree. They made a nice composition, and Belle, remembering her obligation to old Mrs Palairet, stopped self-consciously and prepared to take their picture.

To her intense relief, Mr Traherne didn't watch as she positioned her camera. He simply held the parasol above her head and gazed out to sea.

Belle tried to concentrate on what she was doing.

The young woman was Celia Palairet – small, dark, and delicately beautiful – whom she and Dodo had admired from afar. The young man was her husband – Alasdair? Adam? Dodo had a crush on him too; but then, Dodo had a crush on everyone.

Right now, the young man had his back to them, and was spoiling the composition. To Belle's surprise she saw that he was angry. She could tell from the tautness in his shoulders, and the way he held his head.

Then he turned round, and the composition improved. Belle forgot Mr Traherne and became absorbed in her task. It was still early enough in the afternoon for strong light and shade, and their figures would be dramatically sidelit. 'Try to bring out the emotion in whatever you shoot,' her mother always said. As Belle took the picture, she thought that maybe this time she'd succeeded. She'd caught the tension between them. Then it occurred to her that they might not thank her for that.

Surreptitiously she glanced at Mr Traherne, who was still gazing out to sea. Perhaps, she thought, we can turn and go back now; back towards the others.

To her dismay, Mr Traherne saw that she had finished, and resumed his walk, slowly up the beach: away from the others, and towards the young couple.

Reluctantly, Belle followed. After all, there were people ahead, so it wasn't as if they would be alone.

'Careful,' said Mr Traherne. 'We're under a manchineel tree. Don't tread on the fruit.'

Belle said thank you, and threaded her way between the small, innocuous-looking green fruits.

Mr Traherne remarked how extraordinary it was that so many of Jamaica's most beautiful plants were so very poisonous.

Belle nodded politely.

'Oleanders,' he went on. 'Frangipani. Even the humble ackee. At least, when the fruit are young.'

She could tell from his voice that he was still annoyed with her for being rude. To smooth things over, she told him about the photographs she'd taken of Dodo the day before.

'Ah, Dodo.' Mr Traherne gave an indulgent chuckle. 'You made a good choice there. That's a very particular type.'

She nodded, although she didn't quite understand. The way he said 'you' to her was incredibly personal. It was scary, but also a little bit thrilling. It made her feel important and grown up.

Up ahead, Celia Palairet left the shade of the almond tree, opened her parasol with a snap, and started towards them. Her husband remained where he was, with his hands in his pockets, staring stonily out to sea.

Celia Palairet wore an elegant white silk tunic-jacket and a narrow hobble skirt, and she moved well, taking tiny steps over the silver sand.

Belle's spirits rose. Now she wouldn't be alone with Mr Traherne any more . . .

Celia Palairet walked past them with the briefest of nods, and continued down the beach to rejoin the others.

'Lovers' tiff,' remarked Mr Traherne when she was out of earshot. 'But to return to what we were saying. Dodo Cornwallis. An amusing little face. But just a trifle – conventional, don't you think?'

'Um,' said Belle. 'I don't know.'

'But surely you'd agree that she doesn't wear clothes very well? The slightest suggestion of a scarecrow?'

They turned and saw Dodo in the distance – tall and coltish in her baggy grey worsted bathing costume – waving at them furiously before launching herself off the diving platform.

'Now you, on the other hand,' said Mr Traherne, starting once more up the beach, 'you wear clothes very well indeed. Because you only just tolerate them.'

Belle, struggling to keep up with him, shot him an uncertain glance.

'For instance, that frock of yours is no more than tolerable, and I notice that your mamma has put in tucks at the bodice and hem to allow for growth, which rather spoils the effect. But on you it looks quite special.'

Belle flushed. The frock was a sponge-cloth tennis dress which she liked for its comfort. She'd never thought of it as having an 'effect'; let alone being 'special'.

'And I see that you've taken off your gloves.'

'To take the pictures,' said Belle quickly.

'Really? I rather thought it was because you hated wearing gloves.'

He was right. She did hate wearing gloves. Since she was ten she'd been having a running battle with Mamma over that, and also over sun hats and shoes. 'A lady is known by her gloves and her shoes,' Mamma would say.

'Then I don't want to be a lady!' Belle would retort.

But how did Mr Traherne know about that?

'If you were mine,' he said quietly, 'I should be very strict indeed about what you could and could not wear.'

She looked up at him in puzzlement.

'In fact,' he went on, 'if you were mine, I don't imagine that I should allow you to wear any clothes at all.'

Belle stopped.

'Perhaps,' he went on, 'just a housemaid's organdie apron, with a fine gold chain about your neck.'

Belle couldn't breathe. She was standing in the wet sand with the wavelets lapping her bare feet. The hem of her frock was salt-stained, and her sun hat had slid to the back of her head. Mr Traherne stood a couple of feet away in the dry sand, with his back to the sun. He wore an immaculate white linen suit and a Panama hat, and was still holding the sun-umbrella in one hand and his cane in the other. Belle felt like a savage who'd just disembarked from her canoe and come face to face with a conquering European.

'You have,' he remarked, 'the darkest, most direct gaze I've ever seen on a girl. It's really rather unfeminine.'

Belle's heart started to thud. The noises on the beach had faded away. The cries of children. The snorts of the horses. The sounds of the grown-ups having tea.

Over Mr Traherne's shoulder she saw the young man still standing under the wild almond tree. He wasn't very far off. If she ran, she could catch up with him easily. Or he could come to her.

Please come over here, she begged him silently.

As if he'd heard her, he glanced towards them, and for a moment she thought that he met her eyes.

Please, she begged him silently.

He turned his back on her and walked away up the beach.

'You have strong features,' said Mr Traherne beside her, 'and quite a strong will. But what you need to remember is that you're still a female. Which means that you act from your emotions, never your intellect.'

Belle tried to be polite, but she couldn't stretch her face into a smile.

'It also means that you are fundamentally immoral. It means that – like all women – you are a coquette even before you fully understand what that means.'

With his cane he began to draw a line in the sand: a slow, wavy line that meandered between them like a snake.

Belle heard the faint rasp as his cane cut through the coarse white sand. She couldn't take her eyes off the wavy snake-like line.

'Don't be frightened,' he said gently. 'I shan't touch you again. I only did it to prove a point.'

'I'm not frightened,' muttered Belle.

'No,' he said, 'of course you're not.' He paused to shake the sand off the tip of his cane, then resumed the wavy line. 'You remind me of your grandmother. Dear Rose. She was wild, too.'

Belle tried to swallow. 'I'm not like her,' she said, barely moving her lips.

'Oh, but you are,' he said. 'And I can prove it. Tell me. That fancy dress competition. Did you choose your own costume?'

Again she tried to swallow. 'Yes.'

'Of course you did. But why did you choose to dress up as the Devil?'

'. . . I don't know.'

'Oh, I think that you do.'

Belle did not reply. He was still drawing the wavy line. With an effort, she dragged her gaze away.

The young man was far away now, stooping for pieces of coral and sending them skimming across the waves. He was much too far away to reach. She had missed her chance. Her eyes returned to the wavy line.

'Ask yourself this,' said Mr Traherne in his steady, old gentleman's voice. 'Why did you *choose* to dress up as the Devil?'

She did not reply.

'Why did you *choose* to let me touch you the other day?'

Belle opened her mouth to protest, but he talked over her.

'Don't pretend. Don't try to deny it. You could have run away, as any normal girl would have done. You could run away now. But you didn't then, and you won't now.'

The sun was hot on her head and shoulders, the sand glaringly bright.

'The other day, you simply stood there, as you're standing here now. You allowed it to happen. Shall I tell you why?'

Head bowed, she waited.

'Because you're different.'

'No,' she whispered.

'Of course you are. I know you. You're that kind of girl.'

'. . . What – what kind?'

'You already know.'

Slowly she shook her head.

'You're the kind of girl who gives stare for stare, like a man. The kind of girl who rides her pony astride, like a man. The kind of girl who crouches in the hayloft to watch the stallion put to the mares.'

He was right about that. But she'd only watched once, and then got bored. After all, she'd known about babies and things since she was ten, when her mamma had taken her aside and explained it, very matter-of-factly, and to Belle's lasting embarrassment. But Mamma had said briskly that she'd suffered from not knowing as a girl, and she wasn't having that for Belle.

Watching the stallion had been a bit frightening, but also slightly exhilarating. Somehow Mr Traherne made it sound wicked.

'You're the kind of girl,' he went on, 'who will find herself in four days' time riding that funny little pony of hers over to Bamboo Walk, where she will encounter a very old friend.'

Four days' time was Thursday, her day for visiting Aunt Sophie. 'I can't on Thursday,' she said automatically – then put her hand to her mouth. That sounded like an acceptance. As if she intended to be there.

'Yes you can,' he said with his genial smile. 'And you will. Teatime, by the guango tree in Bamboo Walk. I shall take it very much amiss if you do not.'

CHAPTER FOUR

A ratbat flitted under the giant bamboo, and Belle's heart jerked.

In the moonlight everything looked different. The river was black. The ginger lilies had a sickly glow. The young duppy tree harboured a fathomless dark.

She hadn't been back here since the day of the Fancy Dress Ball. She hadn't wanted to come back. But now she had no choice.

She opened her satchel and took out the ingredients for the spell. A baldpate's egg. A parrot's beak. A hammer and a handful of nails. A blue clay ball which she'd found under Grace McFarlane's porch, and guiltily squirrelled away.

She took a deep breath. The air smelt stale and diseased, and the heat lay heavy on her skin. Jamaica is full of ghosts. They're called duppies, and they live in duppy trees, and they can be mischievous, or downright bad. Tonight it felt as if all the duppies in Trelawny were watching her.

She set her teeth. The spell had to work. She'd tried everything else.

She'd been silent on the drive home from Salt River, but luckily Aunt Sophie was in a thoughtful mood too, and she didn't notice. Dodo was asleep.

As the dog cart rattled over the dusty red roads, Belle watched the tangled verges flashing by. Mr Traherne was right. The plants she'd grown up with were all poisonous. Rattleweed. Kill-buckra. Jamaica nightshade. These were the flowers she'd stuck in albums; the leaves she'd picked for playing boil-pot with the pickneys. What did it mean?

She shut her eyes and wondered what to do. Today was Sunday. He'd told her to be in Bamboo Walk on Thursday afternoon. He hadn't given her a choice. He'd just said to be there.

Ought she to do as he said? Or should she stay away, and risk his disapproval?

She longed to ask someone – some grown-up who could tell her what to do. But who?

The one thing she knew was that Papa must never, *ever* find out. If he did, he would know that she was different: not the normal daughter he thought she was, but a *female*. A female who let a gentleman put his hand on her breast. If Papa found out . . . Even thinking about it made her skin prickle with dread.

So that ruled out telling Mamma, who would of course go straight to Papa. And it also ruled out telling Aunt Sophie, because she would go straight to Mamma.

Which left only her uncle Ben, and her terrible old relative, Great-Aunt May.

She went to see Ben.

More than anyone else she knew – perhaps even more than Papa – Ben Kelly knew his way about. He never talked of his past, but Belle had picked up enough rumours to know that he'd done things she couldn't even imagine. He'd grown up in the London slums. He'd been a miner in Brazil. He'd lived rough in the Cockpits, and befriended the mountain people. The servants liked and respected him, but they feared him too, and sometimes they told stories about him when they didn't think the carriage folk could hear.

Belle adored him.

On Monday morning she was lucky, and she had him to herself. Aunt Sophie was in Falmouth making calls, and Dodo had baulked at the eight-mile ride, and stayed at Eden to play with the twins.

'So what's up, Belle?' said Ben as they strolled across the lawns.

As always when she went to Fever Hill, they'd begun by looking over the work on the new house, then shared a jug of her favourite freshly pressed cane juice, with a slip of ginger in it for bite. Now they were on the lawn at the back. Belle's pony, Muffin, was tethered under a breadfruit tree, but Ben's mare, a gleaming thoroughbred called Patsy, ambled behind him like a big, docile dog. At Fever Hill, the horses had the run of the grounds.

'What's up?' he said again.

Belle wondered where to start. 'If a gentleman,' she said slowly, 'asks a lady to take a ride with him, do you think she ought to accept?'

Ben put both hands in the pockets of his shooting jacket, and his green eyes became thoughtful. 'Depends on the gentleman. And on whether he really *is* a gentleman.' He paused. 'Not too many of those about, I'm afraid. You'd better watch yourself, love.'

She was relieved that he didn't ask any questions, but also alarmed. Surely there were lots of gentlemen? Every man of her parents' acquaintance was a gentleman – unless he was a servant or a field hand or a shopkeeper. 'How does one tell the difference?' she asked.

'By what they do.'

She thought about that.

'Belle,' he said gently. 'Whatever's bothering you, talk to your mother.'

'I can't.'

'Yes. You can.' The mare nuzzled the back of his neck, and he gently pushed it aside. 'You may not realize it, but your mother's an amazing woman. You can tell her anything. Believe me, I know.'

'But I *can't*. That's why I came to you.' She bit her lip. 'I was sure that you'd know what to do. Aunt Sophie says that you've seen and done practically everything, both good and bad.'

Ben looked startled. Then he burst out laughing. 'Did she now? Well, unfortunately for you, she also made me promise not to tell you anything about it. At least, not till you're a lot older than you are now.'

'Why?' demanded Belle.

He sighed. 'Because you need to do some growing up first. Sweetheart, I know you're at the age when you're getting – well, curious about things—'

Belle's face burned.

'—and that's fine,' he added quickly. 'But I'm not the one to talk to. Believe me, I'm not.'

'But—'

'Talk to your mother, Belle. It's the best thing to do. It really is.'

Of course she didn't do as he said. How could she? But by ignoring his advice, she had the horrible sense that she was putting herself irretrievably in the wrong.

The next day, Tuesday, she went to see her only other relation. Great-Aunt May.

Great-Aunt May, or Miss Monroe as she was known to all Trelawny, was Belle's great-great-grand-aunt, and unimaginably old. She lived in a town house on Duke Street, and never went anywhere. She sat all day in her upper gallery – a dim, shuttered chamber that smelt of camphor and old age – and not even her servants knew how she passed her time. But somehow she found out everything that went on in Trelawny. And despised most of it. She and Mamma hated each other – Belle didn't know why – although Mamma still took Belle to visit her once a year, as it didn't do to fall out with family.

It was precisely *because* Great-Aunt May hated Mamma that Belle thought she might safely ask her advice. Great-Aunt May would sooner take poison than give Mamma the time of day.

It took some inventiveness to see her alone, but on Tuesday morning Mamma took Dodo to call on Mrs Herapath, who lived round the corner from Duke Street, and Belle managed to get away.

'So, miss,' said Great-Aunt May in a voice like cracked ice.

Belle perched on the edge of her chair and forced a smile. Her heart was thudding. She could feel the sweat trickling between her shoulder blades. She'd always been frightened of Great-Aunt May. And she wasn't alone. Most people in Trelawny were frightened of Great-Aunt May.

As always, the old lady sat absolutely straight on an upright mahogany chair, with her gloved talons atop her malacca cane. Her face was shrunken and bloodless after a lifetime spent indoors, but her eyes were little blue pits rimmed with red. Despite the heat, she wore a high-necked gown of stiff grey moiré, and long kid gloves the colour of flint. Great-Aunt May always wore gloves. According to legend, she'd donned them at the age of eighteen, in disgust at the world after her only London Season, and had never taken them off. Shortly afterwards, Mr Traherne's father, Addison Traherne, had asked her to marry him. She had been outraged, for he was descended from a blacksmith. She'd hated the Trahernes ever since.

'So, miss,' she said again. 'What brings you to me?'

Belle swallowed. 'How are you, Great-Aunt May?'

The old lady treated that with the contempt it deserved. Clearly she had no intention of making this easy for Belle.

Belle drew a deep breath, and launched into a halting account of the bathing party at Salt River, although she didn't mention any names.

Great-Aunt May listened in unnerving silence. 'So,' she said at last. 'It appears that you have a *beau*.'

Belle jumped. She wasn't sure if 'beau' meant what she thought it did, but she didn't dare ask.

'A *beau*,' repeated Great-Aunt May with grim relish. 'At the age of thirteen. How extraordinarily vulgar.'

Belle's hands tightened in her lap.

'What is his name?'

Belle licked her lips. 'Mr – Mr Traherne.'

The ancient face went very still. The gloved talons tightened on the cane. 'Which one?' said Great-Aunt May. 'The elder – or the younger?'

Belle could not bring herself to say.

'Ah. *Indeed*. The elder.' Surprisingly, the inflamed blue eyes gleamed with pleasure.

Belle was alarmed. She'd been wrong to come. What were her troubles to Great-Aunt May, except the source of grim amusement? Great-Aunt May didn't care about her. She'd been Belle's age at the time of the great slave rebellion of 1832, when she'd watched the hangings in the square. She'd seen the corpses piled by the side of the road in the cholera epidemic of 1850. She'd witnessed hurricanes, earthquakes and floods. She didn't *care*.

'I don't know what to do,' said Belle.

'Why come to me?'

'I thought—'

'You thought that I might help you. Why?' With her cane she rapped the parquet. 'The Trahernes have been a stain on this parish for years,' she went on, 'and before I die, I intend to see them removed, *root and branch*. However, *I* shall choose the time when that shall come to pass. And I say that that time is not yet come.'

'But—'

'I shall not corroborate your story, miss. Upon my word, I shall not. And without me, who would believe you?'

Belle stared at her.

'*Why* should they believe you?' said Great-Aunt May, leaning forward. 'They would simply say that you have a pretty skill at weaving a falsehood, just like your mamma.'

It was so unexpected that Belle's jaw dropped.

'Oh, yes,' said Great-Aunt May. 'Your mother is a liar, as was her mother before her.'

'No,' protested Belle.

Again Great-Aunt May rapped the floor with her cane. 'Do not interrupt! You are liars, I say! All Durrants are. Feckless. Loose. It is *in the blood*.'

'I'm not lying,' said Belle, who didn't know what feckless meant. 'I'm telling the truth.'

But was she? Or had she got everything disastrously wrong? Did Mr Traherne simply want to *help* her, because she was different? After all, he'd promised that he wouldn't touch her again. And she believed him, for he was a gentleman, and gentlemen always keep their word.

'*Lies*,' repeated Great-Aunt May with relish. 'That is what people will say. Wicked, wicked lies.'

Belle leapt to her feet and fled.

By the afternoon the heat had become intense. Tempers frayed. People scanned the sky in vain for rain clouds. Belle and Dodo stayed on the verandah, flicking through back numbers of the *Weekly Gleaner* and getting on each other's nerves.

To make matters worse, Dodo had developed a crush on Ben, and insisted on going through the albums again. And when she wasn't doing that, she wanted to talk about kissing.

It turned out that although she still played with dolls, Dodo Cornwallis knew a surprising amount about kissing, but nothing whatever about what came after – although she thought that she did.

'A girl at school told me all about it,' she said as they were dressing for dinner. 'It's really quite simple. There's something men need to get rid of from time to time, so they give it to the Piccadilly women.'

Belle paused with a petticoat in her hands. 'Who are the Piccadilly women?'

Dodo rolled her eyes. 'You *know*.' When Belle still looked blank, she leaned forward and said in a hoarse whisper, 'Bad women. You know.'

Belle didn't. And the term worried her. She'd never thought about it before, but now she realized that there was a hierarchy. There were 'ladies' like Mamma and Aunt Sophie; and 'women' like the servants and the market women; and 'bad women', whatever that meant. And then there were 'females'. At Salt River, Mr Traherne had called her a female. Was that like a Piccadilly woman, or was it even worse?

Wednesday dawned hotter than ever, and she still hadn't decided what to do. Then at breakfast she had a brilliant idea.

What if she did what she was told, and went to Bamboo Walk – *but Mr Traherne wasn't there*? What if he was taken ill? Not seriously ill; just enough to make it impossible for him to go for a ride. Then she would have fulfilled her obligation, and at the same time avoided anything happening – *and he couldn't possibly be displeased.*

It was simplicity itself. Why hadn't she thought of it before? All she needed was a little obeah. And she knew just the person to help.

Her teacher, Evie McFarlane, was a beautiful mulatto lady who'd been friends with Aunt Sophie since they were children. She'd married a coloured planter, Mr Walker, and now lived on his estate at Arethusa, on the other side of Falmouth. But everyone still called her Miss McFarlane, or 'the Lady Teacheress', as she'd once been the schoolmistress at Coral Springs.

She'd given up teaching school on her marriage, but still tutored Belle as a favour to Mamma, who couldn't face sending Belle away to Miss Woolmer's academy at Kingston. But the best thing about Evie was that she wasn't only a teacher, but also a witch.

Her mother, Grace, was also a witch – the most powerful obeah-woman in Trelawny – and she lived by herself in the old ruined slave village at the bottom of Fever Hill. But not even Grace could do what Evie could. Evie was four-eyed. Evie could see ghosts.

'Can you see the future, too?' Belle asked casually after Evie had arrived in her little dog cart and they'd settled down for a half-hearted history lesson. Dodo had gone back to her aunt at Running Gut, and they were alone on the verandah.

'No, I can't,' said Evie with a wry smile. 'Why? Can you?'

This was a setback. Belle had been hoping that Evie might simply tell her whether or not she was going to go to Bamboo Walk tomorrow. Then at least she'd know, and she wouldn't have to ask Evie to do a spell to make Mr Traherne ill. Clearly it wasn't going to be that simple. She said, 'But you do know how to set a curse, don't you?'

Evie's face closed.

'I mean,' floundered Belle, 'that's what people do when they make obeah. Isn't it? Nailing a person's shadow to a duppy tree, or putting hand on someone, or setting a snake on—'

'Belle,' said Evie in her low, soft Creole voice. 'Obeah is not a game.'

Belle coloured. 'I know. I do know that. I didn't mean—'

'It's dangerous. Do you understand? You meddle with obeah, even just a little, and it'll fire back on you so fast—' she broke off, shaking her head. 'So fast that it's like a broken rope snapping back in your face.'

Belle swallowed. She'd never heard Evie talk with such feeling. It frightened her. 'It was only to make him ill,' she said in her defence.

'Who do you mean?' said Evie.

Belle shook her head.

Evie thought for a moment. 'So this man,' she said. 'I suppose you've got something of his? You know enough about obeah to know that you need a personal effect?'

Belle nodded.

Evie held out her hand.

Reluctantly, Belle reached into her pocket and brought out Mr Traherne's handkerchief, that he'd given her to bind up her hand. It was fine white lawn, but it bore no initial. Evie would not be able to tell to whom it belonged.

'Consider this confiscated,' said Evie, sounding very much the teacher as she tucked it into her hand-bag. 'And now I want you to promise me – *promise* me – that you won't try anything on your own. Belle? I'm waiting.'

Belle heaved a sigh. 'All right,' she said at last. 'I promise.'

But twelve hours later here she was, standing in the moonlight by the river, getting ready to break that promise.

A hot breeze rustled the dry leaves of the giant bamboo. Fearfully she looked about her. The night was full of spirits. Who would protect her now? She'd broken faith with Ben, and now she was about to break faith with Evie McFarlane. She was about to put herself beyond the protection of one of the most powerful witches in Trelawny.

But what choice did she have? Even without Mr Traherne's handkerchief, she'd picked up enough obeah from the servants to make a stab at a spell. At least, she had to try.

She turned back to the sliding river. A fish broke the surface with a plop. A mosquito whined in her ear. The night-song of the crickets was low and musical.

Suddenly, to her surprise, her spirits lifted. These sounds were as familiar to her as the sound of her own voice. This was her *home*. Eden would protect her. Eden would make her spell work.

Thursday morning dawned hot and windless, but Belle didn't mind, for the omens were good.

A mongoose crossed her path as she padded to the bath-house. In the night, Mr Anancy the spider had built his web in a corner of her bedroom – and he didn't do that for just anybody. The spell had worked.

Then a boy came with a note from Aunt Sophie. Would Belle mind postponing her usual Thursday visit for a couple of days? Another good omen, for Belle had been wondering how to put off her aunt without arousing suspicion. Now she was free to ride to Bamboo Walk and fulfil her obligation, and Mr Traherne couldn't possibly be angry with her. She would do as she was told; but because of the spell, he would not be able to come. Her spell would see to it that he stayed away.

She had no difficulty getting away, for the twins were being impossible, and Mamma had her hands full. But Belle had to ride slowly because these days Muffin tired easily, and it took an hour to get to Bamboo Walk.

The cane-pieces lay stunned under the heat. Even the crickets sounded exhausted. Muffin wheezed irritably with every step. Already the good-luck charm of rosemary and Madam Fate which Belle had fixed to the bridle was wilting, and so was the sprig she'd pinned to the lapel of her dust-coat.

She reached Bamboo Walk, and reined in. Nothing. At the far corner of the cane-piece, she spotted the guango tree beside a clump of giant bamboo. She put Muffin forward.

Not a breath of wind stirred the cane. The Spanish moss

hung limp from the branches of the tree. The bamboo was utterly still.

Weak with relief, Belle dismounted and tethered Muffin to the tree. She would take a quick look round, so as to be able to say that she had, and then water Muffin at the irrigation ditch, and get out of—

He was waiting for her behind the giant bamboo.

CHAPTER FIVE

'Belle? Belle!' Mamma tapped on the bath-house door. 'Are you all right in there?'

Belle froze. In the looking-glass her face was sweaty and pale. She looked like a stranger. Would Mamma guess what had happened? Would she *smell* him on her?

Belle could. She'd been in here for hours, and she still couldn't wash him off. She would be dirty for ever. She'd never be clean again.

On the other side of the door, her mother said, 'Moses tells me you came back from your ride in a dreadful lather. Poor little Muffin's quite done in. Were you taken ill?'

Belle glanced at the wet combinations in her hands. It was no use. She'd never get rid of the blood. 'Just a bit seedy,' she called. 'Nothing to worry about. A little too much sun.'

In the looking-glass, the huge-eyed girl mouthed the words. She thought, from now on, this is who you are. A girl who lies to her mother. Who lies to everyone.

'You can't ever tell anyone,' he'd said afterwards, as he straightened his tie. 'You know that, don't you? It's our secret.'

Then he'd taken out his handkerchief and wiped himself clean, and mounted his horse, and given her a grandfatherly smile and tipped his hat as he put the big chestnut into a leisurely trot and headed for home.

'Belle?' said her mother. 'I really think you ought to come out. At once.'

Belle heard Scout the mastiff scratching and snuffling at the door. She heard the unease in her mother's voice. She rolled the damp combinations into a ball and stuffed them into the pocket of her dressing gown. Then she smoothed back her hair and unlocked the door.

Her mother gasped. 'Good heavens, Belle, you look like a ghost. Whatever's wrong?'

Belle met her eyes, then glanced quickly away. Mamma hadn't guessed. She was merely worried in an everyday sort of way that her daughter was looking peaky.

Belle felt a jolt of terror. If not even Mamma could guess what had happened, then what he'd said must really be true: they were in the secret together. Just the two of them. She would never escape.

'Belle?'

She swallowed. 'I'm fine,' she mumbled. 'I told you, just a bit too much sun. I'm fine.'

'You don't look fine. Not at all.'

Scout nosed at the pocket of her dressing gown. She pushed him away. 'It's just a sick headache. I think I need to lie down.'

Her mother laid a cool hand on her forehead. 'You've a touch of fever, too. Bed for you. Straight away. No argument.'

Belle had no intention of arguing.

She lay curled up in bed beneath the mosquito curtain, and tried to think of nothing. But the thoughts squirmed in her head like worms. She couldn't get rid of them. He was inside her now, and he was never coming out.

He had been so *strong*. That wet, red lizard tongue filling her mouth and making her gag. Those scaly, liver-spotted hands holding her down. That hard body tearing into her.

How could she ever have thought him noble, like a Roman senator?

And he'd been so calm afterwards. Shaking out his white lawn handkerchief. White. Immaculate.

'Remember,' he'd said as he smoothed back his hair, 'you came to me. Not the other way round. Because this is who you are. I merely saw what was in you and brought it out. But don't worry,' he'd added, his voice very gentle. 'It's our secret. I shan't ever tell. We wouldn't want you to be found out, now would we?'

She shut her eyes and ground her face into the pillow. It never *happened*.

But it had. The evidence was all over her. The scratches on her arms. The chafe-marks on her thighs. The throbbing soreness inside.

And worst of all, his smell. Stale tobacco and oniony sweat, and a sour man-stink that made her want to retch. She'd washed and washed but she couldn't get rid of it. He'd left his mark on her, like an alley cat spraying his territory.

It's our secret.

She wondered if there was some way to break free of it. Wild images thronged her mind. She saw herself stealing a rifle from the gunroom and shooting him dead on the steps of Parnassus. Or paying Grace McFarlane to put hand on him so that he'd sicken and die. Or running away from Eden to somewhere far away where nobody knew who she was. Or simply walking into the deep, green, salty, cleansing sea.

Her mother came in with a headache powder. Belle drank it and lay back again and shut her eyes. She felt her mother's hand stroking her hair back from her temples. Then she heard the rustle of her skirts as she went out, closing the door softly behind her.

Belle lay on her side and watched a patch of sunlight moving slowly across the terracotta tiles.

After a while, a small hand tugged at the mosquito curtain, and Douglas appeared, solemnly holding out his favourite toy: a kaleidoscope.

Wordlessly, Belle took it and twisted the tube for him. After a while she took a turn, glancing through the viewfinder at the hundreds of brightly coloured fragments, endlessly breaking and rearranging. She thought, you break something, and even though you put it together again, it's never the same.

Douglas grew impatient, took back his toy, and left.

It's our secret.

Some time later – she knew it was later because the patch of sunlight had moved a couple of tiles – the door creaked again, and Dodo Cornwallis peered in. 'Oh, phew, you're not asleep.' Timidly she perched on the edge of the bed. 'Poor *you*. I came with my aunt. We were hoping you'd come back with us to make a four for croquet and stay the night. Bad luck, old thing.'

Belle watched her friend's lips. It was as if Dodo were speaking a foreign language.

'Your mamma says it's just a touch of the sun,' Dodo went on, looking hopefully at Belle. 'But I expect you'll be well enough by Saturday, won't you?'

Belle struggled to marshal her thoughts. What was happening on Saturday?

'Mrs Traherne's musical afternoon? I'm playing my piece, and you promised to come. I'll die if you're not there.'

Belle blinked. A musical afternoon at Parnassus. His house. His wife. His son and his grown-up daughters and his grandchildren. Mr Cornelius Traherne. The gentleman.

To get rid of Dodo she said she'd do her best, while inwardly resolving that no power on earth would make her go.

The patch of sunlight moved further across the tiles, then faded to darkness. Scout nosed the door ajar and sniffed her mosquito curtain, then padded out. The crickets' song deepened. Ratbats flitted past the louvres. She heard her father come home. She pressed her face into the pillow. She would never be able to face him again.

She listened to the table being laid, then to her parents talking over dinner.

'. . . But you've got to hand it to old Cornelius,' her father said, 'he always manages to keep his head above water. Two years ago I wouldn't have given a shilling for his chances, but now – with a couple of merchant bankers in his pocket—'

'—not to mention the Clyne marriage,' Mamma said drily. 'Poor little Sibella. Sacrificed on the altar of—'

44

'Yes, but she went into it with her eyes open,' said Papa.

So did I, thought Belle. Does that mean it's my fault?

But she hadn't known what he would do. She hadn't known.

Was this how it was for everyone? Being held down and hurt, like a lump of meat? Was this how it was between all men and women? Between Aunt Sophie and Ben? Mamma and Papa? Was this the poisonous truth beneath the pretty make-believe of tea parties and musical afternoons?

Night deepened. The moon rose. Finally, she slept.

She awoke around midnight, and lay blinking at the moonlight on the tiles.

Then she shook out her slippers, pulled on her dressing gown, and padded across the hall to her father's study. The doorway glowed golden in the light from the lamp on his desk.

'You're working late, Papa,' she said.

He raised his head and stared at her. 'Who are you?'

She swayed. 'I'm Belle.'

He frowned. 'No you're not. You're not my daughter, you're a stranger.' He got up and came round the side of the desk, towering over her. His light grey eyes were glassy with anger. 'Who are you? What are you doing in my house?'

She couldn't breathe. This was a mistake. Any second now he'd break into a smile and tell her it was a joke.

'What have you done with my daughter?' he demanded. 'Where's Belle?'

She awoke with a shuddering start in a tangle of damp bedclothes. The old nightmare. But this time it had felt real.

Outside, an owl hooted. She caught her breath. To hear the voice of Patoo means that something bad will happen. But something bad already had. Was there more to come?

Feeling sick, she shook out her slippers, pulled on her dressing gown, and padded across the hall to her father's study. The doorway glowed golden in the light from the lamp on his desk.

This is *not* a dream, she told herself. He will recognize me. He will. I may be tainted, but I'm still his daughter.

He glanced up and saw her, and gave her the almost-smile that was habitual with him. 'Hello, Belle. Feeling any better?'

Relief broke over her like a wave. She nodded, and went to her usual spot on the Turkey rug, and tented her nightgown over her legs.

Scout, sprawled beneath the desk, lumbered to his feet and came over to sniff her ankles, then lumbered back and slumped down again.

Papa said, 'I don't think rum and water's really in order, do you? Would you like a glass of seltzer water instead?'

She shook her head.

He studied her for a moment, then nodded, and went back to his books.

She looked about her at this big shabby room that hadn't changed since she could remember. The battered mahogany desk under which she'd camped when she was six, and refused to come out. The infamous moth-eaten Turkey rug which Mamma annually threatened to discard. The golden satinwood walls blotched with old damp-stains from the years when her father had lived here alone, and much of the house had lacked a roof.

She'd been coming here since the first nightmare when she was five. She would lie on the rug and gaze at the painting of the old house at Strathnaw, and pester her father about Scotland.

'Why are the trees all bare?'

'Because in the winter it's too cold for the leaves to stay on.'

'But where do the birds make their nests?'

'They don't. They leave the country.'

'Aren't there any birds left at all?'

'Yes, some stay behind.'

'Which ones?'

'. . . Robins.'

'But without nests, where do the robins sleep?'

'No idea.'

Now Belle watched her father writing in the big leather-bound estate book. The lamplight threw sharp shadows across his strong-boned face. *Not exactly refined*, Mrs Herapath had once remarked, *but so attractive.*

But *why* do people think he's so attractive? wondered Belle. Is it because he's strong and kind, and we think he'll keep us safe?

But is that true? Is he really kind? After all, he was once a soldier in the Sudan. He was in battles. He killed people.

It was a horrible thought. He was her father, but she didn't know him.

And he didn't know her.

'Why, Belle, dear,' said Mr Traherne as he stood on the steps to welcome his guests, 'you're looking positively grown-up.'

Belle blinked. Bracing herself, she waited for him to say something more, or for some flicker of unease or guilt to show on his face. But he merely passed his hand over his waistcoat, and turned to her parents with a smile. 'Madeleine, Cameron – *delighted* you could come. You know how much these things mean to Rebecca.'

He looked just as he always did: genial, grandfatherly, and entirely at ease. No covert glance at Belle when Mamma wasn't looking. In fact he'd already turned away to greet someone else.

Belle broke out in a cold sweat. *Navvies sweat*, Mrs Herapath would have admonished her, *ladies glow*.

But I'm not a lady, thought Belle. I'm a female.

She mumbled an excuse to her mother and stumbled from the sunlight into the cool marble gloom of the vast entrance hall. She found the bathroom, pushed past the bemused maid, and slammed the door. Then she bent over the water closet and heaved until there was nothing left to bring up.

But what did you expect? she told herself angrily. An apology? A guilty start? This is *Cornelius Traherne*.

She thought of her pathetic, childish attempts to cast a spell with the help of the duppy tree. What a fool she had been, to imagine that Eden would protect her.

And just as childish and pathetic was the impulse which had brought her here today. The need to confront him – or at least to find out what he would say.

Well, now she had her answer. He hadn't said anything. He didn't need to. Because as far as he was concerned, it had never happened.

Shakily she went to the washbasin and splashed cold water on her face. The girl who stared out from the looking-glass was a stranger.

From now on, she thought, you're somebody else. It doesn't matter who. You've just got to pretend.

'One can always trust Rebecca,' said Mrs Herapath, deftly capturing a petit four from a passing footman, 'to do these things *well*.' Mrs Herapath was the arbiter of taste in Trelawny, for before her marriage she'd been the Honourable Olivia Fortescue. The ladies of Northside society lived in terror of her pronouncements – which, fortunately, were usually benign.

And she was right, Rebecca Traherne did do these things well. The Montego Bay String Quartet was playing Schubert on the upper terrace, while down on the lawn a gentle breeze was fluttering the awnings. In the surrounding gardens, cool green arbours harboured enticing little gilt tables, and everywhere there were flowers: great banks of oleanders, plumbago and frangipani.

And all of it poisonous, thought Belle.

Anger burned her stomach like bile. Jamaica – Trelawny – Eden. Not the paradise she'd always believed it to be. Not with all this poison bubbling underneath.

As a sleeper in a dream she moved unnoticed between the guests. Everywhere she looked she saw dishonesty and pretence.

Mamma and Papa and Aunt Sophie listening to old Mrs Pitcaithley's interminable laments, and pretending not to be bored.

Mrs Clyne handing back her scared little boy to his nurse, and pretending to smile when she was really annoyed.

Mr Traherne patting Dodo's cheek, and pretending to be the genial old host. Dodo pretending to like it. Mrs Traherne in her Bath chair, pretending she hadn't noticed.

Lyndon belligerently asking Belle for a dance, and pretending not to care when she said no.

Everyone pretending. Playing a part.

What part should she play? The docile little miss admiring the pretty ladies and the handsome gentlemen? Or the 'female' who knew what lay beneath?

Over by the balustrade, lovely Celia Palairet was flirting with Georgie Irving, while casting sharp little glances at her husband to see if he'd noticed. Adam Palairet – tall, reserved and stony-faced – was grimly pretending that he hadn't.

Belle pushed her way through to him. 'Why do you pretend?' she demanded. 'If you don't like the way she's behaving, why don't you stop her?'

He looked down at her with surprisingly warm brown eyes that seemed curious rather than annoyed. 'Why should I?' he asked.

'But she's flirting,' Belle said angrily. 'Your wife is flirting with another man.'

For a moment he studied her face, as if he was trying to work out why she was acting like this. Then he said gently, 'You're very young. Do you really know anything about it?'

It wasn't the response she wanted. She wanted anger or outrage. She wanted someone else to feel what she was feeling.

Without a word she turned on her heel and left him. She stalked down the steps and into the garden, and from the corner of her eye she saw Lyndon Traherne emerge from behind a potted orange tree and follow at a discreet distance.

She turned into the rose arbour. It was stuffy and deserted. Mrs Traherne's prized eglantines were dropping their petals in the heat.

Lyndon came after her with his hands in his pockets. Poor lanky, unattractive Lyndon. It seemed inconceivable that only a couple of weeks before, they'd had a spat over who would get first prize in a fancy dress competition.

She turned and waited for him to catch up.

Belligerently he thrust out his jaw, but she could see that he was shaking with nerves. 'Don't you care to listen to the music?' he said.

'No,' she replied. She plucked a rose and started shredding it.

'I say, don't do that. Mamma won't like it.'

'Then you'd better not tell her, had you?'

'Don't.' He put out his hand and grabbed hers.

She let her hand go limp in his, to see the effect.

His face went red. She could feel how his fingers shook.

She thought, so this is what it feels like if you don't get involved. It's easy. You simply take yourself outside, and watch. She said, 'Do you want to kiss me?'

His face flamed. His narrow chest rose and fell. 'You oughtn't to say things like that.'

'Why not? You do want to kiss me, I can tell. You think about kissing all the time, don't you? I heard that last Sunday you asked Becky Frobisher if she wanted a kiss. Our cook said that you—'

'That was different.'

'Why? Because Becky's a servant's daughter?'

He looked confused. 'Because I'm a boy, and boys – we can do things that girls can't.'

'Oh, yes,' she said drily, 'I know all about that.'

He threw her a startled look. Then he blurted out, 'But I have kissed a girl, you know.'

She snorted. 'When?'

'At school. I mean – in Town. And once she let me put my hand down her blouse—'

'She let you, or you did it anyway?'

He looked appalled. 'Oh, I say. I'm not a cad.'

'Not yet, perhaps.'

He swallowed, and she watched his Adam's apple going up and down like a table-tennis ball. In the dim green shade he looked extraordinarily young. She could see the sweat slicking his forehead; the down on his upper lip where he was trying to grow a moustache. If he hadn't been a Traherne, she might have pitied him.

Awkwardly he leaned forward and pressed his lips against hers. When she didn't push him away, he put the tip of his tongue hesitantly into her mouth. It wasn't unpleasant and he wasn't at all rough; merely clammy and over-eager. She thought, he's doing this because he knows he can. Because I'm a female.

It is in the blood.

Emboldened still further by her non-response, he took hold of her by the waist and pressed his body against hers. He was pushing her back against the roses – which fortunately lacked thorns – and making odd little moaning noises in his throat. She fought the urge to laugh.

'Gorgeous, gorgeous,' he mumbled as he slid his sweaty face down her neck. One hand came up and touched a button on her frock.

She let him. Why not? What did it matter?

But he was so clumsy that she had to help him undo the buttons. 'Gorgeous,' he moaned as he pressed his face against her breast. 'Gorgeous, gorgeous.'

No I'm not, she thought irritably. She watched an aphid from the roses alight on his head and start clambering over the curly black hair.

The aphid had almost reached his ear, and Lyndon's other hand was working its way up under her frock towards her thigh, when she glanced over his shoulder and saw a man enter the pergola. Shock burst inside her.

It was her father.

CHAPTER SIX

'I need to know why,' said Papa.

He looked exhausted, as if he hadn't slept.

Well, neither had she.

It was the morning after. They stood side by side on the river-bank: close but not touching. Belle watched the steam rise from the great tattered leaves of the philodendron, and wished she was far away, where nobody could find her.

At Parnassus under the pergola, he hadn't said a word. He'd simply gone very still, and looked at her – a penetrating, adult look she'd never seen before – then turned on his heel and walked back the way he had come.

She hadn't run after him. What could she have said? Instead she'd stayed with poor shattered Lyndon, who'd sunk to his knees and burst into tears.

Now her father threw his cigar in the river and turned to face her. 'Why?' he said again.

Again she did not respond.

'My God, Belle, you're only thirteen years old. What made you behave like that?'

She crossed her arms tight across her chest and thought, please let this be over soon. Please, please, please.

'Do you think – do you imagine that you're in love with him?'

She flinched. 'With Lyndon? Of course not.'

'Then are you merely – attracted to him?'

'No!'

'Then why?'

'. . . I don't know.'

He took a few steps away from her along the path, then turned back again. 'What's wrong? What's happened to you?'

The old dread rose in her chest. *Where's Belle? What have you done with my daughter?* She pushed it back down.

What could she tell him? The truth? That she'd been with a sixty-six-year-old grandfather – a man thirteen years older than himself? If he was this upset about Lyndon kissing her, then how would he feel about what Mr Traherne had done in Bamboo Walk?

No, the truth was impossible. It was a wall between them. And in a strange way, that made her angry with him. Because now she would have to lie to him for the rest of her life.

With the heel of her boot she hacked at the rotten earth. 'Have you told Mamma?' she said in a low voice.

'No. And I don't intend to. It would kill her.'

No it wouldn't, she thought angrily. People say these things but they don't really mean them. Why can't you say what you mean? Even you, Papa? Even you?

He rubbed a hand over his face.

Such a depth of sadness and pain. And she was the one who had done this to him: the person she loved most in the world. She couldn't look at him any more.

Across the river the heliconia flamed in the harsh sunlight. That's the true Eden, she thought. Cruelty and poison masquerading as a flower. She said, 'I can't stay here any more.'

'Wh–at?'

She turned back to him. 'I can't. I *can't*. I want to go away.'

'Belle – what are you talking about?'

'I want to go – to England. Yes, England. You'd like that, wouldn't you? You and Mamma are always telling me that it'll soon be time for me to go to boarding school.' She cast around for support. 'What's the name of that place where they have the school where Aunt Sophie went?'

'Cheltenham.'

'Yes. Cheltenham. I want to go to the school at Cheltenham.'

She'd only just thought of it, but now it seemed perfect. A faraway place where nobody knew who she was. Far away across the deep, green, salty, cleansing sea.

But a part of her longed for him to reject the idea out of hand – to say, 'Don't be ridiculous, Belle darling, Eden's your home. No arguments. You're staying here with us, and there's an end of it.'

But he didn't.

He said yes.

The carriage rattled at speed through the streets of Kingston, sending john crows flying up from the gutters and goats clattering away on tiny delicate hooves. Shoppers and tourists waved away clouds of dust and cast them disapproving looks for going too fast.

Mrs Sibella Clyne dismissed them with a regal toss of her golden head. As far as she was concerned, she was late for the steamer to Southampton, and that entitled her to go just as fast as she liked.

Belle, sitting opposite, stared at her numbly.

Mrs Clyne – a plump, still-pretty blonde with her father's slightly protuberant blue eyes – was travelling back to England, and had agreed to chaperon her. Mrs Clyne, who lived in a fashionable town house in Berkeley Square, where Belle would be spending her holidays. Mrs Clyne, the younger daughter of Cornelius Traherne.

And Belle had actually thought that she'd be getting away from him.

She gazed out of the window and tried not to think about home. About Papa.

He'd accompanied her to Kingston to see her off, but had had business on the quayside and left the hotel early, saying that he would meet them by the gangplank ten minutes before the *Atalanta* was due to leave.

She'd already said her goodbyes at home – to Poppy and Old Braverly and Moses and the others; then to the twins and Aunt Sophie and Ben and Mamma. Mamma had been crying. Mamma never cried. 'Why do you have to go? You don't have to go, you can change your mind and stay here and forget all about this wretched, wretched school!'

That was when Lachlan had pressed his parting present into Belle's hand. A finger-length sausage of river clay, sun-dried and painted yellow. He'd given it a pointy tail and a flat head with two shiny duppy-seed eyes. 'Ellosnake,' he'd told her severely. A yellow-snake. For luck.

She had it now in her pocket, wrapped in her handkerchief. She touched it with her finger and swallowed tears.

Beside her, the nursemaid threw her a curious glance. Mrs Clyne's toddler, Max, simply looked scared.

'*Such* heat,' said Mrs Clyne, fanning herself aggressively. 'One always forgets how appalling Jamaica can be before the rains.'

Beside her, Max scanned the sky with a worried gaze, as if the deluge might come upon them at any moment.

Mrs Clyne flicked him an irritated glance, then returned to Belle. 'I'm afraid you'll find it rather cold at Cheltenham. I know I did.'

Belle was surprised. 'Did you go to school there too?'

'Heavens, yes. I was there with Sophie. Didn't she tell you?'

Belle shook her head.

'The food was too dreadful for words,' said Mrs Clyne. 'So utterly without flavour that one had to guess what kind of meat it was by the sauce that went with it. And all sorts of ridiculous rules. Don't speak on the stairs. Don't walk more than three in a row. I was always forgetting. And of course, I was a hopeless dunce. Not at all clever, like Sophie.'

'Were you – were you homesick?'

'Oh, dreadfully. At first.' She paused, as if she'd said too much. 'But I had Sophie. You'll have Dodo. One gets over these things, you know. One gets over anything.'

Belle thought about that.

Mrs Clyne gave her an appraising look that was hard to read.

'Your mamma,' she said, 'doesn't want you to go.'

'I know,' said Belle.

'She's frightfully upset.'

Belle did not reply.

'Don't you care?' asked Mrs Clyne.

'Yes,' said Belle.

Mrs Clyne sighed. Then she quoted softly under her breath, *'How sharper than a serpent's tooth it is to have a thankless child.'*

'I'm not thankless,' said Belle.

'Perhaps not,' said Mrs Clyne. Then her face fractionally softened. 'Oh, don't mind me, dear. That's just something my father used to say to me whenever I didn't do exactly what he wanted.'

Belle did not reply. It had not escaped her notice that while Mrs Clyne had said that Mamma was upset, she hadn't said anything about Papa. Did he think that she was thankless? Did he *want* her to go?

To avoid the traffic, the driver had taken a route down South Camp Road, and now the carriage turned right into Harbour Street. They were approaching the junction with Fleet Street, which Belle knew from the servants' gossip was where the country girls ended up if their dreams of a respectable position in the city went wrong. It was where the Piccadilly women lived.

The carriage lurched to a halt to make way for a streetcar, stopping directly in front of the infamous street. Mrs Clyne ostentatiously looked the other way. Belle did not.

On the corner of the street, she saw a girl. She was pretty, with smooth, coffee-coloured skin and liquid dark eyes; and she was quite clearly looking for customers. Belle had never seen her before, and yet she felt a jolt of recognition.

She could be me, she thought.

She wondered if Mr Traherne visited Fleet Street when he was in Kingston on business. Perhaps he even visited this very girl.

Suddenly, Cheltenham Ladies' College and tasteless school dinners seemed utterly unreal. How was she going to fit in? How was she going to avoid being found out?

The carriage lurched forward, and the girl on the corner was left behind.

Belle caught sight of herself in a shop's plate-glass window: a transparent ghost overlaid by the busy faces of shoppers and passers-by. *Where's Belle? What have you done with my daughter?*

Then suddenly they were at the quayside, and everything was happening at once. She was stepping down into the blinding sunlight amid a sea of white, brown and black faces and a chaos of noise. Fishermen in blue cotton dungarees and jippa-jappa hats splashed water over their catch and yelled their prices at the top of their lungs. Fat market women in brilliant print gowns jangled duppy-seed necklaces in the faces of frightened tourists. 'Ripe pear!' yelled the higglers with piled trays on their heads. 'Cherry mango! Black jangla, fresh-caught this day!'

And suddenly Papa was sweeping her up in a bear hug and kissing her hard on the cheek, his moustache scratching her skin. 'It's not too late,' he said in her ear, 'you can still change your mind. We'll go back to Eden together and forget about this.'

She hugged him tight and shook her head.

Slowly he set her down, and put his hands on her shoulders. 'Belle. There's still time.'

She looked up into his light grey eyes, then quickly away. 'No,' she said. 'I want to go away.'

He sighed, and took his hands from her shoulders.

A porter lumbered towards them pushing a trolley piled high with trunks. Belle stepped back to get out of the way, and Papa disappeared behind the trolley. She felt a clutch of panic.

'Belle, dear!' called Mrs Clyne from the gangway. 'Come along now, we really ought to be getting aboard!'

The porter trundled on with his trolley. Papa was still there. The relief was so great that her knees buckled.

'Write,' said Papa, his eyes glittering. 'A long letter. Twice a week without fail.'

She nodded. 'You too. And Mamma. And Aunt Sophie and Ben. And the twins – as soon as they learn how.'

He nodded. Frowning, he cleared his throat. 'Well, then. You'd better be on your way. We don't want them to leave without you, hm?'

'Papa—'

'Better be getting on now, Belle. No sense prolonging things. Look, Mrs Clyne is waving at you to join her. Off you go.'

'Belle!' called Mrs Clyne. 'We really ought . . .'

Belle glanced over her shoulder to tell her she was coming, and when she turned back, Papa was walking away through the crowd.

'Papa!' she screamed.

But at that moment the *Atalanta*'s whistle went, and he didn't hear her.

At any rate, he didn't turn round.

PART TWO

CHAPTER SEVEN

Loos, France, September 1915 – three years later

'The question one has to ask oneself,' whispered Adam Palairet's brother officer as they waited to go over the top, 'is whether one will fight or funk?'

Adam did not reply. To distract himself from that very question, he'd been struggling to concentrate on the scuffling of the rats in the darkness, and the sucking sounds as the men shifted nervously in the mud.

He thought, if I don't reply, Cornwallis is bound to shut up . . .

Cornwallis didn't. 'I mean, one never actually knows until one's tested, does one? I've heard of chaps who were simply raring to go, and then the next instant they were in an absolute blue funk, and—'

'Shut up,' hissed Adam. He jerked his head to indicate that the men were listening. The nearest, an eighteen-year-old bank clerk called Nathan, was clutching his rifle and looking sick.

Chastened, Cornwallis fell silent. With his large nose and anxious brown eyes, he reminded Adam of a red setter he'd had as a boy in Scotland.

That made him feel bad. Why shouldn't Cornwallis talk if he wanted? After all, there was really nothing to choose between them. Both were recently gazetted second lieutenants fresh from the OTC; both were distinctly New Army: part of the ragtag of lawyers, office workers and colliers who'd come out to swell the ranks of the regulars after a hasty training at Aldershot. Both had only been at the Front for a matter of weeks – and had, by various quirks of chance, not yet seen any action. And both had brothers to live up to: brothers who were very much 'proper soldiers'.

Only in my case, reflected Adam with the familiar dull ache, my brothers are all dead.

Ever since he'd received the last telegram – the one about Erskine – he'd thought of nothing but getting out to the Front. He needed to be where it had happened. He needed to honour Erskine and Gordon and Angus: to honour them by suffering as they had suffered.

And perhaps, too, he needed to carry on the tradition. For over two hundred years there had been a Palairet in the Black Watch. Long after the family had relocated to lowland Galloway, their allegiance to the Highlanders had remained. There had been a Palairet at Charleston and Corunna; at Cawnpore, Tamai, and Magersfontein. Now it was Adam's turn. His first 'big show', as Cornwallis would have put it: a night raid on the German lines, to start promptly at 3.25 a.m., with a barrage of supporting shell-fire to blow up the enemy wire ahead of them. At least, that was the plan.

Adam glanced at his watch. 3.20 a.m.

Christ, he thought, I hope I don't get the wind up in front of the men.

Cornwallis was right. The question was simple. Would one fight or funk?

This waiting was the worst. He kept running over details in his mind. Had anything been left undone? Were the signallers in place, and the stretcher-bearers and the chaplain? Did the guns have the right range?

The telephone rang. Everyone jumped out of their skins.

Further down the trench, he heard Captain Goodwin talking briefly and softly, then fall silent.

'That'll be Division,' muttered Sergeant Watts, a couple of men to Adam's right. 'Wanting to know if everything's in place.'

3.25 a.m.

The night exploded. The earsplitting crump of shells; lights flaring up ahead – greenish yellow, purple; the red and white of flares. Captain Goodwin gave the order to advance, and Adam's heart lurched. He thought about wishing Cornwallis luck, but suddenly there was no more time, for they were starting to climb. As he struggled to reach the top, he heard the rasp of his breath and the blood pounding in his ears; the grunts of the private next to him, whose muddy kilt kept slapping his knees.

Then they were up and running across the churned-up waste of No-Man's-Land, and all was weirdly calm. A warm, velvety night with bright moonlight and myriad stars. The crump and whine of shells flowering in the distance. Then, from the German trench that was their objective, a loud, hollow popping of rifles.

As he ran, Adam snapped off his revolver at where he guessed the enemy must be, but he knew he couldn't possibly hit anyone. It was a hot night. Insects buzzed past his ears.

Another one whipped past, and slowly it dawned on him that it wasn't an insect, but a bullet. He was surprised by his obtuseness, and his lack of fear.

Around him the men were running forward, heads down, kilts swinging. He saw someone lob a rifle-grenade, and thought, it's too soon for that, you fool, you'll never reach them.

Cornwallis slipped and lurched against him, nearly knocking him into a shell-hole. Private Nathan put out a hand to steady him, and as Adam glanced at the boy's pale, intent face, another bullet cracked past his cheek, and a neat red hole blossomed in Nathan's forehead. He crumpled to the ground like a rag doll.

Adam saw it, but he didn't feel it. He ran on.

Suddenly the air split apart. A deafening roar – a crackling of bullets like a swarm of angry bees. The Boche machine-guns had opened up on Madagascar Point.

Still Adam wasn't frightened. Those bullets weren't meant for him.

He saw Captain Goodwin waving his arm and yelling a command – couldn't hear it – but it must have been 'Take cover!' because several men threw themselves into a shell-crater.

Adam followed. He hurled himself into the bottom of the crater and landed beside Cornwallis, who was clutching his revolver and shaking. Cornwallis's revolver was a spanking new Webley Mark VI with a bayonet fitted to the barrel. Adam shifted slightly to the right to avoid being jabbed by mistake.

A rising shriek coming towards them.

'Pineapples!' yelled Sergeant Watts. 'Heads down, lads!'

As Adam pressed himself into the stink, the shriek came closer – unbearably loud – then a shattering noise burst inside his skull – he was choking on acrid fumes – and a column of earth shot skywards, spattering him with mud and blood and chunks of flesh.

As the spattering subsided, he glanced round for Cornwallis, but he wasn't there any more. Instead there was only freshly turned earth and an officer's boot, topped with pulpy bone and blackening flesh.

Is that how it happens? wondered Adam blankly.

More shells screaming overhead. Columns of earth shooting up around him. Bullets hissing and snapping like whips. Choking on lyddite, not knowing where he was going, Adam scrambled past Sergeant Watts to the edge of the hole – and slipped, and put his hand on something spongy. Puzzled, he registered that it was a face: a Frenchman by the uniform, and dead for some time.

A bullet opened up a long red furrow across the back of his hand. He blinked at it in astonishment. Good Lord, he thought, they're aiming at *me*. I'm part of the target.

But he had no time to take it in. Goodwin was ordering them to advance.

Adam scrambled over the lip of the shell-hole and ran forward.

Six hours later, he sat on an old Fray Bentos crate in his dugout, smoking a cigarette and trying to shake off the feeling that at any moment his brother Erskine would walk in, and he could tell him all about it.

About how they'd managed to take their objective – messily and haphazardly, and at the cost of fifteen men and poor

Cornwallis. About Sergeant Watts briskly making sure of the German trench, then slapping a field dressing on Adam's hand and offering to take him to the Regimental Aid Post. About him waving away the sergeant's help and stumbling back to his dugout, where his batman, Brewster, had brought him a mug of tea that he couldn't taste and two letters from home which he hadn't yet read, before taking himself off for a spot of well-earned souveniring.

Above all, Adam wanted to tell his brother how strange it was that he couldn't seem to *feel* anything any more. Nothing at all. He couldn't even taste this bloody cigarette . . .

He blinked at the letters in his lap. Neither was from Celia, which wasn't unexpected. She hadn't written for a fortnight, and her last letter had been one long complaint. *I didn't marry a soldier, I married a barrister . . . I detest Cairngowrie Hall . . . I wasn't meant to moulder away in some dismal Scottish backwater . . . I'm moving back to London . . .*

At the time, he had been wild to go to her; hadn't eaten or slept for worrying that she might leave him. But that had worn off surprisingly quickly. If she hated Scotland, then of course she should move back to London. He could afford it – just. Besides, if she was in London, it would be easier to see her when he was home on leave.

So he didn't experience more than a twinge of pain when he saw that the letter was not from his wife, but her brother. *Sorry I'm not Celia,* wrote Drum in his disarming, schoolboyish hand, *but you know my sister, not a great one for letter-writing. Don't suppose you've heard, but I got my blighty last week: nice clean bullet in the wing. Spot of luck, don't you think? Good old Boche! I was quite deaf for three days afterwards, which was a bit rum. Doctors said it was nerve exhaustion (me!), but I just told them what rot, and now I'm running straight again, although am still beastly weak, hence the brevity of this note. Chin up, old chap, stay sharp, and write if you feel like it. Best wishes and all that, Drum.*

'Good old Drum,' murmured Adam.

That was what everyone said about Drummond Talbot. Big, bluff, blond, hearty Drum. Such an unexpected brother for small, dark, secretive Celia.

The second letter was from Sibella Clyne. Adam was surprised. He knew Sibella only distantly – her first husband had been a Palairet, one of his Jamaican cousins – but after she was widowed she'd swiftly married again: a merchant banker who had died soon afterwards, leaving her wealthy. She'd stayed on good terms with the family – particularly with the Palairet matriarch, Great-Aunt Louisa – and was a favourite of Adam's younger cousins, as she gave the best dinners in Town. But although Adam liked her, they'd never been close. He found her exhausting, and he knew that she found him 'frighteningly reserved'.

Dear Adam, she wrote in her swift, elegant copperplate, *as your great-aunt is indisposed (albeit not seriously), she has asked me to write with the news from home . . .*

Adam felt a flicker of irritation. The conspiracy between the two women could not have been more transparent. 'The poor boy's wife won't write to him, so we jolly well ought. Keep up morale at the Front, that sort of thing. Our duty as Englishwomen.'

I'm told, wrote Sibella, *that they're having a rather trying time out in Jamaica. Last month a hurricane hit the Northside; apparently it seemed at first as if it was going to miss them altogether, but then at the last moment it swung round and flattened a great swath of the coast; that's hurricanes for you! Cocoa and coffee absolutely destroyed, and everyone who got out of sugar is now bitterly regretting it, especially with the War sending the prices sky high. Of course, your great-aunt isn't seriously affected at Salt River, but my people seem to have made somewhat of an error, have not they?*

Adam noted the undercurrent of glee. 'My people' meant Sibella's father, Cornelius Traherne, who'd recently turned over many of his cane-pieces to coffee, and must now be facing a difficult year. It was widely known that he and Sibella did not get on.

Still, she went on crisply, *I'm delighted to say that Eden is doing well at last. So glad for dear Madeleine and Cameron! And of course that means that darling Belle can finally afford some decent clothes, which has been fun. You remember Isabelle Lawe?*

Adam raked his memory and came up with an angry school-girl who'd once berated him for lack of honesty about something or other. She'd been friends with Dodo Cornwallis, St John's little sister.

St John Cornwallis. The smoking crater. The boot . . .

Adam lit another cigarette and inhaled deeply. What the devil was Captain Goodwin going to tell St John's people? He could hardly write and say that their youngest son had been blown apart by a shell, leaving only a boot.

Pushing the thought away, he took refuge in Sibella's letter.

Of course as it's term-time, she went on, *darling Belle oughtn't to be with me at all, but she's run away from school (again!), and I simply didn't have the heart to send her back. Besides, London is so exciting at the moment! The streets are filled with uniforms, the Boy Scouts look adorable cycling along sounding the All Clear on their bugles, and the Zepps are really rather pretty, and far too slow and clumsy to be frightening. Besides, they only ever bomb Dover and the East End.*

Of course, there are inconveniences. Those horrid new paper pound notes; and the fact that everything's so frightfully expensive; and the fashions are too drab for words – some people seem to think that if one's not in khaki, one's being unpatriotic – although the dear little aeroplanes on the veils are rather sweet.

Unsurprisingly, everyone is absolutely rabid *about German spies. They've even talked of banning Beethoven (which came to nothing, of course), and anyone with a German name is finding things rather trying. I'm only thankful that my poor little boy is safely down in Sussex, as he'd never hear the end of it with a name like Maximilian – and you know how timid he is. Or perhaps you don't? I can't remember if you've ever met . . .*

How can she imagine that I want to hear all this? wondered Adam with some amusement. He skipped to the last page: . . . *and poor little Bobby Mordenner was killed last week, such a trial for his mother. But enough of that. Your cousin Osbourne is staying with us, charming boy, and he seems to be quite taken with Belle. So agreeable to have a man about the house again; something I've sorely missed since dear Freddie had an attack of patriotism and got himself a commission. Although what Freddie could possibly achieve against the Boche, I cannot imagine . . .*

She had a point. Freddie Austen, who was widely known as

'Sibella's faithful swain', having adored her hopelessly through both her marriages and beyond, was a sweet, sensitive scion of minor Irish nobility, whose talents leaned more towards bird-watching than combat. But then, reflected Adam, the same could be said of a lot of us.

'Ready for you, sir,' said Sergeant Watts, making him jump.

'What?' Adam said blankly.

'Burial, sir,' said the sergeant. Like any seasoned soldier, he didn't hesitate to tell his young officers what he thought they needed to know. 'Detail's just come back, sir; chaplain's at the ready, and Cap'n Goodwin likes to see all his officers turn out for the service.'

Adam was still stuffing his letters in his pocket and straightening his tunic as he followed the sergeant through the winding communication trench and up over the duckboards to the little patch of churned earth where the service was to be held.

The day was turning out fine, and some late ox-eye daisies brightened the spot where the men had gathered. Overhead, a skylark was going crazy in the sunshine.

The chaplain was waiting in his surplice with a Bible in his hand, while behind him stood the other officers and a handful of men. The man nearest the chaplain carried a half-filled sandbag.

As Adam took his place beside Captain Goodwin, the chaplain began the service, and the private with the sandbag lowered it carefully into a freshly dug hole. Beside the hole lay an empty whisky bottle, securely corked, containing a handwritten luggage label.

The sergeant saw Adam looking at it, and whispered in his ear, 'Cap'n Goodwin's little system, sir. Marks the grave till the crosses come through.'

'How many names on the label?' Adam whispered back.

'Five, sir.'

Five, thought Adam. The sandbag contains the remains of five men.

But what about Private Nathan? He hadn't been blown up, just shot through the head. And what about St John Cornwallis's boot? There didn't look as if there was enough room in the sandbag for that. Why hadn't they found Nathan and Cornwallis?

Adam made a mental note to say something afterwards. Or perhaps he ought to write a report to the War Graves Commission? HQ was always sending out reminders about that. *It is of the greatest importance to civilian morale that the location of all temporary graves be reported at once . . .*

Once again, Adam saw the red hole blossoming in Nathan's forehead. One moment he'd been a boy of eighteen, intent on not losing his nerve, and the next – he was simply dead. Nothing human left. Just a lump of meat on the ground. And now the chaplain was thanking God in His mercy . . .

Adam struggled to take it in.

He hadn't believed in God since he was eight, when his mother had died of the Russian influenza. He'd flatly refused to go to Sunday School, and there had been a family row about it, with his older brothers siding with Pa against him, while three-year-old Erskine looked on with round blue eyes. Surprisingly, it had been the Sunday School teacher who had taken Adam's part, by declaring that he must be given time to find his own way. That was Aunt Maud for you. Rigidly conventional for most of the time, and then occasionally . . .

With a twinge of guilt he realized that his mind had drifted away from the service. How could he be so callous? How could he care so little about a brother officer whom he'd known ever since Winchester, and four of his own men?

And yet, try as he might to conjure up some sadness, all he could feel was a vast disbelief.

He looked about him at the grey faces of the living, and the yawning black hole with the sandbag at the bottom; at the barbed wire stretching into the distance, and the tender blue sky. He thought, what are you doing here? How could you possibly *imagine* that this has anything to do with your brothers? How could you think that by running over a few hundred yards of torn earth waving a useless revolver, you're honouring their memory? They're dead. They're gone. What's left of them is no different from those chunks in the sandbag.

He glanced down at his bandaged hand, and remembered the

feeling of surprise when he'd been shot: when he'd realized that he was part of the target.

He ought to find that frightening, but he didn't.

Oh well, he thought numbly. Perhaps I'll be one of the lucky ones. Perhaps I won't feel fear.

CHAPTER EIGHT

Berthonval, August 1916 – one year later

A doctor was visiting the battalion. As his practice had been in Galloway before the War, Adam asked him to dine in his dugout: an impulse he regretted on learning that the doctor was making a study of shell shock.

After heavy losses at Longueval and Delville Wood, the battalion had spent two weeks behind the line, then taken over No. 1 sector at Berthonval. The trenches were deep and dry but not revetted, so they needed shoring up to prevent a collapse when it rained. As the line was quiet and the weather good, Adam drew up a rota for the men, and they got on with it.

Normally he enjoyed this sort of work, but now he found himself snapping constantly at the men, and cursing their slowness. What was wrong with him? Presumably this confounded doctor meant to find out.

The dinner was a good one, for Sibella Clyne, who seemed to have adopted Adam as one of her causes, had sent out another parcel. After tinned oysters and cold partridge, they had a chocolate cake from Rumpelmayer's, washed down with two bottles of Graves, and plenty of whisky. The doctor was excellent company, but Adam knew that he was being observed, which made him even edgier than usual. When his batman came in with more coffee, he snapped at the man to get out.

There was a silence after the batman had gone. The doctor lit a cigar, while Adam rearranged a matchbox on the collapsible writing desk which doubled as a dinner table. When the silence had become intolerable, he said, 'So what's the verdict?'

'What do you mean?' the doctor said mildly.

'Well, it's quite clear that you've been sizing me up. What's the verdict?'

The doctor smiled. He had a square, freckled face, and small grey eyes that gave nothing away. 'Your CO is becoming concerned about you. That's all.'

'So he told you to check me out.'

'Something like that. He seems to think you're showing signs of wear and tear.'

Adam barked a laugh. 'Enough for a ticket home?'

'Probably not.'

'Ah. I didn't think so.'

'Often a man simply needs time out of the line. And sleep.'

'I don't want sleep,' said Adam. 'When I sleep, I dream.'

'Nightmares?'

'Well, of course.'

There was a pause, which the doctor seemed content not to fill. Adam finished his cigar and lit another, then refilled their whisky tumblers. He caught the doctor's eye and shrugged. 'I know, I'm drinking too much. And my nerves are shot, and I look fifty instead of thirty. So do we all. Must be something to do with sitting like rabbits in holes, waiting to be blown to blazes.'

'That could be it,' agreed the doctor.

'So why is the CO picking on me? Everyone's got the wind up.'

'You're one of his best officers.'

Adam snorted. 'Then he's in trouble. If a shell bursts a mile away, I have to steel myself not to cringe. I curse anything and everyone. I talk too fast, and always about the War. Each new gas attack, each new calamity, I have to talk about it. It's as if — as if I'm trying to *infect* everyone else with my own fear. And that's what it is, doctor, it's fear. We call it "windiness" or "wear and tear" because we can't bear to use the real word. It's despicable.'

'I don't think so.'

'Well, I do.' With his fingertips he drummed on the table. 'Do you know what I hate most? It's the ones who *don't* get the wind up. We had one last month, a transfer from C Company. Big fellow, good officer, no imagination. No fear. "Life in the line", he told me on his first morning, "affects me very little. I've found that if you can just steady yourself the first time you're shelled, then you never have any trouble again." ' Adam took a long pull at his drink. 'God, how I hated him! I hated him far more than I've ever hated the Boche – whom, as it happens, I don't hate in the least.' He took a deep breath. 'Poor fellow was caught by a sniper two days later. So after all that about shellfire, he—' He broke off. 'You see? I'm talking too much. And before the War they used to chaff me for not talking enough – for keeping my feelings to myself.' He paused. 'So tell me, doctor. In your expert opinion. Is it shell shock?'

'We don't use that term any more—'

'I don't care what you call it!' Adam burst out. 'Is it shell shock?'

The doctor studied him. 'No. The thing is, Palairet, in war, men wear out. Like clothes.'

Again Adam snorted.

'I mean it,' said the doctor. 'Courage can be spent. But yours isn't, not by a long chalk. All you need is rest.' He reached for another cigar. 'And I'd watch your drinking, if I were you. If it gets out of hand, it won't much matter whether you've broken down because you drink, or drink because you've broken down.'

That made Adam laugh in earnest.

The doctor didn't join in. He said, 'I understand you haven't been home on leave for quite a while.'

'I've been on leave. Only recently I spent a couple of days in Paris.'

'But you haven't been home. You haven't seen your wife.'

Adam gave him the blank smile that used to infuriate his older brothers.

'What about letters? Getting plenty of those?'

'Oh, yes, plenty of letters.'

'From your wife?'

Adam set down his glass and rubbed his temple. Once he'd started, he couldn't stop. 'The odd thing is, people keep asking me to look after them. As if I can. As if I have any sort of control over what happens.'

The doctor waited for him to go on.

'Last week I had a letter from my great-aunt out in Jamaica, asking me to "keep an eye on" my cousin Osbourne. He's just been conscripted by what she calls "this dastardly new law", and she's heard that he's somewhere in my neck of the woods. Apparently his mother became hysterical when he was called up; "quite inconsolable".'

'That's understandable.'

'Why?' snarled Adam. 'He's still alive, isn't he? And anyway, what do they *imagine* I can do to keep him that way? Why does everyone keep coming to me?'

The doctor put his head on one side. 'Perhaps – because you do feel fear, and yet, somehow, you still carry on.'

Adam threw him a disbelieving look.

'Some men,' began the doctor, 'men like your unfortunate transfer, for example, never experience fear. Others do, but they carry on. In my experience, it's the latter kind of man to whom people look for help. It's the same in a unit. The men know that such an officer understands what they're going through, and yet can be depended upon to lead them—'

'But that's just it,' cut in Adam. 'I can't be depended upon.'

The doctor was silent for a moment. Then he said, 'What do you fear most?'

Adam did not reply.

'Is it shellfire? Is that what you fear?'

'Doesn't everyone?' He downed the rest of his drink. 'The worst death of all. Blown apart. Crude. Shattering. No dignity. Just clods of flesh.'

The doctor studied him. Then he stubbed out his cigar and got to his feet.

'Leaving so soon?' Adam asked with a curl of his lip.

'You'll be all right,' said the doctor. 'I shall recommend you for some Divisional Rest. In the meantime, keep busy.'

Adam burst out laughing.

'I mean it, Palairet. Spot of activity does wonders to steady a man.'

'Well, jolly good,' said Adam, raising his glass, 'because I've a patrol at five in the morning. I dare say that'll be just the ticket.'

His orders were to take seven men and scout out the enemy line. 'Shouldn't take you more than an hour or so,' said his CO. 'Pleasant day for a walk in the woods.'

Adam sent two scouts fifty yards ahead, with two more as flank guards a hundred yards on either side, keeping Sergeant-Major Watts with him. They were to take as little as possible: just rifles, and a bandolier to each man.

They soon reached the woods, where their progress slowed, as they had to climb over so many fallen trees. They lost sight of the line behind them. The War fell away.

The woods were deep and cool, the glades bright with purple teazels and magenta willowherb. Adam thought of the woods around Cairngowrie Hall. Yesterday he'd had a letter from Maud McAllister; in the margin she'd sketched a squirrel nibbling a pine cone. Celia no longer wrote at all, and he didn't expect it, but he looked forward to his aunt's brisk little notes about the daily goings-on in Galloway. And he'd developed a taste for Sibella Clyne's breathless torrents of gossip: they seemed so much more real than reality, and required no response from him except distant amusement.

His great-aunt's letters were welcome for a different reason. She was the only woman he knew who could fill several pages with nothing but disapproval. *Sugar has made that dreadful man Kelly a millionaire all over again,* she had written in her last, *although much good may it do him, as he is now somewhere on the Somme, having persuaded a cavalry regiment to take him; I cannot conceive of how. In my day, officers were gentlemen, not street Arabs made good.*

Eden, too, prospers wonderfully, but I do not begrudge them their success, for at least Cameron Lawe is a gentleman, of sorts. I understand that his wife is active in the War Contingent Fund, which is to be admired, although she has been heard to speak disapprovingly of the War itself, and this I find reprehensible. Sadly, their daughter Isabelle does them no credit. On dit *that she has joined a fast set in London, and leads poor Sibella a merry dance; a stranger to war work, as she will be to her reputation, should she continue in this vein . . .*

Dear me, thought Adam as he clambered over a tree trunk, a young girl who prefers parties to war work. Whatever is the world coming to?

A snap of branches up ahead, and one of the advance scouts came running back. He'd spotted a system of trenches guarded by barbed wire.

Adam went forward with Watts, and found to his surprise – for this sector had supposedly been recently scouted – that the trees had been cleared to give a field of fire in front of the wire. He sent one scout back to warn the flankers, then with Watts and the other man he crawled under the wire.

To his relief, the German trench was empty. It was also scrupulously tidy: four rifles neatly lined up against a wall, a little pile of bombs, a stack of blankets, and some tinned provisions.

While Watts heaved the supplies into the bushes, and the scout went off to bury the bombs, Adam made a quick sketch of the trench system. *NB*, he wrote at the bottom, *cavalry will not be able to circumvent this.* The thought nearly made him smile. 'That dreadful man Kelly' would be disappointed. Adam had only met him a couple of times in Jamaica, but he'd never forgotten seeing him ride.

The scout returned and chatted quietly to Watts, who was lighting his pipe, while Adam finished his map by sketching the lie of the land. To the west the ground dipped sharply, but he couldn't see for the trees how far down it went . . .

A German observation balloon rose silently into the sky and came to a stop directly above him.

It was no more than a hundred and fifty feet overhead, and Adam could clearly see the two men in it. One of them was looking down at him through his field glasses, while the other jabbered excitedly into a telephone: reporting their position, no doubt.

With a sense of unreality, Adam pocketed his map and quietly ordered the men to fall back into the woods. Beside him, Watts swore under his breath, and extinguished his pipe. Together they plunged into the trees.

The Germans lost no time. Adam had scarcely entered the woods when three guns opened up from the German line, and three shells came shrieking towards them, exploding several hundred yards to the right. Adam yelled at the men to run. More heavy crumps, this time a little closer. Shrapnel whistled through the trees. Black smoke billowed closer. The Germans were getting the range . . .

As they ran, a line of men suddenly loomed up ahead through the drifting smoke. Adam drew his revolver, then recognized Captain Anstruther of B Company, Lieutenant Cardinal, and four of their men.

'What the hell are you doing here?' yelled Anstruther.

Briefly, Adam told him about the observation balloon, then asked the same question.

'Wire-cutting party,' yelled Anstruther, ducking as another crump passed overhead. 'No idea there was anyone else in here! Another bloody mix-up!'

Another shell wobbled towards them, and they threw themselves to the ground. When it was over, they got up and ran like hares.

Watts had been hit in the leg. Adam went back for him, and together they struggled on. By now the German battery was putting big crumps right across them. He heard the dreaded whirr-crump, and he and Watts threw themselves under a fallen tree.

The shrieks became deafening. Adam pictured the shell wandering malevolently through the sky, seeking them out. This is the one, he thought, as he always did these days. The fear squirmed in his stomach. He felt it crawling up his chest, seizing hold of his heart. He set his teeth . . .

The shell burst. Shrapnel thudded around him. Watts grunted. Adam hugged the earth.

Shaking so hard that he could hardly stand up, he struggled to his feet. Watts was dead. Adam glanced round. Anstruther and Cardinal were dead too. The men were crouching in the willowherb, looking up at him. It dawned on him that he was now the senior officer.

Should they make a break for the lines, or take cover and wait till it was over? He didn't know. He could see the terror in the men's eyes. *Officer getting the wind up* . . .

Once, Watts had told him what he called the 'soldier's motto'. 'If in doubt, sir, do *something*. Anything. Don't much matter what.'

'Head back to the line,' said Adam. 'Come on, up with you! Back to the line, sharp!'

The men leapt up and followed him.

As he ran, Adam felt his nerves steady. The fear was still there, but it was no longer in charge. He thought, my God, that doctor was right. Spot of action. It's just the ticket.

He received a citation for 'great coolness and gallantry', which made him laugh. It sounded as if they were talking about some-one else. He also got four days at Divisional Rest, and an invitation to dinner with the divisional commander.

HQ was a different world. The huts were daintily camouflaged, there was none of the usual rubbish lying around, and the duck-board path was neatly covered in rabbit-wire to prevent people losing their footing. Even the sandbags were superior: beautifully hand-stitched gabardine in cheerful colours, which had obviously been made by a ladies' sandbag club. Adam felt like a tramp.

Towards the end of dinner, while they were waiting for the brandy and cigars, he could stand it no longer, and excused himself.

He went out into a field at the back. It was still light, and ox-eye daisies glowed in the last of the sun.

If Erskine were here, he thought, how he'd laugh at that citation. And those sandbags!

He watched a ladybird negotiating a grass stem, and tried to picture his younger brother's face. He couldn't. Erskine had been the cleverest of the three: the wittiest, the most fun. Adam's favourite. His best friend. And now he couldn't even remember his face.

Inside him, something broke. He sank to his knees and the sobs burst from him. Wrenching, painful. Frighteningly loud.

He cried for what seemed like hours. At last the sobs subsided, and he was able to get to his feet and straighten his clothes. He glanced at his watch, and saw to his amazement that he'd only been crying for three minutes.

In a ditch, a frog began to croak. A breeze stirred the ox-eye daisies.

Adam brushed the grass seeds off his knees and took a deep breath. He felt drained, but curiously calm. His face was stiff as a mask.

Yes, he thought, a mask. Because it's all about acting, isn't it?

He went back inside. Had coffee with the divisional commander, told a couple of jokes. Listened to DC's stories with every appearance of enjoyment.

This is what you've got to do, he thought as he lit another cigar. You've just got to become a bloody good actor.

CHAPTER NINE

Gouzeaucourt, March 1918 – eighteen months later

He was shot through the heart, wrote Adam, *and died instantly. I am certain that he felt no pain.*

The boy in question had crawled fifty yards with his intestines hanging out, before falling into a shell-crater and drowning. Adam signed off with his usual expressions of regret.

He wrote three more letters along similar lines, adding little details about the weather for verisimilitude, then sat back and rubbed his temple. On his writing desk was a stack of the men's letters awaiting censoring, and a half-finished report on Enemy Dispositions. He decided to ignore them, and finish his letter to Maud McAllister – although most of that would be lies, too.

Since you asked about my domestic arrangements, he wrote with false jocularity, *I can tell you that I'm not too badly off. It's chilly outside, but quite snug in here, for we have a charcoal brazier and four officers in close quarters to warm things up.*

The brazier existed, but not the charcoal; Adam's eyelashes were sticking together with cold. But the four officers were accurate enough, although one was a German who'd been dead since the summer. His ribs poked between the revetments like a broken birdcage.

You will also be pleased to learn, Adam continued, *that I have a dog: a black and white mongrel who followed me home last week. I have dug him a small recess by my bunk, and put in a couch of sandbags, and he seems quite comfortable. He accompanies me on my rounds, and has developed a fondness for corned beef, particularly the W. H. Davies variety.* The dog also enjoyed fresher meat, of which there was plenty about. But Adam saw no need to trouble Maud with that.

Last night we had a gas attack, which was rather boring. For an hour we bumbled around in our rubber snouts, then bumbled back to bed. According to Birtwhistle, the Boche put over about 1500 gas shells (there's a fad at the moment for counting these things), so we were lucky to lose no more than two men. Ten others had been carried away to cough up their lungs at the base hospital; but why tell her about that?

As it's a little damp, some of the men are down with what they call 'three day fever', which resembles influenza. I had something similar at Arras, the Christmas before last; here's hoping I steer clear this time!

He frowned. He mustn't overdo the tone, or Maud, who was no fool, would smell a rat. *If the above sounds strained,* he added, *then please forgive me. We're waiting for this 'great German offensive' they're all talking about, and it's wearing us down – not least because we've fetched up a bomb's throw from Delville Wood; yes, the same Delville Wood over which we played tug-of-war two years ago. That should give you an idea of precisely how far we've come.*

Again he frowned. He oughtn't to have written that. It didn't do to be too honest, not even with a sixty-one-year-old ex-Sunday School teacher. Besides, if the censors ever got wind of it . . .

Swiftly he signed off and sealed the envelope, which, like all officers' stationery, bore the printed message: *I certify on my honour that the contents of this envelope refer to nothing but private and family matters.* Despite what he'd written about their position, Adam signed his name underneath with a flourish.

It was time to go round the line. With Dog at his heels, he made his way through the winding trench, walking with his habitual back-aching stoop to keep his head below the parapet. It was one in the morning, and all was quiet. After the bitter skirmishes of the past three days, the men were exhausted, and those off duty were fast asleep, but as Adam neared the end of his sector, he sensed that something was up. Then he heard it: a burst of uproarious singing, swiftly suppressed.

Sergeant Duckworth came round a bend in the trench, looking harried. 'Ration-carriers, sir. Roaring drunk, the lot of them.'

Adam sighed. 'Why?'

'Poor devils got lost, sir. Wandered about half the night, then decided they couldn't find us because we'd all been blown to smithereens, and sat down to drown their sorrows with the rum rations.'

It was just as the sergeant said. Two of the ration party had passed out on the duckboards; two more were slumped beside them in tears; and another four were beaming up at Adam, incapable of anything else. They were rough, filthy, and achingly young. Their kilts were stiff with mud, and most had souvenirs tied to their waists: a bayonet scabbard, a coalscuttle helmet, a belt buckle marked *Gott mit Uns*.

Sergeant Duckworth cleared his throat apprehensively. 'Do we arrest them, sir?'

'And then what?' said Adam. 'If we sent them down the line, we'd only bring shellfire on them and their escort.' Again he sighed. 'Let those two sleep it off, and do what you can for the others. We'll stand to as normal, at five o'clock.'

The sergeant blew out a long breath. 'Thank you, sir.'

Adam had just turned back for his dugout when he was almost flattened by a young staff officer.

'Captain Palairet,' panted the officer, 'thank heavens I've found you!'

'Keep your head down,' said Adam. 'Snipers in this sector, or didn't you know?'

Alarmed, the staff officer bent double. 'Brigadier McClaren will be visiting the lines at three a.m., sir. He wants your men turned out so that he can inspect their rifles.'

'What?' said Adam wearily. 'Why does he want to do that?'

The staff officer was eyeing Private Morrish, who was sprawled at his feet, snoring gently. 'Brigadier likes to see the men well turned out, sir,' he said doubtfully.

And mine aren't, thought Adam. But if his men were filthy, their rifles were not; he himself inspected them regularly. What was the point in waking them for nothing?

Sergeant Duckworth came up to see why Adam was still there. Behind him there was another burst of singing, rapidly hushed.

The staff officer looked startled.

Adam didn't blink. Squaring his shoulders and sticking out his chin, he put on his best martinet act. 'Very good, lieutenant,' he snapped, 'I shall have the men turned out by three. But be so good as to ask the brigadier to send me that order in writing. *If* you please.'

The staff officer swallowed, and Sergeant Duckworth bit back a grin. They both knew that Adam had every right to request a written order, but that by the time the message got through the brigadier would probably have lost interest, thereby giving the men a couple more hours' much-needed sleep.

Further down the line, a shell burst. The officer ducked. Adam didn't. The officer straightened up, visibly impressed. He was too inexperienced to appreciate that Adam wasn't being brave; he simply knew by the sound that the shell wasn't close enough to do any damage.

'That's shell sense, that is,' Adam heard Sergeant Duckworth telling the officer as he and Dog started back for the dugout. 'Captain Palairet knows what he's about.'

No he doesn't, thought Adam. Nobody does. That's the point.

Back at his dugout, he poured himself a drink, then snatched half an hour's sleep.

He awoke with a start. All was quiet, save for the scuffling of the rats and the distant crump of the shells. He knew he wouldn't sleep again, so he got up, fed Dog, and took out his sketch pad. At the entrance to the dugout, a trio of skulls poked through the mud like mushrooms, and on one of them sat a rat as big as a cat, nibbling something clutched in its paws. Adam settled down to draw.

He was working on the tail when Birtwhistle came down the steps, drew his revolver, and spattered the rat across the duck-boards.

'I was drawing that,' Adam said mildly.

'Sorry, old man,' said Birtwhistle. He threw himself onto his bunk and began immediately to snore.

Adam stooped to retrieve the *Danger de Mort* sign which had been knocked off the table by a fragment of rat. He didn't feel like starting another sketch. Time to open the parcel he'd been saving.

Sibella had been more than usually generous: four bottles of cognac, a dozen pocket classics, five cashmere shirts, a little glass tube of quarter-grains of morphine, and an expensive-looking box from a Mayfair chemist containing a dozen gelatine sheets impregnated with cocaine. *A useful present*, said the label, *for friends at the Front.*

Adam set aside the cocaine to give to Birtwhistle, and arranged the other items on the writing desk. Then he opened Sibella's letter.

It's a bribe, of course, she wrote disarmingly, *but my younger brother Lyndon will shortly be joining the battalion, so be a dear and keep an eye on him? Oh, and I expect you've already heard, but your cousin Osbourne has got his blighty at last! A decent wound to the calf, nothing too horrific . . .* Which is hardly surprising, thought Adam with wry amusement, since Osbourne had inflicted it on himself.

He is great friends with dear Belle, Sibella went on, *and I fancy that he would like it to develop into something more . . .* Adam broke off reading with a frown. He didn't like the sound of that at all. What the devil was Osbourne playing at? *. . . which would be awfully sweet, don't you think? Belle, of course, isn't letting on whether she has feelings for him or not, and I've given up asking. With Belle one never really knows.*

But we're having such fun *now that she's out! And she does dress divinely. Some people frown on that, and say that these days it's bad form even to dress for the theatre. Personally, I consider it a duty to look decent for the troops. Besides, it's not as if the dear girl is turning into one of those appalling 'flappers', who smoke in public and lunch out alone. And having lots of boyfriends cannot of itself make one fast, now can it?*

And now some complaints, so if you're feeling low, you'd better stop reading right away. This rationing is getting out of hand. I now have a 'meat card', a 'food card' (isn't meat a kind of food?), and a 'sugar card'. I got into the most frightful muddle the other day when Cook was down with the 'flu. It seems so bizarre, the notion of sugar being rationed! Why, even in quite decent restaurants, the waiters refuse to leave the sugar bowl on the table, in case one steals the lot. And when I think of the acres of the stuff we had at Parnassus! But of course, if one can afford it, one can still get practically anything on the good old BM, so perhaps I oughtn't to complain.

Although on reflection, yes, I think I ought. These air raids are no longer amusing. Only a few months ago – did I forget to mention it? – a bomb fell just yards from Piccadilly Circus! Blew out all the windows of Swan & Edgars, but left Eros unscathed. Perhaps one should read something into that, though I can't think what.

Anyway, the whole thing is unutterably beastly, so hurry up and deal with the Hun. PS – I almost forgot! You remember Dodo Cornwallis? Of course you do, you were with her youngest brother when the poor sweetheart was shot. Well, dull little Dodo has gone and snared herself a duke! Dodo! *Isn't it killing?*

'Killing,' murmured Adam with a smile. Darling Sibella. What would he do without his weekly dose of gossip? Over the years, her letters had grown far more addictive than poor Birtwhistle's cocaine.

He knew that this was not a flirtation in the traditional sense. Sibella Clyne relished her independence as a wealthy young widow far too much to endanger it; and she must be aware, as was he, that they had nothing in common. But he suspected that she liked the notion of corresponding with an officer at the Front, and he pictured her telling her friends, 'The poor dear absolutely *depends* on my letters, it's really rather sweet.'

'Eh?' grunted Birtwhistle in his sleep. 'What's that?'

'Shut up,' said Adam, 'you're asleep.' He opened the second letter.

It was much shorter than Sibella's. *I hear that the divorce has gone through,* wrote Drum Talbot, *and that you're now a free man. I just wanted you to know that if I ever had to choose between you and my sister, I should choose you, every time.*

Adam twitched in irritation. Drum wasn't playing the game; he was being too honest. *If you need a billet on your next leave,* he went on, *do look me up. In fact, please do anyway. The thing is, old man, I've been a bit of a muff, and got myself into a spot of bother. I could use your help. Or at least, your advice. You're so much cleverer than I. I can never seem to . . .*

Adam put down the letter. The prospect of his next leave was beginning to weigh on him. The last time, Drum had met him at Waterloo Station, and whisked him off to an endless whirl of parties and jazz clubs. Dodo, Clive, Binty, Sibella . . . they'd all been there, although as usual he'd just missed meeting the infamous Isabelle Lawe, who'd been at a house party in Somerset. Through it all he'd smiled and laughed, and felt like a Martian. The idea of doing it again made his head ache.

Pocketing his letters, he stood up. There was a report to make on the state of the concertina wire in front of the trenches. He whistled to Dog, and together they set off down the line to find Sergeant Duckworth.

Because of the snipers, Adam had to use a periscope to view the wire. As he was leaning it against the top of the parapet of the first section to be surveyed, with Sergeant Duckworth standing by to take notes, a bullet cracked through the sandbag an inch from Adam's jaw.

If the sergeant hadn't been with him, he would have sunk to the ground in shock. Instead he merely remarked, 'Rather close, that one.'

'As you say, sir,' said the sergeant. 'Looks like the parapet's only one sandbag thick just here. Best watch out.'

'Quite.'

With Dog padding after them, they proceeded slowly along the line. It was a clear night with a white frost, and the stars were bright. Far to the west, they were shelling the German lines. Adam watched a yellow flare trail like a comet across the darkness; crimson cloudlets of shrapnel shells; green shellfire bursting in long, dreamlike arcs.

It was breathtakingly lovely. For a moment, Adam forgot that he was standing up to his bootstraps in stinking trench mud; he forgot the scuffling of thousands of rats. Through the periscope he watched a glowing green wave of gas beginning to unfurl and roll slowly towards the line. It was too far off to threaten his men, and as he watched its silent progress it was hard to believe that it might be bringing agony and death to others. 'Beautiful,' he murmured.

'What's that, sir?' said the sergeant with a start.

Officers weren't supposed to say that sort of thing. But suddenly Adam felt too tired to put on an act. 'The gas,' he said. 'It looks so beautiful. The colours. They're almost—'

Something hit him in the chest like a sledgehammer.

He felt no pain. He spun round and sat down heavily in the mud, and the War simply dropped away.

CHAPTER TEN

Kyme Castle, Lincolnshire, September 1918

Dodo sent Belle a note by a footman, asking her to come to her rooms after tea, and Belle went, bursting to share her news.

'Not a *word* to anyone,' Osbourne had told her. 'Not a word, infant. I shall need time to square it with my people.'

Of course she'd agreed. To keep the secret, she'd hung his ring on a chain round her neck, and tucked it under her bodice. But as she followed the footman down the endless passages, she kept putting her hand on it to make sure it was real.

A secret engagement. How like Osbourne to come up with something so romantic. Although 'secret' presumably only meant not telling the outside world. Dodo must be told at once. And Belle couldn't wait to write to Eden. She'd already drafted the letter hundreds of times in her head.

They would adore Osbourne. Everything about him was so *right*. For a start, he was a Palairet. And he had money of his own, which proved that he wasn't after hers. And he'd been in the army, so Papa was bound to approve.

Now at last she could go home. After six years of thinking up reasons why she couldn't possibly go back to Jamaica even for a visit, she could finally dare to try. Once she was married to Osbourne, she would be safe. She would persuade him to take her to Jamaica for the honeymoon, and they would stay at Eden, and she'd get to know the twins, and see Mamma. And Papa would smile at her as he used to when she was little. He would be proud of her again . . .

The footman opened the doors and she found herself in an enormous, gloomy apartment with hangings of glacial blue silk.

'*Belle!*' Dodo ran to her and threw herself on her neck. 'It's so *amazing* at last to have you to myself!'

'Steady on, Dodo!' laughed Belle. 'I've been staying with you for over three weeks!'

'Oh, you know what I mean!' Dodo seized her hand and dragged her into a small, cosy antechamber hung with rose damask.

Belle threw herself onto a sofa and fanned herself in mock exhaustion. 'I had no idea Kyme was so vast!'

Dodo gave her a slightly strained smile. 'I know, isn't it the end? On our first night back from the honeymoon I had to ring for the butler, just so that he could lead me down to my guests.'

'Guests?' said Belle. 'But you'd only just got back from your honeymoon.'

Dodo's smile tightened. 'We had forty-eight for a Saturday-to-Monday. It'd been arranged beforehand, but no-one had told me.' She sucked in her lips. 'Of course, Esmond was no use at all. "Over to you, old girl." That's what he said.' She went to the window seat, and sat gazing out across the park.

It was unlike Dodo to talk so much about herself, and Belle wondered what was wrong. She decided that the news of her engagement could wait. 'It's a shame we haven't been able to talk,' she said. 'Let's make up for that now.'

Dodo turned back to her and smiled. Beside her, half hidden beneath a cushion, lay something small and book-shaped wrapped in a pink silk scarf. She put her hand on it, then drew back as if it burned. 'It's odd,' she remarked, 'but when we've only six or seven to stay, it's always much harder to get away. Now that we've over sixty it's easy, because nobody knows where I am.'

'Is that when you come up here?' asked Belle.

Dodo nodded. 'My sanctuary.'

Belle looked about her at the rose-covered sofas littered with magazines and half-finished petit point. She didn't envy Dodo her exalted position, or this vast, cold mansion on the Lincolnshire coast, but she envied her her stability. Being married must bring such peace.

This, thought Belle, is how married people live. No more endless rounds of packing and unpacking, and trailing about the country for interminable house parties. No more slipping in and out of gentlemen's rooms; no more having to get rid of them afterwards. This is what I'll have when I'm married. I shall be safe.

From her window seat Dodo said, 'You're such a brick for agreeing to put in another week. This fancy dress party tonight. I don't think I could stand it without you.'

'Oh, Dodo—'

'Did you manage to square it with Sibella?'

Belle raised her eyebrows. 'Not exactly sure. I sent her a wire two days ago, but haven't had a reply. But don't worry, it's not like her to sulk for long.'

There was silence between them. Then Dodo put her hands in her lap, as if to mark a change of tone. 'Well,' she said breezily, 'let's talk about you. You look as if something amazing has happened. Or should I say someone?'

Belle studied the lines of strain on her friend's face. 'Let's start with you,' she said. 'After all,' she added with a smile, 'you're the duchess.'

Dodo did not return her smile. She'd put on a little flesh since her marriage, and someone – perhaps the dowager duchess – had persuaded her into pastel muslins of unimpeachable dullness, which did nothing for her colouring. Belle thought she looked as if she was about to fade into the wallpaper. If, that is, anything so vulgar as wallpaper could have been found at Kyme.

'Belle,' said Dodo with a frown, 'I have the most tremendous favour to ask of you.'

Belle got up and went to sit beside her. 'Anything. What is it? You're not – in some kind of trouble?'

But what sort of trouble could Dodo be in? Gambling debts? A lover? Sniffing too much snow? None of that seemed to fit. Dodo had always been the good one at school.

Dodo was shaking her head. Then she took a deep breath, and drew the silk-wrapped parcel from under the cushion, and put it in Belle's lap. 'There. I need you to hide this for me.'

Belle looked down at the parcel. 'Of course. But – am I allowed to see what it is?'

To her surprise, Dodo blushed scarlet. Then she gave a tight little nod.

Belle unwound the crêpe de chine – and relief bubbled up inside her. It was a brand new copy of *Married Love*. She tried not to laugh. 'Marie Stopes? But Dodo, why on earth—'

'I had the most frightful time getting hold of it,' said Dodo in a rush. 'In the end I had to ask Celia, and she—'

'But why couldn't you just buy a copy? Everyone's reading it, it's in all the shops.'

Dodo gave her a wan smile. 'Darling, duchesses don't go into shops. They have things sent up, or they sit outside in the Bentley, while the shop man comes out in a morning coat and takes their instructions.'

'Oh,' said Belle. 'I see what you mean.'

Dodo twisted her long hands together. 'Besides, I haven't any money. I mean, I have if I want it. All I need to do is send down a cheque, and someone goes to the bank and brings back the money. But then I've got to write everything down in the accounts book, and every second Monday I've got to go to Esmond's study and have them vetted. I'm such a muff at sums, I always get them wrong. So I've sort of – given up.'

'I'm sorry,' said Belle. 'I didn't understand. Of course I'll hide this for you, if you want. But – won't that be inconvenient? What about finding somewhere in here?'

'I couldn't possibly. The maids would find it. Besides, a book would stand out like a sore thumb. Esmond detests bookish women.'

Belle began to feel guilty. Compared to Dodo's, her life was so free. She had the whole of the second floor at Berkeley Square, and Sibella was a chaperon in name only. Belle went where she pleased, did what she pleased, with whom she pleased. She wasn't exactly happy, but she was at least busy. And now this sudden chance with Osbourne . . .

'The thing is,' said Dodo, cutting across her thoughts, 'I thought it might help.'

Belle looked at her blankly.

'The book. That's why I got it.'

'Oh,' said Belle. Then understanding dawned. 'Oh,' she said again. Suddenly she wanted to be anywhere but here. She and Dodo had never talked about 'that sort of thing'. Belle had never talked about it with anyone. The mere thought gave her a hot, prickly, crawling sensation all over; a sick feeling that she was about to be found out . . .

'You see,' began Dodo, going scarlet again, 'Esmond's not awfully keen on – well, on that side of things.'

'Dodo, don't—'

'No, no, please, I have to tell someone.'

It was Belle's turn to twist her hands in her lap.

'I suppose,' Dodo went on, frowning at her feet, 'you could say that he's – well. Not very good at stud. At least, he isn't with me.' She picked an imaginary thread off her afternoon gown. 'At this rate I can't imagine how I'll ever get with foal. And then what shall I do? That's what I'm here for. I mean, that's why he married me.'

'Darling, no!' protested Belle. 'Esmond – loves you.' She coloured. They both knew that was a lie. Esmond had never loved anyone. He'd never shown the slightest inclination to marry until he'd turned fifty, when the dowager duchess – 'the DD', as everyone called her behind her back – had finally put her foot down, in the interests of ensuring the continuance of the ducal line, and a perfunctory engagement to Dodo had been the result.

Dodo raised her head and looked at her with brimming eyes. 'Oh, Belle. You're so beautiful and brilliant and popular. I've never understood why you've been such a good friend to me.'

'Because you're the best person I know,' said Belle, and this time she spoke with total conviction. 'I've never heard you say an unkind word about anyone. I can't imagine being like that. I know I couldn't do it, not even for a day.' She put her hand on the book. 'I'll hide this in my trunk. Whenever you want it, just send to borrow my "Poiret scarf".'

But Dodo seemed to have forgotten about the book. 'I dare say one just has to soldier on,' she said, still picking at her skirt. 'But I had no idea it would be so hard. So many rules.' She paused. 'Last week I was in one of the glasshouses, and I picked a peach. There was the most fearful row. Wainwright – he's the head gardener – he complained to the butler, who complained to Esmond, who absolutely . . . Well. Apparently one's not supposed to interfere with the glasshouses. Or the gardens, or the kitchens. I've never even seen Cook, she just sends up the menus every week for me to mark up. Although of course I never dare. I spend my days rushing about the countryside, leaving cards on people, and hoping against hope that they won't be in, because the visits are the worst. If one wasn't born out here, one's a foreigner for ever.'

'Come and stay at Berkeley Square,' said Belle. 'You know Sibella's always glad to see you. We'll have fun.'

Dodo shook her head. 'Esmond would never allow it. I haven't been up to Town since we got back from the honeymoon. At first he said it was because of the 'flu; and when that died down, he said there were too many fast women on the streets. He means women with jobs, like conductorettes and postwomen. He thinks they're an abomination. It's why he resigned from the Athenaeum, because they'd taken on a waitress. And now of course the 'flu's back again, so that's that.'

'But I hear it's only the old people who are going down with it,' said Belle. 'And they say that you're fine if you stay indoors, and drinks lots of fizz. Besides, it can't last more than a couple of weeks, can it? It'll be over by October. Just like the War. You can come then. We'll make plans.'

Dodo nodded, but Belle could see that she was only pretending to cheer up for her benefit.

Belle squeezed her hand. 'In the meantime, 'let's just enjoy the house party—'

'Oh, don't,' said Dodo with a shudder. 'I've made a hash of that too. Esmond's absolutely incandescent.'

'Why, what have you done?'

She met Belle's eyes. 'I've gone and invited Adam Palairet.'

Belle looked at her without understanding. 'I'm afraid I don't— Oh, you mean Osbourne's cousin? But what's wrong with that?'

'Belle! *He's Celia's ex-husband!*'

Belle blinked. 'Oh. Oh, dear.'

'Exactly,' said Dodo. 'And you know how protective Esmond is of Celia. She's so beautiful, and he's known her for ever. Even the DD adores her.' She swallowed. 'That was why I invited her, you see, to please them. But then I became so frantic with all the arrangements that I got . . . absent-minded, and invited Captain Palairet, to please Drum. They were at school together, and I really didn't see the harm. Besides, he's had such a frightful time – Captain Palairet, I mean – in and out of hospitals for months. And he wrote such a lovely letter when poor St John was killed. I simply didn't *connect* . . .'

'Can't you write and put him off? I'm sure he'd understand if you told him Celia's here.'

'No he won't, he'll come down and cause a scene. At least, that's what Celia says. She's in a fearful tizz about it, and so is Esmond. Besides, it's too late to put the Captain off. He's arriving tomorrow.'

Belle bit her lip. 'Perhaps he won't turn up.'

'Yes he will,' said Dodo. 'He wrote and asked if Osbourne would be here. Apparently he needs to see him urgently. Oh, Belle, it's *such* a muddle! And I was only trying to please everyone!'

Belle felt guilty all over again. Thank heavens she didn't have to please anyone but herself. And Osbourne, of course.

She stood up and slipped Marie Stopes into the pocket of her afternoon gown. 'I'm sure Osbourne can handle his own cousin,' she said. 'I'll get him to write and put him off. And if that fails, then Osbourne and Drum shall form a guard of honour around Celia, and stop the dreaded captain getting anywhere near her. And just to make sure, I'll be on the lookout from dawn tomorrow, so that I can head him off at the first sign of trouble. How's that?'

Dodo leapt up and gave her a hug. 'What would I do without you?'

'Promise you won't worry any more?'

Dodo nodded. Then she caught her lip in her teeth. 'What about Esmond?'

'Bother Esmond! The dreaded captain isn't coming down till tomorrow, by which time Esmond will have forgotten all about being incandescent, he'll be too speechless with admiration after your wonderful party. And it will be wonderful, Dodo. I know it will. Now let's go and dress, and start enjoying ourselves!'

CHAPTER ELEVEN

Belle's costume for the party was a housemaid's afternoon dress: a deep green alpaca with a white organdie apron, and a little organdie cap with green velvet ribbons. The dress was authentic, but she'd drawn the line at housemaid's slippers, opting instead for high-heeled glacé kid with pearl-buttoned straps.

But it was surprisingly hard to persuade her maid into one of her evening gowns.

'It just don't feel right, miss,' Jenny said stubbornly.

'But that's the whole point!' said Belle. 'It's a master and servant party. We dress up as servants, and you wear evening dress.'

Esmond had thought it 'screamingly funny' when Celia had first mooted the idea, and at the time Belle had thought so too. Now, though, seeing Jenny's discomfort, it struck her as snobbish and hard.

Pushing the thought aside, she flung open the wardrobe and scanned her gowns. 'This one,' she said, pulling out a Poiret evening frock of silver gauze over mauve brocade, which would complement Jenny's delicate colouring.

Jenny looked even more doubtful. 'I couldn't, miss. That's one of my favourites.'

'All the more reason. Now off to your room to dress. And don't forget the shoes that go with it, and the headdress and the gloves.'

That made Jenny laugh. 'That's my job, miss.'

When she had gone, Belle threw her dressing jacket over her maid's costume, and sat down to make up.

At Kyme, electricity was restricted to the state rooms, and bedroom lighting meant smoky oil lamps and an overhead gasolier. The lamp on the dressing table was an old-fashioned one, which reminded Belle of Eden – although Eden, she reminded herself, had electricity now. *But we hardly use it*, Mamma had written in her last letter. *The generator makes too much noise, and the lights attract too many mosquitoes.*

Mamma wrote once a month: sprightly, amusing letters which couldn't mask the occasional note of wistfulness. Over the summer she'd been worrying about air raids, and urging Belle to move to Sibella's house in Sussex until the War was over. More recently she'd seen a report in the *Gleaner* about moral laxity, and tentatively suggested that Belle should beware of jazz, and avoid what she quaintly called 'paint'.

Papa wrote at Christmas and Easter and on Belle's birthday, in November. His style was brisk and informative, and he always covered exactly four sides of notepaper. By the end, Belle knew a great deal about how the estate was going on, and nothing whatsoever about him.

Don't think of that, she told herself firmly. Think of the party. Think of having fun.

She was annoyed to find that her hands were shaking as she reached for her little crystal pots of rice powder and *rouge à lèvres*. What was wrong with her? Since leaving Dodo's rooms, she'd become aware of a vague, creeping dread.

It's probably *because* of Dodo, she told herself. Poor Dodo. Whatever had possessed her to marry Esmond?

'Because he proposed,' Dodo had told her when Belle had finally plucked up the courage to ask. 'Because the family wanted it. Because I wanted to please them. I don't know. Because.'

Belle's hand went to her breast, and beneath the alpaca she found Osbourne's ring. With us it'll be different, she thought. It'll be all right. Once you're married, you'll be safe.

As if summoned by an invocation, Osbourne opened the door. He looked resplendent in a footman's full-dress livery.

'Why, infant,' he exclaimed as he closed the door behind him. 'What an adorable costume.'

She leapt up and ran into his arms, and he bent and kissed her lightly on the mouth.

The dread was gone. She was safe. Osbourne treated her with a gentleness she adored: as if he thought she was made of porcelain. Yes, a porcelain doll.

'Darling infant,' he murmured against her mouth. Then he kissed her more deeply.

They broke apart for breath, and he stooped to check his appearance in the looking-glass.

Belle sat down to reapply her *rouge à lèvres*.

As Osbourne straightened up, he looked about him and gave an elegant shudder. Then he cast himself onto the bed and flung a corner of the counterpane across his legs. 'Your room's even colder than mine.'

'I'm aware of that,' said Belle with a smile. In the looking-glass they exchanged amused glances. Dodo had thoughtfully given them rooms in the same wing. 'Follow the green carpet till you reach the Grecian urn,' she'd told Belle in a conspiratorial whisper, 'then turn left at the blue Persian rug. But do try to make it back to your own room by six, or you'll embarrass the servants.'

On the bed, Osbourne propped himself up on his elbow and yawned. 'Kyme is *such* a trial. Why can't Dodo get the appointments right? My room has rose-water instead of a shaving mirror, while yours has an ash-stand and no pincushion. Why do we put up with it?'

Again, Belle smiled at his reflection. At twenty-eight he was nearly ten years her senior, but looked younger, his fair hair as golden as a boy's, his grey eyes full of light. For his costume he'd chosen the Kyme house colours of sea-green and blue: dark blue breeches and patent pumps, a green satin waistcoat, and an immaculate cutaway coat of green broadcloth with crested silver buttons. He looked so beautiful that Belle's heart swelled with pride. To mask her feelings she said, 'We put up with it because we're Dodo's friends.'

'Ah, is that why,' he murmured. His gaze wandered to the bed-side table. 'What's this?' He picked up *Married Love.* Then he burst out laughing.

'It's not mine,' Belle said quickly.

'I can see that. Dodo's written her name on the flyleaf.' Another snort of laughter. '*Dodo* and Marie Stopes? Isn't that exquisite?'

'Don't mock,' said Belle. She was annoyed with herself for failing to hide the book before he came in.

'Oh, do listen to this,' said Osbourne, leafing through the pages. '*The frequent troubles which arise in physical intimacy cannot be said to be the fault of our educated girls, composed as they are of virgin purity enclosed in ignorance, but rather result from the insensitivity of the male . . .*'

'That's enough,' snapped Belle.

Osbourne blinked. 'Kitten, I'm sorry. I keep forgetting that you're new to all this.'

By 'all this' he meant slipping into each other's rooms, and the loss of 'virgin purity'. He couldn't be more wrong. Belle hadn't been new to it since she was thirteen. But it had been easy to persuade him that he'd been the first. It always was.

'What's the matter?' asked Osbourne.

She shook her head.

'Now let me guess. Something's up with Dodo. That's why you were closeted with her all afternoon.'

'It's nothing you need to know about,' said Belle.

'What does that mean?'

'Women's secrets,' she replied, softening that with a smile. Then she said, 'Actually, there is something you ought to know. Your cousin Adam is arriving tomorrow. Dodo invited him by mistake. Then she remembered Celia, and got herself in a tizz. I've told her that you and Drum will guard Celia with your lives.'

She'd spoken lightly, but to her surprise, Osbourne's face had gone still. 'Adam's coming here?' he said in an altered voice.

Belle paused with her scent bottle in her hand. 'Yes. Why?'

Osbourne ran his thumb thoughtfully across his lower lip. 'How fearfully tiresome,' he said.

'Why?' Belle said again.

He heaved a sigh and threw himself back against the pillows. 'Because he's always trying to drag me down to Scotland. Because he wants me to run the estate, and I simply won't. It's an absolute ruin after all the death duties. Because—'

'Why does he want you to run it?'

'Kitten, it's far too complicated for you to understand. The point is, we shall have to leave before he arrives.'

Belle turned and stared at him. '*What?*'

'I can't see Adam now. I simply cannot.' He propped himself up on his elbow. 'I'm frightfully sorry, infant, but there it is. We must leave first thing tomorrow. I shall order the motor for six. Can you bear to be ready by then?'

'But I can't leave Dodo.'

'Of course you can. Dodo's married. Dodo can look after herself. I, on the other hand—'

'But why do we have to leave?'

'Kitten, do *try* to pay attention! Cousin Adam wants me to be a farmer. How could we possibly marry if I were herding sheep on some ghastly hillside?'

'But he couldn't make you do that.'

'I expect he could. He's the head of the family.' Once again he lay back and stared at the ceiling. 'He probably wants me to go down there at once, so that he can marry me off to some appalling laird's daughter with ankles like tree trunks.'

Belle knew perfectly well that all this talk of sheep-farming and lairds' daughters was just a smokescreen; Osbourne often made up stories when he wanted to avoid the truth. But she also knew that it was best not to come right out and confront him.

Busying herself with her hairbrush, she said, 'But why should it matter what Captain Palairet wants?'

He was silent for a moment. Then he sighed. 'Because – because, kitten darling, I fear that he wouldn't quite approve of our engagement.'

Belle set down the hairbrush. 'He wouldn't *approve*? Why not?'

Again Osbourne sighed. 'It's just the way he is, darling. Grim and dour and disgustingly moral. All the Scottish Palairets are. Apart from me, of course. I'm the glorious exception.'

He was trying to throw her off the scent. 'Why wouldn't he approve of me?' she said quietly.

'Oh, Lord. It's just— If you must know, he's got something into his head about your mamma's family. The Durrants. But it's really nothing . . .'

Bell felt her face growing hot. The old taint rising to the surface. *It is in the blood . . .*

'It's ridiculous, I know,' said Osbourne with a yawn. 'And don't worry, I'll square it with him eventually. But now do you see why, just at the moment, I need to stay out of his way?'

Belle thought about that. She felt torn between her loyalty to Osbourne, and her promise to Dodo to stay at Kyme. 'Osbourne,' she began. 'About Dodo—'

'Oh, Lord—'

'But I don't see how I can leave her. She's having such trouble settling into her new role. She needs me.'

He got up and came over to her, and pulled her gently to her feet. 'We'll talk about it later,' he said, taking her in his arms. 'After the party, you can come to my room, and we'll play master and servant.' His hand moved down to her breast. 'I've always wanted to roger a maid.'

Belle twisted sharply out of his grip. 'That isn't funny.'

He dropped a kiss on her nose. 'It wasn't meant to be funny, darling. It's the truth.'

When he had gone, Belle sat down at the dressing table and put her head in her hands. She felt shaky and sick. *I've always wanted to roger a maid . . .*

One sentence was all it took to bring it back. Just one sentence.

You wear clothes well, because you only just tolerate them. If you were mine, I don't imagine that I should allow you to wear any clothes at all. Perhaps just a housemaid's organdie apron, with a fine gold chain about your neck.

She shut her eyes, and willed the memory back down again. Why hadn't she seen it sooner? The housemaid's costume. The creeping dread . . .

She opened her eyes and stared at her reflection, and a mask stared back at her. Painted lips. Rouged cheeks. Glossy dark bob beneath the little organdie cap. She was looking at Isabelle Lawe, and at Belle, and Dodo's best friend, and 'infant' and 'kitten' and 'maid'. She was looking at anyone – or no-one.

A sheen of sweat had broken out on her forehead. Mechanically, she repaired the damage with powder; but nothing could hide the fear in her eyes. The mask was beginning to crack.

Wrenching open a drawer, she took out the flat lacquer box that she took with her everywhere. Inside, beneath a bundle of her parents' letters, was a child's clay model of a yellowsnake, and a plain morocco travelling case for photographs. She took out the case and opened it, and stared down at the image inside.

This was the only way she knew of pushing the memory back down again, but it never really worked. Because in invoking Eden, she was invoking the memory, too. Eden was where it had begun. Like her, it was tainted for ever.

A knock at the door. She started. The photograph case fell to the floor.

'May I come in?' said Celia Talbot.

Belle nodded. She didn't like Celia. But Celia was better than no-one.

'You're fearfully pale,' said Celia. 'Are you all right?'

'I'm fine,' said Belle. 'Just a little tired.'

Celia looked wonderful. She'd dressed as a lady's maid, in a gown of dove-grey taffeta, with neat white collar and cuffs, and a small embroidered muslin apron tied by a black velvet ribbon. With her sleek black marcelled hair and clear blue eyes, she managed to look both disturbing and demure.

'You've dropped something,' she said, stooping for the picture frame. Then she gave the photograph a longer look. 'Heavens, what an attractive man. Who is he?'

Belle swallowed. 'My father.'

As Celia studied the photograph, she gave a slow smile. 'Isn't that odd? Such a strong face, and yet – his eyes are rather similar to Osbourne's.'

'No they're not,' Belle said quickly.

'Oh, I rather think that they are. That very clear, light grey? Although your Papa's eyes are – harder.'

'No,' said Belle. 'Papa isn't hard.'

Celia's smile widened. 'Of course not. Do forgive me.' She handed back the photograph. 'Do you know,' she said, curling up on the counterpane, 'I fell for Adam for exactly the same reason. Because he reminded me of my papa.'

'But that's not why I—'

'No, darling,' said Celia soothingly, 'of course it isn't.' She ran a finger along the satin ribbon which threaded the counterpane. Then she frowned. 'Oh, don't mind me, I'm simply out of sorts. I suppose you've heard? Adam's arriving tomorrow.'

Belle was relieved to be back on safer ground. 'Don't worry,' she said, 'we're all rallying round. Osbourne will be on guard with Drum, and I shall cause a diversion at the least sign of a scene.'

'Darling Belle,' Celia said perfunctorily. 'But I hardly think Osbourne's a match for Adam. He can be – relentless. And I ought to know . . .' She gave a delicate shudder, and Belle realized that she was enjoying herself immensely.

'Of course, he's still mad for me,' Celia went on. 'Terrified that he's lost me for ever.'

Belle could think of nothing to say to that. She glanced at her reflection. To her relief, she saw that the mask was back in place. No-one would guess that it had a crack in it.

In the looking-glass she watched Celia open her evening bag and take out a slim gold compact. 'Do you sniff?' Celia asked as she opened the compact and withdrew a tiny gold spoon.

Belle shook her head.

Celia raised her eyebrows. 'Well, I think you ought to try it, just this once.'

'Thanks, but I don't—'

'No arguments, darling. You seem *distraite*. A touch of snow will do you no end of good.'

Belle met Celia's eyes in the mirror. Why am I even hestitating? she thought. It's not as if I'm a model of purity. 'Perhaps you're right,' she said. 'Perhaps just this once.'

CHAPTER TWELVE

Dinner passed in a glittering haze.

Belle flirted outrageously with Drum Talbot, and laughed too hard at Esmond's jokes. She drank too much champagne and barely touched her food – although the turbot, lobster and duckling were the best that the 'good old BM' could muster. Belle didn't care. Celia's snow was fizzing in her blood like wine.

As the ices were brought in, she leaned forward and gazed down the length of the fifty-foot dining table: at the dazzling damask and the shining silver; at the towering *compotières* of orchids and pineapples and grapes. Brittle laughter dinned in her ears. The glitter of crystal hurt her eyes.

Everything was the wrong way round. She saw housemaids in sequinned evening frocks offering cigars to butlers and gardeners; footmen in white tie and tails dispensing liqueurs to housekeepers and grooms.

Her chemical elation drained sharply away. We're actors in a play, she thought with a twinge of unease. The flowers and the fruit are the props, and the servants are the stagehands. But where is the audience?

At the other end of the table, Dodo rose to her feet, and like brilliantly coloured shards in a kaleidoscope her guests rose too, and drifted towards the ballroom, where the ragtime band was already striking up. Beyond the ballroom was the Long Gallery, where bridge and bezique awaited the older guests; then there was the Blue Antechamber and the Peacock Salon and the billiards room, and so on and on. There would be Murder and Coon Can until dawn, as well as other, less salubrious games . . .

Suddenly, Belle wanted no part of it. She let the others flow around her like a bright, noisy river, and watched them as if from behind a sheet of glass. She watched them playing their parts.

She saw Esmond leading Celia out for the first dance – although in truth, all he really wanted was to get her alone in some shadowy corner of the library. She saw Celia pretending to have fun. She saw Dodo gamely chatting to the DD as they headed for the bridge tables.

All of them acting, thought Belle. She was puzzled. She hadn't felt like this in years. Six years ago. Rebecca Traherne's musical gathering at Parnassus . . .

Suddenly she needed to be alone.

But as she made her way through the chattering throng, a man grabbed her arm. 'Belle!' Drum had to raise his voice to be heard above the din. His handsome, boyish face was flushed, and he'd rolled up the sleeves of his gardener's overalls. 'Be a sport and help me round up a posse for charades!'

'Later,' said Belle, removing his hand from her arm.

'Oh, go on, be a *sport*!'

'I said later!' she snapped.

Drum blinked in surprise: a big, bluff golden retriever who didn't understand why he'd been told off.

'Later, Drum darling,' she murmured, patting his shoulder by way of apology. Then she slipped through the throng and let herself out of a side door onto the terrace: out into the sweet, cool, forgiving September night.

The din of the party fell away. She moved to the balustrade and put both hands on the cool stone.

It was a warm, still evening, and the air smelt faintly of roses. Behind her, a gibbous moon crested the turrets and cupolas of Kyme. Below, the great double curve of steps swept down to the carriageway, reminding her disturbingly of Eden. Beyond that stretched the shadowy vastness of the park, washed in blue moonlight, and dotted with dark trees like men standing guard.

To her left, the terrace was banded with gold from the tall Georgian windows. Through the nearest she caught a glimpse of Osbourne. He was dancing with Binty Sheridan, but swallowing a yawn, while surreptitiously casting around for her.

She felt a little better. Darling Osbourne. But perhaps she would just let him wait a little longer . . .

Down in the carriageway, a motor started up. Wheels crunched on gravel. Turning, Belle saw the beam of headlamps as it drove away, leaving its passenger standing at the foot of the steps. Quietly, Belle withdrew behind a marble urn.

The man who had just arrived stood some twenty feet below her, gazing up at the house. He was in uniform, with a greatcoat slung over one arm, and a valise at his feet. Belle couldn't see him clearly, but she made out that he was tall and very slender, with an air of contained watchfulness which, even after six years, was instantly familiar.

She felt cold. Adam Palairet. But he was not supposed to arrive until tomorrow.

Over her shoulder, she saw Osbourne detach himself from Binty and move through the dancers towards the windows. He was looking for her. If he spotted her and came out, he'd find himself face to face with his cousin: just the man he was desperate to avoid.

Belle glanced down at the man in the carriageway, and heard again what Osbourne had said. *Wouldn't quite approve of our engagement . . . got something into his head about your mamma's family . . .*

Anger tightened her chest. If Osbourne wanted to avoid him, then avoid him he would.

Adam Palairet had picked up his valise and was starting up the steps.

Belle moved forward to intercept him.

He'd reached the top of the steps when the sound of her heels tapping across the flags made him stop.

A burst of jazz came from the ballroom. At the noise, he flinched, as if to avoid a blow. Then he gave himself a little shake and squared his shoulders, and waited in silence for her to approach. 'I seem to have arrived in the middle of a party,' he said. Then he astonished her by taking off his cap and holding it out to her along with his greatcoat. 'Would you please find a footman to show me up to my room?'

She'd accepted his things automatically, but now she handed them back.

He took them with an air of slight bemusement.

'I'm afraid,' she told him, 'I'm not a maid. This is a master and servant party. I'm Isabelle Lawe.'

Adam Palairet studied her in silence, and in the golden glow from the great front doors his face gave nothing away. He looked utterly unlike Osbourne. Brown hair, brown eyes beneath strongly marked brows, and a firm, unsmiling mouth. It was a clever face: thin, thoughtful and reserved, but he didn't look as if he'd laughed in a very long time. In fact, he looked spent. Belle had seen that look before, in men who'd returned from the Front. It was as if a light had gone out.

'I'm sorry,' he said, although he sounded tired rather than sorry. 'I didn't realize who you were.' He held out his hand. 'How do you do. I'm Adam Palairet.'

'I know,' said Belle, just touching his hand with the tips of her fingers. 'I recognized you. We met once before, years ago. You wouldn't remember.'

'I remember,' he said. He made no attempt to pretend that the memory had been a pleasant one.

She glanced over her shoulder and saw to her horror that Osbourne had spotted her – but not, it seemed, his cousin, for he was making his way purposefully towards the entrance hall.

'We thought you were arriving tomorrow, Captain Palairet,' Belle said loudly. Out of the corner of her eye she saw Osbourne freeze.

'I decided to come early,' said Adam Palairet. 'I need to see my cousin Osbourne rather urgently. Do you know where he is?'

Belle had the uncomfortable feeling that he'd guessed exactly what she was up to.

She lifted her chin. 'I'm afraid I've no idea,' she said crisply. 'But I'm not at all sure that he wants to see you.'

'I'm quite sure that he doesn't,' said Adam Palairet.

Behind him Belle saw Osbourne slip across the hall and disappear into the library. 'Then perhaps,' she said, 'whatever it is that you want to see him about can wait till tomorrow.'

'It concerns you too,' said Adam Palairet, startling her. 'I understand that you – that you're a rather close friend of his?'

'I don't like your tone,' she said sharply. 'Who told you that?'

'Does it matter?' He stooped for his valise. 'When you see him, would you tell him I've arrived? Would you ask him to look me up?'

'No, I don't think I shall,' said Belle. 'Besides, I have things to attend to. For one thing, I'm supposed to stop you from accosting your ex-wife and causing a scene.'

He turned back to her. 'Celia? Is she here?'

'Please don't try to make out that you didn't already know.'

'As it happens, I didn't,' he said mildly. 'But why should I wish to cause a scene?'

'Apparently you used to beat her. Or something equally sordid.' She felt herself colouring. Spoken out loud, it sounded ludicrous.

Adam Palairet seemed amused. 'Is that what they say?'

'Yes, it is. Why do you smile? Don't you even care?'

'Should I?'

'Why do you always answer with questions? It's most uncivil.'

'I'm sorry,' he said, not sounding sorry at all. 'I suppose it's because for the last four years I've been giving orders – that's what one does in the army – and it's a relief not to have to do it any more.' He gave her a brief smile which only made him look more tired. 'Now if you'll excuse me, I'd better find Dodo and reassure her that I'm not about to make a scene.'

She stood in the doorway and watched him walk away across the echoing marble hall.

Something about the way he moved reminded her powerfully of that day on the beach at Salt River. She remembered standing in the sand with Cornelius Traherne, willing the young man who'd just quarrelled with his wife to come towards them. Please,

please, she'd begged him silently, and for a moment, when she'd caught his eye, she'd thought that he would. But then he'd turned and walked away, leaving her alone with Traherne.

If only he'd joined them, everything would have been different. Traherne wouldn't have been able to carry on talking to her; he wouldn't have had the chance to order her to meet him in Bamboo Walk; and then she would have stayed a child, just a normal child, and Papa wouldn't have looked at her as if she were a stranger, like in the old nightmare . . . And all because this remote, unsmiling man had walked away.

And now, because of his prejudice against her family, he meant to make trouble for her and Osbourne.

On impulse, she ran after him. 'Why did you have to come here?' she cried. 'Why do you have to spoil things?'

At the sound of her voice, a footman peered from a doorway, then discreetly disappeared.

Belle didn't care.

Adam Palairet stood looking down at her with his tired, steady brown eyes that gave nothing away.

'What good does it do?' cried Belle. 'We're so happy! Why must you ruin everything?'

Adam Palairet opened his mouth to say something. Then he seemed to think better of it, and turned on his heel and walked away.

Osbourne wasn't in the library, but a maid told Belle that he'd been seen leaving the West Gallery, heading for the glasshouses, so she set off in pursuit.

Osbourne had chosen an excellent hiding place. Kyme had four enormous glasshouses from which an army of gardeners kept the house supplied with oranges, grapes, pineapples and peaches; it also had a gardenia house, a conservatory and an orchid room. All were far from the party, being across the lawns from the house, and only dimly lit by gas.

As Belle made her way through the first glasshouse, she began to feel better. And she regretted her outburst at Adam Palairet. She'd made a fool of herself. Besides, what could he actually *do*?

Osbourne was of age, and had his own money from some sort of trust. Let the dreaded captain do his worst.

She searched the conservatory and the gardenia house, then the other glasshouses. All in vain. Osbourne, she thought with a smile, knows how to hide.

Grapes hung overhead in luscious clusters bloomed with pearl. She passed a tree laden with the infamous peaches which had got poor Dodo into trouble. She picked one and took a bite. It tasted incredibly sweet and juicy.

With the peach in her hand, she reached the orchid house. Here the sound of ragtime had faded to an insect whine, and a fountain in a white marble basin made its own gentler music. Orchids twined naked green stems about the hairy trunks of palms beaded with moisture. Belle breathed in a draught of hot, humid air. She smelt jasmine, and the heavy sweetness of Dames de Noces . . .

The scent of Jamaica.

For the first time in years, she thought of her secret place by the Martha Brae. The giant bamboo creaking and whispering overhead; the young duppy tree snaking its folded roots towards the green water . . .

A sharp sense of danger swept over her. Eden had been ruined for her, ruined for ever. She could never go back. Would it be like that with Osbourne? Would Adam Palairet find some way of ruining that too?

She threw away the peach. Broke off a sprig of jasmine and inhaled its heavy, funereal perfume. Then she caught another scent.

Cigar smoke.

In the far corner, through the fronds of an enormous umbrella palm, she made out a faint blue haze of smoke; a corner of a rattan armchair; a man's hand resting on the arm. Even from this distance she could see that it wasn't Osbourne.

That smell of cigars . . .

If she shut her eyes she could almost see her father. 'Hello, Belle,' he would say when she padded into his study in her nightgown. And if the nightmare had been particularly bad, he'd pour her a tiny glass of rum and water, and she'd lie on the Turkey rug gazing up at the great oil painting of Strathnaw, and ask him impossible questions about robins and snow . . .

Shaking off the memory, she walked the length of the orchid house, and drew aside the palms.

The gentleman in the armchair turned his head, recognized her, and gave a delighted smile.

'You? But how extraordinary,' said Cornelius Traherne.

CHAPTER THIRTEEN

She was back in Jamaica, and nothing had changed.

Dodo, Sibella, Osbourne – they'd all been a dream. Once again she stood before Cornelius Traherne in the moist half-darkness, amid the dripping palms and the jasmine. Its heavy perfume caught at her throat. The trickle of the fountain was a distant echo of the Martha Brae.

He hadn't changed. By now he must be in his early seventies, but his lips were still a plump, vigorous red, and his pale, slightly protuberant blue eyes were as avuncular as ever – until one noticed the pupils, as blank and black as a goat's.

'It really is you, isn't it?' he said with the kindly, old-gentleman smile that she remembered. 'Little Isabelle Lawe from Eden.'

Her blood thudded in her ears. For a moment the urge to run was almost overwhelming. But if she ran, he would have won. He would know that he still had power over her.

There was a lamp on the cane table at his elbow: a hurricane lamp with a tall glass shade, like the ones on the sideboard at home. Reluctantly, she moved forward into its light. 'What brings you to Kyme?' she said.

'The dear old DD,' he replied, tilting back his head to draw on his cigar, and regarding her through lowered lids. 'We've been friends for ever. Although as you can see, I've eschewed this notion of dressing as a servant in favour of a dull old evening coat. More befitting for an elderly duffer like myself. Don't you agree?'

Belle did not reply.

'But tell me,' he went on, 'how is your papa? And your beautiful mamma?'

Another silence, which he affected not to notice. 'And my daughter? How is Sibella? I take it that you left her well?'

She licked her lips.

'Such a pity that I never seem to see her when I'm in Town.'

'I thought it was rather that she would not see you.'

He chuckled. 'It amounts to the same thing, doesn't it? And how is my grandson? How does Max go on?'

'I really can't say. Sibella has him down in Sussex with a governess.'

Traherne nodded sagely. 'Safest place for him. Such a sickly child. And always rather fearful, as I recall.'

Belle swallowed hard. She wondered why she didn't just leave. What was keeping her here, standing before him like a supplicant?

For years she had imagined this moment. She had planned precisely what she would say to this man who had ruined her life; this man who haunted her nightmares and infected her mind.

Sometimes in her fantasies, she destroyed his reputation before an awestruck crowd with a few well-turned phrases. Sometimes she achieved it with an icy, contemptuous glance. More recently, her daydreams involved cutting him dead as she walked in un-impeachable respectability on the arm of her handsome new husband, Osbourne Palairet.

But none of the fantasies worked. None of them could take away that sense of being for ever tainted. That deep conviction that only he really knew who she was.

Like a supplicant she stood before him in her maid's uniform – dear *God*, in her maid's uniform, just as he'd once told her she would. She was inside his fantasy. The intervening years had been a dream . . .

'I must say,' he said, 'you're looking uncommonly well. And that costume is rather a success. You make a very fetching maid.'

'You can't do this,' said Belle.

He blinked. 'I beg your pardon?'

'I'm not a child any more.'

'What an odd thing to say.' He paused. 'But then, you always were an extraordinary little girl.'

'No,' said Belle. 'No I wasn't.' But she knew that her voice lacked conviction.

'Oh yes, quite extraordinary. You seemed to know things at thirteen which most grown women—'

'You ruined me,' she said.

He reached over to the ash-stand at his elbow and ground out his cigar. Then he drew another from his dinner jacket, rolled it between his fingers, lit it, and leaned back with a sigh. 'I rather fancy,' he said, 'that you're confusing me with someone else.'

Belle stared at him. She opened her mouth to speak, then shut it again.

'Oh, you needn't trouble to apologize,' he said gently. 'It's easy to do. One's memories of childhood are so unreliable, aren't they? Events run together. Faces blur.'

'You can't do this,' she whispered.

'However, because you're the daughter of an old friend,' he went on, 'I'm inclined simply to draw a veil over such a regrettable mis-understanding.' Frowning slightly, he picked a fleck of tobacco off the tip of his tongue. 'Although if I've understood you correctly – if it's true, as I hope it is not, that something unfortunate happened to you when you were a child – then for the sake of the regard I have for your parents, for the sake of their standing in society, and indeed for the sake of the respect I have for you – then you have my word as a gentleman that it shall go no further.'

There was a roaring in her ears. She put out a hand to steady herself, and beneath her palm the window pane felt clammy and cold. 'In all these years,' she said, 'it never occurred to me that you might lie about it.'

The pale goat-eyes met hers steadily. Patient. Unassailable. She could see that he did remember, but that he would never allude to it.

You can't ever tell anyone. You know that, don't you? It's our secret.

Of course she knew it. If anyone found out – if Osbourne got to hear of it – the engagement would be over, and her last chance of safety would be at an end.

And yet – it appalled her that he could pretend like this.

'You used to tell me,' she said in a low voice, 'that I was born to play the part of a maidservant.'

'Whatever are you talking about?'

'You used to say that if I was yours, you would see to it that I wore nothing but an apron—' her voice broke.

He looked genuinely puzzled. 'But how extraordinary. I have no recollection of that whatsoever.'

With astonishment she realized that at least in this, he was telling the truth. He'd forgotten all about his own fantasy. He'd simply *forgotten*. Somehow that was more humiliating than if he'd remembered. And more frightening. It was like being rubbed out.

'I was thirteen years old,' she said, her voice shaking. 'And you did – that.'

He rose to his feet, looking down at her with polite concern. 'You clearly are a most unfortunate young woman,' he said, his voice full of sympathy. 'You seem to have created some sort of terrible fantasy in your mind, and for some reason which escapes me, you have woven me into it.' He gave her a brief, pitying smile. 'I wish you well, my dear. I truly do. And I hope that in time, you will recover your sense of proportion.'

He moved past her, and she pressed herself against the panes of the glasshouse to avoid touching him. But as she did so, she heard men's voices on the lawn outside. She spun round.

Traherne stopped with his cigar halfway to his lips.

Through the window, Belle made out Drum Talbot hurrying towards them up the path that skirted the glasshouse. He seemed agitated, talking urgently to another man behind him whose face she couldn't see. Plainly, Drum didn't know they were there, watching him from behind the glass.

'An altercation,' murmured Traherne. 'Dear me, what very poor taste.'

Belle turned back to him. 'You need to be clear on one thing,' she said. 'If you ever try to speak to me again, I shall cut you dead.

I don't care who's there to see it. I don't care if the whole world knows, and it causes the most dreadful scandal.'

Traherne raised an eyebrow. 'You're more likely to make a fool of yourself than to cause a scandal,' he remarked. 'Although of course, you must act as you think best.'

He was right. If she cut him, she would only bring ridicule on herself. She was powerless. There was nothing she could do.

Once again she turned her back on him, and this time she saw Drum pleading with his companion. In the moonlight she recognized Adam Palairet.

As she watched, Palairet glanced over Drum's shoulder and saw her. For a moment his eyes held hers; then his gaze flicked to Traherne beside her. She could tell by his stillness that he was puzzled to see them together. Then he turned and spoke to Drum, and put his hand on his arm and led him away. There was a gentleness in the gesture which surprised her. It was as if he were soothing a troubled child.

Beside her, Traherne was watching the little pageant on the lawn with amusement. 'I wonder what that's all about.'

She took a breath and put her hands together. 'Don't ever speak to me again,' she said.

He raised an eyebrow. 'My dear girl—'

'I'm not your dear girl. I'm engaged to be married.'

'Congratulations.'

'If you try to spoil things, I shall—'

'Yes?' he broke in gently. 'You shall what? Try to make people believe in some bizarre misfortune which never took place?'

'Where have you *been*?' said Osbourne when she reached the safety of his room.

She shut the door behind her and leaned against it, breathing hard.

'Good heavens,' he said, 'you're shaking. What the devil has happened?' He drew her into his arms and she leaned against him. 'Is it Adam?' he said. 'Has that brute—'

'No, no, it's—'

'Has he been interrogating you about me?'

117

'Take me to London,' she said fiercely.

'What?'

'You said you wanted to get away. Well, now I want it too.'

'But – what about Dodo? I thought you couldn't possibly leave her?'

'I'll square it with Dodo.'

He smiled. 'Ah, the inconstancy of woman!' He bent and kissed her mouth. 'We shall leave at dawn,' he murmured. 'It's already arranged.' He kissed her again, more deeply, but she twisted her head away. 'Darling infant,' he whispered as his arms tightened about her.

'Osbourne, not now . . .'

'Darling, darling infant.'

'*No . . .*'

But in the end, she let him. She didn't want to. But neither did she want to be alone.

As she lay beneath him on the counterpane, she caught sight of her maid's costume lying crumpled on the rug. It looked like a sloughed-off snakeskin.

'Darling kitten,' gasped Osbourne, squeezing her breast.

She remembered the flick of the yellowsnake's tail as it disappeared round the tree trunk; just before Traherne put his hand on her breast . . .

Later, when Osbourne had rolled off her, she lay staring up into the darkness. She saw again that avuncular, old-gentleman smile.

It was a chance encounter, she told herself. It means nothing.

Beside her, Osbourne had fallen asleep. She turned on her elbow to look at him, and he suddenly seemed unfamiliar: a handsome, golden-haired stranger who had wandered into her life and promised to make everything better.

And it *will* be better, she thought. Everything will be better once we're married.

CHAPTER FOURTEEN

Sibella was in a state of 'utter distraction' when they reached
Berkeley Square. This meant that she was reading a novel on her
favourite peach-coloured sofa, and looking the *dernier cri* in a
gauzy mauve afternoon gown which suited her fair hair and
plump figure to perfection, while a cold three-course luncheon
awaited them in the dining room.

'My new walking costume is a *disaster*,' she announced briskly
as she offered her cheek to Belle and then to Osbourne. 'Addisons
sent it round yesterday, and they've used the most ghastly
machined lace in the panels. I'm minded to send it straight back.
Added to which, Max's wretched governess is ill; what am I to do
if it's serious and he has to come up to Town? I've a skeleton staff
here as it is: Cook's in an isolation ward at the Nuffield, and Mary
and Jim are threatening to run off and nurse their relations.
Osbourne, darling, do go down to Sussex and sort things out.'

'Sort out what?' said Osbourne.

'Max!' cried Sibella. 'I can't have him with me, not with half the
world falling ill of this beastly 'flu. Even the doctors are going
down with it. They're so short-staffed that they're talking of
calling in the veterinary surgeons.'

'I'm afraid I can't,' said Osbourne. 'I've affairs of my own to sort
out.' He caught Belle's eye and winked. On the drive up from

Kyme, he'd spoken of finding them an apartment for after they were married. 'Something quiet and delightful, in one of those pretty little streets off Cheyne Walk.'

Belle gave him a tight smile. She hadn't slept well, worrying about Traherne. 'But you will be staying with us, won't you, darling?' she said. 'That's all right, isn't it, Sibella?'

'I'm counting on it,' said Sibella. 'We need a man in the house at times like these.'

Osbourne sighed. 'I can't possibly.'

'Why not?' Belle said uneasily. The prospect of being without him alarmed her. It was no use telling herself that Traherne would never come here – and that even if he did, he wouldn't be admitted; that Sibella hated her father, and the servants had permanent instructions to say that she was not at home.

'I simply can't,' Osbourne said again. 'This is the first place Adam will look.'

Sibella rolled her eyes. 'You're not still avoiding him?'

He looked pained. 'It's rather a case of him hounding me.'

'Well, I don't know anything about that,' said Sibella, 'but I do *wish* he were here to sort things out about Max. Adam's the kind of man who gets things done.'

'The solid, dependable type,' said Osbourne with a yawn.

Sibella gave him a wry smile. 'That's not quite what I mean.'

'Well, as I'm not the solid, dependable type,' he said, rising to his feet, 'and I've an obscene amount to do, I'm off to my club.'

Belle's hands tightened in her lap. She had an irrational sense that things were slipping away from her; that Traherne had been only the beginning . . . 'Shall we be seeing you tomorrow?' she said, hating how clinging that sounded.

'What barnacles women are,' murmured Osbourne. 'Kitten, I shall come if I can. But really, I—'

'Luncheon,' Sibella said crisply. 'One o'clock. Don't be late.'

When he'd gone, Sibella cast herself onto the sofa with a sigh of relief. 'Actually, I'm rather glad he's gone. Now we can have a quiet time on our own.' She threw Belle an appraising look. 'What's wrong? Have you two had a tiff?'

Belle shook her head. 'Everything's fine. And you? How are you?'

Sibella threw her a look that said she knew she was being fobbed off; then went along with it. 'Yet another proposal from dear old Sir Monty,' she said. 'Honestly, Belle, why do they *imagine* I want to become a wife again? It's so much more fun being a widow. But speaking of wives, how's Dodo?'

Belle told her, and Sibella listened avidly. She had an unquenchable appetite for gossip, and a starkly unromantic view of relations between men and women, which her enemies called callous. When Belle had finished, she reached for the bonbon dish. 'It sounds,' she said, 'no different from most marriages I know.'

'Isn't that a bit harsh? After all, this is Dodo.'

Sibella shrugged. 'She's tougher than you think. She'll get over it. One can get over anything, darling. Even marriage.'

Belle studied her for a moment. Then she broke into a grin. 'Oh, Sibella. What would I do without you?'

She meant it. It always struck her as bizarre that the Trahernes should have furnished both the man who'd shattered her life, and the woman who'd put it together again. Sibella Clyne was shrewd, pragmatic and unsentimental, but she'd been briskly kind to Belle: never questioning her hatred of school, and lying fluently to the headmistress on the numerous occasions when she'd run away. She'd never once badgered Belle about her lack of involvement in war work, and in recent months she'd turned a discreet blind eye to the affair with Osbourne.

To the outside world she was a plump, gossipy socialite who gave excellent dinners and talked amusing nonsense. But sometimes Belle caught a flash of another woman underneath: a woman who'd 'got over' two deeply unhappy marriages; who treated her wealth with disdain and her friends with quiet generosity; who rebuffed her numerous suitors with firmness and grace.

'Belle, what's wrong?' Sibella said again.

Belle hesitated. She was longing to tell Sibella all about her engagement, but something held her back. With a shock she realized what it was. She didn't know if Sibella would be delighted or appalled. 'Nothing's wrong,' she said.

Sibella gave an unladylike snort.

'If you want to know,' Belle said lightly, 'while I was at Kyme, I had a bad bout of homesickness.' She paused. 'And I happened to run into your father.'

'Oh Lord, no wonder you're out of sorts.' Sibella leaned back and stared at the ceiling. She'd never told Belle what lay behind her animosity to him, and Belle had never asked. It was simply a given between them. 'I'd heard he was in the country,' she said at last. 'No doubt he's seeing to poor Lyndon's affairs.'

There was a silence while they thought about that.

Sibella got up and went to the looking-glass above the chimney-piece. Suddenly her face showed every one of her thirty-four years. 'It's so odd,' she said in an altered voice. 'I never thought I cared for Lyndon when he was alive; he was simply my odious little brother. But now that he's gone . . .' She sat down again, shaking her head.

Belle went to sit beside her.

'This wretched war,' Sibella said shakily.

Belle took her hand.

Sibella gave her a watery smile. 'Don't worry about me. I'm just a bit down. So many gone. It's so – so hard to *accept* . . .' She gave a little snort of laughter. 'Do you know, this morning I was reading quite an amusing piece in *The Times*, and I actually made a mental note to cut it out and send it to Freddie? The poor man's been dead for over a year, and I still can't . . .'

'I know,' said Belle.

'It's not as if I loved him,' said Sibella. 'People like me aren't capable of love. But I was *used* to him. With him I never had to pretend.' She took a ragged breath, then put both hands to her hair. 'Heavens, I must look a perfect fright.'

Belle stood up. 'Let's go and have lunch,' she said. 'Then we'll see about this disaster of a walking costume. And if there's the slightest doubt about it, I shall take it back to Addisons myself.'

The costume did need altering, and the next morning Belle seized on it as an excuse to get out, and made her way to Bond Street, leaving Sibella laid up with a headache.

Belle had slept badly, for Osbourne had neither telephoned nor sent a note. She couldn't shake off the sense that her house of cards was about to come tumbling down.

Having declined Sibella's offer of the motor, she made her way on foot, in the hope that the walk would lift her spirits. As she turned into Bond Street she was engulfed by the familiar crowds in khaki and mourning: the Tommies and the officers, the conductorettes and munitions workers; the Dominion troops whose dark faces always evoked Jamaica. She saw VADs pushing the wounded in Bath chairs: pale, shrunken young men in jaunty blue flannel suits and red neckties. She passed a newspaper stand where headlines screamed of the Allies' triumph in driving the Germans back beyond the Antwerp–Metz railway.

She felt the familiar twinge of guilt. Her mother and aunt worked hard for the Jamaica War Relief Fund; Dodo sent books to officers in the trenches; even Sibella organized parcels to the Front. But she herself had resolutely avoided all that. It was as if any involvement in war work might bring her too close to reality – to the reality she'd been running from since she'd left Jamaica. In London she had her mask: her identity as Belle Lawe, the irrepressible socialite. If she gave that up – even temporarily – then real life would intervene, and she might be found out . . .

She saw to the alterations at the dressmaker's, then, as the anxiety still hadn't worn off, she decided to cheer herself up with a visit to the park, and hailed a cab: one of the aged hansoms that had been pressed back into use now that the motor-taxis and omnibuses were on restricted service.

As they drove, she realized quite how much London had changed while she'd been down at Kyme. Here and there in the crowd, she saw people wearing white surgical masks as protection against the 'flu, which was worsening day by day, and beginning to be spoken of as an epidemic.

No-one else seemed to find the masks alarming. No-one else even noticed. The cab rattled past a mother and child on the pavement, both wearing masks. Their eyes met hers blankly. They were used to this. But to her it didn't seem real. She began to feel like a ghost.

'Oh, people are dropping like flies,' the cabbie told her with gloomy relish. 'It's ten times worse than it was in the summer, and now it's mostly the young as are falling off. They're saying it's the Kaiser's secret weapon, but I don't know. I remember the Russian 'flu of '89, and you're not telling me *that* was down to the Kaiser. Still,' he added, belatedly remembering his tip, 'you'll do all right just so long as you smoke enough, and carry a pocketful of salt.'

Belle paid him off and got out. It was a beautiful, soft September day, and although there were no flowers in the flower beds it was a relief to see grass and trees. She almost managed to ignore the two great anti-aircraft guns positioned at Hyde Park Corner. But as she passed a newspaper stand, she noticed that the billboards carried only tidings of the War, and said nothing about the epidemic. So how *could* people be 'dropping like flies'?

And yet, there was the public telephone booth at the corner of Grosvenor Street, padlocked shut '*to prevent infection*'. And as she walked down South Audley Street she passed red and yellow flags tied to the railings, with home-made signs tacked to the doors: *Influenza; Tradesmen leave provisions on step; Doctor walk in, don't knock, all in bed.*

It was past one by the time she reached the house, but despite Sibella's invitation to luncheon, Osbourne wasn't there.

'He's gone, miss,' whispered Jenny, who in the absence of the rest of the staff was acting as housemaid, cook and footman.

'Gone?' said Belle. 'Do you mean he was here, and he—'

'Left, miss.' Jenny leaned closer. 'Slipped out by the basement,' she hissed. 'Mistress has a visitor he didn't wish to see.'

Belle thought of Cornelius Traherne, and her stomach turned over.

'They're in the drawing room,' whispered Jenny, and before Belle could stop her she'd opened the doors and stood aside to let her pass.

'Ah, Belle,' said Sibella.

'Hello,' said Adam Palairet.

Ignoring his outstretched hand, Isabelle Lawe made her way to the window seat and sat down. 'You didn't waste much time,' she said, with no attempt at courtesy.

'No,' replied Adam, ignoring her tone, 'I didn't.' He watched her take off her hat and shake out her sleek black bob, then cross her legs and jiggle her foot slowly up and down. He found that irritating, and resolved to ignore it.

Sibella was watching them with amusement. 'Well, I gather that you've already been introduced; although I must say it's amazing that your paths didn't cross years ago. Shall I see about some tea?'

'Not for me,' said Isabelle Lawe.

'Thank you,' said Adam at the same time.

Biting back a smile, Sibella left the room, shutting the doors behind her.

The silence lengthened. Isabelle Lawe went on jiggling her foot. She wore a tailored coat-frock of forest green, with calf-length buttoned boots of dark blue Russian leather. The strong colours suited her, and her figure was more than good enough to take the severity of the cut, but Adam thought she looked sulky and unappealing; and she'd painted her wide mouth too dark a shade of red.

He reminded himself that she wasn't yet twenty, and that her animosity was mostly defensive. In fact, he ought to feel sorry for her. None of this was her fault.

It didn't work.

'I've been meaning to ask,' she said. 'Why are you still in uniform? Sibella tells me that you're some kind of invalid.'

Refusing to be needled, he gave her his blandest smile. 'I'm in uniform,' he said, 'because I'm a soldier. Although I may shortly become an ex-soldier, which is presumably what you mean. It's up to the doctors to decide.'

'You don't look ill.'

'I got shot in the lung. It's now quite healed, but it's still a bit troublesome.'

'So you're broken-winded. Like a horse.'

He ignored that. 'I'm waiting to hear if they'll let me go back.'

'Rather a pity if they don't,' she said, still jiggling her foot. 'You'll miss the end of the War. Everyone's saying the Germans will throw in the towel any day now. That they're simply holding out to improve the terms of surrender.'

'Is that what everyone's saying?'

She flushed.

He knew what she was doing. She was keeping him talking until Sibella returned. But what did she hope to achieve by that?

Suddenly he felt tired. Why do I bother? he wondered. She doesn't want to be helped, and I've no interest whatsoever in her welfare. I'm only doing this out of some outdated notion of family honour, in which I've long since ceased to believe.

'I suppose,' she said, 'being in uniform has the advantage that no-one will give you a white feather. And presumably you enjoy trying to make people like me feel guilty for not doing our bit: for not knitting comforters or dispensing sandwiches to the troops at railway stations.'

'And do you feel guilty?'

She hesitated a fraction too long. 'No,' she said.

'Then there wouldn't be much point in my trying to make you, would there?'

She studied him with frank dislike. She had clear olive skin and direct, very dark eyes that some men would have found challenging. Adam didn't. He said, 'Miss Lawe, I do appreciate that you're not—'

'While you were at Kyme,' she broke in, 'did you get to see Celia, after all?'

'No, I didn't. After all. Now please, I—'

'What a pity. People say that we look rather alike, she and I. Do you think that's true?'

'There is a resemblance,' he said, rubbing his temple.

'Only I'm not nearly such a beauty as Celia.'

'That's true,' said Adam, 'you're not.'

Her lip curled mirthlessly.

'Now can we get to the point? I need to see Osbourne.'

Her chin went up. 'I know you do.'

'Do you know where he is?'

'Yes.'

'Will you tell me?'

'No.' Her hands had moved to her lap, and she'd lost her air of brittle assurance.

He sat forward with his elbows on his knees. 'Miss Lawe, what you need to understand—'

The doors opened, and Sibella came in. She glanced from one to the other, tasting the atmosphere with relish. 'Oh dear,' she said insincerely, 'did I come back too soon? Ought I to—'

'No, don't,' said Isabelle Lawe. 'We've just finished.' She got up and walked to the door. 'Goodbye, Captain Palairet,' she said. 'And jolly good luck in the War.'

Adam sat back with a sigh.

Sibella plumped down beside him, her blue eyes agleam with mischief. '*What* was that all about?'

'How do you stand her?' said Adam.

'Belle? Oh, I'm inordinately fond of her. She has such spirit! Why, was she uncivil?'

'Yes. Very.'

She gave a snort of laughter. 'You poor darling.' She paused. 'You know, you're looking awfully tired. Why don't you stay to lunch?'

'No, thank you, Sib. I don't think I could take another dose of Miss Lawe.'

She studied him with concern. 'They're not going to send you back to the Front, are they?'

'I don't know. I had a note from Clive this morning.'

'Your doctor friend?'

He nodded. 'It seems the medical board's so short-staffed that they're drafting him in to help. He's seeing me tomorrow. Then they'll decide.'

'If they do send you back, shall you mind terribly?'

He thought about that. 'I don't know. In a way it'll be a relief. Things are simpler over there.'

'Whatever do you mean?'

He glanced at her, then shook his head. How to explain that he was getting tired of people seeking his help? First there was Drum, sending him a plaintive wire begging him to meet for dinner; then a call from Maud McAllister with some worry about the Home Farm that couldn't possibly wait; and on top of all that, he still had to track down wretched, *bloody* Osbourne, and somehow persuade him to . . . 'I just want to go somewhere very very quiet,' he told Sibella, 'and be alone for ever and ever.'

Sibella burst out laughing. 'Oh, Adam, I don't think that's going to happen! You're far too attractive to be alone!'

Despite himself, he laughed. 'Now you're trying to embarrass me.'

'Heavens no,' she said, handing him his tea. 'I gave that up aeons ago.'

There was a companionable silence while they drank their tea. Then Adam said, 'I really do need to see Osbourne.'

'About what?'

'I'm afraid I can't tell you. Not just yet. But perhaps you can tell me . . . This friendship between him and Miss Lawe. Is it serious?'

Sibella raised her shoulders in a shrug. 'These days, who can say? I doubt it. Although they do seem fond of one another. Why?'

He sighed. 'I wish I'd never . . . Why do people keep coming to me for help?'

'Because you're so good at giving it, darling.'

'Well, not any more. As of now, I'm renouncing all that. No more help. Why do you smile?'

'Because that's simply not in your nature.'

'It's not in yours to be analytical,' he pointed out, 'but it's not stopping you at the moment.'

That made her chuckle. 'Perhaps I shall become a philosopher in my old age.'

He got to his feet. 'Well, then you have a great many years in which to decide.'

'Flatterer,' she said as she accompanied him to the door.

But as they went out into the hall, she faltered for a moment, and on instinct he put a hand under her elbow to steady her. 'Are you all right?' he said sharply.

She gave herself a little shake, and smiled up at him. 'My dear Adam. My cook is in hospital, my son's governess will shortly be joining her, and I've hardly a shred of respectable clothing to my name. Of course I'm all right. Why shouldn't I be?'

CHAPTER FIFTEEN

Sibella was late for breakfast, and as Belle was finishing hers Jenny came clattering down the stairs, fighting back tears. 'She's bad, miss. You'd better come.'

Sibella lay in a storm of bedclothes, her pretty hair tangled, her face flushed and glistening with sweat. Sibella, who was always immaculately turned out; who never even 'glowed'.

When she saw Belle, she forced a grin that was painful to see. 'I know,' she gasped. 'Frightful nuisance. Could you – call Dr Steele? And don't – *don't* come any closer.'

Belle raced downstairs and telephoned the doctor. No reply. Cursing under her breath, she shouted for Jenny.

The girl appeared at the top of the stairs, twisting her hands.

'Fetch Dr Steele,' said Belle. 'Don't just stand there, run and fetch him! And don't come back without him!'

While Jenny got her hat and coat, Belle ran upstairs to the bathroom and ransacked the medicine cupboard. She didn't know what she was looking for. What did one give someone with influenza? What was influenza, anyway?

Dimly, she remembered her mother dosing her with quinine when she was little. Quinine was her mother's answer to everything. Perhaps it would work on the 'flu? She grabbed the bottle and an armful of others, and turned to see Jenny in the doorway.

'My mum swears by garlic tea,' said the girl as she jammed on her hat. 'And wrapping them in wet sheets to bring down the fever, and hot toddy for the heads.'

Belle forced a smile. 'Sibella will like the toddy.'

Jenny's eyes filled with tears.

'You'd better go,' said Belle.

'Dr Steele,' muttered Jenny. 'Right away.'

When she'd gone, the house lapsed into funereal stillness. Clutching an armful of phenacetin, Dover's powders and tincture of quinine, Belle elbowed open the bedroom door.

Weakly, Sibella waved a hand to warn her back.

'Dr Steele will be here soon,' said Belle as cheerfully as she could. 'In the meantime, I'm afraid you're stuck with me. So no more nonsense about not coming any closer.'

Jenny did not come back. Perhaps she couldn't find Dr Steele. Perhaps she'd given up looking for him, and was too frightened to return. Whatever the reason, Belle stopped listening for the latchkey, and rolled up her sleeves and got on with it.

Sibella was running a fever of one hundred and five. Her face was a mottled puce, and she kept taking great hungry gulps of air, but it was never enough. Her breath rasped like a bank note being crisped in someone's hand.

Belle asked her where it hurt.

'Everywhere,' she moaned. 'When I move – when I'm still . . . Oh, Belle, give me something for the pain . . .'

All Belle could do was wrap her in wet sheets to bring down the temperature, and dose her with quinine and phenacetin. None of it seemed to have the slightest effect.

Around noon, Sibella had a coughing fit. Belle held her shoulders and prayed that it wouldn't lead to convulsions. Then Sibella started to retch. Belle ran for a basin. To her horror she saw that it wasn't vomit Sibella was bringing up: the basin was spattered with greenish-yellow pus.

'Poor – you,' gasped Sibella between bouts of coughing, while Belle held her head. 'How – perfectly vile.'

'Hush, darling,' murmured Belle. 'You need every ounce of strength.'

At last the coughing subsided, and Belle laid her back on the pillows, where she fell into an exhausted sleep.

Belle crept out to the bathroom and rinsed the basin, trying not to gag. Then she tiptoed downstairs and rang Osbourne's club. He wasn't there, and they didn't know where he could be reached. At least, that was what they said.

She stood in the middle of the hall, wondering whom she could call. A hospital? The police?

A faint moan from the bedroom settled it for her. No time to telephone. She ran back upstairs.

It was eight in the evening when Dr Steele finally arrived, accompanied by a shamefaced Jenny. 'I couldn't *find* him,' she whispered. Belle silenced her with a look.

The doctor was red-eyed with exhaustion, but to her astonishment he spent a scant five minutes with Sibella before leading Belle back onto the landing. 'I've seen worse,' he said brusquely. 'She may pull through.'

Belle was aghast. 'But you're not leaving already?'

'My dear Miss Lawe. I've seen several dozen cases in the past few hours, and by morning I shall have seen several dozen more. I cannot afford to linger.'

'But—'

'Keep dosing her with phenacetin at four-hour intervals for the pain,' he said as he started down the stairs, 'and here's morphine to dry the lungs and slow the breathing. You did well with the wet sheets and the quinine.'

Belle clutched his arm. 'But I don't *know* anything! How will I know if she's getting worse?'

'You'll know,' said the doctor wearily. He turned and gave her an appraising look, as if wondering how much more she could take. 'To tell you the truth, Miss Lawe, your guess is probably as good as mine. In thirty years I've never seen anything like this. There are no rules. Every case is different. Sometimes their lungs fill with pus and they drown within hours. Sometimes the heart gives out. Sometimes there's delirium. Sometimes they go deaf or blind. Sometimes they have great gushing nosebleeds – black blood, pints of it. That's either the turning point to recovery, or aneurism and the end . . .' He broke off, shaking his head. 'I'm sorry. Unforgivable to sound off like that. But I've never been so powerless. It makes me angry.'

'What about Sibella?' said Belle in a small voice. 'Will she . . .'

'I don't know. I really don't know.'

At the door he turned and handed her a sixpenny booklet. 'Take this. It'll tell you more than I've got time for.'

'Will you be coming back?'

'Some time tomorrow. If I can.'

She swallowed. 'Thank you, Dr Steele.'

'You're a good nurse, Miss Lawe. Common sense. Good nerves. Strong stomach. You'll muddle through.'

'Poor Freddie,' murmured Sibella in one of her lucid periods. 'He really loved me, you know.'

'I know he did, darling,' said Belle as she sponged Sibella's face and throat, where the skin had broken out in hundreds of tiny purple blood blisters that burned to the touch.

It was past midnight. Belle's face felt stiff with fatigue, and she'd been clenching her jaw so hard that it ached. Dr Steele's booklet lay unread on the rug beside the bed. She hadn't had a moment to look at it.

She and Sibella were alone in the house. Jenny had disappeared hours ago, leaving an ill-spelt note to the effect that her mother had been taken sick, and her brothers and sisters needed her. Belle hardly noticed her absence. She had enough to do fighting her own fears without having to calm Jenny's as well.

'You know,' breathed Sibella, 'he – proposed to me. Just before I married Clyne. But it – would never have done. I couldn't have made him happy.'

'Hush, Sib, please . . .'

'You see – I never knew *how* to love. Didn't have the knack.' She paused for breath. 'I'm glad he died before me. Wouldn't want him – to see me like this.' Suddenly she frowned. 'Good heavens, what's Lyndon doing in my room?'

A couple of hours later, she began to breathe more freely. Hardly daring to hope, Belle gave her another sponge bath – and saw to her alarm that the blisters had spread to her back and arms. What did that mean? A quick skim through the booklet was no help at all. It didn't even mention blisters.

'What happened to your uncle?' asked Sibella abruptly.

Belle was startled. 'Ben? He's on the Somme, darling. Do you remember? We had a letter from Sophie in the summer.'

'Oh – yes.' Her blistered lips parted in a smile. 'Sophie was furious when he joined up. Why did he? He was the last man I'd have . . .'

'I'm not sure,' said Belle. 'He said he owed it to his country, but perhaps he was joking. With Ben you never really know.' She was puzzled. Sibella never talked about Ben.

'I hated him for years,' said Sibella. She shut her eyes. 'But I wanted him, too.'

Belle stared at her. '*Ben?*'

Sibella fixed her with fever-bright blue eyes. 'Don't worry, darling. Sophie knows all about it. But – it's true. I've never wanted any man as I wanted him. Not love. Just – the other thing.' Her face contorted. 'Belle, it's not *fair*. I'm going to die, and I've never loved anyone.'

'You're not going to die,' Belle said fiercely. 'You're going to—'

'No, no. I – I shan't get over this.' She clutched Belle's hand. 'Make sure I look decent? The blue bedjacket with the Valenciennes trim? And don't – don't let Max see me. It'll only frighten him—'

'Don't talk like that!'

By three in the morning, the blisters had spread to her entire body, and all Belle could do was dose her with whisky and quinine, and hold her down to prevent her fighting off imaginary suitors. 'For the last – time, I will *not* marry you! I won't – marry – anyone!'

At half-past three she became abruptly quieter, and her colour improved a little. The blood blisters began to fade, and her temperature dropped to one hundred and three. Belle swallowed tears of relief. She was getting better.

'My father,' Sibella said suddenly, 'is a terrible man.'

Belle folded a napkin and set it on the bedside table. 'I know,' she said.

Sibella looked at her. Her eyes were clear. 'You're the strong one,' she said. 'You're like your mamma.'

'Hush, darling, don't talk any more. You need to rest.'

'Sophie once told me what Madeleine did when she was young, to keep them together. Extraordinary . . .'

'You need to rest,' Belle said again. She smiled. 'You're getting better, Sib. The fever's coming down.'

Sibella shut her eyes. 'Find a *good* man, Belle darling. They do exist, you know.'

CHAPTER SIXTEEN

Adam's patience was wearing thin as he mounted the steps of number seventeen, Berkeley Square. After a frustrating two days of unanswered wires and 'missed' telephone calls, Osbourne was still contriving to elude him. So to hell with Osbourne. There was now no option but to have it out with Miss Lawe; and if she thought she could stonewall him yet again, she'd find that—

To his surprise, she answered the door herself.

He knew immediately that something was wrong. Her face was scrubbed clean of make-up, which made her look about fifteen, and there were dark shadows under her eyes. Her once sleek hair was dull and uncombed, and her haphazardly buttoned blue gown looked as if she hadn't taken it off in days.

'Captain Palairet,' she said, giving him a distant stare as if she was having trouble focusing. 'What are you doing here?' She didn't say it rudely; she simply didn't understand.

He began to be worried about Sibella. 'May I come in?' he said.

'No, I don't think—'

'Please. I need to speak to you. It won't take long.'

She blinked. Her eyes were red-rimmed, although whether from fatigue or crying, he couldn't tell. The last of his irritation drained away. 'Please,' he said again. He felt like a bully.

With a sigh she turned on her heel, leaving him to close the door after him. He followed her into the drawing room, and watched her seat herself on Sibella's peach silk sofa by the window. She didn't ask him to sit down, so he remained standing – then realized that he was looming over her, and took the armchair opposite.

'Where are the servants?' he asked.

She rearranged the cushions beside her, picked one, and placed it on her lap, as if for protection. 'They're gone,' she said. 'They had relations to nurse.'

'Where is Sibella?'

Her hands tightened on the cushion.

'Is she – ill?'

She took a breath. 'Sibella died this morning.'

A light breeze stirred the curtains. From the square came the sound of a child laughing. Adam looked about him at this room which bore traces of its owner everywhere. The *Tatler*, with one of the pages turned over to mark the place. A rather daring Elinor Glyn, lying open on a side table. The little Fabergé bonbon dish – 'my *downfall*,' she would drawl, as she helped herself to yet another violet cream.

It wasn't possible that she was gone.

He watched Isabelle Lawe take up the Elinor Glyn, close it, and replace it carefully on the table. He went to sit beside her and tried to take her hand, but she turned herself away, and he gave up, abashed.

'I'm – so sorry,' he muttered. He was uncomfortably aware that his apology could apply equally to his blunder, or to Sibella. Somehow that seemed to trivialize Sibella, although he knew that she herself would have been vastly amused at his expense. 'Darling Adam,' she would have chuckled, 'what a muff you can be, for all your cleverness! And you're simply *appalling* at showing your feelings.'

He was surprised by how deeply her death affected him. He'd seen hundreds of men die at the Front. But it shouldn't have happened to her. Not pretty, elegant, amusing Sibella, who existed to distract from the harsh realities; not to succumb to them.

'It was just before dawn,' said Isabelle Lawe, tucking a lock of hair behind her ear in a gesture he found oddly moving. 'She'd been quiet in the night. Just sometimes humming songs from her childhood, Jamaican nursery rhymes. But then – her breathing got worse again.' She shook her head. 'That *sound*. Like paper being crackled. I tried everything. Nothing was any use.'

'What about doctors? Didn't you have any help?'

Again she shook her head. 'Dr Steele came a couple of times, but he wasn't any use either. He said so. Nothing's any use.' She blinked rapidly. 'Around four in the morning, she opened her eyes, and took a great deep breath. Then she – died.' Sucking in her lips, she stared fiercely at the cushion, clearly willing herself not to cry.

Feeling powerless, Adam waited while she got herself under control. Then he asked if Sibella was still upstairs.

'Yes, but you can't see her. She wouldn't want—'

'I won't be long,' Adam said quietly, 'but I need to see her. To say goodbye.'

The curtains were drawn and the bedroom was in half-darkness, but a lamp cast a golden glow that was not unbecoming. Poor Sibella would have been pleased.

But no amount of flattering light could conceal the ravages of the disease. Her pretty face was gaunt, and she looked older and grimmer than she had in life. Not for the first time, Adam reflected that it's a pious myth that the faces of the dead take on an unearthly serenity. That's asking too much of them, he thought. The dead are simply dead. They show their pain, like anyone else.

Isabelle Lawe had done a surprisingly good job of the laying out. Sibella wore a lacy pale blue bedjacket, and her golden hair was neatly combed and arranged around her shoulders in becoming curls. Her hands clasped a pink rose, obviously taken from the garden in the square. It was a heartfelt touch that he would not have expected from Isabelle Lawe. Perhaps she was capable of deeper feeling than he had supposed.

'Goodbye, Sibella,' he murmured. 'Be at peace.' Then he bent and kissed the cold brow, and left her to her rest.

In the drawing room, Isabelle Lawe was standing at the window, looking out into the square with her arms clasped about her waist. At Adam's arrival she turned to him. 'She wouldn't have wanted you to see her like that,' she said reproachfully.

'I'm sorry,' said Adam. 'But she wouldn't have wanted me not to say goodbye, either.'

She made no reply.

Adam cleared his throat. 'Perhaps I can help with – well, with arrangements? Her father is a member of my club. I could find him and break the news, if—'

'No,' she said with startling vehemence, 'Don't do that.'

'But surely—'

'I said no!' She paused, still cradling herself. 'Sibella didn't get on with her father.'

'I'm aware of that, but—'

'She left instructions with her solicitors,' said Isabelle Lawe, her voice rising. 'I telephoned them this afternoon. They're seeing to all the arrangements for the . . .' she took a breath, 'for the funeral. But she was very clear about one thing. Mr Traherne is not to be admitted either to the service or to the house in Sussex, or to this house.'

Two spots of colour had appeared on her cheeks, and her knuckles were white. For some reason, she didn't like Cornelius Traherne any better than poor Sibella. Adam remembered her pale face staring at him from the darkened conservatory at Kyme as she had stood beside Traherne.

'What about her mother?' he said. 'I don't think her dislike extended—'

'I've sent her a wire,' she replied. Then she fixed him with her direct dark gaze. 'What did you want to see me about?'

The change of subject took him by surprise. 'Nothing,' he said.

'It can't be nothing,' she said, 'you've been hounding us for days.'

'Actually, I was hounding Osbourne. I thought it'd be better coming from him. And I still think so, which is why—'

'Tell me what it is.'

'No.'

'Yes.'

He stood irresolute, wondering what to do. Then he sat down and put his hands on his knees. 'Osbourne's married,' he said.

He'd read in novels of the blood draining from a person's face, but until now he'd always thought it was just a literary convention. Now he watched in amazement as the vigour drained out of her. Even her lips turned pale. Without the red lipstick, her mouth looked vulnerable and raw.

He watched her move to the peach silk sofa and sit down, and put her hands together in her lap. 'Tell me everything,' she said.

He wondered how to begin. 'It was last year,' he said slowly, 'when he was stationed in Arras. She – his wife – she's the daughter of the woman in whose house he was billeted.'

She blinked. 'What is she like? That is – if you know.'

He hesitated. 'It's a respectable family. Wine merchants. The father's dead, the brother runs the business. Or he did, before the War.' Why am I telling her all this? he thought savagely. What possible good does it do?

He blundered on. 'Her name is Françoise. Eighteen years old, but seems younger. Sheltered. Shy. Quite pretty, in a conventional sort of way.'

'You've seen her?'

He paused. 'When Osbourne left, she had no money. She didn't know where he was. She – needed help. Her brother was away fighting, still is, and her mother had recently died. Somehow she'd got hold of my name. She wrote to me. On my next leave, I went to see her.'

She stared at him without understanding. 'You mean – Osbourne simply left her?'

Again he hesitated. 'I imagine he thought he could get a divorce. But of course she's a Catholic. Then, perhaps, he decided that if he just sent her money—'

'But you said that she had no money, so he can't have done.'

'Perhaps he intended to,' he said unconvincingly. Christ, he thought angrily, why am I trying to defend him? 'I don't know, Miss Lawe,' he said brusquely, 'because so far I haven't been able to find him and have it out.'

There was a silence while she considered that. Then she said, 'Now I understand why he wanted us to keep it secret.' She glanced at him. 'You see – we were engaged to be married.'

It was his turn to stare. 'Oh. Oh, God. I – didn't know.'

'Of course you didn't. No-one did. That's what I'm telling you.' She paused. 'He wanted it to be a secret. He said that he needed time to square it with his people. He meant you.'

'Ah,' he said.

'Apparently,' she said, her voice hardening, 'you wouldn't have approved of me.'

Adam looked blank. 'I don't understand.'

'Don't you? Well. Perhaps that was a lie, too.'

Another silence.

Then she said. 'There's something else, isn't there?'

He shook his head. 'I think you've had more than enough already—'

'I'll be the judge of that. Tell me. I need to know everything.'

He frowned at his hands. 'There's – a child.'

A soft intake of breath.

'A little girl,' he said. 'Ten months old.'

Isabelle Lawe put her hands by her sides and stared down at the rug. 'Well, that's it, then,' she said to herself.

Adam didn't know how to reply.

It was very still in the drawing room. The breeze had subsided, and the curtains hung motionless. The clock on the chimney-piece had stopped.

The telephone rang.

Adam jumped. Isabelle didn't move.

On and on it rang: loud, insistent, everyday. Adam stirred. 'Shall I—?'

She did not reply.

He went out into the hall.

The woman on the other end of the line sounded both flustered and aggrieved, but as she was a housekeeper she kept a lid on her temper when she learned that she was speaking to an officer. She seemed anxious to make it clear that she was *not* a governess – the governess having so far neglected her duties as to have ended up in hospital with the influenza – which now left the lone housekeeper singlehandedly running the household, *and* looking after Master Max, whom she was plainly desperate to get off her hands, so that she could go to Brighton and nurse her sister. 'I'm a *housekeeper*', she complained for the tenth time, 'not a governess . . .'

Quietly, Adam told her what had happened.

She made a clucking noise, but showed no real distress, and Adam could hear her reckoning the extent to which this would make it harder to ditch Max. He felt a flash of pity for the boy, whom he vaguely recalled meeting before the War.

Through the open door he saw Isabelle Lawe sitting silent and still by the window. 'Well he can't come here,' he told the house-keeper, putting a little military steel into his voice to fend off the expected protest.

'But I'm a *housekeeper*, not a—'

'Who else can take him?'

'Well . . . there's Mrs Pryce-Dennistoun. Mrs Clyne's friend? They play bridge together. I telephoned her when I couldn't get through to you' – somehow she made that sound as if it was his fault – 'but she can only take him for a couple of days, she was most particular about that—'

'Good enough,' said Adam. 'See to it.'

'What, me? But sir, I can't—'

'Mrs Clyne's solicitors will reimburse your expenses,' he said briskly. 'I'll make sure that they know the boy's whereabouts.'

'But sir, can't you—'

'No,' he said, and replaced the receiver.

Back in the drawing room, he told Isabelle Lawe. She listened without seeming to take in a word.

Adam said, 'Is there someone I can call?'

She blinked up at him. 'What do you mean?'

'Someone to be with you? You shouldn't be here on your own.'

'I don't want anyone.'

'There must be someone.'

She shook her head. 'Not for people like me.'

He threw her a sharp glance. What did she mean? 'I can't just leave you,' he said.

'Very well,' she said wearily. 'I've an aunt. Aunt – Mildred. I shall telephone her directly you've left. There. Does that satisfy you?'

He guessed that Aunt Mildred had been invented on the spot to get rid of him, but decided to go along with it. After all, Isabelle Lawe was no relation of his. He wasn't responsible for her, and she didn't want his help. Besides, he'd done what he'd set out to do, he'd warned her about Osbourne. Duty discharged.

He moved to the door. 'I'll call tomorrow morning to see—'

'Please don't,' she said between her teeth. 'I'm sorry if that sounds uncivil, but I shall be fine. I don't want your help.'

He inclined his head. 'Very well.'

'I shall be fine,' she said again, as if to convince herself. 'There are worse things than losing a lover.'

'I'm sorry,' said Adam. That was so inadequate that he coloured. 'I'll – let myself out.'

She did not reply, or even turn her head.

On the steps, he glanced through the window and saw her still seated on the sofa, just as he'd left her. She hadn't moved at all.

CHAPTER SEVENTEEN

'Where to, miss?' said the cabbie.

Belle stared at him.

'Where d'you want to go?'

'I don't care,' she said. 'Just take me away from here. Take me somewhere – poor.'

It was his turn to stare.

'The East End,' she said on impulse. 'Take me to the East End.'

He hesitated. 'Big place, miss. Whereabouts?'

'Just drive.'

With an eloquent shrug he shut the roof hatch and clucked to his horse to walk on.

Belle drew down the blind, and sat back against the greasy green plush. She was so *tired*. It had been all she could do to cram a few things into a valise, turn off the gas, and lock the front door. Now, as the cab rattled off, she shut her eyes. She didn't want to see number seventeen slipping away, or the last of Berkeley Square. She was finished with all that.

Or rather, it was finished with her. The duppies had caught up with her at last, just as she'd always feared they would. No more Sibella. No more Osbourne. No more being the popular socialite, Miss Isabelle Lawe. The duppies had cast her out into darkness.

And there wasn't a minute to lose, for Cornelius Traherne would come to the house as soon as he heard the news. Sibella had been wealthy. Many times she'd told Belle that Max would inherit it all; that she'd left instructions with her solicitors that 'if anything happened', her father was to have no control over the boy. But Belle knew that that wouldn't stop Traherne. He was not a man to be deflected by a woman.

You did the right thing, she told herself as the cab swayed through the streets. But she couldn't shake off the feeling that yet again, she was running away from Traherne.

She tried to put that from her mind, and at last slid down into uneasy dreams.

'Where now?' said the cabbie, startling her into wakefulness. The roof hatch was open, and the harsh daylight made her blink.

'I told you,' she said blearily, 'the East End.'

'We're there, miss. Where now?'

What did it matter? Why couldn't he leave her alone?

'I'm not allowed to just drive around, miss,' he said testily. 'You know that well as I do, it's against my licence. Sides, there's a war on.'

'Give me a moment to think,' she said.

Heaving a sigh, he pulled up at the kerb.

Belle raised the blind and peered out. They were in a narrow street overshadowed by grimy tenements, and criss-crossed with soot-speckled washing. She smelt stale cabbage and sewerage. Yes, she thought. The dirtier the better.

But where should she go?

A memory surfaced from long ago. She was twelve years old, standing with her aunt and uncle on Fever Hill, inspecting the new great house which was nearing completion.

She'd always loved those visits. Aunt Sophie made a point of listening to her ideas, and sometimes even implemented one or two; and Ben let her hold out a handkerchief to gauge the wind direction, so that they could ensure that the new house would be as cool as possible.

This particular afternoon, a strong land breeze had been blowing from the hills, and the three of them had been standing in the carriageway, admiring the splendid new porticoed verandahs.

Suddenly, Ben had snorted a laugh. 'It's bloody enormous,' he'd said, earning a curious look from Belle and a warning glance from his wife. 'Well, it's a long way from East Street, isn't it, sweetheart?' he'd said to Aunt Sophie.

Belle was intrigued. 'What's East Street?'

'Where I grew up,' he replied. 'Well, part of the time.' He gave her a lopsided smile. 'Not your kind of place, love. Not at all.'

'Is East Street in London?' said Belle. 'Are your mamma and papa still there?'

'Oh, no, they're long gone,' he said softly. 'Nobody in East Street remembers the Kellys now.' Then he'd lapsed into Cockney, which he did sometimes to make her laugh. 'We 'ad two rooms to ourselfs an' an ahtside privy for twenty-four fam'lies. An' look at me now, eh?'

Belle was puzzled. 'Only two rooms? But where did you keep all your horses?'

This time, Aunt Sophie laughed, too.

'No horses,' said Ben, 'not in those days. Still, we thought we were doing all right. Two whole rooms, with a bit of curtain in between for privacy, and a separate bed for us kids—'

'Ben, that's enough,' said Aunt Sophie.

Then he'd given his wife a wolfish grin and a kiss that nearly swept her off her feet, and after that he'd challenged Belle to race him to the stables . . .

'Where *to*, miss?' snapped the cabbie.

'East Street,' said Belle.

'You sure?'

'I'm sure.'

Why hadn't she thought of it before? The slums. It was where she belonged.

'I just don't *belong*,' said Drum Talbot as he worked his way through yet another brandy.

The waiter came and offered more, and Adam waved him away. Drum had had quite enough already.

'I'm putting on an act all the time,' Drum went on. 'It's so damnably hard, Adam. I can't tell you how much I loathe it.'

'I know,' said Adam. 'That's why I think you could do with a rest. A chance to get away.'

Drum blinked rapidly. 'You're a good sort, Adam. One of the best.'

Adam sipped his coffee in silence. He didn't feel like 'one of the best'. He felt callous, unfeeling, and faintly guilty because he wanted Drum to go away.

As he listened to his old schoolfriend warming to his theme, he reflected how deceptive appearances could be. Drummond Montague Talbot was one of the finest specimens of manhood England could produce: blond, brawny and brave. But Drum had a tragic flaw. He was gentle.

Poor old Drum. He'd had the most dreadful time at Winchester. He might have been bigger and stronger than most of the other boys, but he could never bring himself to fight back. He simply couldn't stomach the violence. He was the sort of boy who rescued ants.

And when he grew up, it was a running joke that at shooting parties he'd do anything to avoid bringing down a pheasant, and was generally to be found chatting to the beaters, or playing with the dogs. Even as a soldier – and he'd been a good one – he couldn't bring himself personally to shoot at the enemy. The lengths he'd gone to to avoid being found out.

So in Drum's case, appearances deceived. And also, thought Adam, in the case of that girl at Berkeley Square. The fragile-looking social butterfly who had singlehandedly nursed Sibella through the ravages of the 'flu; who had sat perfectly still without uttering a word while he'd torn down all her hopes.

Osbourne's married. What an unbelievably crass, insensitive way to break the news. If only he'd known – or even assumed – that Osbourne had meant more to her than a casual flirtation. But instead he'd conveniently told himself that she didn't really care; that girls like her were incapable of strong feelings; that all he had to do was tell her the truth, and then wash his hands of the whole sorry affair.

So like a playground bully he'd blundered in, and now he was saddled with this nagging sense of responsibility. Simply to have *left* her like that, in that silent house, with Sibella lying dead upstairs . . . Caddish did not begin to describe it. It was downright cruel.

And how odd that while everyone around him seemed to be clamouring for his help, that girl, who seemed to need it more than most − or at least, to need *someone's* help − had been the only one to refuse it.

'Maybe you're right,' said Drum.

'What?' said Adam.

'About Scotland. You're a damn good fellow,' he said, blinking rapidly. Adam saw to his horror that he was close to tears. '*Damn* good fellow. All I can say is, the service will be worse off without you . . .'

'Let's not go into that,' said Adam.

'Sorry. Sorry. Still a bit raw, eh? Course you are. Quite understand. Damn shame that you'll miss the final push.'

Adam rubbed his temple and took another sip of his brandy. The truth was, he didn't know if he minded being out of the army or not. Clive had seen him that afternoon, and broken the news. 'You're done with it,' he'd said without preamble. 'Lung's shot. No more fighting for you, not even home service. Oh, you're perfectly fit for normal wear and tear, and I still wouldn't give a penny for my chances against you on the polo field. But you won't be racing across No-Man's-Land any more. So buck up. You're well out of it. If I were you I'd go home and crack a bottle of fizz.'

But Adam hadn't felt like cracking a bottle of champagne. Clive was right, of course, and in the rational part of his mind he knew that. But the stubborn, irrational part of him − the part which perhaps still harboured a vestigial sense of honour − that part told him that he ought to be at the Front with his men; not fighting for King and Country, but fighting for them. And that by not being there, he was letting them down.

Just as he'd let down that girl in Berkeley Square. *Hell*, why couldn't he forget about that?

'Here's to you,' said Drum, raising his glass, which he'd contrived to refill while Adam had drifted away.

Adam rose to his feet. 'Would you excuse me for a moment,

Drum? I've just remembered a telephone call I have to make.'

The telephone attendant gave him a knowing smirk as he settled himself in the booth, for he'd already spent much of the afternoon in there. Perhaps the attendant thought he was conducting an affair. If so, he'd be surprised to learn that those calls had concerned a dead woman and a seven-year-old boy.

First, and not without difficulty, he'd traced Mrs Pryce-Dennistoun, whom he vaguely knew, and ascertained that Max had indeed arrived safely. Then he'd spoken to Sibella's solicitors, checked that they had the funeral arrangements in hand, and told them of Max's whereabouts. To his surprise, they already knew. Isabelle Lawe had sent them a note.

So, clearly, he told himself now as he dialled Sibella's number, she's more competent than you give her credit for. Stop worrying. She'll be fine.

There was no answer at number seventeen.

Adam swore under his breath.

It wasn't yet nine o'clock, so she probably hadn't gone to bed. Perhaps she was out. Or perhaps she didn't feel like answering. And who could blame her, after what she'd been through over the past three days.

With a troubling sense of unfinished business, he went back to his table, where Drum had reached the maudlin stage. 'You're the only one I can talk to, old chap. The only one who *understands . . .*'

It was another half-hour before Adam got his friend safely bedded down in one of the club's spare rooms, and himself into a cab bound for Berkeley Square. If he could just check that she was all right, he could put the whole thing out of his mind.

There was no moon, and the streets were bathed in a dim blue glow from the few streetlamps which had been lit. There wasn't much traffic, only the odd omnibus with its windows heavily curtained; but on the pavements, people were out for an evening stroll, admiring the searchlights and that peculiarity of wartime London, the stars.

Number seventeen was in darkness, and when he rang the bell, no-one came.

'Looks like she's out,' said the cabbie cheekily.

'So it does,' said Adam between his teeth.

Back at the club, he slept badly. There was nothing new about that; since the War he always did. But this time he was trapped in an infernal loop. Again and again he saw the blood drain from her face. *Well, that's it, then.* The way she'd said it.

Dawn was breaking and the milk chariots were starting on their rounds when he set off on foot for Berkeley Square, feeling oddly conspicuous in his civilian clothes. Better get used to it, he told himself. You've no longer any right to wear the uniform. But it still felt wrong. He even missed the feel of the identity disc round his neck – which for the first time in four years lay discarded on top of his bureau.

Again there was no answer at number seventeen.

'She's gone,' said a girl's voice below him, making him start.

Glancing down, he saw a housemaid craning up at him from the basement of number sixteen. Sharp, intelligent blue eyes assessed him with frank curiosity.

'Do you know where she went?' he asked.

She shook her head. 'But she'd a bag with her, so it must of been an overnight visit. And she didn't take Mrs Clyne's motor, she took a cab.'

Adam's heart sank. She could be anywhere.

Something must have shown in his face, because the girl took pity on him. 'There's a cab rank round the corner. One of them'd probably know.'

It turned out that, for a shilling, 'one of them' did indeed know; and for another, he was willing to take Adam there.

'But this can't be right,' said Adam, when the hansom drew up outside a dingy tenement in Walworth.

The cabbie insisted. 'I remember 'cos it was so rum, lady like her wanting to put up in a slum like this.'

What the devil is she playing at? thought Adam. She has money. Why not put up at an hotel?

The front door was on the latch, and above it hung a grimy sign which had seen better days: *Lodgings, weekly or monthly rates, Mrs Arthur Jugg.* Beneath that were traces of another line, *Dinner by arrangemt,* but this had been scrubbed out – presumably, thought

Adam with a flash of pity for Mrs Jugg, because she was having trouble with rations, and couldn't afford the black market.

He told the cabbie to wait, and went inside.

It was dark in the hall, and the gasolier hadn't been lit. In the gloom, Adam made out peeling wallpaper spotted with rosebuds and rust.

A door opened to his right, and a child peered out. From the oversized trousers and the cap jammed down over its red hair, Adam guessed it to be a boy, although the small, grimy face was delicately androgynous.

Adam said, 'I'm looking for a lady.' He felt in his pocket and held out a sixpence. 'Young, dark, very pretty. Has she been here?'

The boy snatched the sixpence, then darted back to the safety of his doorway. 'Numberate, forfflor,' he muttered.

'Thank you,' said Adam.

What the devil is she playing at? he wondered as he climbed to the fourth floor. He was beginning to be faintly irritated. This precipitate flight from Mayfair to the slums, with only a carpet-bag for luggage . . . It smacked of self-pity. Was she trying to 'throw herself away', like a character in a penny dreadful? And why? Because Osbourne was married? Somehow, that didn't seem to fit.

He'd almost got tired of knocking at number eight when she answered the door. His irritation vanished. The blue frock hung off her. Her eyes were swollen, her face flushed and blotchy. He thought, so she can actually look plain.

'You,' she said blankly. Then she glanced behind him, as if she'd expected someone else.

'I was worried,' he said. 'I wanted to see if you were all right.'

'I'm fine. Go away.'

'I can't do that. I've a cab outside. I'll take you to an hotel.'

She was watching his mouth as if she was having trouble following. 'I'm staying here,' she said. 'It's where I belong.'

'You can't stay here.'

'Please go away.' She took a step back and stumbled, and instinctively he put out a hand to steady her. Her wrist was feverishly hot.

He felt a flicker of alarm. 'You're burning up. How long have you been ill?'

'I'm fine,' she muttered. Then her knees buckled and she went down.

For a moment, Adam stared at her in astonishment. Then he picked her up and carried her inside.

CHAPTER EIGHTEEN

The world was falling away, and she was spinning into darkness. A band of red-hot iron was crushing her skull. Burning needles pierced her eyes. Someone was trying to smother her with a blanket: someone strong. 'Go 'way!' she moaned, clawing at his hands.

'Try to lie still,' said a voice, infuriatingly calm.

How could she lie still when every breath, every blink, sent the burning needles shooting through her?

Down, down she fell, into the churning black tide . . .

She awoke to the certain knowledge of evil. Before she even turned her head she knew what it was. There in the corner: a massive yellowsnake. Malevolent. Waiting to strike.

She moaned in terror.

'It doesn't exist,' said the voice, as unruffled as before.

'Yes it does,' she retorted. She could see every scale on the flat, monstrous head; every lightning flicker of the black forked tongue. In horror she watched as it uncurled its bloated coils and slithered towards her . . .

'*No!*' she screamed.

'Don't be such a silly,' said Sibella, bending over her and brushing her face with the sleeve of her lacy blue bedjacket. 'Yellowsnakes are harmless. Surely you know that?'

'But Sibella,' said Belle. 'You're dead.'

'Oh no I'm not,' chuckled Sibella. 'That was just a joke they played on you. You children can be such vicious little brutes.'

'But I'm not a child,' said Belle.

'Yes you are,' said Cornelius Traherne, coming to stand beside Sibella. 'You're an extraordinary child. You are aware of things which most grown women—'

'Go away!' she screamed. 'Don't *touch* me!' Raising herself on her elbow, she fought him off with her other arm.

The strong hands took hold of her shoulders and gently pushed her back onto the pillow.

Again she clawed at them. 'Don't – touch me!'

'You seem,' said Traherne, 'to have created some sort of terrible fantasy—'

'It's not a fantasy!' she shouted. 'It really happened!'

'It's not real,' said the voice. 'There are no snakes.'

She was sobbing with fury. How could he deny it? How could he sit there and *deny* it? He was in league with Traherne, and so was Sibella. They were all in league against her.

She opened her eyes, and the daylight stabbed her like shards of glass. There he sat, Adam Palairet, calmly telling her that she was making it up. Adam Palairet, who had killed Sibella, who had chased Osbourne away; Adam Palairet, who had told the duppies where to find her . . .

'It's your *fault*!' she screamed. 'It's all your fault!'

He knew that he wasn't helping her; he was making things worse. She needed doctors and a hospital bed, not a bug-ridden mattress and a man she couldn't stand. She needed help.

After her outburst over the snake, she'd collapsed in a dead faint. That was a relief, but it wouldn't last long. He knew that much from the past seven hours. And he knew, too, that he couldn't just sit here any longer, hoping she would get better. He had to go and find help.

Praying that she wouldn't wake up and fall out of bed while he was gone, he raced downstairs and hammered on the landlady's door. No answer. He tried the other doors, working his way back upstairs. Most swung open on cramped, empty rooms. One bore an *I* sign, but its occupant was either away from home, or too ill to answer.

Cursing under his breath, Adam ran out into the street. It was only two in the afternoon, but the place was eerily quiet. He hammered on doors, and still no-one came. There was no-one about. It was like the dreams he used to have before the War, when he knew that he had to reach some vitally important goal, but obstacles kept springing up, each more impossible than the last.

At the end of the street he spotted a public telephone booth. Salvation. But when he reached it, he snarled in frustration. It was chained shut '*to prevent infection*'. He cast around for something to snap the chain.

A piece of luck. The landlady's boy was back, hunched in a doorway, watching him with unblinking blue eyes.

'Crowbar,' said Adam, tossing him a sixpence. 'Fast.'

The boy caught the sixpence one-handed and sped off, returning a few minutes later with a length of iron railing. 'You'll get done for that,' he muttered as he watched Adam breaking into the booth.

'Quite probably,' said Adam. 'Here's a shilling. Run up to number eight and keep an eye on the lady till I get back.'

The telephone exchange was undermanned and maddeningly slow, and it took for ever to get through to St Thomas's Hospital. They didn't have a bed to spare, and seemed astonished that he was even asking. He tried the Lambeth Infirmary; then the two doctors whom they recommended. Still no good. All were awash with patients, and scoffed at the very notion of a private nurse. Adam began to feel like a man trying in vain to get rid of an unwanted stray.

He telephoned Clive. By some fluke, his friend was at home, snatching a quick meal before hastening out to see more patients. 'Sorry, old man, but I'm up to my eyes in patients of my own.'

'But what am I supposed to do?' said Adam in disbelief.

'See her through,' said Clive.

'But I'm not a doctor!'

'Listen, old man. You won't get her into hospital, and you won't

154

find a nurse for love or money. It's down to you. You've done a spot of medicine in the trenches; it's not that hard. Besides, one way or the other, it'll be over in a day or so.'

Adam cut the connection, and leaned against the side of the booth. How could this be happening? A simple visit to see if an acquaintance was all right, and now he was marooned in the slums, dizzy with fatigue, with claw-marks throbbing on the backs of his hands – and he didn't even *like* the girl.

It's down to you, Clive had said.

Bloody *hell*, thought Adam.

Through the open door, a flash of yellow caught his eye. It was a shrine: one of tens of thousands which had sprung up on street corners since the start of the War. A wooden tablet surmounted by a simple cross bore the names of those from the street who had been killed at the Front. A ledge below held flowers: in this case, chrysanthemums in a jam jar.

Suddenly, Adam felt ashamed.

Back at number eight, he found Isabelle Lawe raving at the snakes, while the boy stood in the doorway, trying not to look scared.

Adam gave him two pounds plus sixpence commission, and sent him off for quinine, phenacetin, a thermometer, and a bottle of whisky. He couldn't remember much about his own bout of fever in Arras, and he wasn't even sure if this was the same illness; but he had a hazy recollection that quinine and alcohol had pulled him through.

While the boy was gone, he ransacked Isabelle Lawe's valise for anything that might help. Among the flimsy silk blouses and the ridiculously impractical lace all-in-ones – didn't the girl know how to pack? – he found some eau de Cologne which would come in useful as an alcohol rub, and a sixpenny booklet entitled *The Nurse's Guide to the Treatment & Management of the Influenza Patient*.

'Not a *child*,' whispered Isabelle Lawe.

Startled, Adam turned round.

The illness was draining her from within. The skull beneath the skin was disturbingly visible: the blue ridges of cheekbones, the sharp line of the jaw. Her eyes were dull and sunken, and they stared at him without recognition. He wondered what she saw when she looked at him. Whom was she trying to fight?

'Right,' he said, and his voice echoed in the dingy little room. 'It's just you and me and the *Nurse's Guide.*'

Then he pulled up the stool and started to read.

'Why are you doing this?' gasped Isabelle Lawe.

Adam stopped sponging her neck, and sighed. Damn, she was awake again. Every time he thought she'd fainted, she came round. If she didn't get some rest soon, her heart would give out.

It was some time after midnight on the second night. She'd been delirious for nearly two days. So perhaps, he thought, it's a good sign that she's regaining her senses? But he wasn't too sure. The *Nurse's Guide* was full of stark warnings about false dawns.

'I'm giving you a sponge bath,' he told her. 'Cold water and eau de Cologne. It's supposed to—'

'No, no,' she muttered, screwing up her eyes at the penny candle on the rickety deal table. 'Why are *you* doing this. Why you.'

'I couldn't find anyone else,' he said bluntly, moving the candle onto the floor where it wouldn't bother her.

'Well, now you can go.' She said it haughtily, as if she were dismissing a servant. It almost made him smile.

He dipped his handkerchief in the bowl and started doing her chest – or as much of it as he could reach while foraging blindly under the blanket so as not to embarrass her. Although, he reflected, she was probably too ill to be embarrassed, so maybe he was doing it to spare his own blushes; and when one thought about it, that was pretty irrational, given that he'd spent months at the Front living cheek by jowl with his men— 'I told you to get out,' she snapped. 'Go away. I want to die.'

'Don't be so melodramatic,' he muttered, 'and drink this.' Holding her head, he poured a few drops of the mixture into her mouth.

She spluttered. 'What on earth is that?'

'Quinine, seltzer, and Scotch.'

'It's horrible.'

'I know. According to the book, you're supposed to have Apollinaris and champagne. But they're a bit hard to come by in Walworth.'

'Where did you get the whisky?'

'Billy,' said Adam. To stop her talking, he explained that Billy was the landlady's boy, and that he'd been a godsend for fetching supplies, and was earning a small fortune in commissions.

She twisted her head away, refusing more to drink. 'Then pay — the landlady to look after me. And *go*.'

'I can't,' said Adam. 'She's dead. Now, no more talking.' To make his point, he stuck the thermometer in her mouth.

While he waited for the mercury to rise, he told her that Billy — whom he'd sent off to bed an hour before — had been hanging around ever since his mother's death three days before. He was waiting for his aunt Lucy from Stoke Newington to come and pick him up — 'Only she never,' he'd told Adam through a well-earned corned beef sandwich. 'I dunno if she ever got word.'

Another one needing help, thought Adam, kneading the tiredness from his eyes. And the worst thing was, there wasn't much he could do for either of them. The best he could do for Billy would be to see him safely to his aunt's. The best he could do for Isabelle Lawe was — what? Watch and wait, and feed her the odd trickle of whisky?

Most of the essentials in the *Nurse's Guide* were out of his reach. Chapter one made a great fuss about gasifying the air with an Alformant lamp, and injecting *liquor strychninae* to calm a racing heart. It was also stern about the need for frequent '*delicate, small meals of nicely made gruel or tapioca pudding, thoroughly cooked*'. Adam had no idea how to make either of those, nicely or otherwise, and he suspected that even if he could, his patient would simply throw it up, as she'd thrown up the phenacetin he'd tried to give her for the pain. But tapioca pudding was beginning to sound extremely good to him, even though he'd hated it at school. He hadn't eaten since the corned beef sandwich, and that had been ten hours before.

'The snake is back,' whispered Isabelle Lawe, spitting out the thermometer.

'It isn't real,' he told her for the twentieth time.

'Then why is it shooting venom in my eyes? Why do you keep lying to me?'

'I'm not lying. I—'

'Get off me,' she snarled, clawing open the scabs she'd gouged in his hands the night before.

'There is no snake,' he said through his teeth. 'Look, I'm throwing a book at it right now, you can see it bouncing off the wall.'

'Stop lying!' she shouted.

'Lie still or you'll—'

'*Stop lying!*'

Black blood jetted from her nose and soaked the bed.

Something had snapped inside her head, and let loose a torrent of steaming black blood. Out it came like water gushing from a tap: pints of it spraying the blanket, the wall, the floor.

Adam Palairet was cursing softly and continuously as he pinned her down with one hand and with the other pressed a handkerchief to her nose. She made a gurgling protest. The handkerchief wasn't stemming the flow, it was sending the blood back down her throat; he was drowning her.

Just when she thought she was going to pass out, he realized what was happening and snatched the handkerchief away, and out spurted the blood, narrowly missing his chest.

The iron band around her ribs tightened unbearably – then snapped. She sank into darkness.

She awoke to feel her face being sponged with cool water. She recognized the smell of eau de Cologne – recognized it, and yet experienced it as if for the very first time. Sharp, clean and cool. She'd never smelt anything so wonderful.

With an enormous effort, she lifted her eyelids a fraction. The light streaming through the open window was soft, the soft light of dawn. It caused her no pain. The burning needles were gone. The iron band was gone. She felt weightless and empty, as if she might float away on the breeze. She felt no pain.

Adam Palairet sat beside her on a rickety little stool, unshaven and red-eyed with exhaustion. He wore a pink, moth-eaten crocheted shawl round his shoulders, and no shirt. His shirt lay in a heap on the floor. It was black with blood.

Belle frowned. 'But – I missed you,' she murmured. 'I know I did.'

He stopped sponging and glanced at her. 'That was the first time.'

She took that in. 'How many . . .'

'Five. But there's been nothing for an hour. I think you're over the worst.'

Belle knew she was, but she felt too weak to say it. Shutting her eyes, she gave herself up to the wonderful, clean smell of the eau de Cologne. She felt incredibly weak but also strangely cleansed.

After a while she opened her eyes a fraction and said, 'Thank you.'

He threw her a glance. 'Do I take it from that that you intend to live?'

'What?'

'You kept telling me to leave you to die. I became rather tired of hearing it.'

She frowned. 'How – melodramatic of me.'

'Quite.'

Another silence, while she lay listening to the sparrows squabbling in the eaves. Then she felt the tears leaking out of her eyes. 'I miss Sibella,' she said.

'I know. So do I.'

With the damp handkerchief he wiped away her tears, leaving trails of coolness. Then he dabbed gingerly at her nose.

Eventually she stopped crying. 'What – happens now?'

He hesitated. 'You must keep very still, don't talk, and try to sleep.'

'No, I mean later. What happens later?'

'I don't know,' he said.

By the following afternoon, Adam had things under control.

With the help of the resourceful Billy, he'd found a Mrs Benson who lived three houses down, who agreed to see to the laundry and 'do for' Belle. He'd obtained a camp cot for himself, and

159

written in guarded terms to Drum, who'd sent on his post and a change of clothes without asking any questions, as well as some much-needed cash – 'Don't mention it, old chap, we'll settle up in Scotland.' He'd also scribbled notes to Maud McAllister, giving her his new address, and to Sibella's friend Mrs Pryce-Dennistoun, who'd left numerous irate messages at his club, without specifying what they were about.

On the evening of the third day, he sat on the camp bed with a whisky on his knee, reading his letters. Belle was asleep, having for the first time taken a little milk pudding laced with Scotch.

The *Nurse's Guide* approved of Scotch. *A daily diet of milk, raw eggs and whisky is most fortifying.* It also approved of Benger's Invalid Food ('*when properly made up, it is never lumpy*') and the food-drug Sanatogen. Mrs Benson, however, sniffed at the notion of special provisions for invalids. Adam suspected that with milk at ninepence a gallon and himself footing the bill, she preferred to make a substantial pudding which would sustain her own brood, too. He didn't mind. He was becoming quite fond of milk pudding.

The first of his letters was a hasty note from Drum, announcing his arrival in Galloway, and thanking Adam for the loan of the tithe cottage, which he anticipated would be 'just the ticket'.

The second was a letter from Maud McAllister, expressing bemusement at his Walworth address, and explaining, with her usual blend of apology and brisk common sense, that she'd got as far as she could with the estate manager, and it was high time Adam tackled him face to face over the running of the Home Farm.

Feeling suddenly tired, Adam put down the note. Maud was right, it was time he went home. And he wanted to. He longed for the peace and solitude of the hills where he'd grown up.

'Is something wrong?' asked Belle.

She lay curled on her side, watching him. Her skin still had the grey cast of sickness, and her eyes were shadowed and sunken. She looked about twelve.

'I need to go to Scotland,' he said.

She closed her eyes. 'So go. I'll be fine here.'

He repressed a movement of annoyance. 'Don't let's go over that again.'

'I've got Mrs Benson,' she said with a frown. 'And if that doesn't satisfy you, I can write to Aunt Mildred.'

'Aunt Mildred who doesn't exist.'

She did not reply.

Adam said, 'There's a sleeper train to Carlisle. I'll get you a berth.'

She opened her eyes and stared at him. 'Absolutely not.'

'Then what do you suggest?' he said irritably. 'You know Mrs Benson can't spare you more than the odd half-hour, not with six children to care for.'

She chewed her lower lip, and he saw to his horror that she was close to tears.

The recovering invalid will be prone to bouts of low spirits, said the *Guide, and should be humoured at all times.*

Oh, Christ, thought Adam, now what do I do?

'I just . . .' she took a shaky breath, 'I just want to be on my *own*.'

He thought about that. 'I understand. I really do. I want to be on my own, too. But I cannot simply leave you here.'

'But—'

'You're four flights up, and apart from Billy, the rest of the house is deserted. You've lost pints of blood, and you're so weak you can't even stand.' He paused. He was beginning to feel like a bully. 'If you don't say yes,' he went on in a gentler tone, 'I shall have no option but to send a wire to your people in Jamaica.'

She looked horrified.

Now he felt even more of a bully. 'Well, then.' He stood up. 'Scotland it is. I'll go down and make arrangements, and then—'

There was a knock at the door.

They stared at one another. For some obscure reason, Adam felt guilty, as if he'd been caught doing something wrong.

'Don't answer it,' whispered Belle. To his surprise, she looked frightened. 'It can't be Billy or Mrs Benson,' she breathed, 'because they never knock. And I don't want to see anyone else.'

Adam went to the window just in time to see a black Daimler almost as wide as the street sliding noiselessly away.

The knock came again, this time more hesitantly.

Adam strode to the door and flung it open.

A small boy stood before him with an expensive leather suitcase at his feet. He had sandy red hair and terrified, slightly protuberant blue eyes fringed with pale lashes.

''e come in a motor,' muttered Billy, who'd followed the boy upstairs, and was eyeing him with blatant hostility.

The boy tried to swallow, and made a gulping sound instead. He was trembling, and his shoulders were up around his ears. 'Cap – Captain Palairet, sir?' he squeaked.

'Yes, that's me,' said Adam. 'Who are you?'

'Um. Maximilian Clyne? Sir?'

Billy snorted. 'Wassortofaname is that?'

Again the Clyne boy gulped. 'This is for you, sir.' Shakily he held out an expensive-looking cream envelope.

With a sense of impending doom, Adam took it and scanned the contents.

It was a note from Mrs Pryce-Dennistoun. She'd only ever said that she could take the child for a very few days, simply out of the kindness of her heart, and it had now been over a week, which was going too far by anyone's standards, and really was too much to expect . . . *Besides,* she finished crisply, *the child is your responsibility, Captain Palairet, for I am reliably informed by the Clyne family solicitors that in her will poor dear Sibella appointed you his guardian.*

'Who is it?' said Belle.

'He's not stopping here,' snarled Billy.

'Um,' said Max, 'where do I sleep?'

Adam stood blinking at the note. Then he folded it and put it in his pocket, and rubbed a hand over his face.

Two orphaned boys and an invalid girl. Great God Almighty.

CHAPTER NINETEEN

Two troop trains had just come in, and St Pancras was heaving with uniforms. The porter cleared a path through the throng, and Adam followed in his wake, pushing Belle in the Bath chair, while Max and Mr Granger, the courier, brought up the rear.

The grim little procession drew some curious glances. As well it might, thought Adam. It must be as clear as day that none of us wants to be here.

'Shall I have to wear a kilt?' asked Max in a small voice.

'No,' said Adam.

'Will the other boys be wearing kilts?'

'There aren't any other boys at Cairngowrie. Now stay here with Mr Granger, and *don't move*. I'm going to settle Miss Lawe in her berth.'

'Miss Lawe doesn't need to be "settled",' snapped Belle as they reached the sleeping-car.

'Please don't argue,' said Adam.

By the time he'd carried her onto the train and put her in her cabin, she was frighteningly pale, and for the tenth time he wondered if he was doing the right thing. The *Nurse's Guide* had strong views on recovering invalids getting up too soon.

'Are you feeling worse?' he said.

'Yes,' she muttered. 'It was the cigarette smoke in the cab. I thought I was going to be sick.'

'I'm sorry. I didn't—'

'Not your fault. It's the 'flu. I used to like cigarette smoke. Now it stinks like burning bamboo.'

Adam stood irresolute in the doorway. 'Shall I ring for the maid to help you?'

'No, thank you.'

He paused. 'Max and I will be in the hotel car. I'll have the concierge send you a tray.'

'Thank you, I'm not at all hungry.'

'You ought to eat something.'

'I shall be fine,' she said between her teeth.

You don't look fine, he thought. You look extremely ill, and rather close to tears.

'What are you going to do about Max?' she said abruptly, as if to deflect his sympathy.

'Max? He'll share a cabin with me. It's—'

'No, I mean, what are you going to do?'

He blew out a long breath. 'I don't know. I haven't had time to talk to the lawyers. Of course, it's impossible in the long term. I shall have to find some relation of his father's to take him on.'

'The poor little thing. Passed from pillar to post.'

That stung. She had a way of doing that: of putting her finger on what was worrying him. 'I wasn't aware,' he said sharply, 'that you cared for him so much.'

'I don't in the least. I'm just glad that he's your responsibility, not mine.'

'You're looking tired,' he said unchivalrously. 'Get some rest.'

Damn her, he thought as he made his way back to the others. And damn Sibella, and damn Max. Damn the lot of them.

Ironically, the only one he wouldn't have minded keeping was the one he'd had to give up. Adam had dropped Billy at the aunt's in Stoke Newington, having made as certain as he could that she was capable, and glad to have him. Adam had given her twenty pounds to start things off. It had made him feel uncomfortably as if he were washing his hands of the boy.

'But what else can you do?' Belle had said when he'd returned to the carriage and they'd started for the small hotel where Granger had found them rooms for the night. 'You can't adopt every orphan who needs you.'

Again that finger on the sore spot. He didn't want to adopt anyone. Especially not Max. It was just that he'd been sorry to see Billy go. And by comparison, Max was a poor substitute. It was something of which Max himself seemed aware, for from his corner of the carriage he'd given Adam a shy, apologetic smile.

The porters were checking the doors by the time he rejoined Granger and the boy on the platform. Max looked as if he hadn't moved an inch, having taken Adam's order literally.

What was Sibella *thinking*? Adam thought angrily. Making me his guardian? The child needs a governess. He doesn't need me.

Max was clutching a large book to his chest, and eyeing a Boy Scout selling flags for the Soldiers' Comforts Fund. Although it was a warm day for the end of September, he was bundled up in a thick worsted coat, muffler and gloves, with a fur-trimmed cap pulled over his ears. As he'd dressed himself that morning in the hotel, this must be either from choice, or the result of remarkably thorough drilling.

Someone – presumably Mrs Pryce-Dennistoun – had sewn a black armband to his sleeve, but apart from that he showed no visible trace of mourning for the loss of his mother. Perhaps he hadn't yet understood that she was gone. Or perhaps he simply didn't miss her.

'I'm afraid I cannot love him,' Sibella had once told Adam in one of her customary flashes of honesty. 'The poor boy is the image of his appalling father, and that gets in the way. I know it's not his fault, but there we are. So it's much better for him if he sees me as little as possible, and then when we do meet I can make an effort to be nice.'

'I'll take it from here,' Adam told the courier, and Granger wished him a safe journey with a rueful smile.

Once in their cabin, Adam and Max unpacked their things in uncomfortable silence. The train moved off. They made their way to the hotel car. Adam ordered cutlets for them both, with a glass of milk for Max, and a much-needed bottle of claret for himself. He also ordered an omelette to be taken to Belle, although he guessed that she probably wouldn't touch it.

'So, Max,' he said, when the silence had gone on long enough. 'You seemed intrigued by that Boy Scout. Are you a member of the Cubs?'

An anxious crease appeared on Max's pale forehead. 'No, sir. I wanted to be, but I have a chest, and Mrs Shadwell said not.'

'Who's Mrs Shadwell?'

'My governess. But I *wanted* to be. In the Cubs, I mean.' He took a quick in-breath which ended in a gulp. 'I'm not a slacker, you know. I wanted to collect silver paper and roll up bandages. Something for the War. But Mrs Shadwell said not.'

'Oh,' said Adam. 'Well, not to worry.' But as he said it, he thought what a stupid thing to say. It was no use telling Max not to worry. Any fool could see that he worried about everything.

After an awkward wait, the food arrived. Belatedly it occurred to Adam that he should have ordered something easier for a seven-year-old to deal with, but to his surprise, Max tackled his cutlet with creditable aplomb.

He seemed older than his years, as is often the case with an only child, but with his pale eyelashes and pinched little face he was not prepossessing. He was the sort of boy whom other boys bully. The sort of boy whose timidity irritates adults.

Adam felt a flash of pity, and asked him what he wanted for his birthday.

'An officer's suit from Gamages,' Max said promptly. 'Only I expect that'll be too much, it's seven and sixpence, so then a regimental badge. Not a real one, of course,' he added, as if he'd overstepped the mark. 'A pretend one made of tin. They're one and sixpence, including postage.'

Adam repressed a smile at the thought of the heir to the Clyne fortune longing for a one and sixpenny badge. 'You seem to know all the details,' he said.

'Mrs Clary, she's the housekeeper, she lent me her catalogue for an afternoon.'

'And what regiment would you like?' asked Adam.

'The Black Watch.' Then that worried look again. 'I know that's your regiment, Captain Palairet, and I'm not saying it because of that. It's always been my favourite.' As if to prove his point, he proffered the book which was his constant companion.

'*Deeds of Pluck and Daring in the Great War*,' Adam read aloud as he took the book. 'Hm,' he said, for want of anything better to say. 'Although of course,' he added, 'the War isn't over yet.'

'Oh no, sir, of course not.'

As Max watched anxiously, Adam leafed through the pages, because that seemed to be expected. An engraving caught his eye: *The Trenches in Winter*. In the background, beyond a stretch of wire as neat as a farm fence, the sky was bright with little red and yellow stars of shellfire. In the foreground, three well-muffled soldiers stood in pristine snow, watching the 'show'. It could have been a fireworks display in Surrey. Adam didn't know whether to be amused or appalled.

'That's the Battle of Loos,' Max said anxiously.

'So it is,' said Adam. He turned to another plate which showed a square-jawed officer brandishing a revolver as he went over the top. *Led by the Young Officer*, the caption read, *the Eager Highlanders Rushed Forward*.

The story seemed to concern the retrieval of a wounded comrade. *The Huns fought gallantly*, read Adam, *but were beaten back by dogged British pluck. The officer succeeded in rescuing his stricken pal, but sustained a bad leg wound himself. Fortunately the wound, though severe, was not fatal. He recovered and was awarded the Military Cross.*

Adam closed the book. He could feel the boy's eyes on him. Some comment seemed required, but his mind had gone blank. That tidy wire fence. Those little red and yellow stars . . .

'So,' he said at last. 'You – like this, do you?'

'It's my favourite book ever,' Max said fervently.

'Ah. Well, good. And – which is your favourite story?'

'I can't decide. Either "The Rescue Of The Wounded Highlander", or "How They Saved The Pets".'

'Indeed,' said Adam. He handed back the book.

For a moment Max looked crestfallen. Then he hugged his

treasure to his chest, as if to reassure it that he still loved it, even if it had been found wanting by a higher authority.

He's not stupid, thought Adam. Damn it, I ought to have said something jolly and approving. Something soldierly.

The waiter brought coffee for Adam, and bread and butter pudding for Max. Max ate some of the currants, but left most of the pudding. Then he took another of his gulping in-breaths. 'You were on the Somme, sir, weren't you, sir?'

Adam gave a wary nod.

'What was it like?'

Adam looked down at his coffee. How the devil was he supposed to answer that? But Max was watching him with those pale, protuberant blue eyes. 'It was noisy,' he said, 'and cold and muddy. Boring for much of the time. For the rest – extremely frightening.'

Max's jaw dropped. 'You were *scared*?'

'Of course. It's frightening when people try to kill you.'

Max swallowed.

Perhaps it wasn't such a good idea to tell the truth. 'But I had a dog,' said Adam, 'and he cheered things up no end.'

Max brightened. 'What was he called?'

'Um – William.' Now why had he said that? But somehow, 'Dog' wouldn't have sounded convincing.

'What happened to William when you came home?'

Ah, thought Adam. Dog had been shot one night by an NCO who'd mistaken him for a rat. 'I had to give him away,' he lied.

'Oh. What a shame. To whom did you give him?'

Adam paused. 'To a little French girl who lived in a pretty cottage well behind the front line. She was awfully glad to have him, as her own dog had died – of old age – the week before.'

'What was her name?'

'Er – Mary. Well, Marie, actually. Because she's French.'

Max's brow creased with a new worry. 'But how will William understand her?'

'Ah,' said Adam. 'Well, you see, he's French too. Having been born in France.' This was getting complicated. To change the subject, he started telling Max about their destination. 'It's a few miles north of Stranraer,' he explained. 'That's a little town by the sea. There's a house on the beach – well, it's not actually a beach, it's the edge of Loch Ryan; which isn't actually a loch, but a very long, narrow inlet.' He paused. 'Anyway, the name of the house is Cairngowrie House, but generally people just call it the House. And about two miles up the hill, through some woods, there's a bigger house called Cairngowrie Hall. That's where we'll be staying, at the Hall. My aunt, Miss McAllister, lives at the House, but she'll be coming up to stay with us at the Hall, to look after you.'

Max laid down his spoon. 'Oh,' he said in a small voice.

'She's very nice, you know,' said Adam.

Which was not, he reflected, entirely true. He pictured Maud's plain red face and gimlet grey eyes. For more years than he could remember, she'd been the terror of the Sunday School at St Anselm's, just outside Stranraer. But she'd always been a good friend to him.

It was just that she didn't care for strangers. She'd met so few in her life: a life of unimaginable dullness, keeping house at the Manse for her father, and then for that dreadful brother, who had followed in the Reverend McAllister's unbearably worthy footsteps. Small wonder that with unfamiliar people she could be brusque.

And yet, thought Adam as they made their way back to their cabin, she is perceptive, loving, and lonely. Surely she will take to Max?

Maud didn't.

They arrived when it was still dark, and she met them in the carriage. She took one look at Belle, who'd woken up briefly, and her face stiffened in shock. Max, who was hiding behind Adam, she grimly ignored. But Adam could guess what she was thinking, for he'd heard her say it often enough. 'If there's one thing I detest, it's a ninny.'

Little was said until Stranraer was left behind, and they'd been out on the coast road for some miles. They approached the turning up Cairngowrie Hill, and Adam recognized the tidy brick bulk of the House, with a glowing line of white beach beyond.

Suddenly from the House came an unearthly shriek.

The horses shied.

Max yelped in fright. 'Is that a monster?' he whispered to Adam.

'Of course not,' snapped Maud. 'It's only Julia.' She turned to Adam. 'I left her at the House, of course, but I shall have to go down to be with her every day. I take it that that'll suit?'

'Of course,' he said. He was puzzled. He hadn't expected her to be thrilled at their arrival, but it was unlike her to be so defensive with him. He wondered if something else was wrong – something, that is, in addition to the arrival of two unwelcome strangers for whom she'd reluctantly agreed to care.

Belle had fallen into an exhausted slumber, and Adam watched Maud eyeing her with icy disapproval. 'She's wearing *paint*,' she hissed in his ear. Belle had applied a touch of rouge stick to her lips. 'What is she, some sort of actress? And where's her luggage? It's hardly decent, arriving with just the one dress basket.'

'I thought I mentioned it in my wire?' said Adam. 'Her trunk is being sent on.'

Thwarted, Maud lapsed into twitchy silence.

But as they drove up the rhododendron-fringed drive towards the Hall, she turned to him again, and laid her hand on his sleeve. 'I'm sorry, Adam. Not much of a welcome for you. You deserve better. It's the shock, you see. You're far too thin. What have they been doing to you down in London?'

He smiled. 'I think that had more to do with the trenches.'

She nodded. Then she returned to the attack. 'Of course I'll do my best for her,' she said in a hoarse whisper, 'but what if she dies? You'll have some explaining to do to her parents, won't you?'

'That,' said Adam, 'had occurred to me.'

'And as for the boy . . . *well*.' She could hardly say any more, as Max was listening with open ears.

This is a mistake, thought Adam as Cairngowrie Hall loomed into sight. A great big, disastrous bloody mistake.

CHAPTER TWENTY

'I *hate* Scotland,' cried Belle. 'It's so appallingly grey. Grey hills, grey sea, grey sky. Hardly ever stops raining. And when it does, *finally*, clear up for a few seconds, that woman informs me that I can't possibly go out unless I sit in a *cart*.'

'Is that what this is about?' said Adam, looking tired. 'The dog cart?'

Belle made a supreme effort to keep her temper. These days, everything got on her nerves. Adam. The boy. The Hall. A great, draughty mausoleum, it lacked electricity, a telephone, and proper staff. All it had was a cook who couldn't cook, and a disapproving maid-of-all-work whose uniform smelt of kippers, and whose hobnail boots curled upwards at the toes like the untrimmed hooves of a donkey.

But what got on Belle's nerves more than anything else was Miss McAllister.

'Perhaps Maud has a point,' said Adam, unwittingly courting disaster. 'Perhaps you ought to rest for a few days more.'

'Why?' demanded Belle. 'Because she says so?'

He did not reply.

She took a deep breath. 'I've been here a week,' she said as steadily as she could. 'I've tried to do what she says. I've stayed in bed. I've forced down the most ghastly nursery food. I've even tolerated this wretched invalid chair. Now I simply want to go for a walk.'

'To the beach,' said Adam.

'All right, to the beach. What's so—'

'It's two miles. If you do that on foot you'll have a relapse.'

'So now you're a doctor?'

'Well, I got you through the 'flu, didn't I?'

'Which of course puts me *for ever* in your debt—'

'I didn't mean that.' A flush stole over his cheekbones, and she knew that she'd hurt him.

She watched him go to the window and stare out across the loch.

Damn. She'd spoilt it again. It was always happening. He would come in to see how she was, and for a few minutes things would go quite well. They would talk about the War, and how Stranraer was coping with rationing and the 'flu. He would tell her about the improvements he was making to the Home Farm, which she liked, because it reminded her of Papa's letters about the estate. Then she would say something mean, and ruin everything.

Why did she do it? What was this compulsion to scratch the surface; to force him to react?

She smoothed the rug over her knees, and wondered how to find a way back. The fire hissed in the grate. Outside, the wind soughed in the pines. On the landing, there was a listening silence. Belle tried to ignore it.

She'd been given one of the guest chambers at the front of the Hall: a large, shabby room with a moth-eaten four-poster bed and gloomy, smoke-darkened oak panelling. It was at the head of the stairs, and the door didn't close properly, so Miss McAllister could hear every word. No doubt the old bat was listening right now, feeding on each fresh outrage that fell from the lips of the Scarlet Woman.

Well, let her, Belle thought savagely. It's not as if we're getting up to anything indecent.

'Would you like to go back to London?' said Adam without turning round.

She stared at his rigid back.

'You could stay at the house in Berkeley Square. I'm sure I could—'

'No,' she broke in. 'I don't want to go back there.' She couldn't stay there now that Sibella was gone. Besides, sooner or later, Cornelius Traherne would be bound to turn up.

'Then what about Dodo?' said Adam. 'You could go down to Kyme.'

Again she plucked at the rug on her knees. 'You don't have to find me a home, you know. I'm not a stray dog.'

He turned and looked down at her, his face unreadable. He had a way of withdrawing into himself – of taking himself out of reach. In another man she would have taken this for moodiness, but with Adam she sensed that it had more to do with self-preservation. She guessed that this was what he'd done at the Front, in order to get by. Of course, she would probably never find out for sure, because he would never talk about it. At least, not to her. Although that was hardly to be expected, when she was being so capricious and ungrateful . . .

She gave herself a little shake. 'You know, you're not under some kind of obligation, just because Osbourne— Just because he . . .' Her eyes began to fill. Not *now*, she thought. Not in front of him. 'What I mean,' she went on, 'is that you're not obliged to look after me, simply because he's your cousin.'

'I don't agree.'

God, he could be stubborn.

'If Maud wants you to go in the dog cart,' he said, 'then I'm afraid that's what you'll have to do. You know we don't have a motor, and the carriage is being repaired. And it's too far to walk.'

'Fine,' she said between her teeth. 'Maud's word is law. Blessed be the Gospel according to Maud.'

Maud opened the door. Her sharp little eyes darted from Adam to Belle, then back again. 'Are you not yet ready?' she said.

'I've only to put on my boots,' Belle replied sweetly.

'I'll leave you to it,' said Adam.

When he'd gone, there was a prickly silence. Then Belle said, 'I suppose you heard that.'

'Heard what,' said Miss McAllister.

'My latest blasphemy.'

The thin mouth tightened. 'What I don't understand,' she said, 'is how you can be so ungrateful to him.'

'Then I don't suppose you'll understand this either,' said Belle, 'but I never actually asked him to help me. He's only doing it out of some misguided sense of family honour.'

The older woman drew herself up. 'I was not aware,' she said stiffly, 'that family honour could ever *be* misguided.'

Belle set her teeth.

'Now come along,' said Miss McAllister. 'The dog cart is waiting, and the boy must have his constitutional. We can't all be waiting on the whim of one sick young woman.'

Maud was so angry that she could hardly speak. *Maud's word is law. The Gospel according to Maud*. It wasn't the blasphemy. It was the mockery. The assumption that because she looked like a dried-up old spinster, that was what she was.

In stony silence they arrived at the beach. Maud stepped down from the dog cart and sent the boy off to walk to the Point – walk, don't run, and don't go within six feet of the water. Then she turned to the girl. 'I shall be at the House for an hour,' she said. 'I suggest that you sit on those rocks and take the air. And don't tire yourself.'

The girl gave her an insolent smile. 'Thank you. I don't need a nurse.'

Maud felt her cheeks growing hot. 'You are a rude, un-principled chit,' she snapped. 'Your mother was just the same.'

That wiped the smile off the lovely face.

'Oh, did you not know?' said Maud, pretending surprise. 'Your mother lived here as a child. Yes, here at Cairngowrie House, with that mother of hers. That Rose Durrant.'

The blood had drained from the girl's face, and Maud wondered if she'd gone too far. But this had been building up all week, and she couldn't have stopped if she'd tried. 'She was no better than she ought to have been, that Rose Durrant, and your mother looked fair to be going the same way. And as for you. Well. You're just the same.'

The girl swayed.

'Do you know what she did, that Rose Durrant? She sent her child to my Sunday School! Oh, yes. You write and ask your mother if she remembers. Ask her if she remembers Miss McAllister the Sunday School teacher.'

She left the girl speechless, and strode up the path towards the House. She felt shaky, and she had the queasy sense that she'd been cruel. She pushed the thought aside.

As she unlatched the gate, the little garden enclosed her with its welcome, as it always did. She could have wept with relief.

She went to the bench in the porch and sat down. It was a bright, sunny October day. To the north, beyond the mouth of the loch, she could just see the rocky mound of Ailsa Craig; to the east, across the water, the bracken on Beoch Hill blazed a rich tawny. Maud took a deep breath, and fixed her gaze on a huddle of oystercatchers bobbing up and down on the water.

It was no use. This afternoon, Cairngowrie had no power to calm her. Her hands clenched into fists. That girl.

No doubt to her, Maud McAllister was nothing but a sour old spinster, fit only to care for other people's children.

Why did people always assume that spinsters love children?

'Of course,' they used to say, 'Maud adores children.' But she didn't. She disliked their selfishness and feared their scorn. It was just that when she was young, she had been too timid to contradict. Her father had told her to run the Sunday School, so she had. And as the years went by, she'd felt more and more like an impostor.

Then one Sunday, while they were all making each other miserable in the name of the Lord, that child, little Madeleine Falkirk, had stood up and calmly told the class about Eden.

'My mamma grew up there,' she'd said, as if reciting a catechism. 'It's a magic jungle, and in the middle of the jungle stands the great Tree of Life.'

She had described it so well. The curtains of creepers that were spangled with fireflies after a rain; the moonflowers and the orchids. Maud had been entranced.

But then the child had fixed her with that beautiful, innocent, corrupted gaze. 'Eden is where I began,' she had said, 'because before I was born, Mamma and Papa used to meet there in secret, under the Tree of Life.'

Maud had burst into tears and fled the class.

Afterwards, people had assumed that she'd been shocked, but that wasn't it at all. What had made her run weeping onto the sands below the Manse was the sudden realization that she was never going to experience the kind of passion that Rose Durrant had experienced under the Tree of Life. That no man would ever look at her with desire.

As she'd stood sobbing in the icy north wind, she had seen herself as others saw her: a twenty-eight-year-old spinster with a lumpy red face and no lips. This was not who she was; not in her heart. But she realized with anguish that the body does not accurately reveal the soul. The body lies. And the world doesn't care.

Ten years later, she had met Adam.

By then her father was dead, and she was keeping house for her brother Randolph at the Manse. The Manse had been her home all her life, but now that it was just the two of them, it closed in on her.

It had always been a dark house, for the lower windows on three sides had been bricked in to avoid the glass tax; and it was cold, for only the living-room fire was ever lit. That afternoon, the house was so quiet that it made her breathless, so she slipped away for ten minutes to watch the cormorants. Then Duncan Ritchie happened along in his cart, and on impulse she did the unthinkable: accepted a lift up the coast road to Cairngowrie Sands. The Sands were only four miles from the Manse, and she could easily walk back when she was ready. But she needed that great curving sweep of buff-coloured sand, that harsh wind clawing at her face and hair.

That was when she'd seen the boy running down from the Hall. A coltish eight-year-old with a tear-streaked face, he'd stood on the beach flinging stones at the sea, and shouting his grief at the sky.

The two branches of the family had never been close, and

Maud didn't know him very well. But she'd been fond of his mother, whom she'd recently nursed through her last illness, so now she felt compelled to do something to help him.

'Have you ever made a sand-angel?' she said.

The way he looked at her. The brown eyes limpid with grief, and wary, like an animal's. Wondering if she would make things better or worse.

'I believe,' she said, 'that you lie on your back and wave your arms in the sand. I've always wanted to try.'

They tried it together, and got covered in sand: gloriously, unforgivably dirty. The angels were remarkable. Adam made a face for his with sea shells, and gave it an angry snarl. Maud gave hers razor-shell claws for skewering fish, and a wild jumble of kelp for hair. 'The bubbles are knots,' she told him. 'Mermaids never comb their hair, and they get the most dreadful tangles, but they don't care, they just cut it all off and start again.'

When it was time to leave, they kicked the angels to bits, then went their separate ways like partners in crime. 'I had a wizard time,' said Adam. Then he gave her a smile that she never forgot. Surprised and admiring. As if he knew who she really was, and liked her for it.

She walked home with a spring in her step, to an outraged Randolph clamouring for his tea. She didn't care. She didn't know it at the time, but she was in love.

On the bench, Maud put her fists to her eyes. Stupid to be thinking of that now. Stupid, stupid old woman.

She opened her eyes and stared across the glittering waters of the loch. It would be dusk in an hour or so, and already the birds were flying in to roost on the sands. Barnacle geese and oyster-catchers, dunlins and widgeon and mallards. But now, finally, what she'd been hoping to see: a trio of cormorants scudding over the waves with contemptuous grace.

Maud loved cormorants. Graceful, green-eyed risk-takers who lived in nonchalant squalor on guano-spattered rocks. 'The slums of the bird world,' Randolph used to sneer. But that was why she liked them. They were so different from herself.

A few hundred yards down the beach, the Clyne boy was

almost level with the tithe cottage. He was no risk-taker. The wind had dropped, and the waves lapped tamely at the sand, but he was keeping at least twenty feet away.

At the other end of the beach, the girl sat on the rocks, staring out to sea. That girl with her scornful, beautiful face. That girl who, with one flick of her long black eyelashes, was about to ruin Maud's world. What did Adam see in her, apart from the obvious? *Why* did he have to bring her here?

After the sand-angel episode, Maud and Adam had become friends. They'd gone on nature walks, and he'd shown her his sketches. She'd saved up little things to tell him.

Then he'd grown up.

She would have been horrified beyond words if he'd ever guessed the truth, but she was too honest to hide her feelings from herself. She knew that what she felt for him was not the affection of an old woman for a much younger nephew, but the love of a woman for a man.

She loved the breadth of his shoulders and the rangy grace of his body. She loved the intelligence which informed every line of his face. She loved the back of his neck, and the warmth of his brown eyes with their little flecks of gold; the catch in his voice when he was moved.

She asked very little in return. All she wanted – all she'd ever wanted – was to live out her days at the House, and to see him now and then.

And for a time, it had looked as if she would get her wish. The War had been kind to her. Wicked even to think that, when so much had been taken away from so many – when Adam himself had lost all three brothers. But it was true. She had mourned the boys, but she hadn't felt the same closeness to them. Adam was the one who had to be saved.

Then poor old Randolph had died. Such a relief. It had even been a relief to learn that he'd left her penniless, for if he'd left her a competence, she would have felt obliged to live as he had lived.

That was when Adam had stepped in and offered her Cairngowrie House.

The *freedom* of it! The unbelievable luxury of keeping house for no-one but herself – of stepping out of the door and going for a walk *whenever she chose*!

Then suddenly Adam was home on leave, bringing Julia with him, to change Maud's life for ever . . . Oh, yes, for a time it had looked quite promising.

But now, in the space of a month, it was falling apart. An old schoolfriend of Erskine's had written to ask if he could rent the House. And since the needs of a young family must always over-ride those of an elderly spinster, Adam had suggested that Maud might care to move up to the Hall.

She had lacked the courage to speak up, even to him. All her life she had been ruled by men. She was too old to change.

And now – the final insult. That girl.

Maud heaved a ragged sigh. The future stretched before her like the cold, cold sea. She would have to leave her beloved House, and go up to the Hall for good, and once again she would keep house for others. For in time, Adam would marry that girl, and then Maud would have to move again. She would be packed off to the tithe cottage with the Clyne boy. The final indignity. To end her days caring for someone else's child.

A huge wave leapt at Max, and he raced up the sand. The sea had nearly got him that time. He would have to watch out.

The beach was a wilderness of terror and strange beauty. Max still couldn't believe that he was being allowed to face it *on his own*. At Rowan Lodge he hadn't been allowed into the garden on his own, and in cold weather he hadn't been allowed out at all, because of his chest. He'd tried to tell Miss McAllister this, but she'd told him not to be such a ninny, the sea air would do him good. What she called 'sea air' was a cold, angry wind that tugged at his muffler and made his throat hurt. He couldn't see how it would do him good.

'You may walk to the rocks beyond the tithe cottage,' Miss McAllister had said in her singsong voice that Captain Palairet said was 'lowland Scots'. As she'd said it, she'd pointed to a distant speck. 'But keep within sight of the House, and stay out of the water.'

Stay out of the water? Max stared at the heaving grey sea; at its white foam claws raking the sand like an angry cat. Did Scottish boys go *into* that? They must be incredibly brave.

He plodded on. You *have* to keep going, he told himself grimly. You *have* to get past the tithe cottage and all the way to the rocks, or you'll be a coward for ever and ever.

But in his heart, he knew that he would never reach the rocks; that he was doomed to be a coward all his life.

'My other charges,' Mrs Shadwell always told him, 'were brave, brawny lads, Boy Scouts every one of 'em. And of course, with the War, they're keeping so busy. Helping in air raids. Guarding the railway bridges against the Enemy Within.'

I could guard a railway bridge, thought Max as he plodded on. And maybe there'd be an attack, and someone would be wounded . . . *The Huns fought gallantly, but dogged British pluck won through, and Max the brave Boy Scout succeeded in rescuing his wounded pal, although he himself expired of wounds soon after, with a heroic smile on his lips . . .*

But Max knew that this was a double falsehood, because he was not brave, and had never had a pal.

And now he cringed whenever he thought of Boy Scouts, because of the one he'd encountered at St Pancras.

The Boy Scout had approached them as Max had stood with Mr Granger on the platform. Mr Granger had bought a flag in aid of the Soldiers' Comfort Fund, and Max had summoned all his nerve and said, 'Hello,' in what he'd hoped was a jolly sort of way.

The Boy Scout had drawn himself up. 'Don't you know,' he'd said coldly, 'that we're not permitted to talk to civilians while on duty?'

Max, the civilian, had been crushed.

And of course he knew what had really caused that withering look. The Boy Scout had seen through his disguise.

'Your papa was a *Boche*,' Mrs Shadwell had once told him. 'Oh, yes. He changed his name from Klein to Clyne. As if *that* would fool anyone.'

That was why the Boy Scout had scorned him. Because he was half German. Almost as bad as being a spy.

The rocks didn't seem to be getting any nearer, and the sand had given way to greenish-grey pebbles strewn with clots of knobbly brown seaweed that smelt of fish. Max stopped for breath, and glanced back the way he had come.

Miss McAllister was still sitting on the bench in her garden, watching him. He tried a small wave. She did not wave back. He plodded on.

It did not surprise him that Miss McAllister disliked him, or that she kept a monster in her house. Ladies who look after children always do, so that they can punish the children if they are bad. Mrs Shadwell had kept a terrible orange cat who could scratch faster than a blink. And as Max had lived on the top floor of Rowan Lodge, there had been no-one to hear him cry.

So in one way, Cairngowrie House was better than Rowan Lodge, because now he slept on the first floor, with the grown-ups. But he didn't expect it to last. He would do something wrong, and be sent to the attic. Either he would make a noise and disturb beautiful, ill Miss Lawe; or he would do something to annoy Captain Palairet, who'd had a bad time at the Front.

And always there was Miss McAllister, pinching in her mouth like a drawstring bag. Max couldn't decide if she was more terrifying than Mrs Shadwell, or about the same. Miss McAllister had big red hands with ropy veins like a man's, and she didn't like Max. But then, the only person who ever had was Uncle Freddie, and he'd been killed at the War.

A seagull landed in front of him on a clump of seaweed. He froze. The seagull had dazzling white wings and a gleaming dark eye ringed with orange. Max was entranced. He loved birds. They were so beautiful and skilful and brave, flying so high and never getting scared.

Uncle Freddie would have liked the seagull. He'd liked birds. He'd even looked a bit like one: like a friendly ostrich with tired eyes. Max had sobbed every night for weeks when he was killed. It still hurt to think about him, but it was also strangely comforting.

The seagull lifted up into the sky and flew away, and Max watched in awe. He resolved to look up its name, if he could find the right book. And perhaps if he saw it again, he could give it a piece of seaweed to eat.

He plodded on. He was level with the tithe cottage. Beyond it the rocks were suddenly much nearer. They were grey and strangely humped. Max felt a flicker of fear.

Then one of the rocks moved.

Max's heart lurched.

In horror he watched its head swing round to look at him. The wind roared in his ears. He couldn't breathe. What if it came after him?

There was no-one to help him. Miss McAllister was too far away. Besides, she wouldn't help a ninny.

Slowly, so as not to alert the monster rock, Max turned his head and stared at the tithe cottage. If he could make it up that little stony path, then maybe a kindly cottager would give him sanctuary, like in 'How They Saved The Pets'.

The monster rock slid into the sea with a splash. Then another and another. A herd of monster rocks. Max's nerve broke and he raced up the path.

He pounded the door. No-one came. He ran to the window, trying not to step on the heather that grew beneath it in clumps.

A lady stood in the parlour with her back to him. She wore a flowery print gown, and looked very sturdy and strong: like Mrs Shadwell, but with short hair. Surely she would defend him against the rocks?

He tapped on the window.

The lady turned.

Max gave a terrified yelp and fell backwards into the heather.

CHAPTER TWENTY-ONE

'Come quickly!' gasped Max, careening into Belle. 'There's someone – I think they're hurt!'

'What do you mean, hurt?' she said.

Max gulped and tried to speak at the same time. 'There's blood on his mouth.'

Belle glanced from the white-faced boy to the cottage, and then to the distant speck of Cairngowrie House. Now what do I do? she thought. After the long walk over the sand, her knees were trembling; what help could she be? Wretched Miss McAllister was right. She'd walked too far.

'You stay here,' she told the boy, 'I'll go and see.'

'Here on my own?' said Max. 'But what about the rocks?'

'What rocks? There aren't any rocks. Just stay here.'

Dreading what she might find, she went up the garden path and lifted the door latch. 'Hello?' she called.

There was no-one in the hall, but she could feel that the house wasn't empty. The door to her right was ajar – presumably it opened into some sort of front room. From inside came the sound of someone breathing.

'Are you all right in there?' she said. 'I'm sorry to intrude, but the boy said—'

'I'm fine,' said a deep, masculine voice. 'Please go away.'

Belle frowned. Something about the voice was familiar. 'Hello?' She put her hand on the door. 'Are you sure you're—'

'No, don't—'

The door swung open, and there was Drum Talbot hunched on the sofa in an orange flowered tea-gown, with a smear of scarlet lipstick beneath his moustache.

'Oh God,' he groaned, and burst into tears.

He cried for ages. Great choking sobs that seemed to tear up his chest.

After the first blank astonishment, Belle went to the sofa and sat down beside him, and put one arm awkwardly round his beefy shoulders.

Eventually the sobs lessened. He pulled a large handkerchief from his flowery sleeve, and blew his nose. Then he wiped off the lipstick. 'I'm so – dreadfully sorry,' he said hoarsely.

Belle didn't know what to say. She'd heard of effeminate men, but she'd never met one; or not knowingly. She felt sorry for him. It must be awful, to be found like this. She couldn't see why he was apologizing.

'Such an appalling shock for you,' he said without meeting her eyes.

She glanced at his tear-ravaged face. He'd missed a bit of lipstick at the corner of his mouth. She repressed the urge to wipe it away. 'Not a shock,' she said. 'Just a surprise.'

He sniffed and tugged at his handkerchief, then ran a hand through his thick fair hair. 'That poor little tyke. Is he all right?'

'Max? He's out in the garden. I'm sure he's fine.'

He frowned. 'Good. Good.'

'Drum – it's all right, you know. I won't tell anyone. I promise.'

He heaved a ragged sigh. 'Thanks most awfully. You see, if it ever got out, they'd send me to prison.'

'Oh, surely not. Not for getting dressed up.'

He gave a hollow laugh. 'Darling Belle, what a sweet way of putting it! No, not for that. For being – what I am.'

There was an awkward silence.

Then Belle said, 'I never guessed, you know.'

His lip curled. 'Oh, I'm good at hiding it. I ought to be, I've had enough practice.' Then his face contracted. 'Everything about me is a lie. Even my nickname. "Drum". So hearty and masculine.' He swallowed. 'I don't expect you to believe me, but I've never actually done this sort of thing before. I mean, getting dressed up.'

'I believe you.'

'You see, out in France, things changed.' He swallowed. 'I – I fell in love. It was the real thing. An NCO in my unit. Although of course I never said a word. I couldn't. He's a big, rough, masculine man. A real man. If he ever found out what I am, he'd be disgusted.' He rubbed a shaky hand over his face. 'I should have been over the moon when I got my blighty, because it prevented me from doing anything foolish. But all I could think was, I'll never see him again.'

She put her hand over his.

'And then, like an idiot, I got into trouble. Had to leave Town, as they say. At least, until things quieten down.'

'How did you fetch up here?'

'What? Oh, Adam, of course. He's been an absolute brick. He knows, you see. He's the only one who does. He lent me this place so that I could sort myself out. And now look at me.' He shut his eyes. 'Don't tell him, will you? I mean, not about this.' He tugged at his sleeve.

'Of course not,' said Belle.

'The worst of it is, I still can't forget that NCO.' He paused. 'All my life I've wanted to be loved by a man like that. And yet I *know* that that's an absolute impossibility, because a man like him – a real man – would only ever love a woman.' With a brawny hand he smoothed the flowered silk over his knee. 'That's why I tried on this frock. I wanted – just once – to see what I'd look like as a woman. To see if – in some other life, perhaps – I'd stand a chance of attracting him.' His face crumpled.

'Oh, Drum,' said Belle. 'I'm so sorry.'

He gave a mirthless laugh. 'I'm sorry too. Sorry that you had to see this.'

'Don't worry about that.'

'And I didn't even know you were in Scotland.'

'I'm staying at the Hall.'

'With Adam? He didn't say anything. In fact, I had no idea you were even friends.'

Belle coloured. 'We're not. Well, we're not anything else, either.' She thought about that. 'It's complicated.'

Drum nodded without understanding.

To change the subject, she told him about Osbourne's being married, and about Sibella, and about falling ill herself.

'I can't believe Osbourne would do that,' he said, shaking his head. 'And then not even to write. To *try* to make amends.'

Her lip curled. 'You're not the only one who isn't what he seems.'

'Do you – do you still love him?'

'No,' she said. 'It's very odd. When Adam told me, I was devastated. Or I thought I was. But then it was like turning off a tap. I'm not even angry. The other day, Adam told me that Osbourne's going to try to make it up with his wife and child. He's bringing them over to England. I felt nothing. Except sympathy for her.'

Again Drum nodded. 'Anyway, Adam's worth ten of him.'

Belle did not reply.

'You're an amazing girl,' said Drum.

'No I'm not.'

'Yes you are. I never thought anyone could be so kind. And I actually feel better, now that you know.'

She squeezed his hand. 'Come up to the Hall for dinner.'

He gave her a watery smile. 'I can't.'

'Yes you can. It'll do you good.'

'No. No.'

'Tomorrow, then. I'll square it with Adam. And the dreaded Miss McAllister.'

He forced a smile. 'Perhaps.'

But she knew that he wouldn't.

He walked her to the door. 'You've no idea what it's like,' he said suddenly, 'to be one person to one's friends and family, and quite another person underneath. To have to live like that, day in and day out. It's so bloody exhausting.'

'Yes,' said Belle. 'I know.'

'I hear you overdid things a bit,' said Adam.

'And now I'm back in this ghastly invalid chair,' said Belle, 'and I'm sure Miss McAllister had a marvellous time telling you all about it.'

'She's not like that, you know.'

'Oh, really,' said Belle.

'Yes, really.' He stooped to put another log on the fire. 'Honestly, Belle, what were you thinking? Walking all the way to the Point?'

'But only part of the way back,' said Belle, rearranging the rug over her legs. 'I felt a little tired, and had to send Max for the dog cart.'

'A little tired' was an understatement. Her knees had given way and she'd had to sit on the pebbles with her head down, while the black spots darted sickeningly before her eyes. When she'd got back to the Hall, it had been all she could do to climb the stairs. Thank heavens that Adam had still been down at the Home Farm.

'How do you feel now?' he asked.

'Fine,' she lied. In fact she felt frighteningly weak. And annoyed with herself for having proved Miss McAllister right. And hopelessly sad about Drum.

It had been horrible, having to leave him in that lonely little cottage. And Max had given her no time to gather her wits. 'Will the gentleman be all right?' he'd asked. He'd been hovering in the porch because of the 'rocks that moved'. Whatever they were.

Yes, she'd told him, the gentleman was fine. He'd simply put on an overall to clean some windows, then fallen and cut his lip. Only don't tell anyone, or he'll be embarrassed.

It was the best she could come up with at such short notice.

'According to Maud,' said Adam, 'you've set yourself back. She wanted to call in Dr Ruthven, but I thought you'd prefer not.'

'Definitely,' said Belle with feeling. Miss McAllister had threatened her with Dr Ruthven before. He'd been an old friend of Adam's father, and was widely respected as a sponsor of the Stranraer Temperance Institute. His daughter Felicity was 'a dear, lovely, *innocent* young lady who frequently accompanies her father on his rounds,' and had known Adam 'for ever'.

'Then in lieu of Dr Ruthven,' said Adam, 'Maud wants you to go to bed, and stay there for at least three days.' He hesitated. 'I know you loathe doing what she says, but in this instance I really think—'

'I know, I know. I'll do as I'm told.' Secretly, she was relieved. It dispensed with any question of her returning to London.

Adam sat down in the easy chair opposite her, and crossed his long legs at the ankle. For a while there was silence as they watched the log beginning to crackle.

Then Belle said, 'Poor Drum. He's so unhappy.'

Adam raised his head and gave her a guarded look.

'I saw him at the tithe cottage,' she explained. 'He told me about himself.'

'Ah.'

'How long have you known?'

'Celia told me.'

She frowned. 'Celia told you? Why?'

'He and I had been friends since school. Perhaps she thought that by telling me, she could change that.'

This was the first time he'd mentioned Celia, and Belle waited for him to go on, but he simply leaned back in his chair and studied the fire, running his thumb slowly across his bottom lip.

'When Celia told you,' Belle said carefully, 'were you surprised? I mean, about Drum.'

'To begin with. Although in retrospect, it made a lot of sense.'

'Had you come across that sort of thing before?'

'Oh, yes.'

She smoothed the rug over her knees. 'I dare say you saw it all in the trenches.'

He snorted. 'I saw it all at Winchester.'

She was silent for a moment. He seemed to accept people so readily for what they were. Did he do that out of tolerance, or because they didn't matter to him any more?

'But didn't you mind?' she said. 'When Celia told you about Drum. Surely you minded?'

'Why should I have minded?'

She swallowed. 'Well. Because someone you knew – a friend –

they'd kept something from you. Something important about themselves.' She was dismayed to find that her voice was shaking. 'Surely that mattered to you? I mean, not being told. Being kept in the dark. Surely it altered how you thought about them – how you felt . . .'

He was watching her closely, as if he'd guessed that she wasn't only talking about Drum. 'Drum had his reasons,' he said.

She dropped her gaze. How would he feel, she wondered, if he ever found out about me? About Cornelius Traherne. About what I am.

Even thinking of it made her feel sick. *Found out, found out.*

Adam uncrossed his legs and leaned forward. 'Are you all right?' 'Yes. Why?'

'You've gone very pale. I think you'd better lie down.'

'No. I'm fine. Just a little tired.'

'I'm sorry, I've worn you out.' But he made no move to go.

She sat staring at her hands. She had the sense that if he didn't go soon, she would blurt out the truth. Or burst into tears. At last she said, 'Nothing fazes you, does it?'

'What? What do you mean?'

She raised her head and met his eyes. 'Drum. Osbourne. Me. Nothing seems to disconcert you.'

He gave her a long, steady look. 'Some things do,' he said.

CHAPTER TWENTY-TWO

The weather closed in again. For three days Belle lay in the big four-poster and listened to the wind soughing in the pines, and the rain battering the windows. To begin with she enjoyed it. Then she became restless, and moved to the invalid chair by the fire. On the fifth day she came downstairs, and had a fight with Miss McAllister.

'What's the *matter* with you both?' said Adam. They'd just finished breakfast, and Miss McAllister had stormed off to her room. 'I've never known her to be like this. And as for you . . .'

'You've never known me to be anything else,' supplied Belle.

Adam sighed. 'I have to go out this morning. I shall be gone all day. Please. Please. Try to get along.'

'I will if she will,' said Belle.

'That's not good enough.' He stood up. 'I know you hate being reminded of this, but I'm going to remind you anyway. In East Street I probably saved your life. The least you can do for me—'

Belle laughed. 'Goodness, you're ruthless! I thought you were supposed to humour the invalid.'

'To hell with that,' said Adam.

The house seemed very quiet when he'd gone. Belle tried to read, but soon gave up and wandered the empty rooms.

According to Adam, the Hall had been built in the late seventeen hundreds by Finlay Palairet, who'd vastly improved the family fortunes by selling his Edinburgh linen-weaving business and moving to Glasgow, where he'd gone into sugar refining and rum distillation. As he'd traded exclusively with the Jamaican Palairets, who were just entering the Golden Age of sugar, he'd prospered mightily. 'Huguenot *savoir faire* crossed with Scottish pragmatism,' was how Adam had drily characterized it.

The combination might have worked well in business, but it made for an odd mix when it came to architecture. Cairngowrie Hall had fine, well-proportioned rooms, and fireplaces that worked – but the plasterwork was slightly too ornate, and it sat uneasily with the whole: like a dress suit on a hoary old sea captain. And clearly, the Hall hadn't been cared for in years. After the death of his wife, Adam's father had left it and his four young boys in the hands of a housekeeper, and travelled abroad.

A dead mother and an absent father, thought Belle as she wandered the rooms. No wonder he was close to his brothers. And now they're all gone . . .

She found Miss McAllister in one of the bedrooms. Wardrobes stood open; chests of drawers spilled clothes; the bed was piled with cricket jumpers, shooting jackets and books. Miss McAllister stood in the middle of the rug, looking oddly lost. But when she saw Belle, her mouth tightened. 'What do you want?'

'I'm sorry,' said Belle. 'I didn't mean to intrude.'

Miss McAllister's gaze drifted to the chaos around her, and she chewed her lower lip, as people do when they're trying to hold something back. 'I'm the one who's intruding,' she muttered.

Belle didn't know what she meant.

'The boys' things,' said the older woman. 'High time that someone sorted them out.'

'By the boys, I take it you mean his brothers?'

'Well of course. Angus. Gordon. Erskine.' She sucked in a breath. 'I was in here yesterday, looking out some of Erskine's things for his fiancée. That's where Adam's gone, to Castle Garth, to see Annis. She's been asking for some mementos.'

'Oh,' said Belle. 'Can I help?'

'No.'

So much for getting along.

'Adam didn't want to go,' said Miss McAllister. She sounded angry, as if it was Belle's fault. 'He's been putting it off.'

'I can imagine.'

'No you can't. Nobody can.' She moved to the bed and touched a pile of cricket jumpers with a rough red hand.

'Well,' said Belle. 'I'll leave you to it.'

'If you hurt him,' Miss McAllister said suddenly, 'you'll have me to reckon with. You just remember that.'

Belle turned back to her. 'I'm not going to hurt him.'

But even to herself, it didn't sound convincing.

She found Max in the cold, fireless drawing room, kneeling on the window seat and staring out at Loch Ryan. From the hunch of his shoulders she could tell that he was worried.

'What are you looking at?' she asked.

He gave a start and nearly fell off the window seat. 'Um. The rocks.'

'But there aren't any, are there?' The grounds around the Hall were dotted with firs and rhododendrons, and the drive led down to the coast road through Cairngowrie Woods, with the grey waters of the loch beyond. Not a rock in sight.

'These ones are different,' whispered Max. 'They *move*.'

Belle remembered something he'd said at the tithe cottage. 'What do you mean? Rocks can't move.'

'These do. I saw them. They went into the sea.'

Belle bit back a smile. 'Max, those are seals. Don't you know about seals?'

He hesitated. 'Yes. I read about them in a book. But I never . . . They moved really fast.'

'I expect they were scared of you.'

'Oh,' said Max. Then his forehead creased. 'But I still ran away. I oughtn't to have run away.'

'You're a child. You're allowed to run away.'

'Boy Scouts don't.'

Belle snorted. 'Oh yes they do. Where I grew up in Jamaica, there was a Boy Scout pack, or whatever it's called, and sometimes I used to climb a tree and pretend to be a duppy, and throw mangoes at them. They ran away every single time.'

Max looked wistful, as if he wanted to believe her. He said, 'Captain Palairet says he was scared at the War.'

'I expect he was,' said Belle. She felt a flicker of envy that Adam had talked to Max, and not to her.

'But he didn't run away,' said Max.

'No, because he's a grown-up and a soldier.'

'And brave,' Max said sadly.

Oh dear. This wasn't going very well. Belle thought for a moment. Then she said, 'Come along. Let's go to the kitchen.'

'*The kitchen*?'

'What's the matter? Don't you like kitchens?'

'I don't know. I've never seen one.'

Belle laughed.

The kitchen was huge and stone-flagged, with an old-fashioned black iron range, and an enormous pine table scoured white by generations of scullery maids. Max was entranced. 'Are we allowed?' he whispered.

'Probably not,' said Belle.

As it was mid-morning and there would only be three of them for luncheon, Cook had 'gone for the messages' to Stranraer, which Belle eventually gathered meant doing the shopping. After some persuasion, Nelly the maid-of-all-work grudgingly agreed to vacate the kitchen, having shown Belle the whereabouts of flour, butter, sugar and eggs.

'We're going to make biscuits,' Belle told Max when Nelly had taken herself off.

'*Make* them?' said Max. Plainly it had never occurred to him that biscuits did anything other than appear on plates at teatime.

'Special biscuits,' said Belle. 'My mother used to make them with us when we were bored. They're called zoo biscuits.'

'Why?'

'Because you make them in animal shapes, and paint them.'

She showed Max how to rub butter into flour, then mixed the 'paints' using egg yolk and food colouring – of which, fortunately, Cook had a good supply. Paint brushes proved trickier, until she found some pastry-glazing brushes: a little too thick, but adequate.

The dough was turning grey under Max's diligent pummelling, so Belle set him to greasing the baking sheets. 'What are your favourite animals?' she asked.

'Birds,' he said promptly. 'Then fish.'

'Birds might be tricky,' she said, 'but I can manage fish.'

'What's all this?' said Miss McAllister from the doorway.

They jumped.

'We're making biscuits,' said Belle, feeling absurdly guilty. 'I asked Nelly. She said we could.'

Miss McAllister gave a disbelieving snort.

Belle said, 'Max was just telling me how much he likes birds.'

Miss McAllister turned to Max and her eyes narrowed, as if she suspected him of trying to humour her. 'What kinds of birds?'

He gulped. 'Ostriches and seagulls. And the black ones with green eyes.'

'Cormorants,' said Miss McAllister.

'Oh,' said Max. 'Thank you. Yes. Those.'

Another sharp look. Then to Belle, 'See that you clear up afterwards. I won't have Nelly overburdened on a whim.'

Belle bristled. 'I was going to anyway.'

'Well, see that you do.'

When Miss McAllister had gone, they worked in silence. Belle rolled the dough flat, and cut out a series of fat fishes, then painted the first one to give Max the idea. 'Red and green,' she said. 'A parrotfish. Sort of.'

Max caught on faster than she'd expected, and painted several orange goldfish with large eyes and tense, unsmiling mouths. Then he got bolder, and painted on some red scales. For the last one, he cut away the lower jaw, then stuck the cut-off piece to the fish's back.

'What's that on its back?' said Belle.

'The dorsal fin.'

'Gosh, that's clever.'

Max went pink. Then he said, 'Can it be striped?'

'Of course. It can be anything you like.'

While the biscuits were in the oven, they washed up. Emboldened by Belle's compliment, Max asked her about Jamaica, and soon she was telling him how to chew sugar cane and spit out the trash, and what bananas look like when they're growing on the tree, and how to attract hummingbirds. It reminded her of the twins, and she felt a wave of homesickness.

'Captain Palairet knows about Jamaica, too,' said Max, polishing the mixing bowl with a corner of the tea towel. 'He used to visit his relations in the holidays, and once he fell out of a breadfruit tree and knocked himself senseless.'

As Belle removed the last baking sheet from the oven, she gave him a curious glance. 'When did he tell you all that?'

'Sometimes he lets me read in his study, and I ask him things.'

Belle was going to ask what sorts of things, when Miss McAllister reappeared in the doorway.

'Still not finished?' she said.

Belle opened her mouth to retort, but Max got in first. 'Look,' he said shyly to Miss McAllister. 'I made you a biscuit.'

'What?' snapped Miss McAllister.

Max's shoulders went up round his ears. 'I hope you like it.' He pointed at the striped fish with the overbite and the dorsal fin. 'It's a tiger shark.'

Miss McAllister seemed oddly flattered by her shark, and told Max that she would have it with her morning tea. She also lent him a book on birds – 'just lent, mind, and you must look after it' – and told him that he might accompany her to the House to meet Julia.

Belle had a shrewd idea that she was being nice to him to spite her, so she asked to come too.

'No,' said Miss McAllister.

Remembering Adam at breakfast, Belle ignored the rebuff. 'Please,' she said. 'I really would like to come.'

Miss McAllister scrutinized her for signs of mockery. 'You'll have to be quiet,' she said, 'and do exactly what I say. Julia doesn't care for strangers.'

Cairngowrie House was a solid, double-fronted Victorian dwelling which didn't look as if it had changed since the old Queen had died. The furnishings were heavy mahogany up-holstered in faded plush, the blinds and drapes of thick damasks in strong colours: purple, forest green, navy blue. Belle found it hard to picture her mother living here as a child, but when she started to ask about that, Miss McAllister silenced her with a look.

'Julia is in the kitchen,' she said, as if to remind Belle of the purpose of their visit. Then to Max, 'Once we're inside, stay by the door or you'll startle her.'

He gulped, and his shoulders rose. Belle took his hand.

An unearthly shriek rang through the house.

Max shrank closer to Belle.

Miss McAllister opened the door, and they entered the kitchen.

Max gasped.

Belle broke into a smile.

'Time for tea,' said Julia, flapping her wings.

She was a good three feet from crown to tail-tip, and her small black eyes were bright with intelligence. Her head and breast and her magnificent tail were a throbbing crimson; her wings were a bright cerulean blue, segueing to emerald and topaz at the shoulder.

'She's *beautiful*,' breathed Max. 'She's the most beautiful creature I've ever seen.'

Miss McAllister tightened her lips and tried not to look pleased.

'I never guessed she was a parrot,' said Max.

'She's not,' said Miss McAllister. 'She's a scarlet macaw. Now sit at the table and don't move while I change her water. And when I let her out for a bit of a fly around, don't try to touch her. And don't open the door or she'll be out. I'm always telling Susan — she's the girl who does the rough. But she never remembers.' She was talking far more than usual, and Belle saw with surprise that she was nervous.

The kitchen appeared to have been pretty much given over to Julia. Presumably food for human beings was prepared in the scullery, but in here the windows and the range had been boxed in and framed in chicken wire, to prevent the macaw from injuring herself. One half of the room had been partitioned off into a walk-in netting enclosure, containing what seemed to be half a tree, a bowl of fruit, and a porcelain baby bath.

Miss McAllister caught Belle looking at the bath. 'She likes to bathe,' she said. 'Every morning. Creature of habit.'

'Does she ever go out into the garden?' asked Max.

'Oh yes, but only when I'm there. She had a bad time of it when she was a young one. Rooks mobbed her. They do that.' Her thin lips twitched with disapproval.

'Have you clipped her wings?' asked Belle.

'Good heavens, no.' She sounded outraged. 'You should see her fly. They swoop low, macaws. It's quite a sight.'

As soon as Miss McAllister undid the padlock, Julia flew out, circled the kitchen, then came to rest on top of her enclosure, watching Miss McAllister with her head on one side. 'Up we get,' she said.

'She's awfully clever,' said Max.

'Yes,' said Miss McAllister, 'she is.'

'How did you come by her?' asked Belle.

Miss McAllister carried the baby bath to the sink and emptied it. 'Adam,' she said at last. 'Two years ago, on leave. He said he had a surprise for me, but that if I didn't like it I had only to say, and he'd find it a good home.' She shook her head as she remembered. 'My heart sank. I thought he'd bought me a cat.'

'I hate cats,' said Max.

'So do I,' said Miss McAllister. She stopped rinsing the baby bath, and gazed at Julia over her shoulder. 'That he should think me worthy of something so beautiful . . .' She scowled, as if she'd said too much.

'May I stroke her?' said Max.

'No,' Miss McAllister said firmly. 'Not for a long while. Weeks. Maybe months. You have to just sit, so that she can get used to you. You have to let her come to you. That's the rule with them. Always let them come to you.'

Max nodded, drinking in every word. Belle could see that he'd found a new cause.

Miss McAllister washed her hands, then squared her shoulders. 'Now out into the garden and play,' she told Max. 'I want to speak to Miss Lawe.'

Belle's heart sank. What had she done wrong this time?

Max drooped. 'But can't I—'

'No. You can come in when I say. Mind you leave quickly, so you don't let her out. And don't forget to wrap up.'

Max gave Julia a last adoring look, and went.

When he'd gone, Belle braced herself.

Miss McAllister, too, squared her shoulders, as if she had an unpleasant task ahead. 'I think,' she said, 'that I ought to apologize.'

Belle stared at her. It was the last thing she'd expected.

'I spoke unkindly of your mother, and it's been troubling me. It was wrong. When I knew her she was a brave little thing.'

'Oh,' said Belle.

The older woman came to the table and sat down heavily. 'What these walls could tell,' she murmured.

'What do you mean?'

Miss McAllister raised her eyebrows. 'But surely you know?'

Belle shook her head.

Miss McAllister sighed. Suddenly she looked old and sad. 'It was a bad business. It was winter, and Rose Durrant was here alone with only her little daughter – your mother – when her baby was born.'

Belle gasped. 'I – didn't know. Mamma never talks of Scotland.'

'Well. Perhaps that's why. Perhaps you should ask her about it.'

Belle thought about that.

'Oh, it was a bad business,' Miss McAllister said again. 'As ill luck would have it, the Hall was empty that winter, for the family was from home . . .' Her voice trailed off.

Belle waited for her to say more, but she seemed lost in thought. Then she placed her hands on the table and pressed down hard, as if to contain the memory. 'So there now,' she said in a brisker tone. 'I've said my piece. Told you I'm sorry. Let bygones be bygones.'

Belle gave a slow nod.

There was silence in the kitchen, broken only by the sound of Julia nibbling at an apple.

At last, Belle cleared her throat. 'Miss McAllister—'

'Maud.'

Belle met the sharp grey gaze. 'Maud. About Adam. I'm not going to hurt him, you know. I would never do that.'

The older woman gave her a small, sad smile. 'But that isn't entirely in your control, now is it?'

Belle did not reply.

'The thing about Adam,' said Miss McAllister, 'is that he's no good at showing his feelings. Or else he's very good at hiding them. I've never worked out which, and I don't think it matters. The point is, the feelings run deep.' She frowned. 'He has lost so many people in his life. It's easy to forget that, because he's so good at coping – or at seeming to cope. But it's changed him. I've watched it happen.'

'How has he changed?'

She did not reply at once. 'After the divorce,' she said, 'I told him something foolish. I said, "Don't worry, you'll marry again." He just looked at me, the way he does, very calm and reasonable, and he said, "People make out that the benefits of loving outweigh the pitfalls. But that's not been my experience. Not at all."'

Anxiously, she peered into Belle's face. 'Don't prove that to him all over again.'

Adam returned just before teatime, but Belle didn't know he was back until she passed the study door and saw him sitting at his desk, staring into space.

His face had the unguarded look of someone who doesn't know he is being watched. Then he became aware of her, and forced a smile. 'Hello,' he said.

'Hello,' she replied. Feeling self-conscious, she took one of the easy chairs by the fire.

'So you and Maud managed to get by for a whole day without murdering each other.'

'Actually, we did.' She told him about the tiger shark, and being introduced to Julia. 'And after lunch, she gave me an old snapshot camera that had been her brother's. She said my grandmother had had a talent for photography, so she thought it might amuse. I was quite touched.'

He nodded, and she wondered how much of what she'd been saying he'd actually taken in.

'Was it awful?' she said.

'I'm sorry?'

'Castle Garth. Erskine's fiancée.'

'Oh. Yes. Yes it was, worse than I'd expected.'

She waited for him to go on.

'She kept asking me to tell her what it was like at the Front. What could I say?'

'What did you want to say?'

He ran a hand over his face. Then he looked at her for a moment. 'It's all just meat,' he said. He raised his eyebrows. 'Hardly a profound epiphany, is it? But that's what struck me most forcibly out there. That when someone dies . . . One moment they're a person, and then they're just a lump of meat. It's really no different from in a butcher's shop.'

Belle thought about that. 'Is that how you see us, too?'

'What do you mean?'

'When you came home. When you were in London. Now. Does it feel strange to see people walking around, and to be so aware that that can happen to them? I mean – that they can just die.'

He studied her. 'In a way, yes. It's hard to explain, but sometimes everything feels so confoundedly *odd*. At first, I couldn't get used to it at all. Sometimes I still can't. I'll be walking down a street, or talking to someone, and suddenly it hits me. The strangeness of it. The narrowness of the gap between the living and the dead. How easily it can be snuffed out.' He paused. 'And it's still going on over there.'

'Do you mean the fighting?'

'Everyone's saying that the War can't possibly last much longer. But they were saying that back in March. It's still going on, and I can't help feeling that I ought to be there.' He shook himself and gave an embarrassed smile, as people do when they think that they've been speaking too much about themselves.

'Do you have nightmares?' she said.

'Of course.'

'Different ones, or the same?'

He put his head on one side. 'What is this, a question and answer session?'

'It's what you do to me. It seems to work.'

A corner of his mouth lifted. 'So now you're turning the tables.'

'Precisely.'

There was a silence. She watched him draw diamonds on his desk with one forefinger. Then he said, 'It's always the same dream. Although oddly enough, I didn't have it at East Street.'

Belle made a face. 'Too busy coping with me.'

'Yes, that must have been it.'

Their eyes met. Belle felt herself colouring. 'You're always helping other people,' she said. 'Who helps you?'

He opened his mouth to speak – and out in the hall, the doorbell clanged.

Belle jumped.

'Who the devil is that?' said Adam.

Maud hurried in, looking worried. 'Oh dear,' she said in a hoarse stage whisper. 'I invited them to tea, and I clean forgot!'

'Invited whom?' said Adam.

'The Ruthvens,' whispered Maud.

CHAPTER TWENTY-THREE

'These days we hardly see Felicity,' said her father with a smile. 'It's either the Belgian Refugee Fund or the Home for Convalescent Officers. And of course they're all in love with her. I keep telling Adam that he'd better look sharp, or he'll miss his chance.'

'Oh, *Daddy*,' said Felicity, blushing furiously. She was small and blonde, with a fresh complexion that had never seen paint, and beautiful, clear grey eyes. Since they'd arrived, she hadn't stopped appraising Belle from under her lashes.

Belle stirred her tea and forced a smile. 'Do you live at Kildrochet all year round, Miss Ruthven?'

'Oh, yes,' said Felicity. 'I don't imagine I could cope with London.'

'Oh,' said Belle.

'One must have to be so . . . tough to handle it all,' said Felicity. 'Don't you agree?'

Belle put down her spoon. 'One gets used to it, you know.'

'I don't think I should,' said Felicity. 'All the parties and the dancing. I shouldn't care for that at all.'

Belle nodded slowly, because she couldn't think of anything to say. She hazarded a glance at Adam, but he was helping himself to a zoo biscuit proffered by Max, and pretended not to have heard.

Dr Ruthven asked Belle what sort of war work she did.

'I'm afraid I don't do any,' she replied.

'Belle has been ill,' put in Maud. 'This dreadful influenza.'

'What a shame,' said Felicity. 'War work can be so rewarding.'

'Actually,' said Belle, 'Maud's being kind. I didn't do any war work before I got ill, either. I suppose all the parties and the dancing got in the way.'

Felicity smiled at her. 'At Kildrochet we lead a very quiet life.'

Ah, now you're overdoing it, thought Belle. Again she tried to catch Adam's eye, but he was staring determinedly at the tea tray.

She kept telling herself to be nice, but it was uphill work. The Ruthvens had arrived twenty minutes ago, but it felt like hours. Dr Ruthven treated her with the elaborate courtesy of someone tackling a foreigner of doubtful intelligence, while Felicity was as edgy as a sheepdog who's just spotted a wolf. Maud sat tensely upright, dispensing the tea but saying very little, while Max was overawed to be allowed at a grown-up tea party. Adam simply looked tired.

Felicity turned to him. 'I called on your friend Mr Talbot the other day,' she said in her low, soft voice. 'I thought it might help if he had someone to talk to.'

'That was kind of you,' said Adam.

'What Felicity is too soft-hearted to mention,' said Dr Ruthven, 'is that the fellow was confoundedly uncivil.'

'Oh, Daddy, please, don't—'

'It has to be said, Felicity. Fellow practically hustled her out of the door.'

'He had a bad time of it at the Front,' said Adam. 'Shattered nerves.'

'Then tell him to come to my surgery,' said Dr Ruthven. 'But it's no excuse to be uncivil to a lady.'

'He just needs to be on his own,' said Belle.

'The poor darling,' said Felicity. 'You see, Miss Lawe, that's what you're missing. I can't tell you the joy it brings, to be able to help these poor, shattered men. You ought to come with me to the convalescent home. Then you'd understand.'

'Thanks,' said Belle, 'but I think I'll stay ill for a bit longer.'

Maud shot her a warning look, and Adam bit back a smile.

'Maud tells me you've had a bad time of it,' said Dr Ruthven.

Belle opened her mouth to reply, but Maud was quicker. 'She's through the worst of it,' she said stoutly, 'and getting better every day.'

'Maud's been wonderful,' said Belle, 'and so has Adam.' She turned to Felicity. 'It was amazing, he simply took charge. Scooped me up from the vice-dens of London, and whisked me up here to clean air and healthy living.'

Felicity opened her eyes wide. 'Surely not vice-dens?'

'Pretty close,' said Belle. 'Dancing till the small hours; drinking too much fizz. And of course, we were all taking the most ridiculous amounts of snow.'

Dr Ruthven frowned at his teacup.

Adam rubbed his temple.

'Did you *eat* the snow?' asked Max.

'No,' Belle told him. 'What you do is—'

'Time for bed,' said Maud.

After Maud had taken Max upstairs, Felicity was the first to break the silence. 'Well, Miss Lawe, I think it all sounds absolutely fascinating. And so very different from the way we live at Kildrochet.'

'Don't you ever get bored?' said Belle.

'That was quite a performance,' said Adam after they'd gone.

'Not as good as hers,' said Belle.

'It wouldn't have hurt you to be civil. Dr Ruthven was one of my father's oldest friends—'

'And Felicity wants to be the next Mrs Palairet. Come off it, Adam. "We lead a very quiet life. I don't imagine I could cope with London." Tell me you haven't fallen for that?'

'She's not normally like that. She was overdoing it because you were.'

'She started it,' muttered Belle. She went to the window and drew back a corner of the curtain to look out at the rain. 'Sorry,' she said over her shoulder. 'But that kind of girl brings out the worst in me.'

'What kind of girl?' said Adam, coming to stand beside her.

With her finger she followed a raindrop down the window pane. 'The innocent,' she said. 'Next to her, I'm damaged goods.'

'Don't say that.'

'It's true. I haven't led a "quiet life" since – well, not for years.'

'I know that. But—'

'No you don't. Not really.' She looked up into his face. 'You are aware that Osbourne and I were lovers?'

'Yes, I had managed to gather that.'

She bit her lip. 'He wasn't the first, you know. Had you managed to gather that, too?'

'Why do you do this?' he said quietly. 'It's as if something comes over you, and suddenly you're determined to show me the worst of yourself.'

She hugged herself in her arms. 'The worst of myself? Oh, I haven't shown you that, not by a long chalk.'

'What do you mean?'

She turned back to the window.

'When I found you in East Street,' said Adam, 'you said something that's stayed with me. You said it was where you belonged. What did you mean?'

Again she looked up into his face. She wanted to tell him everything. She really did.

'I don't remember,' she said.

Dinner was awkward, but mercifully brief, as neither Maud, Belle nor Adam felt inclined to talk. Afterwards, Belle sought him out in his study.

'I'm sorry about the Ruthvens,' she said bluntly.

'Jolly good,' said Adam. 'Would you care for a brandy?'

'Yes. Thanks.'

As he handed her the glass, he met her glance and smiled.

She smiled back. Suddenly her heart swelled with happiness. She loved the little flecks of gold in his warm brown eyes, and his tallness, and the way that he moved, and the lines at the sides of his mouth, but it wasn't only that. For the first time since Cornelius Traherne, she was with a man whom she didn't have to charm or seduce or fear. She just wanted to know him. And she wanted him to know her.

At least – she wanted him to know some things about her. But not all.

He went to the fire and threw on another log, then straightened up. 'Belle—'

'I've just realized,' she said nervously, 'these days, I never see you smoke.'

'I gave it up.'

'Why?'

He shrugged. 'You said the smell made you ill.'

She thought about that. Then she said, 'I meant it about the Ruthvens. They're your friends and I was horrible.'

'It doesn't—'

'I'm sorry I embarrassed you. And it wasn't Felicity's fault. It was mine. Next time I'll try to be more . . . gracious.'

'Gracious?' said Adam. He burst out laughing.

'I haven't heard him laugh like that in years,' said Maud as they walked on the beach the following morning. The weather had changed again, and Cairngowrie was experiencing an Indian summer. It was so warm that Max had been allowed to take off his shoes and socks, and now he stood at the shoreline, fascinated by the feel of the waves sucking the sand from between his toes.

'Poor little Felicity,' said Belle, trying to sound as if she meant it.

'Bother Felicity,' said Maud. 'She's a sly little thing. I've never cared for her.'

'Then why did you invite them?'

Maud sighed. 'I invited them a week ago, to spite you. Then I forgot all about it.'

Belle laughed.

Maud didn't even smile. 'I wish I had your courage,' she said in a low voice.

Belle threw her a surprised look. 'What do you mean?'

'It takes courage to say what you think.'

'You mean, to be rude.'

'To say what you think. I don't have that kind of courage. Not really. I believe that's why Adam's fond of you.'

Belle stopped. 'No he isn't.'

'Of course he is.'

'You're wrong. He only—'

'If he wasn't fond of you,' said Maud, 'why did he bring you to Cairngowrie?'

'Because I was ill, and there was no-one else.'

'Of course there was,' said Maud. 'There's that duchess friend of yours down in Lincolnshire. He could have taken you there. But he didn't.'

Belle hacked at the wet sand with the heel of her shoe. Despite her denial, she knew Maud was right. Adam was fond of her. She didn't want to put it any higher than that, but she felt it to be true.

And yet – what then? How could it possibly work?

There was too much she hadn't told him. And when he found out, he wouldn't be fond of her any more. How could he? It would be like learning to be fond of an entirely different person.

The answer came to her in a flash.

So don't tell him anything. After all, why does he need to know? What good would it do?

Her heart began to pound. It could be done, she told herself. It really could be done.

She looked at the sun-diamonds on the blue waters of the loch, and the purple heather on Beoch Hill. Scotland was utterly beautiful.

She turned her head to find Maud watching her. The older woman's expression was anxious and a little sad. Belle said, 'If you're right about Adam; and if I – if I felt the same way. Should you mind?'

Maud turned and glanced back towards Cairngowrie House. 'I don't know,' she said. 'It depends on how it turns out.'

They walked on in silence. Then Maud went back for Max, and Belle stayed behind, to sit on the beach and think.

The sun was warm on her back, and the sea lapped and sucked at the sand. In the shallows, a flock of terns was diving for sand-eels. Belle watched them for a while, feeling the hope growing inside her. Then she took off her shoes and stockings and walked barefoot in slow circles.

She glanced towards the Point and the tithe cottage, where poor Drum was struggling to deal with the secret he could never reveal. She looked back towards Cairngowrie House, where her mother had lived with parents who'd done their best to keep their secrets from the world. She seemed to see herself walking down the long stretch of beach: or rather, a succession of selves in all her different disguises.

'You're an extraordinary child,' Cornelius Traherne had told her, just before he'd made her into someone else. Since then she'd been so many different people. Schoolgirl, innocent, demi-mondaine; 'infant', nurse, and 'sick young woman'.

Now what? Could she perhaps simply be Belle?

She walked down to the water and watched the waves wash away her footprints. That gave her a strange sense of renewal. One moment there were her tracks, and the next – only clean, smooth sand.

You were right not to tell him the truth, she thought. It can all be washed away. It can be as if it had never been. You *can* start again.

Adam woke with a start. His heart was racing. He didn't know where he was.

You're at the Hall, he told himself as his heartbeats returned to normal. It was only a dream.

He got up and went to the window, and drew back the curtains. The grounds were awash with moonlight. On the lawn, a trio of fir trees was standing guard.

It was only a dream, he thought.

Except that it wasn't. It was the nightmare. He hadn't had it since before East Street, but now it was back.

He's crouching in the shell crater with St John Cornwallis: crouching in rottenness, with shells screaming all around. A whizz-bang is coming towards them, getting louder and louder. He turns to warn St John to get down – but it isn't St John any more: not Dodo's younger brother, but his own. '*Get down!*' he tries to yell – but he can't make a sound, and Erskine doesn't hear. Then the world explodes. Adam is pitched forward into the mud. When he gets up, Erskine isn't there. Where he'd been there is just a boot, and a gobbet of blackened flesh.

It's a *dream*, Adam told himself as he stared at the moonlit garden.

Yes, but why now?

He thought of Belle as she'd looked when she'd come back from the beach that morning: flushed and laughing at something Max had said.

She could be so utterly different. Sometimes the polished Miss Lawe with the porcelain skin and the perfectly painted mouth. Sometimes the difficult, impulsive invalid. Sometimes the wry, perceptive Belle. He never knew who she would be next, and the change was fascinating. Confusing. Exhilarating.

But he knew now why he'd had the dream.

It was a warning.

Careful, Adam, it said. You lose the things you love. You know that. You always do.

CHAPTER TWENTY-FOUR

A week had passed since the Ruthvens had come to tea, and Belle had hardly seen Adam.

He now spent most of his time at the Home Farm, and when he was at the Hall he was polite, considerate, and utterly un-communicative. Something had changed between them. She couldn't work out what. Suddenly her optimism on the beach seemed wildly misplaced.

The *Dumfries & Galloway Standard* had reported that the influenza was finally on the wane, so Maud announced that she was taking Max to Stranraer to see the boats. 'And it wouldn't do you any harm to come too,' she told Belle. 'You want to watch yourself, or you'll turn peaky again.'

Belle surprised herself by saying yes. She couldn't face a day alone in the house, wondering what she'd done wrong.

As the weather was fine, they took the dog cart instead of the carriage, and as they trotted along the coast road she looked about her at the glittering sea and the rich green pastures which came right down to the beach; at the sleek red cattle and the white terns mewing overhead, and the gentle heather-clad hills. The charm of Cairngowrie had crept up on her unawares. She didn't ever want to leave.

She glanced at Maud, who sat beside her, showing Max how to

hold the reins. Over the weeks, the older woman's face seemed to have softened. She didn't tighten her lips so much, and although she rarely smiled there was a light in her grey eyes now and then, particularly when she looked at Max, or spoke to Adam.

Max, too, had visibly changed. He'd filled out a little, and was becoming talkative; and he no longer gulped. His love for Julia was undimmed, and he spent every available moment in the kitchen at Cairngowrie House, 'sitting still as a stone,' as Maud told Belle, 'determined to win her trust. And I've no doubt that he will. He's got the patience. And the determination.'

Belle felt a wave of love for them both. I don't ever want to leave you, she told them silently. And I don't ever want to leave Adam.

Why had he changed? What does it mean?

Maud felt herself observed, and turned her head. 'What is it?' she asked.

'Nothing,' said Belle. 'Actually, no, I want to ask you something. It's about Adam.'

Maud's face went still.

'The past few days, he's been different. Withdrawn.'

'He's done that since he was a boy,' said Maud.

'But I get the feeling,' said Belle, 'that it's something I've done.'

Maud turned back to Max. 'Don't tug on the reins. Just enough to feel the pony's mouth. That's it.' With her eyes still on the boy, she said to Belle, 'I'm sure you're wrong about that.'

'Then why do I feel that he's avoiding me?'

Maud hesitated. 'Adam has a lot on his mind. A lot of responsibilities.'

'I know, but—'

'No,' said Maud with startling firmness. 'No, I don't think I can talk to you about Adam. I'm sorry, but there it is.'

'Maud, please—'

'I'm sorry, Belle.' She softened that with one of her rare smiles. 'I like you, and I want things to go well for you. But I cannot – I cannot get involved in this. No, that's more than I can do.'

They were approaching the outskirts of Stranraer, and Max was exclaiming with delight at the sight of some fishermen digging for lugworms on the flats. There was no more time for talk.

The outing was a success. Max loved every minute of it. He loved it when the big steamer set off for Ireland from the New Pier; he loved it when a fishing boat came in from the foreshore with a cargo of oysters. He loved the vanilla ice which Maud bought for him at the kiosk on Harbour Street, and he insisted on reading aloud the legend stamped on the stone bottle of ginger beer which Belle bought him to wash down the ice: *Drink Fedele Bonugli's High-Class Ginger Beer, Stranraer.* Belle enjoyed his enjoyment, and for a while she almost forgot about Adam. The worry returned as soon as they started for home.

Maud got out with Max at Cairngowrie House, as they hadn't yet paid the daily visit to Julia, and Belle drove on alone to the Hall. She arrived in time to catch Drum, who was on the point of leaving.

'I came to say goodbye,' he told her as they walked in the grounds.

Belle threw him a surprised glance. 'Goodbye? Where are you going?'

He pulled down his mouth in a mock grimace. 'Where do misfits usually end up? The colonies, dear girl.'

'You're leaving the country? But – isn't that a little extreme?'

He shook his head. 'Best thing for me. In fact, I'm looking forward to it. Fresh start. New faces. It's what I need.'

'Where will you go?'

'Ah, now, I think you'll approve of that. Adam's helped me find a position on his great-aunt's estate.'

Belle stopped. 'You're going to Jamaica?'

He grinned. 'I shall be a sugar planter, like your papa. Do you think I'll be any good?'

She was too astonished to speak. Astonished, and oddly disturbed. 'Of course you will,' she said at last. 'It's just – well, to be honest, I'm jealous.'

He laughed. 'Well, then you shall have to come out and see me, very soon.'

She swallowed. 'I don't think I shall be doing that for a while. I haven't been back for years.'

'Oh. Oh dear. Not trouble at home?'

She hesitated. 'Sort of.'

He seemed to sense that there was more to it than she wanted to talk about, for he gave her shoulder an awkward little pat. 'Bad luck, old girl. But maybe – it's none of my business, I know, but maybe you should just *think* about coming out? Might do you some good. You're looking a little . . . well, down.'

She did not reply. She'd been thinking about going back ever since East Street. She'd had daydreams about introducing Adam to her father. She could see how it would be in every detail. They were on the verandah overlooking the cane-pieces: Papa and Mamma, and herself and Adam, standing at the balustrade among the tree-ferns and the bougainvillea, laughing at the twins playing on the lawn with the dogs.

You're such a *fool*, she told herself savagely. Why even think about it? It's never going to happen.

'I hear old Ma Palairet's a bit of a dragon,' said Drum, dragging her back to reality.

'Old Louisa?' she said with an effort. 'She wants to be, but she isn't really. Unlike my Great-Aunt May, who really is a dragon, and best avoided.' She paused. 'I'll write to my people and tell them you're coming. They'll like you. And I think you'll like them.'

'Thank you,' he said. 'I'm sure I shall.'

They walked on in silence. Then she said, 'Have you seen much of Adam, these days?' She'd tried to speak lightly, and was annoyed to hear the tension in her voice.

'Now and then,' he replied.

'Drum, what's the matter with him?'

He threw her a curious look. 'I don't know. I thought you'd know. I thought – well. I thought he was fond of you.'

'So did I,' she said.

That evening, Belle made a special effort. She wore a gown that Adam hadn't seen before, of deep purple satin which made her feel sophisticated and ready for anything. She knew it was a success because he didn't look at her once when they met for drinks before dinner.

Luckily, Maud was in a talkative mood, and didn't seem to

notice that Belle hardly said a word. 'I'm letting Max come down and say goodnight,' she told Adam. 'It's a reward for persistence. Julia let him stroke her wing this afternoon.'

Adam handed her her sherry, then returned to the side table to top up his whisky. 'I wouldn't let him get too attached,' he said quietly.

Maud paused with her glass halfway to her lips. 'Why not? A boy ought to get used to being with animals. It's—'

'That's true,' said Adam, 'but he'll only get upset when he leaves.'

Belle and Maud exchanged startled glances.

'What are you talking about?' said Belle.

Maud put down her glass on the side table. 'Why should he leave?'

'He can't stay here for ever,' said Adam. He went to the chimney-piece and stood looking down at the fire. 'I had a letter from his father's sister.'

Maud put her hand to her cheek.

'She used to live in Lübeck,' Adam went on, 'but now she's settled in Somerset. Married to an attorney. They seem decent people, and they've two boys of their own. If we can sort it out with the lawyers, they're willing to take him.'

'I should imagine they are,' Belle said drily. 'Exactly how much *is* Max worth these days?'

'That has nothing to do with it,' said Adam over his shoulder. 'All the assets are in trust till he's twenty-one; no-one can get at them. Sibella saw to that.'

'But . . .' began Maud. 'He can't leave now.'

'Sooner or later,' said Adam, 'he'll have to. It's either Somerset or boarding school.'

'*Boarding school?*' cried Belle and Maud together.

'But – Adam,' said Maud, her voice shaking with emotion, 'boarding school is the very last thing that child needs.'

'Maud's right,' said Belle 'He's just finding his confidence. If he went now it'd be disastrous. The other boys would eat him alive.'

'I don't agree,' said Adam. He ran his hand over the chimney-piece. 'School would toughen him up.'

'You don't seriously believe that,' said Belle. 'Adam, what's this about? Why—'

The door opened, and in came Nelly with Max. He was shiny-faced from his bath, and clutching a book to his dressing gown. Belle noticed that *Deeds of Pluck and Daring* had given way to *Langley's Illustrated Birds of Scotland*.

Maud saw her looking at it. 'It was Adam's when he was a boy,' she explained. Then she turned to Adam and said stiffly, 'I take it that you've no objection to his having it?'

He opened his mouth to speak, but then thought better of it.

Max approached him with a shy smile. 'Look, Captain Palairet.' He'd been keeping his place with his finger, and now he opened the book at an engraving of a small brown bird sitting on a rock. 'I saw one just like it this afternoon, sitting on a rock *in exactly the same way.*'

Belle looked at Adam over Max's head. 'Adam, you can't—'

'Now is not the time,' he cut in.

'Captain Palairet,' said Max, frowning at the engraving. 'When you were my age, what was your favourite bird?'

'It'd be the worst thing possible,' said Belle. 'Surely you couldn't—'

'Was it a cormorant, like Miss McAllister's?'

'I'm being realistic,' said Adam between his teeth.

'Captain Palairet—'

'*What?*' snapped Adam.

There was a shocked silence.

Very carefully, Max closed the book and hugged it to his chest. His shoulders crept up round his ears.

'Don't take on, now, Max,' said Miss McAllister. 'Captain Palairet's merely tired. Come along, let's go upstairs.'

But Max didn't move. He drew a deep breath which ended in a gulp. 'Is it not all right that I have the book?' he whispered. 'Do you want me to give it back, sir?'

Adam rubbed his temple. 'Of course it's all right,' he said. 'Now take the book and just – go along to bed.'

★

'That,' said Belle, 'was unforgivable.'

Adam did not reply.

She'd come downstairs and found him standing at the drawing-room window with his hands in his pockets and a half-full tumbler of whisky beside him on the window sill.

'To snap like that without reason,' she said. 'You know how he worships you—'

'Aren't you making a fuss over nothing?' he said without turning his head.

'It isn't nothing to Max. I went to say goodnight to him just now. Do you know what he said? He said he quite understands that he oughtn't to keep the book, because you're a soldier and brave, and he's not . . .' She swallowed. 'Adam, don't you see? You mean so much to him—'

'So shoot me,' Adam said brusquely. He turned to face her, and she felt a flicker of alarm. 'Well, now you know,' he said. 'I drink too much, and I snap at children. Not quite the paragon you seemed to think I am.'

'I didn't think you were a paragon,' she said. 'But I did think that you—'

'I cannot be a father to that boy,' he said with such violence that she took a step back. 'I cannot *love* him. I cannot – love anyone.'

As he said it, he met her eyes. Then he turned and reached for his glass.

In the fireplace an ember cracked.

Adam flinched.

Belle didn't move.

'I think . . .' she said at last, 'I think I understand.'

He did not reply.

'How stupid of me,' she said. 'I was beginning to think that you— Well. That you might be starting to— But you've made it very clear. You can't love anyone. My mistake.'

Still he said nothing. He simply stood there, staring down at his glass.

'But please,' she said. 'Just because I've made a mistake, don't take it out on Max.'

Somehow she managed to turn and walk away, and get out into the chill gloom of the hall.

He didn't come after her, and he didn't call her back.

The next morning, Maud took a subdued and silent Max down to the House. Adam worked in his study. Belle stayed in her room, packing.

No more prevarication. No more deluding herself. For whatever reason, Adam had reached a decision about her. He didn't love her. So it would be best for everyone if she left.

Maud and Max did not return for luncheon, and Belle couldn't face going downstairs on her own. Adam didn't send to ask if she wanted a tray, which was just as well. There was a knot in her stomach. She couldn't have eaten a thing.

Around four, she heard a door slam, and urgent voices in the hall. She went to the top of the stairs and leaned over the balustrade.

Maud and Adam stood facing one another in the hall. Plainly, Adam had just come out from his study, and Maud had run in from outside. She was hatless and out of breath, her shoes and stockings spattered with mud. She looked as if she'd run all the way from the House. 'Oh God,' she gasped, 'Oh God oh God—

'What's happened?' said Adam, taking her elbow and leading her to a chair. 'Is it—'

'That *stupid* girl!' Maud burst out. She slumped onto the chair and gripped the sides with both hands. 'I *told* her never to leave the door open—'

'What girl?' said Adam.

'Susan!' cried Maud. 'Stupid, wretched, stupid—'

'Maud,' said Adam, 'what are you talking about?'

Maud clutched his arm. 'I couldn't *find* them,' she said. 'I followed the tracks in the sand towards the Point and then – then I lost them. And the tide's coming in, and – I couldn't – I couldn't *find* them!'

'Find who?' said Belle.

Adam glanced up and met her eyes.

'Julia's gone,' said Maud. 'And so is Max.'

CHAPTER TWENTY-FIVE

Max of the Black Watch was going over the top to rescue his pal, and if he had to die heroically to save her, then so be it. He knew she was out here somewhere. He'd seen her swooping low over the sand, and he'd heard her cries as the dastardly Boche ravens launched their attack . . .

But he couldn't *find* her. The sea mist had crept up on him when he wasn't looking, and he didn't know where he was.

Miss McAllister would be furious. He'd rushed out without hat or coat or mittens, and now he was so cold that his teeth were chattering. He couldn't even feel his toes. He was going to get most awfully told off.

'*Never* go out of sight of the House,' she always warned. But he was so far out of sight that he couldn't tell where the coast road had gone. He was in a deadly world of swirling mist and threatening seals; he was facing an icy, heaving sea that quite possibly contained tiger sharks.

The fear was an iron band round his chest. He couldn't breathe. But he couldn't turn back. His pal needed him.

'Julia!' he cried. 'Where are you?' The mist muffled his voice as if he were under water.

A distant squawk. But was it raven, seagull or macaw? And which way?

The wet sand dragged at his feet. Water slopped into his boots.

The sea was getting closer and closer in a way he'd never seen before: each wave clawing a little higher up the beach, as if it were after him.

A gust of wind parted the mist like a curtain, and he saw a finger of rock sticking out into the sea – and on it a flash of red amid a flurry of black.

'*Julia!*' he shouted. 'I'm coming!'

Grabbing a stick of kelp to beat off the marauders, he leapt onto the rocks.

They were slimy with seaweed. He slipped and went down, banging his knee painfully. Cold waves slapped him in the face, making him splutter. He grabbed at the rocks to push himself upright. His hands were so cold that he didn't know he'd cut them until he looked down and saw the blood.

A seal bobbed out of the water and stared at him with bulging black eyes. It was huge. Max gripped his kelp stick, and prayed that Miss Lawe was right about seals never attacking humans.

'Go away,' he cried, waving his stick.

The seal disappeared beneath the waves, then bobbed up again.

Through the mist, Max saw Julia flapping her wings and lashing out with her formidable beak; the ravens lifting in a tattered cloud.

'Go *away!*' Max yelled at the seal, brandishing his stick. He lost his footing and crashed into the sea.

If anything happens to that boy, thought Adam as he pulled on the oars. If anything happens . . .

The mist was so thick that he could hardly make out the prow. Rocks loomed with alarming suddenness. He could feel the incoming tide dragging at the boat. With each pull on the oars, the old wound in his chest ached savagely.

'No more racing across No-Man's-Land for you,' Clive had told him, 'but you're fit enough for ordinary duty.' Adam wondered if rescuing small boys and parrots qualified as ordinary duty. Judging by the pain in his chest, probably not.

The next moment, he saw them. A small figure cowering at the tip of the promontory, clutching what looked like a baby wrapped up in cloth.

'*Captain Palairet!*' yelled Max, trying to stand, and nearly toppling into the sea. 'Here I am!'

'I can see you,' called Adam. 'Don't move, I'll come and get you.'

The tide was running fast, but the sea was no more than choppy, so it wasn't too hard to bring the boat about and get near the rocks. As Adam approached, Max tried to hold the bundle out to him, and nearly lost his balance. 'I found Julia,' he said unnecessarily. Now that help had arrived, he seemed more excited than scared. 'I wrapped her up in my jacket, like in "How They Saved The Pets".'

'Max, listen to me,' said Adam. 'I'm going to come alongside and you're going to pass me Julia, then climb in yourself. Got that?'

Max nodded.

As Adam drew closer, he saw that the boy was soaking wet, and shaking so hard that he could hardly stand.

'Change of plan,' said Adam. 'Just stay there and don't move.' With the oars out of the water, he stood up, bracing his legs against the sides, then leaned over and lifted boy and bundle bodily into the boat. Then he whipped off his own jacket and wrapped it round Max.

'B–but you'll catch cold,' stuttered Max.

'No I won't, I'm rowing. Did you fall in?'

Max nodded. 'I was warding off a seal and I slipped. But I climbed out, and then I got Julia. I think she was glad to see me, but I had to wrap her up to stop her scratching.'

'That was brave,' said Adam.

Max wiped the seawater from his face. 'The ravens were scared of me,' he said. 'They flew away.'

The boy had been given a warm mustard bath and was tucked up in bed with two hot water bottles and a mug of steaming milk before Maud allowed herself to hope that he might survive.

'You look as if you could do with a drink, too,' said Belle, who was seated at the foot of the bed. 'Why don't you go downstairs? I'll stay with him till the doctor arrives.'

Maud hesitated.

'You'll come back soon?' said Max with an anxious frown. He looked very small in her bed, incongruously wrapped in her warmest flannelette nightdress, and with both hands bandaged. He seemed embarrassed at the fuss he'd caused, and it had taken some time to reassure him that he wasn't going to be told off.

'Of course I shall come back,' Maud told him. 'This is my room. Now no more talk, and drink your milk.'

'Come back *soon*,' he mumbled.

Maud managed to get herself out onto the landing before her knees gave way and she sat down heavily at the top of the stairs.

She'd never fainted in her life, but she'd come close to it when she'd seen Adam striding out of the mist with that terrible, limp bundle in his arms.

And now here they all were, safely back at Cairngowrie House, and waiting for Dr Bailey. Julia was downstairs in her enclosure and, from the sound of it, giving Adam merry hell; and the boy was tucked up in her bed, and requesting that she come back *soon*.

He was asking for her; not for Adam or Belle. He was sticking like a limpet to plain old Miss McAllister.

'Like a limpet,' she murmured in astonishment.

Another squawk and a muffled curse from downstairs. She was needed in the kitchen. She put her hand on the balustrade and pulled herself to her feet.

She knew now what she had to do. She only hoped she was brave enough to go through with it.

No more shirking, she told herself grimly. You've been putting this off for long enough. That boy has just shown you the meaning of courage. If he can do it, so can you.

She found Julia hunched on her branch, bedraggled and furious, but otherwise unharmed by her ordeal. 'Off you go,' she squawked at Adam, who was standing at the sink, holding a bleeding forefinger under the tap.

'She can bite, can't she?' he said over his shoulder.

Maud sat down with a sigh at the kitchen table. 'That was only a playful nip,' she said. 'A proper bite would have taken your finger clean off.'

He snorted a laugh.

She placed both hands on the table and pressed down hard. 'Adam—'

'Here you are,' he said, setting a steaming mug before her. 'Tea and sherry. I couldn't find any whisky.'

'Thank you,' she replied. The tea tasted vile, but she found it curiously strengthening. Dutch courage, she reflected, has something to be said for it.

'Shall you be all right tonight?' asked Adam. 'Or would you like me to stay?'

She shook her head. Without looking at him she said, 'You take Belle back up to the Hall.'

'Very well.'

'But if you could send Nelly down, it'd be a help. And she can bring some of my things.'

'Of course.'

For a while, neither of them spoke. Adam stood silent and thoughtful, while Maud sipped her tea and covertly observed him.

He was leaning against the range with his arms crossed over his chest. His shirt was still damp and clinging to his shoulders, and his dark hair was tousled and dripping seawater. As she watched the little drops sliding down his neck, something twisted in her heart. She knew what it was. It was the ache of farewell.

It's a sort of a bargain, she told herself. You have to give him up to Belle, which is as it should be, if she can make him happy. And in return, you may have your reward. Yes. It's a bargain. That made her feel a little better.

'Adam,' she said again.

He raised his head and looked at her with a slight lift of his eyebrows.

'When I say what I'm about to,' she began, 'you may well assume that I'm not thinking straight; that I'm still upset by what's just occurred. But it's not that at all. I've been meaning to say this for some time. I've given it a great deal of thought. So please listen without interruption.'

His face went still.

Maud took a deep breath. 'That boy,' she said, 'must not go to boarding school. Nor must he be sent away to live with some aunt whom he's never met.' She paused. 'Cairngowrie is good for him. He's just beginning to come out of his shell. If he went anywhere else, he'd go right back into it again.'

Shells again, she thought distractedly. First limpets, and now more shells . . . 'And when I say Cairngowrie,' she went on, 'I mean this house. Not the Hall. That boy needs to stay *here*. And so do I. It may be wicked and selfish to say so, but I don't want that young friend of Erskine's having this house for his family. *I* want it. I don't want to go anywhere else, not ever again. I want to die in this house.'

Adam looked at her for a moment. Then he came and sat beside her and took her hands. 'I had no idea you felt like this,' he said. 'Of course you shall have it. I'll write to the Taliskers at once and put them off. I'll do the same for Max's aunt. I'll put them all off. It shall be exactly as you say.'

Maud stared at him in stunned silence. All the months of anguish. The conversations in her head; the arguments, the deliberations. And all she had to do was tell him.

'Thank you,' she said quietly. A great weight had lifted from her shoulders. She felt exhausted.

Slowly she pushed herself to her feet. 'That sounds like the doctor now. And you need to take yourself off to the Hall and change out of those wet things.' She paused. Then she said, without meeting his eyes, 'Take Belle with you. She needs her bed.'

CHAPTER TWENTY-SIX

The mist had cleared and the stars were coming out in a luminous blue sky as the dog cart made its way up the hill towards the Hall.

After giving Belle the travelling rug and suggesting that she wrap up warmly, Adam didn't speak again. He seemed pre-occupied. She wondered if he'd had some sort of altercation with Maud.

'You must have got pretty chilled down on the beach,' he said when they reached the Hall. 'You might want to take a bath to warm up.'

'What about you? You're the one who got wet.'

'I'll be fine.' He paused with his hand on the pony's neck. 'I'll take the dog cart round to the stables.'

An hour later she came downstairs to find him in the drawing room. A brisk fire was burning, and he was pouring drinks.

She noticed that he'd changed into tweeds and a thick blue fisherman's sweater. His shirt collar was up at the back, and she repressed the urge to turn it down and free the dark hair trapped beneath.

'What was all that about with Maud?' she said as she took the glass from his hand.

He lifted his eyebrows. 'A series of demands. She wants to stay on at the House. And she wants Max to stay with her, and no more nonsense about Somerset or boarding school.'

'Ah. And did you accede?'

'Of course.'

'Good. I'm glad she finally found the courage to speak up.'

'So am I,' he said.

A log cracked, and they both jumped.

'I'd forgotten', said Adam without looking at her, 'that it's Cook's night off. She's gone to stay with her sister in Stranraer.' He paused. 'Maud wanted Nelly down at the House, so I'm afraid it's just us.'

'Ah,' Belle said again. She was suddenly sharply conscious of the bitter-sweet smell of the pinesmoke, and the way the firelight caught the line of his jaw.

Adam seemed to feel it too, because he was making a determined effort not to meet her eyes. 'She's left us some cold ham and salad,' he said to his whisky. 'Will that be all right?'

'Fine. Actually, I'm not very hungry.'

'You ought to eat something. You didn't come down for luncheon.'

'I was busy. I was – well, I was packing.'

She waited for him to say something, but he didn't. He simply nodded slowly, still without meeting her eyes; then he put down his tumbler on the chimney-piece, and ran his thumb over his bottom lip.

Say something, she thought in exasperation.

When the silence had gone on long enough, she told him Dr Bailey's verdict on Max. 'Mild exposure, some nasty scratches to the hands and knees, but nothing a spell in bed won't cure.' She flushed. Why did she have to mention bed?

'You were right about Max,' he said suddenly.

'What do you mean?'

'When I talked about boarding school, I was taking it out on him. I shouldn't have done that.'

She glanced down at her drink.

'Belle—'

'It's all right,' she said quickly. 'I understand.'

'Do you?' He crossed the room to the window and stood looking out at the grounds. 'The thing is,' he said without turning round, 'over the past few years, I've learned to be a pretty good actor. I've had to be. Over there – at the Front – one's always acting. In front of the men. With one's fellow officers. One's superiors. Always putting on a show.'

'I know,' she said. 'I'm quite good at acting, myself.'

He turned and met her eyes. 'What I'm trying to say, very badly, is that I don't want you to go.'

She swallowed. 'I thought you couldn't love anyone.'

He ran a hand through his hair. 'Last defence of the about-to-be-vanquished. Can you forgive me?'

'No,' she said.

Again that slow nod. But this time he was smiling.

Belle wasn't. She was so nervous that she could hardly stand. It was extraordinary. Over the years she'd been pawed by dozens of men who meant nothing to her, and she'd never suffered from nerves – never *felt* anything. Yet now that she was with a man for whom she really cared . . .

Then he was coming towards her, and she was putting her tumbler on the chimney-piece and going to meet him, and he was taking her in his arms and kissing her.

That first touch of his mouth on hers, that first taste of his breath, altered her perception of him for ever. She sank her fingers into the softness of his hair; she felt the muscles of his jaw tense as he kissed her more deeply; she tasted his taste of whisky and spring water, and breathed in the sharp, peppery tang of his skin.

They drew apart for breath. She tightened her arms about his waist, unwilling to let him go.

Very gently, he placed his hands on her shoulders and put her from him. 'I think', he said, smoothing her hair behind her ears, 'that you've had about enough for one day.'

'*What?*' she said.

His eyebrows drew together, and his gaze dropped to her mouth. She could see the hunger in him; feel the tension and the holding back.

She guessed what was troubling him, and gave his shoulders a little shake. 'Adam, you are so old-fashioned.'

'Am I?'

'You don't want to "take advantage of me". That's it, isn't it? Because I'm here in your house, alone with you, and you don't want to abuse your position.'

'Am I that transparent?'

'As spring water.'

His lip curled. 'Well. But I still think you need to rest.'

'God, you're stubborn. Can't we—'

'No. No we can't.' His smile broadened. 'Maud would never forgive me if you had a relapse.'

She half expected him to come to her room, but he didn't.

Biting back her frustration, she undressed and slipped on her nightgown, and washed her face at the wash-handstand.

Down in the hall she heard him locking the door, then coming upstairs and turning off the lights. He didn't even pause outside her room, but passed on down the corridor to his own.

Now what do you do? she wondered.

She stared at herself in the looking-glass. Her eyes were bright, her lips swollen and slightly parted. She could still taste him; still feel the roughness of his cheek against hers.

Suddenly, out of nowhere, she had an unwelcome flash of another time when she'd stared at herself in a looking-glass. Years ago, when she'd rushed home from Bamboo Walk after meeting Cornelius Traherne. She'd been in the bath-house, desperate to wash the blood from her underthings, when Mamma had knocked at the door. *Belle? Are you all right?* In horror she'd raised her head and stared at the blank-faced stranger in the glass.

Why think of that now? she thought angrily. This is utterly, utterly different.

She blew out her candle and climbed into bed.

Sleep was impossible. She lay staring up at the canopy, straining for the least sound that might mean that Adam was coming to her. All she heard was the wind in the pines, and the creaks and groans of the old house settling in its sleep.

Around midnight she couldn't stand it any longer, and went to his room.

She was shaking with nerves, but somehow managed to open the door without making any noise.

Instantly he turned his head. The curtains were open. He was lying on his back in a patch of moonlight. In silence he raised himself on one elbow and looked at her.

'I thought you might be asleep,' she said.

He shook his head. 'Not possible.'

'Me too,' she said, her teeth chattering.

He drew back the covers. 'Get in, you'll catch cold.'

Somehow she crossed to the bed and climbed in beside him. He drew the blankets around her and pulled her against him, and for a moment she lay still, breathing in his warmth. Then she slipped her hand under his pyjama top and felt the smooth hardness of his chest; the long ridged scar to the left of his heart.

He tensed.

'Does it hurt?' she whispered.

He gave a slight smile. 'No. Your hand's cold.'

She withdrew it and blew on it, then unbuttoned his top. Her hand moved over his chest to the ridge of his collarbone, then down to the curve of his biceps.

'Belle—'

'Sh . . .' she whispered.

She dug her fingers into the back of his neck and drew him towards her, and his mouth came down on hers.

It felt so right, so easy, to be pressing her body against his, to feel his warm hands caressing her hips, her flanks, her back; so right that she felt a piercing sadness in her breast: a twist of physical pain that made her wince. 'If only we'd met years ago,' she whispered.

She felt him smile against her throat. 'We did. On the beach at Salt River, remember? But I'd just married Celia, and you were about twelve years old. A little young for this sort of thing, don't you think?'

Again that twisting pain. To chase it away, she buried her face in his chest, breathing in his warmth. It didn't work. She kept seeing Cornelius Traherne holding the sun-umbrella over her, and smiling his courteous old-gentleman smile.

She wasn't in bed with Adam, she was on the beach at Salt River in the glare of the silver sand, hoping against hope that the tall young man up ahead would turn and walk towards them, so that she wouldn't have to listen any more . . .

The pain in her chest broke free and burst from her in a sob. To her horror she realized that she couldn't stop. On and on it went: great heaving, wrenching sobs.

After the first frozen astonishment, Adam held her close and stroked her hair, while she lay sobbing and shuddering against him. 'It's all right,' he murmured. 'It's all right. I won't do anything.'

She tried to tell him that she was sorry, but she was crying so hard that she couldn't get the words out. She lay sobbing help-lessly against him till her throat ached and her eyes were swollen and sore, while he smoothed her hair and told her over and over that it was all right, that everything would be all right.

She awoke before dawn to the cries of seagulls on the lawn.

She was alone in the bed, curled up under warm blankets that smelt faintly of Adam. Her face was stiff, her eyes scratchy. She felt fragile, as if any sudden move might shatter her to pieces.

Adam had fallen asleep in an easy chair drawn up by the side of the bed. He'd pulled on the fisherman's sweater over his pyjamas and thrown his greatcoat over his legs. Despite the dark shadow of a beard, he looked like a schoolboy, his hair tousled, his eyelashes shadowing his cheeks.

After a while he opened his eyes and met her gaze and smiled.

'Why didn't you stay in bed?' she said.

He sat up, rubbing the back of his neck. 'I'm afraid,' he said, 'that would have been more than flesh and blood could stand. How do you feel?'

'So–so. I probably look dreadful.'

'Well, your eyes are red, and you're very pale. But you look a damn sight better than you did when you had the 'flu.'

She tried to smile. 'How about you? Did you get much sleep?'

He yawned. 'Not really. The age of chivalry is vastly overrated.'

'What do you mean?'

'I read about it once. Apparently medieval knights used to prove their devotion to their lady by spending a night alongside her without lifting a finger. Or anything else. I can't imagine they got much sleep, either.'

'Adam, I'm so sorry.'

Again he smiled. 'I've spent worse nights, believe me.'

'I want to be with you. I really do. It's just that . . .' Her voice trailed off.

'I have to admit that I've never had that effect on a woman before.' His face became thoughtful. 'It did make me wonder why.'

She tensed.

'I think – at least, I get the sense,' he went on, 'that some time in the past, some man gave you a bad time of it. Am I right?'

Her skin began to prickle. He was getting too close. 'In a way,' she said.

He hesitated. 'This is going to sound completely absurd. But was it – it wasn't – Cornelius Traherne?'

Her stomach turned over. '*What?*'

'It's just that I saw you with him in the glasshouse at Kyme, and you seemed – well, the way you seemed together. As if there was something . . . It made me wonder, that's all.'

She couldn't breathe. Her skin was prickling and hot. *Found out, found out.* 'Good heavens, Adam,' she said, 'I've known him since I was a child. He's older than my father.'

'Sorry. Sorry. Absurd even to think it. God, what a relief. It's strange, the things that seem entirely plausible in the middle of the night.'

'I know,' she said quietly.

'I'm sorry,' he said again. He looked at her for a moment, as if he was wondering whether to fling back the bedclothes and join her. Then he seemed to come to a decision, and got to his feet. 'I'll go and make us some tea.'

'You could come back to bed,' she said.

He shook his head. 'I think it's a bit soon, don't you?' Stooping, he kissed her cheek, and she reached up and stroked his hair.

'We'll be all right, won't we?' she said.

He smiled and kissed her again. 'Of course we will.'

When he'd gone, she curled on her side and lay staring at the grey sky. Drum Talbot had said once that it was tiring, telling lies all the time.

No it's not, thought Belle. It's easy.

While Adam was downstairs, Belle had a bath and dressed. She felt exhausted, and more like an invalid than since arriving at Cairngowrie. But it'll be all right, she told herself. There's nothing in the way. Not really.

As she was brushing her hair, a motor crunched on the gravel. By the time she reached the window, whoever it was had gone inside.

The car in the carriageway was an expensive one, a Daimler or a Bentley; she couldn't tell which from this angle. So not the Ruthvens, she thought with a vague sense of unease.

She opened the door and went out onto the landing. Voices in the drawing room. Slowly she went downstairs, and paused with her hand on the door handle.

'I wish you'd let me know you were coming,' she heard Adam say curtly.

'I didn't know I was until yesterday,' the other man replied.

Belle's hand tightened on the door handle. It can't be, she thought.

'. . . but it seemed the natural thing to do, to stop by and see my grandson,' said Cornelius Traherne.

CHAPTER TWENTY-SEVEN

'I'm afraid that Max is from home,' said Adam.

Why did you let him in? thought Belle, shifting uneasily on the sofa. Why can't you just tell him to get out?

With every second that Traherne stayed, her sense of danger grew. Couldn't Adam feel it too? How could he stand there, calmly talking to this man? How could he not see through the avuncular façade to what he really was?

'What a pity,' said Traherne, leaning back in his chair and studying Adam with amusement.

Belle could see him noting Adam's red-rimmed eyes and unshaven cheeks, just as he'd taken in her own hastily brushed hair and lack of make-up. No doubt he was adding two and two together and making five. No doubt he would make use of it if he could.

'If you'd be so kind,' he said to Adam, 'as to tell me where I can find the little fellow, I should so much like to see how he goes on.'

'I'm sure you would,' muttered Belle.

Traherne ignored her.

Adam threw her a glance. 'Since you're in the area for a while,' he said, turning back to Traherne, 'perhaps something can be arranged, but not yet. Max isn't well.'

'I'm sorry to hear that,' said Traherne with every appearance of concern. 'Not this dreadful influenza, I hope?'

'Nothing like that,' said Adam. 'He got into a scrape on the beach, and needs to rest for a couple of days.'

Why did you have to tell him that? thought Belle.

'Mr Traherne,' said Adam, 'forgive me for being blunt, but you are aware of the terms of your daughter's will?'

Traherne sighed. 'Poor dear Sibella. All that energy, wasted in needless antipathy. But really – and do call me Cornelius – there's nothing in the will to prevent my simply calling on my grandson. Now is there?'

'Not as such,' Adam conceded, 'but—'

'Well, then.' Traherne smiled. 'And now, Palairet, you must forgive *me* for being blunt in my turn, but I feel it my duty as a grandfather to register my concern. I arrive in London only to be told by my daughter's solicitors that my grandson has been whisked away to some remote and not altogether healthy Scottish outpost. I take the first available train, as any grandfather would, only to be told that the little chap is "from home", whatever that means, having been laid up after a "scrape" while in his new guardian's care—'

'Adam was the one who rescued him,' Belle cut in.

'He needed to be "rescued"? Dear me, how very unfortunate. Although perhaps it's as well that he *is* from home, given that arrangements here at Cairngowrie Hall seem so extraordinarily . . . well, informal.'

Belle felt her cheeks growing hot.

Adam's face went stiff. 'Now look here, Traherne—'

'But I shall say nothing of that,' said Traherne imperturbably, 'for I'm well aware that times have changed, and it is only old fogeys such as I who still have any regard for the proprieties . . .'

Belle's jaw dropped.

'. . . although as a friend of the family's,' he went on with a fatherly glance at her, 'it occurs to me to wonder, Belle dear, what your papa and mamma would say if they knew what you were up to. By the way, they were both well when I saw them last, as were the twins. Your mamma's efforts at quarantine appear

233

to be keeping them clear of the influenza, at least for the present.'

Belle gripped the edge of the sofa. 'But – there isn't any 'flu in Jamaica.'

Traherne opened his eyes wide. 'My dear girl, where have you been? It's been ravaging the island for weeks. Tens of thousands have died.'

'Miss Lawe has been ill herself,' said Adam. 'She's only just regained her strength.'

'I'm so sorry to hear that,' said Traherne. 'And my apologies, Belle, if you misconstrued what I—'

'I don't want your apologies,' snapped Belle. 'I want you to leave.'

'Belle,' said Adam, 'there's no need to—'

'Why don't you tell him to leave?' she cried. 'We all know he wouldn't even be here if Max wasn't rich.'

'Oh, I say,' murmured Traherne, 'now that simply won't do.' He caught her gaze and held it, and as she stared into the fathomless pupils she knew that she was being warned to back down.

'I think you'd better go,' said Adam.

Traherne released Belle from his gaze and rose to his feet. 'I don't very much care for your tone,' he told Adam. 'It reflects badly on you, Palairet. Very badly indeed.'

'My apologies,' said Adam insincerely. 'Now let me show you out.'

For a moment they stood facing one another. Traherne was a head shorter than Adam, and clearly did not relish the difference. 'Well,' he said, running a liver-spotted hand down the front of his waistcoat. 'I shall be in Galloway for a fortnight. I shall return when it suits.'

In silence, Adam opened the drawing-room doors.

Belle ran to the window and watched as they waited on the steps for the chauffeur to bring the motor. She felt angry and sick, but more than that, she felt afraid. All these weeks at Cairngowrie, and the thought of Traherne had hardly crossed her mind. She'd been safe here. Safe with Adam. But now, she realized with a sensation of falling, they had been found out. Nowhere was safe. How could it be, when Traherne was Max's grandfather, and Adam was Max's guardian? They would never be free of him.

The Daimler slid away. Adam came in and closed the drawing-room doors behind him, and leaned against them.

Belle turned to him. 'You shouldn't have let him in.'

He studied her in silence. 'What was I to do?' he said quietly. 'Turn him away from my door, like some Victorian patriarch?'

'Can't you see that he was sneering at you? He thinks you're weak. Can't you see that?'

'I don't care what he thinks. My only aim is to protect Max.'

Cold with shock, she paced the room.

'Belle,' he said. 'Let's not quarrel about this. It isn't—'

'Why must you be so considerate?' she cried. 'Can't you see what he is? People like him take advantage. That's what they do.'

'People like him?' He put his hands in his pockets and went to the fire, and stood looking down at it. 'You seem to know him rather well.'

She caught her breath. 'He's a friend of my father's. Well, not a friend so much as a fellow planter. I've known him all my life.'

'You're telling me too much,' he said in a low voice.

'What do you mean?'

Still with his hands in his pockets, he turned to face her. He appeared perfectly calm, but there was a stillness about his face which frightened her. 'You're giving me too much information,' he said. 'It's what people do when they're hiding something. Were you his mistress?'

The suddenness of it took her breath away. 'His – mistress?' She tried to laugh. 'What an old-fashioned word to use.'

'Don't take refuge in semantics. Did you sleep together?'

Once again, she felt as if she were falling from a great height.

'Did you sleep together?' he said again.

She licked her lips. 'Yes.'

He took it without flinching. Almost, she thought, as if he'd guessed it all along. 'So this morning,' he said slowly, 'you were lying to me.'

'. . . Yes. But Adam—'

'Why? Why did you lie?'

She did not reply.

She watched him go to the sofa and sit with his elbows on his knees, staring down at the rug. His face was too calm. She could see him retreating into himself. 'Were you in love with him?' he said, still without looking at her.

'Of course not.'

'Then why?'

Her throat had closed. Panic constricted her chest. And yet she knew that this was her chance. All she had to do was tell him the truth. Right now. Just tell him. *It's not what you think. I was a child. I was a child . . .*

She couldn't do it. She couldn't bring herself to say the words. If he knew the truth, he would know that she wasn't who he thought she was, but someone else altogether. Not a lady, but a 'female' – the kind of female who lets a man like Traherne put his hand on her breast . . . She would be *found out*. And then he wouldn't love her any more.

'Tell me why,' Adam said again.

'I – I can't.'

'Why not? It can't be that hard. After all, there can only be a number of reasons why a beautiful young woman would sleep with a repellent old man.'

As she watched him sitting there, struggling to take it in, she knew that it was impossible between them. Traherne would haunt them for ever. There would always be this threat hanging over them. This ghost at the feast.

The sense of loss took her breath away. She had woken that morning feeling fragile and tired, but also full of hope. Adam had told her they would be all right, and she had believed him. But it wasn't all right. It would never be all right.

'*Why?*' Adam said again. 'Just tell me why.'

'I can't,' she said.

He shut his eyes in pain.

She wanted to go to him, but she knew that it wouldn't do any good. Instead she clasped her arms about her waist and walked past him, out of the drawing-room and up the stairs, and into her room.

He did not come after her.

★

Dear Maud,

You asked me once not to hurt Adam, and I said that I wouldn't. I'm afraid I have to go back on that. I'm leaving, and it's going to hurt him; but not nearly as much as if I were to stay. I can't explain, but there are reasons why being together would be impossible. I managed to ignore them for a while, because I was at Cairngowrie, and I had Adam and you and Max to think about and to care for. But I can't ignore the reasons any more, so I'm leaving. If this makes you hate me, I'll understand. But please *believe that I'm doing this for Adam's sake, not my own. I'll write to you when I know where I'll be.*

Your friend,

Belle Lawe.

P.S. Please would you give the enclosed note to Max. I'm sorry I couldn't see him to say goodbye, but it's best for everyone if I go quickly.

It had been ridiculously easy to get away.

While Adam was down at the House warning Maud about Traherne, she'd sent the groom to Stranraer for Ritchie's cart. By four o'clock she was at the railway station, sitting numbly on a bench and watching the rain streaming down the window panes, while the elderly gentleman who was the only other occupant of the First Class waiting room covertly assessed her potential as weekend entertainment.

He was a dapper little attorney with a small, domed stomach, and white hair brushed carefully over his bald spot in a manner which his wife probably told him looked distinguished. As he seated himself at the other end of Belle's bench and offered her his newspaper, she pretended not to notice when he slipped off his wedding ring and tucked it into his watch pocket.

He probably thinks he's a man of the world, she thought as she answered his opening gambits. What is it about me that attracts such men? Is it something they can sniff out, as a dog scents a bitch in season?

She felt too hollow and exhausted to care. What did it matter? What did any of it matter? If only the train would come, she could get this over, and start the rest of her life without Adam.

'But my dear young lady,' exclaimed the little attorney, 'what a delightful coincidence! I too have just missed the London train, and am waiting for the four thirty to Newton Stewart. Such a nuisance, these restricted services! Newton Stewart hardly seems worth it, only what, twenty-five miles distant? Were it not for the fast train in the morning, one would scarcely bother.' He paused, then added with what he clearly thought was a mischievous twinkle, 'We shall have to put up for the night at the Station Hotel. Such a nuisance.'

'Goodness me,' she murmured.

'Oh, it's quite decent for a small town,' he added hastily, as if he feared he'd gone too far. 'And *highly* respectable.'

She let the silence grow.

Eventually the little attorney said, 'Such a bore, this rain, don't you agree? They say that we're set for the most dismal November.'

'What a bore,' she echoed.

'However, permit me to say,' he added with leaden gallantry, 'that in such company, no-one could notice the clouds for long.'

She inclined her head in acknowledgement and thought, what fools men are. How readily they deceive themselves that a woman finds them attractive. What does he actually see when he looks at himself in the glass? What does he think I see?

And what shall we do about him? she wondered. Shall we send him off with a flea in his ear? Or shall we give him a dirty little secret to take home and finger when he's sitting with his wife?

At last the train for Newton Stewart pulled into the station. Porters ran to place steps at the doors. People alighted and hurried off beneath umbrellas. The little attorney had just patted his plump thighs and announced that he would run and ensure that the porter found them a congenial carriage – when a shadow cut across him.

'I need to speak to the lady alone,' said Adam.

The little attorney gave a start.

Belle clenched her hands in her lap.

Adam was hatless, his greatcoat streaked dark with rain. He was making no attempt at civility, and the little attorney bristled.

'Alone,' Adam repeated in a tone that Belle had never heard him use before.

The little attorney went very red. Gathering his things, he hurried from the waiting room without a backward glance.

Adam watched him go, then took his place at the end of the bench. From inside his coat he took a small square package, and placed it on the bench beside her. 'This arrived from Berkeley Square after you left. Letters from Jamaica. I thought you should have them.'

She took the package and clasped it on her lap.

'I got your note,' he said.

She nodded.

'It didn't tell me anything.'

'Only that I'm leaving.'

'Yes. Only that.'

'That's all there is to say.'

His face was wet with rain. He wiped his forehead with the back of his hand. 'That man just now. He seemed to think he was onto a good thing.'

She flushed. 'We were going to share a carriage to Newton Stewart.'

'And then? What then?'

She did not reply.

'Would you have slept with him, too? Is that what you meant in East Street, when you said that you belonged in the slums?'

'. . . Perhaps.'

'I don't believe you.'

'Then why did you ask?'

On the platform, train doors were being slammed shut. The porter glanced in Belle's direction and indicated her carriage.

She stood up. 'The truth is, Adam, you don't really know me.'

'Yes I do. I do know you.'

She moved to the door, but he stepped in front. 'What you told me about Traherne,' he said. 'It doesn't matter.'

'Of course it does.'

'No. No. I can forget about it.'

'Well, I can't.'

He drew a deep breath, and she saw what this was costing him. To watch him in such pain was unbearable. She pushed past him and ran out onto the platform. She saw the porter holding open the door of her carriage, and made for it as if for a refuge. To her relief, the little attorney was not inside. Presumably Adam had frightened him off for good.

She tried to shut the door, but Adam held it open. He shot a look at the porter and the man withdrew.

'You're getting wet,' said Belle. 'Please don't—'

'When Celia asked for a divorce,' he cut in, 'I said yes straight away. It never occurred to me to ask her to stay. What would be the point in humiliating myself—'

'Adam—'

'Belle. Please. I'm asking you. I'm *asking* you to stay.'

'Don't do this. I tried to explain—'

'I don't want you to go,' he said. 'I can't—' His voice broke. 'I can't lose you.'

She took his hand and put it from the door. 'Please. Adam.'

The train began to move. The rain was running down his face. 'Belle, don't—'

'Goodbye, Adam,' she said. 'Don't try to find me. There isn't any point.'

CHAPTER TWENTY-EIGHT

The Station Hotel at Newton Stewart must once have been a cosy little place, but four years of war had taken their toll. Coal rationing, lighting restrictions, food shortages, and a staff decimated by influenza meant that it could only provide Belle with a chilly little chamber furnished in stained velveteen, and a cold supper of herring in oatmeal.

The waiter clearly disapproved of young women travelling alone, and gave her a draughty table by the kitchen. She was directly in sight of the little attorney from Stranraer, who was also dining alone, but to her relief he buried himself in his newspaper, and pretended not to see her.

For company, she'd brought along the package of letters from home, but she found that she still couldn't bring herself to open them. She wouldn't be able to cope with homesickness on top of everything else. Pushing aside her unfinished herring, she rose and went up to her room.

The next morning she came down early to pay her bill, but was beaten to it by a noisy party of commercial travellers. The harried clerk asked her to wait in the lounge, and she acceded without a word, and found herself a chair.

Her eyes felt scratchy with fatigue after a sleepless night spent reliving events at Cairngowrie in an endless, exhausting loop. She kept seeing Traherne's pale, goat-eyed stare; Adam's face as he ran alongside the train.

Now, as she waited in the lounge, she half hoped that he would come to find her; that he'd make one last attempt to persuade her to go back with him. But deep down, she knew that he wouldn't. It had cost him too much to ask her to stay. He wouldn't ask again.

Out in the reception, someone was calling her name.

Belle frowned. The clerk had said he'd bring the bill to her here, so why . . .

Her heart skipped a beat. It wasn't the clerk. Behind the commercial travellers, a woman was jumping up and down, waving to catch her attention. She was in her thirties, slender and elegantly dressed in a tailored travelling costume of sea-green serge, with her cloudy light brown hair pulled haphazardly back. There was a determined look on her narrow, arresting face as she fought her way through the throng.

Belle stood up. It couldn't be . . .

'Thank *heavens* I've found you!' cried her aunt Sophie, giving her a breathless kiss on the cheek, then throwing herself into a chair. 'Captain Palairet told me you were here, so I came at the gallop. Literally. He lent me his dog cart.'

Belle's head was reeling. 'What are you doing here?'

'Looking for you, of course,' said Sophie. 'My God, Belle, I don't know whether to kiss you or box your ears! Not even to send us a wire! People dropping like flies from the 'flu, and no word from you for *weeks*. Your poor mother's been out of her mind with worry.'

Belle's hands flew to her mouth. 'Oh, God. God. I didn't think.'

'Clearly not,' said Sophie with a wry twist of her mouth.

'I don't – I mean – I thought you were in France, on some sort of war work.'

'I was. I am. But I come over now and then. And when I do, I go straight to Berkeley Square.' She pressed her lips together and frowned. 'You can't imagine my shock when I found no-one at the house. Just a black wreath on the door.'

Belle swallowed. She'd been so caught up in her own concerns that she hadn't given a thought to Mamma and Papa, or Sophie and Ben . . .

'Anyway,' Sophie said briskly. 'I went back the next day, and this time there was a maid, and a lawyer making an inventory. He told me where you were, and – well, he filled me in on the rest.' She blinked. 'Poor Sibella. Poor silly, unhappy, darling Sib. We had our ups and downs over the years, but we always stayed in touch. We shared secrets. We . . . Well. You're going to have to tell me all about it.'

Belle wondered where to begin.

'I don't mean now,' said Sophie. 'You look all in.' She glanced at the package of letters in Belle's lap. 'Ah, good, so they sent them on.'

'I only got them yesterday afternoon,' Belle said defensively. 'I'm afraid I haven't read them yet.'

'Probably just as well. Oh, everything's fine at Eden,' she added quickly, seeing Belle's expression. 'And as soon as I knew that you were too, I sent them a wire. But be warned about that package; it contains several increasingly irate notes from me, telling you to contact them *at once.*'

Belle's hands tightened on the package. 'Was Mamma very worried?'

Sophie rolled her eyes. 'What do you think?'

'I can't believe it never occurred to me. Not even when I was getting better. It was just . . .' She fought back a rising tide of tears.

It never occurred to you, she added silently, because you felt safe at Cairngowrie. Because you'd run away from the rest of your life.

'Don't take on,' said Sophie. 'After all, you did have an excuse. That handsome Captain Palairet told me how ill you've been.' She studied Belle's face with concern. 'My poor little Belle,' she said quietly. 'I'm so glad I've found you.'

'Oh, Sophie,' said Belle, and burst into tears.

Sophie took charge of everything. Somehow she found a better hotel on the edge of town, and organized the move. 'No sense rushing off to London,' she said. 'Not when you're at such a low ebb.'

Somehow she persuaded the proprietors at the new hotel to ignore the Public Meals Order which prohibited meat on certain days of the week, so that by two o'clock they were sitting down in their new suite to a very respectable luncheon of beefsteak and champagne. 'My private supply,' explained Sophie, raising her glass. 'These days I never travel without it. "In victory you deserve it. In defeat, you need it."'

'Who said that?' asked Belle with her mouth full.

'Napoleon. Now drink up.'

An hour later, they were sitting over coffee. Feeling better than she had in days, Belle leaned back in her chair and watched her aunt giving orders to the maid.

Clever, independent, acid-tongued Aunt Sophie; always so well-informed and in command. It was only when Belle looked more closely that she noticed how her aunt's cheeks had thinned; how the lines had deepened at the sides of her mouth.

Belle felt a stab of concern. 'How's Ben?' she asked when the maid had gone.

'I've no idea,' said Sophie. She spoke calmly, but Belle saw how her jaw tightened. 'He's on Special Services. Whatever that means. All very secret, and behind enemy lines.'

'It sounds dangerous.'

'Oh, I've no doubt it is. He calls it "taking risks". As if that makes it more acceptable.' She got up to poke the fire. 'His next leave's in a fortnight. November the eighteenth. We're supposed to meet in Paris, but he hasn't written to confirm. In fact, he hasn't written at all for the last six days.' She put down the poker and sat down again, her face taut with anxiety. 'What I can't forgive is that he volunteered. If he survives, I shall kill him myself.'

Belle made no reply. Nothing she could have said would have given any reassurance.

'Still,' said Sophie, pressing her knees with both palms, as if to tamp down her anxiety, 'I don't want to talk about that. I want to talk about you. You and Captain Palairet.'

Belle glanced down at her coffee. 'How did you guess?'

'The way he talked of you. Or rather, the way that he didn't. He's very self-contained, isn't he? Not the sort of man to wear his heart on his sleeve. And yet I got the impression . . . that inside, he's shattered.'

Belle's eyes grew hot.

'Is it that you don't care for him?' Sophie asked gently.

'No. It isn't that at all.'

'Then what?'

She took a ragged breath. 'I just – I had to leave him. That's all.'

'Why?'

She shook her head. 'There were reasons. Things – things I did. When I was younger.'

'Good God, Belle, you're only twenty years old! Just how—'

'I couldn't tell him, Sophie. It would always have been between us.'

There was a silence. Then Sophie said, 'Whatever it is, sooner or later, you're going to have to tell someone.'

Belle did not reply.

Sophie sighed. 'Very well. Don't tell me. But could I suggest that if you can possibly bring yourself to do it, you should write and tell your mother? She's the family expert on secrets.'

Belle stared at her. 'Mamma?'

'Heavens, yes. When we were younger, her whole life was one huge secret. It's how we survived.' A corner of her mouth lifted. 'Even now, I don't think she's quite broken the habit. Sometimes it drives your father wild.'

Belle didn't want to think about home. Especially not now, when she'd caused so much needless worry by not getting in touch.

'So you left him,' said Sophie, returning with characteristic single-mindedness to the subject under discussion. 'It's a risky thing to do, Belle. And I know. I walked out on Ben once.'

'*What?* But – you've always been so happy.'

'Oh, this was before we were married. He was a groom at the time. Desperately unsuitable.' She shook her head. 'Leaving him was the biggest mistake of my life. Well, one of the biggest. I've made quite a few in my time.' She glanced at Belle, and her honey-coloured eyes were bright with concern. 'What I'm trying to say is that I don't think you ought to go rushing off to London when you're feeling like this.'

'You don't understand. I—'

'Just listen to your aunt, and pretend for a moment that she knows best. Here's what we're going to do. We're going to stay in Newton Stewart for another few days, to give you time to think. Perhaps you'll reconsider and go and see him. Sort things out.'

Belle thought about that. She thought about Cornelius Traherne, who would be staying in Galloway for a fortnight. She thought about Adam's face as he'd stood in the rain watching her go.

She said yes.

For three days they stayed in Newton Stewart. The weather closed in, and Belle remained in the suite and read her letters, and let Sophie cosset her like an invalid.

The earliest letters dated from mid-September, when she'd been staying with Dodo at Kyme. *Your father is as usual doing too much*, wrote Mamma, *although heaven knows he can at last afford to slow down. But old habits die hard. He's planting out the whole of Bullet Tree Walk with new stock from Trinidad, and only ratooning Orange Grove . . .*

The first note of alarm crept in about a week later. *I don't like the sound of this new influenza*, wrote Mamma. *I know I'm being ridiculous, but I'm keeping the twins on the estate. They're furious, they've only just joined the Falmouth Wolf Cubs, but there we are . . .*

Then a gap of two weeks. *Belle, are you all right? It's just that it's been so long since you wrote, and we hear such dreadful things about the epidemic in London. Although at least the authorities there recognize that it is an epidemic, unlike the Governor over here, who pigheadedly maintains that 'the danger is grossly exaggerated'. Meanwhile, seven thousand have died. Your father's issuing emergency rations to the field workers, and we fumigate the twins' room with carbolic nightly. Grace McFarlane died last week. Grace! The most powerful obeah-woman on the Northside! Poor Evie is very much affected – perhaps more than she would have expected – and you can imagine how deeply this death has shocked the country people. If the fever can take a Mother of Darkness . . . But I'm wittering. Write soon and reassure us that you're well . . .*

By mid-October, the anxiety was no longer concealed. *Belle, what's* happening *over there? Please* please *write and tell me you're safe. Here the 'flu's still raging, the hospitals are overflowing, the schools and churches shut to prevent infection. I worry terribly that your father will go down with it, as he spends his days riding all over the parish, directing the relief efforts. (He sends his love, but is too busy to write.) Your aunt Sophie will be in London soon, and she's sworn to track you down. If anyone can, she will. I can't remember if I told you, but she's now rather high up in something called the Graves Registration Commission . . .*

The final note was dated 28th October. It was smudged, disjointed, and obviously written in haste. *This terrible, terrible epidemic. If I believed in a god, I'd be on my knees begging him to keep us all safe and well. Rebecca Traherne is dead. They say it was the 'flu, but I think she died of grief, for it was only a few days after she got your wire about poor Sibella. Captain Palairet wrote to her and told her how you cared for Sibella at the end, and I know that poor Rebecca was deeply grateful to you. I think it eased her mind to know that her daughter died with a friend by her side. I'm proud of you, Belle. Although I could have wished that you'd found time to send me a wire, as well as poor Rebecca . . .*

Belle put down the last letter and sat staring out of the window. It had stopped raining at last, and above the grey tiled roofs of the little town the sky was a pale, washed-out blue.

Not as blue as Jamaica, she thought. Never as blue as that.

Her poor mother. Always so strong, so practical. And yet in that last letter she'd sounded isolated and fearful.

Belle shut her eyes. If only she'd thought to send her a wire. If only she hadn't been so absorbed in her own concerns . . .

Sophie came in, and Belle collected herself with an effort.

Sophie wasn't fooled, but she pretended not to notice, and rang for the maid to order luncheon.

Belle shuffled the letters into a pile. 'Mamma says you're something high up in the Graves Registration Commission,' she said. 'I'm afraid I don't even know what that is.'

Sophie made a face. 'Not many people do.' She stooped to put another log on the fire. 'It was set up in the second year of the War, and I sort of stumbled into it a few months ago.' Brushing off her hands, she curled up on the sofa opposite Belle. 'I'd been approached by an old colleague from a charity where I used to work. He wanted to trace the whereabouts of his nephew's grave, and couldn't afford to go to France himself, so I said I'd do what I could. Someone put me in touch with the Commission.' She opened her hands.

'Did you find the nephew's grave?' asked Belle.

'It turned out there wasn't one. He'd been blown up, poor lad. Nothing left.' Her face became thoughtful. 'Half a million graves, Belle. Another half a million men missing, but with no known grave. And back home, all the mothers and brothers and sisters wondering where to lay their flowers.' She shook her head. 'People have this deep need to know where their loved ones are buried. Even if they can't visit it, they need a mark on a map, or a photograph. Something. Anything.'

Belle had never thought about that. 'And you,' she said, 'what do you do out there?'

Sophie gave her crooked smile. 'Well, for quite a lot of the time, we hare about the countryside, planning cemeteries and planting shrubs.'

'Shrubs?'

'I know it sounds ridiculous, but it makes a difference. There are people who are paid to take photographs of graves for those back home, and believe me, it's much more of a shock for the relatives if all they see in the background is mud and shattered tree trunks, compared to a tidy patch of grass and a viburnum bush. But of course, I don't do much gardening myself. Mostly, I register the graves.' Her smile faded. 'All those names. Carved on little wooden crosses made from bits of packing case; scrawled on scraps of paper tucked inside old bottles. Sometimes I feel as if I'm playing a sort of game of Russian roulette. Whose name will I find this time? Will it be someone I know? Will it be Ben?'

Belle leaned forward and covered her hand with her own. 'You miss him terribly, don't you?'

'All the time.' She paused. 'Sometimes I get so *angry* with him. I have these terrific rows with him in my head. And this is going to sound even stranger, but I dread it when he comes back on leave, because I know it'll be so unutterably awful when it's over, and we have to say goodbye again . . .'

There was silence between them. Then Sophie gave herself a little shake. 'But let's not talk about this. I came to tell you that I've hired a motor-taxi, probably the only one in Newton Stewart, and after lunch we're going for a drive. We're going to visit an officers' convalescent home.'

Belle remembered Felicity Ruthven, and her heart sank. 'Sophie, it's kind of you, but I really don't want—'

'I know you don't,' said Sophie, 'but this is important. There's something I want you to see.'

CHAPTER TWENTY-NINE

The pinewoods were silent and still. Only a crow flew down onto a branch and fixed Belle with a beady black eye.

Sophie had told the motor-taxi to wait at the lodge, so that they could continue on foot. She said she wanted Belle to have time 'to take it in'.

'To take in what?' Belle asked warily.

'Wait and see,' replied Sophie.

It was a clear, cold afternoon, with a light breeze blowing from the south. The sound of the wind in the pines reminded Belle of Cairngowrie.

'Your mother used to love pinewoods when she was a child,' remarked Sophie. 'Did she ever mention that?'

Belle shook her head. 'She never talked about her childhood.'

'She adored Scotland, you know. The beach. The seals. She and Mamma used to take endless photographs. Rose was rather a talented photographer. Did you—'

'Yes,' cut in Belle. 'I did know that.'

Sophie smiled at her. 'I'd forgotten. You used to help your mother in her darkroom, didn't you? Although when you were very small, you had something of a love-hate relationship with photographs. I remember once you took against your mother's portrait of you. "Put it away," you said. "I don't like me looking at me."'

Belle remained silent. She was beginning to wonder what Sophie was up to.

'It's funny how some things run in families,' said Sophie.

'Is it?' muttered Belle. 'What are you—'

'Oh. look. Here we are.'

Through the trees, Belle glimpsed daylight. Then the woods were left behind, and parkland opened out before her. She gasped.

From where she stood, the carriageway swept down towards a wide ornamental lake fringed with bulrushes, then up a long hill guarded by a line of stern marble knights towards a great stone mansion at the top. The severity of its frontage was increased by a line of massive stone columns which gave it a forbiddingly cage-like appearance, and its windows threw back the coppery glare of the sun like eyes. It looked just the same as it had in the oil painting in Papa's study.

'Strathnaw,' said Belle. 'That's Strathnaw.'

'Your mamma's "family seat",' said Sophie. 'At least, that's what poor Sibella liked to call it. Although of course the Monroes never were gentry. Merely gentleman farmers who made good in Jamaica.' She paused. 'Your great-great-great-grandfather Alasdair – May's father – terrible old man – he built it to show off his money and spite his friends. He planted these woods to obscure his neighbour's property, so that whenever he looked out of his window he could say that he owned everything in sight.' She chuckled. 'He'd turn in his grave if he knew that the whole thing had been sold off, and was now a san for convalescent officers.'

Belle was silent. She was back in her father's study, lying on the Turkey rug and gazing up at the huge old oil painting of a snow-bound Strathnaw. Pestering Papa with questions about robins.

That scene was so vivid in her mind. It was like looking down the wrong end of a kaleidoscope, and watching the tiny, brilliantly coloured shards, impossibly far away.

'Your grandfather Ainsley,' Sophie went on, 'used to come here in the school holidays. As did your father.'

'Papa? Papa came here?'

'But you knew that, surely? My grandfather – Jocelyn Monroe – he adopted your father when he was orphaned as a child.'

'Oh, I knew about that. I just didn't know that he ever came to Strathnaw.'

'Well, here's something else that perhaps you didn't know. This is where your parents first met.'

Belle stared at her.

'Your mother was ten years old. Came here in the middle of winter on some secret errand of her own, and saw your father down there by that statue. He was on a white horse, standing so still that for a moment she thought he was a statue himself.' She paused. 'Apparently he wore a long grey cloak which she found impossibly dashing.'

'You said she was a child.'

'And he was a young officer about to go out to the Sudan. After that, they didn't meet again for years. Not till we moved to Jamaica.'

'Sophie,' said Belle in a low voice, 'why are you telling me all this?'

Sophie glanced at her. 'It's a little hard to explain. But I've been thinking about what you said the other day; about your having done something when you were younger that prevents your being with Captain Palairet.'

Belle felt the familiar hot, prickling sensation that told her someone was getting too close.

'I've no idea what you meant,' went on Sophie, 'and since you're not inclined to tell me, I shan't ask again. But looking back, it does seem to me that it explains why you've never been home. You're running away, aren't you?'

Belle began to feel breathless. 'I don't know what you mean.'

'Yes you do,' Sophie said gently. 'You're running away. Goodness, I ought to know. I tried it once myself.'

'Did it work?'

'Of course not. Just another one of my mistakes.' She hesitated. 'None of which answers your question: why did I bring you here?' She turned her head and gave Belle her bright, observant stare. 'Our family has strong roots, Belle. The Monroes. The Lawes. They go back a long way – here in Scotland, and out in Jamaica. Forgive me for lecturing you like this – I always loathe it when people do it to me – but I can't see you going wrong without saying something. You can't keep running away. The family, Jamaica, Eden. It's part of who you are. You can't run away from yourself.'

'No,' agreed Belle. 'But you can become someone else.'

Sophie gave a wry laugh. 'Oh, you're impossible! You sound just like your mother!'

Sophie wanted to go back and retrieve the motor-taxi and drive on to the house, but Belle put her foot down. 'I don't want to go inside,' she said. 'I've seen Strathnaw, and you've given me your lecture. That ought to be enough.'

Sophie realized that she meant it, and gave in. 'I suppose I can't blame you. I've never liked sanatoriums either. And I've always found this one particularly intimidating. It's officers only, so there's a rule that all the nurses must be ladies.' She pulled a face. 'They're all desperately pretty, and desperate for husbands.'

Belle thought of Felicity Ruthven.

'Apparently,' Sophie added drily, 'it's a marvellous place for courting. Before the war they had dances; now they have sans.'

'But some of the officers are very ill, aren't they?'

'Oh, heavens yes. Tremors, mutism, memory loss. But those poor fellows just give the nurses the chance to appear angelic in front of the more able-bodied patients.'

Belle smiled. 'Goodness, you're cynical.'

Sophie laughed.

They turned and started walking back through the trees.

Sophie became thoughtful again. At last she said, 'There's another reason why I wanted you to see the san.'

Belle turned to her, wondering what was coming next.

'In a couple of days, I shall be going back to Flanders. I was hoping you'd have second thoughts, and make things up with Captain Palairet. But clearly that isn't going to happen.'

Belle flinched.

'Where will you go, Belle? You can hardly go to Berkeley Square now that poor Sib . . . What will you do? Shall you go home to Eden?'

'No,' Belle said quickly.

'Then where? I'm sorry to press you, but I think I must. I can't just leave you.'

'Yes you can.'

'No. I cannot.'

Belle turned and walked on a few paces. She'd been wondering about this herself, but so far she hadn't progressed beyond a vague plan of staying with Dodo for a while.

She had no family in England other than Sophie, and no occupation. She had money, Papa had always seen to that – but as an unmarried girl of twenty, she could hardly set up home on her own without putting herself for ever beyond the pale. The War might have changed things immeasurably, but not to that extent.

'We could use you in Flanders,' said Sophie. 'Plenty of hospitals, of course; less glamorous than Strathnaw, but they might suit you better. Or you could come and help me in the GRC.'

'Planting shrubs. Yes, I suppose I could manage that.'

'We need more help than just planting shrubs.'

'Such as what? I wouldn't be able to do anything else.'

'Nonsense. I've already had one or two ideas.'

'What do you mean?'

Sophie shrugged. 'Nothing I'd care to go into just yet. The point is, will you come?'

Belle thought for a moment. 'No,' she said. 'Thank you, but no.'

Sophie did not press her further, and they drove back to Newton Stewart in companionable silence. When they reached the hotel, Sophie went upstairs to write letters, and Belle went outside for a walk.

It was getting dark, and as she wandered the little streets that were only dimly lit by blue-painted street lamps she attracted curious glances from shopkeepers drawing down their blinds. She ignored them. Walking in the dark helped her think.

Damn Sophie for being so shrewd; for reminding her of where she came from.

Rose Durrant, her grandmother, had given up everything to be with the man she loved. She'd thrown away her good name and followed him halfway across the world. Sophie herself had defied society to marry Ben, and as a result had permanently shut certain

254

doors against her. Even for Mamma, there had been sacrifices and heartbreak, although Belle didn't know the details. Compared to all that, what were her own doubts and misgivings?

Turning it over in her mind, she walked on. But the more she thought about it, the more certain she felt that nothing had changed. She could never bring herself to tell Adam the truth. She couldn't risk watching his face change as he realized that she was not the woman he believed her to be.

It was after seven by the time she returned to the hotel. She expected to find Sophie dressed for dinner and awaiting her impatiently in the lounge, but she wasn't. The clerk said that he hadn't seen Mrs Kelly since they'd come in from their drive. Some letters had arrived for her in the afternoon post, including (he couldn't help but notice) an official-looking one from the Front.

With a twinge of alarm, Belle mounted the stairs to their suite.

As soon as she opened the door of their sitting room, she knew something was wrong. The fire had been allowed to burn low, and the lamp on the table was guttering. Sophie sat in the half-darkness, clutching a letter. Her hair was awry. There were traces of tears on her cheeks.

'Oh God,' said Belle. 'Ben.'

Sophie turned her face and looked up at her as if she was having trouble focusing. 'Missing in action,' she said.

PART THREE

CHAPTER THIRTY

Flanders, 11th November 1918

The War had ended that morning, and Arthur Winsloe was taking it personally.

He'd got his blighty at the battle of Lys, and returned home to find that his wife had gone off with another man: a catastrophe he liked to describe in blinding detail to anyone who would listen. Adam didn't always listen, but he didn't walk away, so Winsloe had attached himself, and could not now be shaken off.

'Bloody Armistice,' he said bitterly as they drove out of Ypres, the lorry lurching over the ruts. 'Too bloody late for me. If only she'd waited. I told her it'd be over soon.'

'I thought she left you back in April,' said Adam, swerving to avoid a cat. In the rear-view mirror he saw it walk calmly to the edge of the road, and curl up on a fragment of shell casing.

It was a peaceful sight on a beautiful, clear autumn afternoon. Hostilities had ceased four hours before. The stillness took Adam's breath away.

'But if she'd known how soon it would end,' Winsloe insisted, 'she wouldn't have left. If only the bloody Boche had caved in weeks ago, when they ought to have done . . .'

Adam stopped listening. Every time he came this way, he remembered how it had looked at the start of the War. At this point the road used to cut through the medieval ramparts, and in

1914 they'd been green and blowsy with trees, and guarded by two splendid stone lions who sat on their haunches like large, sleepy house cats. Beyond the ramparts, as one headed into town, the road had narrowed as it passed between tall Flemish houses with stepped brick gables, then on towards the proud old Cloth Hall and the magnificent cathedral.

Now the ramparts were gone, the cathedral lay in ruins, and the shattered skeleton of the Cloth Hall reared stark against the sky. The lions had long since been blasted to oblivion. Adam wondered if they would be replaced, now that peace had come. Peace. It was too huge to take in. He gave up trying, and concentrated on driving.

They rattled over tramlines and light railways intersecting the road; past the railway yard, and on towards the hamlet of Dickebusch – or rather, towards the pile of rubble which corresponded to that name on the map. Again Adam was struck by the stillness. There were people about – farmworkers in clogs pulling hand carts, and little parties of soldiers – but they moved slowly. Everyone seemed subdued.

That morning they'd stopped at a café on the outskirts of Ypres – a *café*, Adam had thought in disbelief, having once again to remind himself that the front line was now beyond Mons, forty miles to the east.

With Winsloe and half a dozen others, he'd sat in the sunshine, listening to some desultory anti-aircraft fire to the north. Then, at ten to eleven, a furious outburst of shelling had opened up in the distance.

An officer of fusiliers had said that it must be a battery getting rid of its shells, in order to avoid having to lug them about.

'Bit rough on the Huns,' another man had remarked, and there had been a general murmur of agreement.

The shelling had lasted until the clock in the café struck eleven, when it had abruptly ceased. The silence which followed was palpable.

Sitting there in the crisp autumn sunshine, Adam had been conscious only of a vast anticlimax. The same feeling was mirrored in the faces around him. There was no cheering, and no hurrahs.

'That's it, then,' someone had said.

Then everyone had gone back to their coffee.

And yet, in the hours that followed, word had filtered through that all over England, towns and villages were going wild.

'Well, *let* them,' Winsloe said bitterly. 'Leave the celebrations to the people back home. They don't know the reality.'

But what reality? thought Adam as he slowed to make way for a farmer's wagon which had lurched out from a side track. London, the influenza, Cairngowrie, Belle – it had all been a dream. He'd never really left the Front.

Although, of course, that was just another illusion. He was no longer in uniform; no longer with his unit. He was with the GRC.

Like Winsloe, he'd wangled his way back to the Front by arguing his intimate knowledge of the region and familiarity with the vagaries of military record-keeping, to land a position in Graves Registration.

So here he was, scarcely ten days after Belle had stepped onto the train at Stranraer, helping to sweep an area from Ypres to Bailleul twelve miles to the south-west: shuttling between basic accommodations in shattered hamlets, where they had to compete with returning farmers and a trickle of grieving relatives, and GRC headquarters in an elegant château just outside Saint-Omer, twenty-five miles to the west.

The task sounded simple enough. Survey the terrain with the aid of mud-spattered (sometimes blood-spattered) records; disinter what could be found; deliver to sorting stations or cemeteries – themselves often bleak, muddy sites still marked out with ropes, where men struggled to erect ranks of wooden crosses in the autumn gales – so that the 'travelling garden parties', as they were affectionately known, might do what they could to prettify things with turf and shrubs before the War ended, and the trickle of mourners swelled to a flood.

'We're putting on a show, d'you see,' an official had told Adam on his first day. 'Scurrying about, turning mud into gardens, before the visitors arrive.'

They had to find their way through a land largely without

roads; past pulverized bridges, and hamlets that had long since ceased to be anything more than marks on a map. The terrain was like a moonscape: riven by abandoned trenches, bristling with thickets of barbed wire, pitted with mine craters, and studded with shell casings. Sometimes they came across pockets of still-lethal gas, and had to beat a hasty retreat. Sometimes they stumbled on unexploded shells protruding from the mud, and had to summon one of the detonation parties which toured the region, touching off discarded ammunition.

It was hard, exhausting, dangerous work. Which suited Adam perfectly. This was why he'd left Cairngowrie. To bury himself in something all-consuming. Something that would stop him thinking.

Winsloe, however, was becoming a problem. He was drinking too much, and talked constantly of his wife. He was also acquiring a reputation for recklessness.

'Got a death wish, that one,' an ex-sergeant had confided to Adam only the day before. 'You watch out, sir. See that package in his greatcoat pocket that he keeps pawing? That's a revolver, you mark my words. If a live shell don't get him, he'll blow out his bloody brains one of these days. No, sir, you watch yerself. Me? I wouldn't go with him for a pension.'

But the ex-sergeant was wrong, Adam was sure of it. Poor Winsloe was the sort who never did more than talk.

They drove through la Clytte, then Dranoutre, where they picked up a party of diggers. Half a mile north-east of the village of Bailleul, Adam turned left onto a track, and pulled up. According to his notes, there should be two clusters of temporary interments about a thousand yards apart, between a strongpoint from the previous year's defences, and a pair of old machine-gun emplacements.

He cut the engine, and the stillness descended. It was so intense that it made his ears throb. He sat for a moment, taking it in, while the men in the back jumped out and stood in the sunshine, chatting in low voices as they lit cigarettes.

'If only she'd waited,' Winsloe said bitterly.

Adam shut his eyes.

'No faith. That's women. They tell you they love you, then they trample all over you.'

Adam thought about Belle – who had never, it occurred to him now, actually told him that she loved him. And if she'd 'trampled all over him', as Winsloe put it, it had only been by mistake.

And yet, he did feel trampled. The pain was far worse than it had been with Celia: a physical ache in his chest that never left him. It was why he'd come to Flanders.

But *why* had she left? What was that self-destructive spark which now and then seemed to flare up inside her and scorch everything to destruction?

He knew that it had to do with what she'd told him about Traherne, but he didn't understand exactly how. And he'd lied when he'd said that it didn't matter. What he should have said was that he could foresee a time when it would not.

'I begged her to stay,' Winsloe said resentfully. 'I begged her.'

So did I, thought Adam. He regretted that now. Perhaps after all he was not so different from poor Winsloe: endlessly going over things he couldn't solve, endlessly angry. Although whether he was angry with Belle or with himself, he couldn't tell.

He was just so bloody sick of thinking about it all the time.

So it was as well to be here, poring over a map spread on the dashboard, instead of home at Cairngowrie. Max and Maud were better off without him. And as Traherne had been called away to London on business, he was unlikely to cause trouble – although if he did, Adam had left instructions with Maud and his lawyers to wire him at once.

'I bet she's celebrating,' muttered Winsloe, fingering his great-coat pocket. 'I bet she's *happy*.'

'Winsloe,' said Adam with his eyes on the map, 'what's the point in talking about it?'

Winsloe ignored him. 'They're all whores,' he muttered.

Adam raised his head and shot him a look.

Winsloe glared at him defiantly. He was a wiry redhead with a pinched face, and pale eyelashes which distantly evoked a grown-up Max; although Max, reflected Adam, had more backbone than poor Winsloe ever would.

'Whores the lot of them,' said Winsloe. 'It's in their nature. Even the young ones.'

'Now you know that's not true,' Adam said wearily. 'What about your daughter? What's her name, Alice? How can a twelve-year-old be a whore?'

At the mention of his daughter, Winsloe's face crumpled. 'Leave me alone,' he said, and his voice broke. 'Just – leave me *alone*.' With an ungainly sob he flung open the door and jumped down, and stumbled off across the moonscape.

With the nagging sense that he could have done more, Adam let him go.

In the rear-view mirror he saw the men exchanging sidelong glances and raising their eyebrows. Time to give them something to do. He got out, slamming the door behind him, and spread the map on the bonnet as he called them over.

'Right,' he said, as if nothing had happened. 'We've got three in this shell crater, by the northernmost Vickers emplacement. Baker, Thomas and Pardue, off you go. I'll catch up with Winsloe and find this lot to the east, at the trench intersection.'

Baker and Thomas picked up their shovels, but Pardue hesitated. He was the ex-sergeant who'd warned Adam about Winslow the day before. 'Want me to go with you, sir?' he said in a low voice.

'No,' Adam said shortly. 'Thanks, but I think I can find him on my own.'

Looking grim, Pardue shouldered his shovel and headed off.

When the men had gone, Adam gave Winsloe five minutes to pull himself together, then started after him.

At least, he thought as he negotiated a tangle of barbed wire, he's heading in the right direction. According to the map, the remains were buried between Sugar and East strongpoints, just to the north of the intersection of four communication trenches.

It was barely seven hundred yards from the lorry, but the ground was so uneven that it soon dropped out of sight. Adam mounted a low ridge – and there below him was Winsloe, cowering on his knees at the bottom of a shell crater.

The crater was a big one, some twenty feet deep and perhaps

thirty feet across, and Adam couldn't see his face, but he could hear his ragged breathing and see his shoulders shuddering.

Adam felt a flash of pity, swiftly superseded by impatience. Not now, Winsloe, he thought.

Then he saw what the other man was holding in his hand, and an icy wave washed over him.

Winsloe had unbuttoned the pocket of his greatcoat, and had taken out what he'd been carrying around for days. A Mills bomb. He was holding it in one hand like a cricket ball, while with the other he gave it oddly tentative little pats. Clearly he was nerving himself to remove the pin.

So Pardue had been right, and Adam had been wrong. Winsloe did not lack backbone. No-one could say that of a man who meant to blow himself up with a grenade.

Feeling bizarrely as if he were intruding, Adam cleared his throat.

Winslow's head jerked up, and he gave Adam an unfocused stare.

'That,' said Adam levelly, 'would be a pretty selfish thing to do. Don't you think?'

'Go away,' said Winsloe. His voice was flat and emotionless: quite unlike his usual whine. He meant to go through with it.

'I can't quite believe,' said Adam as he started down the crater, 'that all this time you've been carrying that thing around with you. Sitting for days in a lorry with a number five grenade stuffed in your pocket. My God, Winsloe—'

'Go away,' Winsloe said again.

'Come off it, old man,' said Adam, disentangling the sleeve of his greatcoat from a length of barbed wire and sliding another foot or so in the mud. 'We've got enough remains to deal with already, without having to scrape up yours as well. Now give that thing to me and let's go and have a drink.'

'I've had enough,' muttered Winsloe. 'I can't go on any more.'

'What about your daughter? What about Alice? She's still a child. She needs you.'

Winsloe waved his free hand, as if to ward off an imaginary daughter.

Adam reached the bottom of the crater and stood with his hands at his sides. The mud was knee deep. He could feel it seeping over his boot-tops. 'For God's sake, man,' he said in a low voice, 'nobody said one has to be happy. One just has to get on with living. Just get through. That's what I do.'

'Get out of here,' snarled Winsloe. 'I don't want to take you with me.'

'Good, because I don't want to go.'

Winsloe pulled out the pin. 'I said, get out!'

'No,' said Adam.

Before Winsloe could dodge out of his reach, he grabbed the bomb and threw it as high as he could over the lip of the crater.

Winsloe gave a howl of outrage. The bomb caught on a tree stump jutting from the crater's edge, and stuck there . . .

Except, thought Adam with a jolt, that it isn't a tree stump, it's a *shell* . . .

Time seemed to slow as he grabbed Winsloe by the sleeve and forced him to take cover. A shell, he thought as they lay face down in the mud. Jesus Christ, I hope it isn't—

There was no time for fear. He didn't even hear the explosion. Something simply clicked in his ear. Then a flash – a blast of heat and suffocating fumes – and a vast upheaval of mud.

Then – nothing.

CHAPTER THIRTY-ONE

Flanders, 23rd November 1918

Number Thirty-Eight Hospital was one of a cluster around Saint-Omer which treated the wounded who came in by train from Ypres, as well as those on the branch line from Armentières, via Bailleul.

The hospital had been established in the second year of the War, in a château a couple of miles north of the city. This was not one of the elegant, slender-turreted châteaux from a Perrault fairy tale, but a plain, squat medieval affair with slitted windows and yard-thick walls for repelling invaders. But it was cool in summer and warm in winter, and had withstood four years of war better than most.

It was a mixed hospital, which meant that it housed wards for 'walkers' and for several grades of the more seriously wounded, as well as three 'nervous' wards for those awaiting transit to the specialist facilities around Boulogne. Many of the patients in these wards were deaf-mutes, stammerers, or afflicted by uncontrollable tremors; many more had been designated 'NYDN', or Not Yet Diagnosed Nervous – that being the catch-all phrase devised by the authorities the previous year to avoid the stigma of shell shock.

Dr McGarry, who ran the hospital, did not believe in shell shock. 'There's a fine yellow line,' he was fond of saying, 'between honourable breakdown and sheer blue funk.'

Dr Hughes, one of his junior associates, was not so sure. Neither was Belle. She found it hard to believe that any of the patients she encountered were acting, particularly the amnesiacs, whom she saw most frequently, since they were the ones she was asked to photograph – either here or at one of the other hospitals near Hazebrouck or Bailleul.

This afternoon, her last subject was a likeable young man with jug ears and a scar which cut a shiny red swath across his forehead and down behind one ear. He was cheerful and talkative, and appeared perfectly normal, apart from the fact that he didn't know his own name, and couldn't remember anything beyond his thirteenth birthday. Since he'd been found wandering naked on a battlefield over a month before, nobody knew who he was.

'It's really most odd,' he said as he entered Belle's little studio in the north tower and took the chair she indicated. 'Everyone tells me I'm nineteen, and sure enough, that's what I see in the looking-glass: a nineteen-year-old stranger. But how can I believe it when I know, I absolutely know, that I'm only thirteen?'

'It sounds extremely confusing,' said Belle, adjusting the tripod. 'Would you mind turning a little to the right?'

The young man did as she asked, but then turned back again, so that she could only see his profile. 'Would *you* believe it?' he said. 'I mean, if you were thirteen, and someone told you that in fact you were really grown up?'

Belle thought of Cornelius Traherne. 'I don't know,' she said. 'Could you turn just a little more to your right?'

Again he did as he was told, and then twisted back. For some reason he seemed to be reluctant to face the camera full on.

Belle noticed that his hands were clenched on either side of his thighs. 'Does the camera remind you of a gun?' she asked quietly.

He looked startled. 'I don't think so. Although now that you mention it, I – I do find it rather scary. Which is a bit rum, I suppose.'

'Try turning the chair round, and leaning your arms on the back.'

The young man tried it. Immediately his shoulders loosened and his fists unclenched. 'Much better,' he said. 'But why d'you want me to face forward, anyway?'

Belle smiled. 'I want your ears to show.'

His face fell. 'Oh, do they have to? The fellows at school will rag me most awfully.'

'Sorry, but the point isn't to take the most flattering picture, it's to capture who you are. And I'm afraid that with you, the ears are part of it.'

'Oh.'

'They might help someone to recognize you. Which would be worth it, wouldn't it?'

He grinned. 'That's sort of the point of all this, isn't it? I was forgetting. I seem to do that a lot these days.'

Without being aware of it, he was now facing the camera full on. Belle took the picture. 'There,' she said. 'That didn't hurt, did it?'

He shook himself and glanced down, as if to make sure that all his limbs were still there. 'Phew. Glad that's over. Do you do this all the time? Take pictures of fellows who don't know who they are?'

'Not all the time. Sometimes I take pictures of graves for relatives who can't afford to visit; or of cemeteries for the GRC records. That sort of thing.'

'Gosh,' said the young man, visibly impressed. 'Well, I suppose I ought to be off, or Sister will be on the rampage.'

'I hope you get better soon,' said Belle.

Again he grinned. 'Oh, I think I shall. When I was picked up, I thought I was seven. Apparently it's called shrinking amnesia. With a bit of luck, it'll shrink some more, and I shall be back to nineteen.'

Belle smiled. 'I hope so.'

She was packing up her camera after he'd gone when there was a knock at the door, and Dr Hughes looked in. 'Finished for the day?'

She nodded. 'In a while the light will start to go. Best to shut up shop.'

With his hands in the pockets of his white coat, he wandered over to the window and leaned against the wall. 'Do you put away your kit every night?'

'Every night,' she replied as she started unscrewing the tripod. 'Just in case they need the room while I'm off somewhere, and forget to tell me.'

He smiled. 'You're beginning to learn the ways of the army.'

'Just a little,' she said wryly.

Idly, he glanced at a stack of photographs in the tray on the shelf. 'You're awfully good at this, you know. This one on top, he's a patient of mine. You've exactly caught the way he is. I mean, not only the way he looks, but his character.'

She threw him a surprised glance. 'Thank you. Actually it was my aunt's idea that I should give this a try. When I came out here I thought I was going to be put to work planting shrubs.'

'But you enjoy it, don't you?'

She thought about that. 'Yes. I do. Very much. It makes a change, to be useful. And to have found something that I'm good at.'

'Oh now, that can't be so unusual for someone like you.'

Something in his tone – a slight added warmth – put her on her guard. As she finished stowing the rest of her things, she felt him watching her.

And yet she'd followed Sophie's advice to the letter. 'Clumpy shoes, shapeless tweeds, and *no* rouge. Some of these poor lads haven't seen a woman in weeks, apart from a nurse. And be warned about the doctors. They're worse than the patients.'

Thinking of Sophie, Belle felt a pang of concern. It was time to get back to their billet. These days, it wasn't fair to leave her alone for too long.

'I don't suppose,' said Dr Hughes, going pink and staring determinedly out of the window, 'that you'd care to have dinner tonight?'

Oh, bother, thought Belle.

'Not just with me, of course,' he added hastily. 'There's a group of us going along, and Sister Martin will be there, so it'll be absolutely . . .' His voice trailed off. His face had turned puce.

He was such a nice man. Belle liked his tired eyes and his gentleness with patients. It was hardly his fault that he wasn't Adam. But she wished that she'd spotted the signs sooner. 'The thing is,' she said carefully, 'my aunt . . .'

'Of course,' he muttered. 'I quite understand.'

There was an awkward silence.

Then he said, 'I take it that there's still no news of her husband?'

Belle shook her head.

'Ah. Well. I dare say he'll turn up.'

'He's been missing for nearly two weeks,' said Belle. 'If he was alive, surely we'd have heard by now.'

'Not necessarily. I don't want to offer false hope, but . . . well, labels get lost, you know. Patients are sent to the wrong hospital. They get mixed up. Either because they're unconscious and the records become jumbled, or, if they're conscious, because they sometimes get . . . well, a little muddled.'

Belle thought about that. 'Thank you,' she said, and meant it. 'Maybe you're right.'

He opened his mouth to say something more, then seemed to change his mind. Pressing his lips together in a smile, he pushed himself off the wall, and wandered out.

Thinking about what he'd said, Belle stowed her things under a bench, then straightened up and looked about her. The light was failing fast, and as she hadn't lit the lamp, a chill grey dusk was seeping into the room.

Suddenly her spirits plunged.

She hadn't been lying when she'd said that she enjoyed what she was doing, but neither had she told the whole truth. She managed reasonably well when she was with patients, because then she had to concentrate on putting them at their ease, which meant forgetting about herself.

It was when she stopped that things became hard. Ever since Ben had been posted missing, Sophie had tried everything to find him, but had consistently drawn a blank. Because he'd been on a mission for Special Services, she couldn't even find out where he was when the 'incident' had occurred – or what the 'incident' had involved.

Through the window the sky was darkening to indigo. An early star was beginning to show. Belle pulled up the chair and sat down, and thought of the long, peaceful twilights of Cairngowrie, and the glitter of moonlight on the waters of the loch.

Despite all Sophie's urging, she'd cut herself off completely from Scotland, not even writing to Maud to let her know where she was. Now, with Ben missing and Sophie fast losing hope, even to be thinking of it felt like an act of disloyalty. But she couldn't help it. She missed Adam so much that it hurt.

She and Sophie had been lucky with lodgings. One of the higher-ups in the Commission had heard that Sophie needed to be near HQ because of Ben, and had pulled strings, so they'd been given a pretty little eighteenth-century town house just off the main square in Saint-Omer.

Belle got a lift into town from a doctor who was billeted a few streets away, and arrived just after six, to find the house quiet, and almost in darkness. The girl who 'did' for them told her that Sophie was in the drawing-room, and that there hadn't been any news of Ben.

The drawing-room door was ajar, so Belle made no noise as she went in. It was a beautiful room, and surprisingly untouched by the War: furnished in a delicate Arcadian style, with a suite upholstered in silvery silk. Belle always thought that Sophie, with her cloudy hair and narrow, distinctive face, fitted in perfectly: like some kind of rational eighteenth-century ghost.

This evening, though, she didn't look particularly rational. She was sitting by the fire with her hair coming down and a pile of paperwork sliding off her knees, staring at her photograph of Ben in its leather travelling case. Belle could only see her face in profile, but the strain was evident. She'd lost weight, and rarely slept more than a few hours a night.

Belle glanced at the photograph on the side table. It had been taken by her mother, and she was only now beginning to appreciate the skill which had gone into it. Her mother had taken it in the grounds of Fever Hill, in the soft shade beneath a guango tree. Ben was in shirtsleeves and riding breeches, with the inevitable horse standing beside him and resting its head peacefully on his shoulder. Ben himself was facing the camera, with his hands in his pockets and the beginnings of a smile just lifting one corner of his mouth. No problems for him in staring at the lens, thought Belle, thinking of her young amnesiac. If Ben had been facing a gun, he'd probably just have stared it down.

God, I hope you're all right, she told the photograph silently.

Sophie felt her presence and turned, and composed her features into a smile. 'I keep thinking about what I said at Newton Stewart,' she said without preamble. 'I said that I'd kill him. Do you remember?'

Belle nodded.

'I wish to goodness I hadn't said that.'

Her eyes strayed to the photograph, and then away, as if it hurt to look for too long.

Belle pulled up a footstool and sat down beside her.

'I keep wondering,' said Sophie, 'if it would feel different if we'd managed to have children. Would that make it easier, or worse?'

Belle stayed silent.

'What if he's gone, Belle? What if we never learn anything more?'

Belle said, 'I was talking to Dr Hughes. He says that the wounded go missing all the time. Labels fall off. Names get mixed up in the records. Patients become muddled. When you think about it, it does make sense.'

Sophie's face cleared fractionally. 'Yes. I suppose it does.' She sounded as if she desperately wanted to believe it, but wasn't good enough at self-deception to succeed.

Belle took her hand. 'Let's go and have dinner.'

Sophie sighed. 'I'm not really—'

'I know you're not, but you still need to eat something.' She stood up. 'I'll run upstairs and change. You put away your papers.'

She was on her way out when behind her, Sophie said, 'Belle – thank you.'

Belle turned. 'For what?'

Again Sophie smiled, but this time it was genuine. 'Just thank you.'

As Belle went upstairs to her room, she thought how swiftly things could change. A couple of weeks before, at Newton Stewart, she'd felt so low that she'd been quite content to have Sophie take charge and treat her like an invalid. Now the roles were reversed.

Sophie was the one who was lost, and she was the one who was found.

Belle spent the night drifting in and out of an unrefreshing slumber, and just before dawn she had a nightmare about Ben.

It was back in Jamaica, years before Cornelius Traherne. She was walking with Ben over the lawns at Fever Hill, while Patsy, his favourite mare, ambled behind them like a large, docile dog. Belle turned to stroke the mare's gleaming neck – and saw to her mute horror that she was stroking a skeleton horse.

'But Patsy's dead,' laughed Ben, showing his sharp white teeth. 'Didn't you know? And so am I.'

Belle woke with a start. The room was in darkness, and very cold. Knowing that further sleep was impossible, she lit a candle, threw on some clothes, and read a book until it was time to go to the hospital.

She was in her studio setting up the tripod when she heard the first patient knock, then open the door.

'You're early,' she said over her shoulder.

'I'm sorry,' he said, sounding aggrieved. 'They told me I'd find you here.'

Belle turned and saw to her surprise that the man standing uncertainly by the door was not in fact a patient – at least, he wasn't in hospital blue, although his leg was in a splint, and he walked with the aid of crutches, to which he was clearly not yet accustomed. He looked to be in his mid-thirties, with short red hair and a pinched, unhappy face. His pale eyelashes reminded her faintly of Max – although there was nothing Max-like about the resentful puckering of the mouth.

'My name's Winsloe,' he declared. Somehow he managed to make that sound defensive, too. 'Arthur Winsloe. And I'm not a patient. I mean, there's nothing wrong with my nerves. Though I dare say I look as if there is.'

'Oh,' said Belle, for want of anything better. 'Well. How do you do, Mr Winsloe? I'm Isabelle Lawe. But I'm afraid there may have been a mistake. You see, I don't do portrait photographs.'

'I know that,' he said irritably. 'I haven't come for a photograph.

274

I'm here because someone told me you knew the whereabouts of Captain Palairet.'

Belle froze. Then she said, 'I'm sorry, I don't—'

'I need to see him,' he said. 'I've only just got out of hospital myself, and I thought he was in the same one as me, but—'

'*What?*' said Belle. 'Are you saying that Adam – Captain Palairet – that he's here?'

'Like I said,' said Winsloe, 'that's what I'm trying to find out. I've been asking around, and this lady at HQ, a Mrs Kelly? She said for me to come to see you.' For the first time he seemed to notice Belle's stunned expression, and his own became uncertain. 'I think I've been misinformed.'

Belle cleared her throat. 'Just now, you said you thought he was in the same hospital as you. What did you mean?'

'Well, I can't be certain,' said Winsloe defensively. 'I mean, we were both in a pretty bad way after the bomb went off.'

Belle swayed. 'The bomb.'

Winsloe wasn't listening to her. 'I couldn't see very well at all. Blood all over me. Him too. He was unconscious, not sure how bad. Anyway, they took us to a clearing hospital, Bailleul, I think. And after that things got fuzzy. That's all I know.'

Belle found her way to the chair and sat down. 'When was this?' she said. 'Did you see him again?'

'A couple of weeks ago,' said Winsloe, 'and no, I didn't. Like I said, things got fuzzy. When I came to, I was at Hazebrouck, no idea where he'd gone.' He paused. 'The thing is,' he said angrily, 'he saved my life. But I didn't *ask* him to. I told him to go away. But now I suppose I've got to live with it, haven't I? I mean, you've got to, haven't you? If someone does a thing like that.'

Belle couldn't speak.

'Why'd he have to go and do a thing like that?' said Winsloe. 'I never even asked him.'

Belle put her cold hands together in her lap. 'Tell me everything,' she said.

CHAPTER THIRTY-TWO

Lights flash painfully in his head. He's awake again. He wishes to God that he wasn't.

'Captain Palairet?' says a woman's voice. Soft, insistent. Infuriating.

He opens his eyes. Shuts them again. The glare is agonizing: shards of glass piercing his skull. Why can't they put out the bloody lights?

He opens his mouth to tell them, but he can't make a sound, just lies there gaping like a fish.

He's been doing that for days. And yet every time he wakes, he has this pathetic hope that this time – *this* time – he'll be able to talk. Each time the disappointment crashes in afresh. He would never have believed it could be so maddening – so all-consuming and *humiliating* – not to be able to speak. It makes him savage: flaring up at trifles, perpetually on the point of losing his temper.

'Captain Palairet? Oh, good, you're awake. Look! You have a letter! Isn't that nice? I'm afraid it's done the rounds: postmarked three days ago; must have been misdirected. Shall I leave it here, where you can reach it?'

Anything, so long as you leave me alone. Oh, and on your way out, Sister Gregory, hand me a revolver, so that I can shoot down that bloody chandelier.

He has a room to himself, for which he knows he should be grateful, but isn't. It has a high ceiling with elaborate plaster mouldings, and sumptuous yellow silk curtains – and, of course, the hated chandelier, suspended directly above him like some baroque instrument of torture. Whose idea was it to turn a casino into a hospital?

Somewhere a door slams, and he twitches so violently that he nearly falls out of bed. Instantly his heart is racing. Cold sweat slicks his skin.

It's only a door, he tells himself in disgust. His body doesn't believe him. His body thinks they're under fire.

Twenty, thirty times a day – whenever a door slams or a trolley creaks, or a train trundles past on its way to Boulogne – he ducks for cover. It's completely beyond his control. And so damned humiliating. It makes him feel like the worst kind of coward.

The doctors say it's only natural that things are so much worse than the last time, when he got shot. 'You see, Captain Palairet, at that time you were at war, and you *expected* to get hurt. This time, you believed that it was all behind you. So of course the shock would be that much the greater . . .'

Is that why I can't talk? Adam had scrawled on his notepad.

'Ah. Well, you see, we're not absolutely sure about that.'

Will I get better?

'My dear fellow, as to that, we really couldn't say.'

They do like to hide behind the plural when the news isn't good.

'Shall I just slit the envelope for you?' says Sister Gregory, hovering.

She's pretty, with flaxen hair and large grey eyes that remind him vaguely of Felicity Ruthven. To get rid of her, he picks up the letter – which in itself is a performance, as he has to prop himself on his good elbow and ignore the pain that blossoms everywhere else. The pain in his thigh is so bad that he nearly cries out, only of course he can't. Not that moaning would lessen the pain. But he still wishes he could.

Sister Gregory makes her habitual clucking noise that sets his teeth on edge, and takes the envelope from his hand as if he's a child, and opens it neatly, and draws out the letter. She makes a great show of not looking to see who it's from, although clearly she's dying to find out.

Adam glances without interest at the sender's address on the back of the envelope. His heart lurches. It's from Belle. *Belle?* In Saint-Omer? What the hell is she doing in France?

Wild imaginings crowd in on him. Somehow she's heard that he got blown up – perhaps Maud sent her a wire? Yes, that must be it – and she's coming to see him. Now everything will be all right. She'll come back with him to Cairngowrie, and they'll pretend that Cornelius Traherne never existed, and . . .

Dear Adam, she writes. Her handwriting is sprawling and emphatic, with several splotches and crossings out. *A strange man called Winsloe told me what happened, and since then I've moved heaven and earth to find you* . . .

Winsloe. Of course. He'd come to see Adam yesterday, having somehow managed to get past Sister Gregory. For half an hour he'd sat beside Adam's bed in accusing silence, before blurting out a resentful 'Thank you', and rushing from the room. He seemed to have taken it as a personal slight that Adam's injuries had been worse than his own.

. . . I had no idea that you were were even in Flanders, and now you're hurt, and when I telephoned the hospital some awful nurse spent ages telling me that she couldn't possibly tell me anything, and that you're not seeing visitors . . .

Of course I'm not. Would you, if you were in this state?

. . . so I'm writing to ask if you'll see me. I know I've no right to expect it after what I did – but I need to see you, Adam. I need to make sure that you're all right . . .

Another door slams, and this time he twitches so violently that his good arm catches the water jug on the side table, sending it flying. The sound of it shattering is like a whizz-bang exploding, so of course he ducks. Bloody *hell*.

That's another thing he misses. Swearing in one's head just isn't the same.

Little Sister Gregory comes running. Of course. Presumably she was waiting on the other side of the door. As she kneels to clean

278

up the mess, she gives him a sweet, sympathetic smile that makes him want to decapitate her.

To avoid her sympathy he glances at the letter crumpled in his fist. Something twists in his chest. He badly needs to see Belle. And just as badly, he couldn't bear for her to see him. Not with one arm shattered in four places, and his head a mass of bandages, and a shard of shrapnel the size of a bayonet sticking out of his thigh, and too close to the artery to remove 'just quite yet', whatever the devil that means.

But he needs to see Belle. He needs to look into her fathom-less dark eyes; to watch that wry twist of her mouth when he's said something with which she doesn't agree. Although of course he wouldn't be able to *say* anything to her at all.

. . . *Adam, please. I need to know that you're all right. Scribble a line – dictate a wire – anything – and I'll be on the next train. I can't bear not to know . . .*

And then what? he wonders. We sit in awkward silence while you do your damnedest not to look horrified? After which, pre-sumably, you go back to Saint-Omer, and I get myself packed off to some convalescent hospital, and we never see each other again?

Because nothing's changed, has it, Belle? There's still something getting in the way of our being together, just as it did at Cairngowrie. And I can't fight it, because you won't tell me what it is. So even if I could persuade you to come back with me – perhaps by making some disgusting plea for sympathy: 'Please don't leave me, the poor, crippled, mute ex-soldier' – sooner or later you would leave, wouldn't you?

And I can't, I just can't go through that again.

The wind tipped over the dwarf cypress, and Belle leaned down to right the pot and position it a little closer to Private Arbuthnot's headstone, so that it would appear in the foreground, and soften the severity.

As she took the shot, she wondered for the twentieth time if there would be a letter waiting for her tonight when she got back to Saint-Omer.

That wretched, wretched nurse.

'Can't you even tell me if he's out of danger?' Belle had pleaded.

'Oh goodness no,' the nurse had said, sounding infuriatingly as if she was enjoying herself. 'I couldn't possibly give out any details whatsoever on the telephone, especially as you're only a friend . . .'

She'd enjoyed saying that, too. And she'd absolutely loved telling Belle that there was no point 'whatsoever' in making the journey to the hospital at Wimereux, because Captain Palairet didn't want visitors, so she'd only be turned away.

'So he's well enough to make stipulations,' Belle had cut in acidly.

The nurse's reply had been shrill. 'Twisting my words will do you no good at all, Miss Lawe.'

'Just let me speak to him—'

'Out of the question. Besides, Captain Palairet *can't* speak.'

'What do you mean?'

A silence at the other end of the line, as if the nurse knew she'd said too much.

'If he's well enough to turn away visitors,' Belle insisted, 'then surely—'

'He can't *speak*, Miss Lawe. He is mute. A lot of our patients are. Now I believe I've already made myself perfectly clear, and I don't think there's anything more to say. You will simply have to write first, or else we shall be forced to turn you away at the door.'

That had been three days ago. Three days of waiting in vain for the post. Had he even received her letter? Or was he too badly hurt to write?

Another gust of wind tipped the dwarf cypress into the mud. Belle blinked at it, and turned up the collar of her coat, and wondered what to do next.

It was freezing in the cemetery – or rather, in the bleak expanse of mud beside the Hazebrouck road which would, when finished, be known by some euphonious name, but was now simply No. 32 on Sophie's map.

Twelve rows of stark new headstones towards the front – priority being given to the named graves – backed by seventeen rows of temporary wooden crosses for the unidentified, who in time would each get their own beautiful stone headstone, inscribed simply *A Soldier of the Great War Known Unto God*. A few of the headstones bore little bunches of coloured ribbons that fluttered wildly in the wind. Somehow they only emphasized the sense of devastation and loss.

At the far end, by the road, a long wooden hut like a seaside pavilion afforded tea for the steady flow of visitors who'd managed to find their way through the mud. Belle could see a clump of them emerging into the wind, clutching their fluttering maps, and moving awkwardly in their new *sabots*, which someone must have advised them to buy in order to deal with the mud. Behind them, a trio of officers had just drawn up in an army motor. No doubt they'd come to pay their respects to an old comrade.

In the corner furthest from the gates, Sophie was fighting a losing battle to make the site less appalling – and to hold on to her temper, which was growing worse with each day that passed without news of Ben.

'But I *told* you to plant them three feet apart,' she cried at her assistant, a hapless young factory worker from Leeds.

At the outburst, several of the visitors turned and stared.

Belle wondered if she ought to go across and intervene. She decided against it. Latterly, a constraint had sprung up between them. Sophie hadn't said anything, but it was becoming clear that she was beginning to lose hope about Ben; while ever since Mr Winsloe's strange, resentful visit, Belle herself had been plagued by an irrational notion that if by some miracle Ben did turn up alive, that would mean that Adam would die.

She told herself that was nonsense, but she couldn't shake off the sense of dread – and the awkwardness when she was with Sophie. It just didn't seem possible that both Adam and Ben would be allowed to live.

A feather-light tap on her shoulder, and she turned to see a visitor – a woman, fortyish, with the stretched look of grief – smiling apologetically as she clutched her hat to her head with one hand, and a crumpled map with the other. '*So* sorry to disturb,' she murmured, 'but I seem to be having a little difficulty . . .'

Why are they always so polite? wondered Belle as she helped the woman find the sector which contained the remains of her only son. Why does the poor thing feel the need to apologize?

The woman was nervous and talkative: she'd come over from Birmingham by herself, on a Tourist Ticket from Thomas Cook's. It gave her just two days to find her son, and she'd already been misdirected twice, and time was running out, not that she was complaining, she could see how hard everyone was working to make it nice . . .

Of one accord, they stopped and looked about them. Sophie's team of gardeners were doing what they could with turf and holly and yew, but nothing could disguise the stark ugliness of the site.

'It's just that I didn't expect it to be so *bleak*,' murmured the woman, softening that with another apologetic smile. 'I mean, a battlefield would seem to imply – well, a field? But I suppose I'm simply being . . . well. But it is so very *bleak*.'

Belle led her to the start of the correct row, then quietly withdrew, to leave her alone with her son.

She was glad that Sophie was too far away to have heard that last remark. From the look of things, she was working herself up into a state.

'Is it really too much to ask?' she cried, brandishing a small yew tree at her assistant. 'All I want is for you to put them in the right way up!'

By the refreshment hut, more visitors turned and stared. At the gate, one of the officers detached himself from his companions and began making his way slowly through the cemetery.

Belle sighed. Sophie sounded worryingly close to tears. Perhaps it was time to persuade her into the refreshment hut.

She was just about to start towards her when something about the officer struck her as familiar. He was very slender, and he moved with a kind of contained and wary grace that she'd seen somewhere before.

Putting both hands on the nearest headstone, she screwed up her eyes to get a better look.

He was still too far away for her to make out his face, but

as he took off his cap she saw that his hair was very dark, and his face pale. With the eyepatch over one eye, he resembled a pirate.

Belle gripped the headstone. It can't be, she thought, as she watched him slowly approaching Sophie's little group of gardeners, stopping every now and then to catch his breath.

Sophie had her back to him and was still busily berating her assistant. It wasn't until the officer had almost reached her that she turned and saw him.

She went very still. Her shoulders seemed to slump. But at her sides, her hands clenched into fists. Then the officer had covered the last few paces between them and was catching her in his arms and holding her tight, and Sophie was crying and hitting him with her fists, then reaching up to touch his face.

Belle got a lift back to Saint-Omer with Ben's fellow officers. Ben and Sophie had urged her to stay with them. 'We'll go out to dinner and paint the town red,' Sophie had said, sounding as if she'd just drunk a whole bottle of champagne. But Belle had firmly declined. They needed to be alone together, she said. She would only be in the way.

But the real reason was deeper and more ignoble than that. After the first wave of elation at seeing Ben safe, her spirits had taken a shattering plunge. She was plagued by that irrational dread that since Ben was alive, then Adam would die.

The town house was silent and still when she reached it, and on the table in the hall two letters were waiting for her.

She did not − could not − pick them up at once. She couldn't even look at them. Instead she made herself take off her hat and coat and gloves, and straighten her hair, before picking them up and walking slowly upstairs to her room. It wasn't going to be good news. She could feel it.

The first envelope was postmarked Wimereux, and she recognized Adam's forthright, slanting hand. She tore it open.

Inside was her own letter, carefully folded and replaced in its envelope, which had been neatly slit. There was no accompanying note. Adam had simply written on the back: *Return to sender. No reply.*

Belle lowered herself onto the edge of the bed, and sat blinking in the gloom. She felt as if she'd been kicked in the chest.

So that's it, then, she thought.

Of all the replies she'd imagined over the past three days – scorn, joy, puzzlement – it had never occurred to her that he would simply send back her letter without one.

Outside, the church bell tolled six. A cart trundled through the square. The room darkened.

It was the cold that roused her at last. She realized that she'd been sitting there for over an hour. And she still hadn't opened the second letter.

Slowly she lit the gas and peered at the envelope. With a little jolt of alarm she saw that it wasn't a letter after all, but a telegram.

Accident at Maputah Works STOP, she read. *Papa badly hurt STOP Please please come at once STOP Mamma STOP*

CHAPTER THIRTY-THREE

Kingston, Jamaica, January 1919

Bad weather caused delays on the passage out, and as a result the steamer docked at Kingston Harbour in the middle of the night.

Belle's first sight of Jamaica was dark and forbidding. Black mountains blotted out the stars. An eerie mist floated on the lagoon. Instead of the boisterous shouts of higglers on the pier, she was welcomed by the dismal slap of the sea against the hull, and the harsh grate of the anchor chain.

And it was cold. Her breath steamed as she waited on deck with Sophie, watching Ben giving instructions to the porters. She'd been away for so long that she'd forgotten how sharp the nights could get in January. She'd been away for so long.

The deck was only dimly lit by the engine lights, and in the crimson glow Sophie's face looked as tense as Belle felt. For the past three weeks they'd become almost accustomed to the worry, but now that they were nearly home, Belle felt a cold settling of dread. Despite all the wires, and Mamma's most recent letter, she wouldn't believe that Papa was out of danger until she saw him for herself.

Those first awful days in Saint-Omer had been almost too busy to allow her to take it in: making arrangements to leave the GRC, sending wires, trying in vain to find out what was happening in Jamaica. Then the journey to London – more wires, more interminable waiting for news, while Ben pulled all the strings he could in order to secure them passage on the first available steamer.

He'd spent a small fortune in telegrams, but it wasn't until Mamma's letter had reached them the night before the *Alveira* left Southampton that they learned what had actually happened.

He's out of danger, Mamma had written, pitching straight in, and addressing her letter, Belle couldn't help noticing, not to herself but to Sophie. *At least that's what Dr Walpole tells me, although I won't actually believe it until we can get him to a proper hospital in Kingston. Falmouth's all very well for a broken arm, but not for this. But I'm getting ahead of myself. I do that a lot at the moment.*

It was ten days ago – feels like ten years – and we'd started crop-time early, because – well, that's just detail. Anyway he was at the works at Maputah (of course), even though there was no good reason for him to be there, he's got a perfectly capable manager in young Neptune, but you know the way he is. He was riding that four-year-old bay that Ben always said had a wild eye (and he was right, as usual; afterwards I had to be restrained from having the wretched beast shot). But there I am, running ahead again.

The weather was getting, well, weathery, as old Braverly would say, and nobody noticed that part of the boiling-house roof – a patch of corrugated zinc that'd been tacked on till the new slates arrive – was working loose. It seems that all at once the zinc lifted, and startled that wretched, stupid horse. It didn't throw Cameron, and he was just bringing it under control when it reared again, overbalanced, and crashed onto its side – with him underneath.

Here Mamma seemed to have broken off, for in the next paragraph the writing was smaller and much neater. *As you can see*, she went on, *I can't bring myself to write about it. So I'll be brief. Luckily, young Neptune had the sense not to move him till Dr Walpole arrived. He – Cameron – was unconscious for three days. Broken ribs. Fractured skull. Dr Walpole suspected bleeding on the brain, but that seems to have been a false alarm, and the cold compresses and this new drug aspirin appear to have brought down the inflammation – although he's still too ill to be moved, so Kingston Hospital remains out of the question.*

Sorry I haven't written before, but I've had my hands full. To be closer to him I've been staying with Olivia Herapath on and off, she's been marvellous; and Evie Walker has taken the twins whenever I ask, an enormous help. And this morning he opened his eyes and smiled at me.

No time to write more, must catch the post. Come soon. No time to say how relieved *and* overjoyed *I was to hear that Ben is safe and well! Oh, Sophie, I can't wait for you to be here. All my love, Madeleine.*

That had been two weeks ago. Since then the wires had been less frequent, presumably because Mamma was spending most of her time at the hospital with Papa – but when news did come through, it was of a steady improvement. Belle almost found herself able to relax on board the *Alveira*. She was going home at last. After years of avoiding it, the decision had been taken out of her hands.

So why now, as she descended the gangway with Sophie, did she feel this fresh bite of anxiety? Was it because she was back on the same stretch of quay where Papa had said goodbye seven years before?

She was shivering in earnest by the time Ben returned with a cab, and the news that the quickest way to reach Falmouth would be to wait until morning, then catch the train to Montego Bay. He'd already taken rooms at the Myrtle Bay Hotel, so that they could lie down for a few hours before going to the station.

They reached the hotel at three in the morning, too late to telephone Eden. 'At least they've finally *got* a telephone,' said Sophie, 'although Maddy tells me they're always forgetting to use it.' Ben sent a wire to Olivia Herapath in Falmouth, advising her of the arrangements; then they went to their rooms and failed to sleep.

As ill luck would have it, the train was late leaving Kingston, then delayed at Williamsfield, halfway down the line. It was nearly dark by the time they finally reached Montego Bay.

Mamma was waiting on the platform, but things got off to an uncertain start. In all the anxiety over Papa, no-one had remembered to warn her that Ben had lost an eye, and when she saw him she burst into tears. It took all his and Sophie's efforts to persuade her that he was fine, and no longer in any pain. Belle stood beside them, not knowing what to say. She felt like a stranger waiting to be introduced.

At last Mamma got herself under control. She blinked at Belle, as if trying to remember who she was.

'Hello, Mamma,' said Belle. Awkwardly she went forward and kissed her mother's cheek.

Mamma put her hands on Belle's shoulders and gave her a little shake. 'Belle,' she said. 'My God. Belle.' Then she brushed Belle's cheek with her lips, briefly enveloping her in the scent of rosewater and rice-powder which instantly evoked bedtime stories on the verandah at Eden. She looked thinner than Belle had ever seen her, and her face had the same stretched, wide-eyed look of the visitors in Flanders.

'I came as soon as I got your wire,' said Belle, unnecessarily. There was so much she wanted to say, but she didn't know where to start.

Mamma seemed to feel it too, because she tried to smile, but succeeded only in compressing her lips. Her hands tightened on Belle's shoulders, but it was to Sophie that she spoke. 'He's taken a turn for the worse,' she said, clearly struggling to keep her composure. 'It was last night. I don't understand it all; you'll be able to get more out of Dr Walpole. There was a swelling. Bleeding on the brain. It subsided, but they think it started an infection. He's running a fever.'

There was an appalled silence while they took this in. There had been brain fever in the family once before. Everyone tried not show that they were thinking of it.

'But he'll be all right,' said Belle.

Mamma turned and blinked at her, and again Belle felt like an intruder who'd spoken out of turn. 'We don't know,' she said.

Mamma had set her heart on their all spending the night at Eden, so Ben and Sophie swiftly gave up any plans of turning off for Fever Hill. No-one asked Belle what she wanted. If they had, she would have found it impossible to explain the sense of dread which dragged at her as they left Falmouth and started up the old Eden Road.

The new motor car only added to the dreamlike sense of un-reality. As they rattled over the bridge at Romilly which marked the edge of the estate, mist floated about the giant bamboo, and the moonlight cast weird, spiked shadows across the road. Belle turned her head and gazed at the black water of the Martha Brae, and thought of yellowsnakes and Cornelius Traherne. Eden at night. This was not the homecoming she'd imagined. Cairngowrie and Adam seemed a million miles away: as if they'd happened to someone else.

They reached the turn-off to the house, and the old guango tree loomed out of the shadows, its great arms lifted to the stars like some fierce guardian spirit. In the moonlight the house looked ghostly and mysterious: the white bougainvillea glowing eerily as it tumbled down the steps, the tree-ferns surging against the walls like a dark primeval sea. Belle thought of the mildewed photographs of the house in the old days before Papa had bought it, when it had still been a ruin. Now in the moonlight it seemed as if once again the forest was about to take back its own.

Fortunately, when they got inside, normality took over. The twins had been allowed to stay up to greet them, and old Braverly the cook – who seemed hardly to have aged in seven years, perhaps because he'd been ancient ever since Belle could remember – had prepared a special dinner in their honour: jerked hog roasted over pimento wood, fried plantain, rice and peas and pickled calabash; and to follow, Bombay mangoes and his famous coconut ice cream. They all did their best, but no-one had much appetite except for the twins, who sat opposite Belle, staring at her.

When she'd last seen them, they'd been cherubic two-year-olds. Now they were lean, handsome ten-year-olds, the image of Papa, with his thick fair hair and unwavering light grey eyes.

More than anything else, the sight of her brothers made her feel like a stranger. Lachlan and Douglas had grown up without her. Eden, Mamma, Papa – it all belonged to them. Not to her.

Throughout dinner, Mamma kept up a steady stream of brittle talk, mostly to Sophie and Ben, but trying when she remembered to include Belle with her eyes, as one does with a guest of whom one isn't quite sure. She kept twisting the rings on her fingers, and asking if they needed more food. Clearly her nerves were stretched to breaking point.

At last, the twins were hustled off to bed by Hannah the nurse. Not Poppy, Belle thought with a pang. Even that had changed. Ben and Sophie discreetly withdrew to unpack, leaving Belle to join her mother for coffee on the verandah.

A silence fell.

It was a chilly night, and Braverly had dragged out the old brazier of black Spanish iron, which threw a red glow on Mamma's lovely, exhausted features as she rearranged the coffee cups on the tray and avoided looking at her daughter.

Belle waited for the expected reproach about not getting in touch when she'd had the 'flu. It didn't come.

'Your friend Drum Talbot,' Mamma said at last, 'is a *great* success.'

'I'm so glad,' said Belle, for something to say.

'Absolutely wonderful with children. The twins adore him, and so does Cam— I mean, so does your papa.'

'It's all right,' said Belle, standing at the balustrade. 'I do know whom you mean.'

There was another silence. Belle looked down at the moonlit garden – at the tumbled mass of the bougainvillea and the distant bulk of the giant bamboo. The poinsettia at the bottom of the steps looked black. Like blood.

'I'm afraid that at some stage,' Mamma went on, twisting her rings, 'you shall have to call on Great-Aunt May. She's been asking to see you.'

Belle frowned. She hadn't seen or heard from Great-Aunt May since that afternoon when she'd tried to tell her about Traherne. 'Why?' she said. 'Why would she want to see me?'

'I've no idea. She's nearly a hundred, you know. Perhaps even she feels that her time will soon be up.' Another twist of the rings. 'I still find it amazing that you ended up at Cairngowrie,' she went on with a lift of her eyebrows. 'And you say that the fearsome Miss McAllister is still there?'

Belle nodded. 'Although she's not really fearsome when you get to know her.'

'Ah. Indeed.'

Another silence.

'Oh, yes,' said Mamma, 'I almost forgot. Your friend is coming out. The Cornwallis girl?'

'Dodo?' said Belle, astonished.

Mamma blinked. 'Um – no. The other one. Margaret?'

Belle's spirits fell. 'That's her younger sister. I hardly know her.'

'Ah,' said Mamma. 'I apologize. I'd forgotten.'

Another pause, while they reflected on that.

Of course she's forgotten, thought Belle. How can one blame her, when she hasn't seen her own daughter for seven years?

'Anyway,' Mamma said with a lift of her eyebrows, 'she's coming out in a few weeks' time for an extended visit to her aunt, and apparently she's hoping to do a little assistant nursing out at Burntwood. Reading to the officers, that sort of thing. You remember the old sanatorium on the other side of Falmouth? Well, now it's an officers' convalescent home. And I thought perhaps they'll be able to find something for you to do, too? I understand that you were an enormous help to Sophie out in Flanders.'

She sounded as if she were talking to an acquaintance. Or trying to find something to do with the prodigal daughter.

'I'm not sure that I'll have time for that sort of thing,' Belle said gently. 'I came to see Papa.'

Mamma looked down at the coffee cups. 'It's just a shame,' she said, 'that it took something like this to bring you home.' She spoke without reproach – it was simply an observation – but Belle felt a wave of guilt and regret.

She watched her mother smooth back her hair from her temples in a gesture she remembered. 'You didn't want to come back, did you, Belle?'

'Of course I did,' Belle said quickly. 'When I got your wire, I was wild to—'

'Oh, of course you wanted to see Papa. But you didn't want to come back here. Not home. To Eden.'

Belle turned back to the garden. 'No,' she said at last. 'Not really.'

'Why not? Can't you tell me?'

Belle tried to breathe, but that hot, prickly feeling was rising in her chest. From where she stood, she could see the giant bamboo down by the river; she could hear it creaking in the breeze, exactly as it had that day when Traherne . . .

It's our secret. We wouldn't want you to be found out, now would we?

Belle ran her hands over the smooth stone of the balustrade. 'It's complicated,' she said over her shoulder.

'Oh, Belle,' her mother said quietly.

Belle stayed where she was, staring out at the garden. Behind her she heard the rustle of her mother's skirts. She felt a sinking sense of failure and regret.

When she turned again, her mother had gone.

The hospital at Falmouth was, as Mamma said, only really equipped for minor injuries, but the staff had done their best by the master of Eden, and given him a private room on the side of the building furthest from the street.

According to Sophie, who'd spent some time talking to Dr Walpole, he'd been right not to move Papa to Kingston. 'Head injuries are so unpredictable,' she said, speaking in the studiedly objective way that people adopt when they're keeping a tight rein on their emotions. 'The infection's flared up again; that's what's causing the fever and the drifting in and out of consciousness. But Dr Walpole believes he can bring it down. And if he can, there's no reason why he shouldn't get better.'

And if not? Nobody wanted to fill in the rest.

Ben took the twins off to Gardner's for an ice, and Sophie asked Mamma if she'd care to come too. Mamma shook her head. 'I'll stay out here till they tell us he's ready to be seen, then go in with Belle.'

'Well, then,' said Sophie, with a glance at Belle. 'I'll leave you two alone for a while.'

Belle sat beside her mother in the corridor, feeling exhausted, and strangely nervous. She'd slept badly, waking often to the sound of the tree-ferns tapping on the louvres, and the north wind whistling through the house. When at last she'd fallen into a fitful sleep, she'd had the old nightmare. She was back in Papa's study, and he didn't know who she was.

'Belle?'

She gave a start.

Mamma had risen to her feet, and was looking down at her curiously. 'Dr Walpole says we may go in.'

Her father lay in a bed by the window. Through the louvres, slatted light gilded his fair head. He was only a little greyer at the temples than Belle remembered, and he didn't look ill at all. Just a narrow strip of bandage across the forehead, and the strapping across the ribs showing at the neck of his nightshirt. The hand that lay on the coverlet looked as tanned and strong as ever.

Mamma went to the side of the bed by the window and pulled up a stool, leaving Belle the chair on the other side. Belle's nervousness increased as she went forward and sat down, and took his hand.

Seven years, and now here she was, holding his hand. It felt warm and strong. When she touched the thick, raised vein on the back, she felt the blood pulsing beneath the skin.

Sadness welled up in her throat. This hand had picked her up when she'd fallen off her swing; it had dried her tears when Pilate the horse had trodden on her foot. This hand had helped her buckle the collar on her mastiff puppy, and held her upright when she sat her pony, Muffin, for the very first time.

As the tears rolled down her cheeks, she felt at last that she was home. How could she have stayed away so long?

After a while he turned his head, and his eyebrows drew together in a frown. Then he opened his eyes and gazed up at her.

Belle saw with a surge of joy that the light grey eyes were as bright and clear as ever. She pressed his hand. 'Papa,' she whispered. 'It's me. Belle.'

'Belle?'

Through her tears she tried to smile. 'Yes, Papa. Belle. Your daughter.'

The frown deepened. 'But – you're not my daughter,' he said. 'Who are you? You're not my little girl.'

CHAPTER THIRTY-FOUR

'Just give him time,' Ben told her as they walked on the lawns at Fever Hill. 'The man's recovering from a head wound. That does things to you. God knows, when I first came round, I didn't even know who *I* was.'

Belle did not reply. After several days of drifting in and out of consciousness, Papa had finally rallied, and been pronounced out of danger. But she hadn't been back to see him. She couldn't bear it if he still didn't know who she was.

'Besides,' said Ben, 'in a way he was right, wasn't he? You're not his little girl any more.'

She threw him a startled glance.

'You're grown up, love. Funny thing is, it's only happened over the past few months.'

'What do you mean?'

He studied her, his eyepatch making him look more like a pirate than ever. 'Something about you. A new assurance? Being out in France did you good. It's as if at last you seem to know who you are.'

'And I didn't before?'

'What, all those years in London?' He barked a laugh. 'Not a chance! You were like a frightened little girl trying on disguises.'

His shrewdness took her aback. But even if he was right . . . 'I just wish,' she said, 'that Papa had known who I was.'

'He will. Just give him time.'

Two days later, she let Ben persuade her to try again.

'In fact,' he said as he handed her out of the motor, 'you're doing me a favour. Sophie's been on at me to visit him, and I've been putting it off. Never liked hospitals at the best of times.'

She knew he was only saying that to make her feel better. And she wished that she wasn't shaking so hard.

Ben pretended not to notice, and almost before she realized it they were at the bedside.

Papa was asleep. He looked the same as he had when she'd last seen him: not ill at all.

Her stomach tightened.

He opened his eyes and studied her for a moment. 'My God, but you've changed.'

Belle swallowed.

Papa's mouth curled in the almost-smile that was habitual with him. 'I was always glad that you were so dark. Like your mother.'

Belle's eyes began to sting. Behind her, she heard Ben get to his feet and leave the room.

She took her father's hand. 'How do you feel, Papa?'

He frowned slightly. 'Oh, no tears, Belle. Please. Never could bear to see a woman cry.'

She nodded, and fumbled for her handkerchief.

'I'm told,' he began, 'that on your first visit, I didn't know who you were.'

'Doesn't matter now,' she sniffed.

'Of course it does. It's just – you look so different. So grown-up and sophisticated.'

Belle tried to smile. Since she'd arrived in Jamaica, she'd made a conscious effort to tone down her make-up and her London grooming, so as to avoid disconcerting her mother. The fact that her father still found her 'sophisticated' was touching. But it also emphasized the gulf between them.

She thought about her life in London. About Osbourne and

the influenza, and Cairngowrie and Adam. There was so much that Papa didn't know.

With a pang she realized that even though he recognized her now, he still didn't really know who she was. She had stayed away too long.

The following month, Papa came home. Dr Walpole allowed it on the strict understanding that he was to get out of bed for no more than two hours every afternoon, and then only to sit on the verandah for a change of scene.

'Change of scene?' growled Papa when Dr Walpole was barely out of earshot. 'What the devil does he mean? Our bedroom looks out onto the verandah, the view's exactly the same. If he wants me to have a change of scene, he should let me go and visit the works.'

He would have done so, too, if Mamma hadn't put her foot down.

Once he was back, Eden became a hub of activity, with Ben and Sophie visiting daily, as well as friends and well-wishers from all over the Northside calling to pay their respects. Belle felt like an onlooker caught up in someone else's family gathering on false pretences.

Eventually she couldn't take it any longer, and moved out to stay with Ben and Sophie at Fever Hill, citing its proximity to Burntwood Sanatorium as an excuse.

The weeks passed.

She got on famously with Ben and Sophie, and visited Eden punctiliously twice a week.

She volunteered for work at Burntwood from Mondays to Thursdays, and was accepted with alacrity.

She befriended Dodo's little sister Margaret, a boisterous, russet-haired fourteen-year-old with the gawky charm of a red setter puppy, who took to following her about and pestering her with questions about photography.

Finally, she mustered the courage to write to Maud. After a long delay, she received a terse note informing her that Adam was 'on the mend' but still couldn't speak, and was now in the convalescent hospital at Farnborough.

March gave way to April, and April to May. Belle tried to put Adam out of her mind, and went on working at Burntwood, and visiting Eden.

She and her father were always polite and even affectionate to one another. He would ask her about Flanders and photography, while she would ask him about the estate, taking care to show that she'd paid attention to his letters over the years, and had kept up with developments. But when all that was dealt with, the silences would grow,and they'd both be relieved when she stood up to leave.

With Mamma, things were worse. In a strange way, it had been easier when Papa was in danger, because at least that had brought them together. Now that he was getting better, the old constraint had re-emerged.

'She's probably just a little confused,' said Sophie as they drove towards Burntwood one morning.

Belle stared at her. 'She hardly gives that impression. It's almost as if she resents my being here. Or else she's still angry with me for not getting in touch during the 'flu. Whatever it is, whenever I see her, neither of us knows what to say.'

The driver swerved to avoid a goat, and Sophie glanced back to make sure that it had survived. 'But, Belle,' she said, 'that's just an impression that she gives. You're not the only one in the family who can act.'

'What do you mean?'

'Well, think about it. She hasn't seen you for seven years, and in all that time it was poor Sib who was more of a mother to you than she. And then when you do come home, it's because of your father, not her; and then you end up staying not at Eden, but with us at Fever Hill. Of course she doesn't understand it. Frankly, neither do I.'

'Fever Hill is closer to Burntwood,' Belle said quickly.

'Only by a couple of miles,' Sophie pointed out.

'Mamma was the one who suggested that I find something to do. She was the one who suggested I help out at Burntwood.'

'Mm,' said Sophie.

Belle said, 'You think I'm avoiding her.'

'I think you're avoiding everyone,' said Sophie. 'Ever since you got here you've cut yourself off. I can't help wondering why.'

Belle began to feel hot. It was a relief when the great iron gates of Burntwood swept into sight. 'Oh, good,' she said. 'We're nearly there.'

Sophie threw her a look.

As they turned into the carriageway, Belle stared stubbornly out of the window. She'd never felt so relieved to reach the sanatorium.

It was an enormous old great house which had originally belonged to Papa's family. In those days it had been called Seven Hills: a monument to the power and prestige of the Lawes in the Golden Age of sugar. But old Duncan Lawe had been savage to his slaves, and in the Christmas Rebellion of 1832 they'd burnt it to the ground. Stubbornly, he'd raised an even larger great house on the original site – bigger than Fever Hill, more magnificent even than Parnassus – and in his bitterness he'd named it Burntwood. He'd died the following year without sleeping a night in his new house, and as the rebuilding had crippled the estate, his heir had been forced to sell soon afterwards.

Since then, it had passed through several hands, and acquired a reputation among the local people for being 'bad luckid'. It was said that when disaster was imminent, a spectral stench of ashes permeated the outer gallery – although this was only discernible to the prescient, or 'four-eyed', as they were called on the Northside.

Belle was not four-eyed, and she'd never smelt ashes in the gallery. But sometimes on overcast days, she thought she sensed an air of misfortune about the place. Margaret Cornwallis, too, seemed to notice it, for recently she'd become subdued, and now spent most of her time winding bandages on her own. Belle was relieved. The pestering had been getting wearisome.

The driver drew up at the foot of the steps, and the old house reared above them like a witch's castle from a fairy tale. It had high, pointed gables, and as the verandahs were enclosed by louvres to make an old-fashioned gallery, a curiously blind façade. But what made it extraordinary was the massive, windowless, wedge-shaped structure of cut-stone and cement which had been built onto the west wing. It was fully two storeys high, and its knife-sharp edge jutted fiercely north, like the prow of an enormous ship.

When Belle had first seen it as a child, she'd been terrified. She'd refused to get out of the carriage until Papa had explained that it was a Hurrycane Cellar, or cutwind: a place of safety in which people used to take shelter from hurricanes.

'There's room for at least ten people inside,' he'd told her. But that had merely set the seven-year-old Belle to wondering how they'd decided *which* ten people had been allowed to survive inside, and which had been left to face the onslaught of the hurricane.

'I think,' said Sophie, gazing up at the windowless stone, 'I finally understand why you like this dreadful place.'

'I don't exactly like it,' said Belle. 'I simply work here.'

'Mm,' said Sophie doubtfully. 'You give the odd photography class, and read newspapers to convalescents. I suppose one might call that work.'

Belle's cheeks grew hot. 'Mamma suggested I come here,' she said defensively.

Sophie brushed that aside. 'The truth is, you've got a lot in common with this place, haven't you?' She craned her neck at the cutwind's blank, forbidding walls. 'Closed to outsiders. Repel all comers. It's no way to live, Belle darling.'

Belle got out of the motor car and closed the door. 'I'll see you this evening,' she said.

Damn Sophie for being so shrewd.

Of course Burntwood was a bolt-hole. That was why she liked it. She *liked* its ugliness and its blind façade; she liked the steady monotony of the work, and the fact that it left her too tired to think at the end of the day.

With an effort, Belle put Sophie from her mind, and spent the morning reading articles from the *Gleaner* to a ward full of blind veterans, and the afternoon teaching the importance of focal length to a trio of mildly flirtatious officers in Bath chairs. By the time she got back to the cubbyhole where she stowed her camera, and which Matron grandly called 'Miss Lawe's office', it was teatime, and there was a letter waiting for her on her desk. She recognized the engraved coat of arms of the Duke of Kyme.

I thought I'd send this to you at the san, wrote Dodo, *as you don't seem to be staying with your mamma (hope nothing's wrong!!). This way it'll be sure to reach you.*

Belle sighed. Not another one who thought she ought to be staying at Eden.

I'm writing with a request for help, Dodo went on with her usual bluntness, *though not for me, for Mags.*

Mags? wondered Belle. Oh, of course. Margaret.

It's just that she's changed so awfully over the past few weeks. I can tell from her letters. She used to draw the most screamingly funny cartoons in the margins, and scribble all sorts of appalling jokes, but suddenly it's just dutiful little notes. I can't think what's got into her, and I wondered, could you bear to have a bash at finding out? She was always the chatterbox of the family, absolutely fearless, ready for anything . . .

Belle felt a stab of guilt. She too had noticed the change in the girl, but she'd been too preoccupied with her own concerns to do anything about it.

. . . and now she's – well, so different. Esmond says it's just that she's not used to the tropics, but privately I don't think it can be that, as she's visited lots of times and always adored it. Of course, if I say anything, Esmond counters it by saying that she's simply growing up. Obviously I tell him that he's right, because there's no point in telling him anything else . . .

Oh, Dodo, thought Belle sadly. Is that the way it's going to be with you from now on? Kowtowing to Esmond for the rest of your life?

. . . but strictly entre nous, I can't help feeling that there must be something else. Sorry to burden you with this when I know your pater still isn't quite well, but I'm really beginning to get a little worried – which with Dodo probably meant that she'd been having sleepless nights for weeks *although of course I'm not asking you to bear the brunt completely. Of all people, old Cornelius Traherne has been absolutely marvellous, and quite taken her in hand; lovely long drives, showing her over his estate, that sort of thing . . .*

The world tilted sickeningly.

Someone knocked at the door.

Belle jumped.

One of the maids put in her head. 'Missy Belle? Miss Evie come by on her way to Fever Hill to visit wid Missy Sophie, an ax to say do you want a ride?'

Belle swallowed. 'Um. Thank you. Yes. Tell her – I'll be down soon.'

The maid glanced at the letter in Belle's fist, and softly withdrew.

Cornelius Traherne has been absolutely marvellous, and quite taken her in hand . . .

The words swam before her eyes. Until now, it had never occurred to her that there might be others.

It can't be true, she told herself. It can't be happening again.

And yet – Margaret Cornwallis was only fourteen . . .

Quickly she skimmed the rest of the letter, but there was nothing more about Margaret; just news of Kyme – to which Dodo seemed to be resigning herself. *Sorry to be such a bore*, she finished, *but anything you can do for Mags would be so very kind . . .*

Anything I can do? thought Belle.

And what *could* she do? He wouldn't stop if I told him to; he'd just pretend that he didn't know what she was talking about. And if I told anyone else, they'd never believe her. And even if they did, it would mean that she'd be found out, too.

Found out, found out. The mere thought made her feel physically sick.

Somehow, she got to her feet and got her things together. Stuffed the crumpled letter into her bag. Found her way out into the corridor.

He's doing it again, she thought. The knowledge pounded through her to the rhythm of her blood. He's doing it to someone else . . .

Teatime was well under way and the corridors were busy with nurses and trolleys as Belle left the sanatorium and went out through the gallery and onto the front steps. Two motor cars were waiting in the carriageway. As there were only eight motors in the whole of Trelawny, the sight had attracted a little cluster of admiring garden boys and porters.

One of the motors was the grey Mercedes-Benz owned by Isaac Walker of the neighbouring estate, Arethusa. In the back, smiling up at Belle, sat his wife, Evie, elegant as ever in a mint-green afternoon gown which perfectly set off her smooth, coffee-coloured complexion.

The other was the mustard-coloured Daimler which belonged to the Parnassus estate. Cornelius Traherne stood beside it, immaculate in a white linen suit and a Panama hat, chatting amicably with the matron, who'd come down herself to greet so important a visitor. He was making no move to go inside. Clearly he was waiting for someone to come out to him.

Margaret? wondered Belle. Surely he can't be waiting to take her on one of his 'drives'?

It felt unreal even to think it. By now he had to be at least seventy-three. *Surely* he couldn't still want to . . .

At that moment, he turned and caught her staring at him, and his face went still.

The shadow of the cutwind sliced across his features, putting half of it in deep shade, and half in harsh sunlight. He certainly looked his age, the liver-spotted skin hanging loose from the jowls; but the full lips were as glistening red as ever, the pale blue eyes as unassailable.

He met her gaze, and inclined his head to her with old-fashioned courtesy. He knew that she knew. He also knew that she would not, and could not, tell.

It's still our secret, the pale eyes seemed to say. *And we don't want to get found out. Now, do we?*

CHAPTER THIRTY-FIVE

'Walk with me,' said Evie when they reached Fever Hill.

Belle didn't have much choice. The maid had told them that Sophie was in Falmouth, although expected back soon, and Ben was down at the stables. Belle could hardly leave Evie all by herself on the verandah.

Together they started across the lawns behind the house. It was a hot afternoon: the kind of afternoon when you can almost see the grass shrivelling before your eyes.

Belle hardly noticed. She was thinking of Margaret Cornwallis, who used to follow her about and pester her with questions, but was now so silent and withdrawn. She was thinking of the shadow of the cutwind carving the face of Cornelius Traherne into light and dark.

He's doing it to someone else . . .

'We'll go up the hill,' said Evie, making her start.

'What?'

'To the Burying-place. Catch a nice cool breeze.'

Belle gave a distracted nod. But as she glanced sideways at her companion, she felt a shiver of apprehension. She liked Evie, but she was also a little afraid of her, for Evie Walker, *née* McFarlane, was unlike anyone else she'd ever met. Evie knew the trick of inhabiting two very different worlds, and she moved effortlessly between them whenever she chose.

On the one hand, she was the beautiful, educated wife of the master of Arethusa: an old friend of Sophie and Ben, and a highly respected schoolteacher (the Lady Teacheress, as the local children still call her), who'd tutored Belle when she was small.

On the other hand, she was the four-eyed daughter of the local witch. She knew more about obeah than anyone else in Trelawny, and was rumoured to be able to see the dead. When she wanted to, she would visit her country cousins up in the Cockpits, where she would lapse into *patois* and spell-weaving as easily as slipping off her shoes.

And there was something else, too. Seven years before, when Belle had been desperate to avoid Cornelius Traherne, Evie had flatly refused to weave a spell for her. Rationally, Belle knew that Evie had been right; but part of her had always resented it. Like anyone else who'd grown up on the Northside, Belle knew the power of country magic. And sometimes she asked herself if things would have been different had Evie granted her request.

Now, as they passed beneath the shade of a breadfruit tree, she glanced at the slender woman walking beside her, and wondered which Evie she was looking at: the one-time teacheress, or the powerful witch.

She didn't have to wait long to find out. They took the path that wound over the crest of Fever Hill and a short way down the other side, to the Monroe family Burying-place. It was a peaceful green hollow surrounded by coconut palms and wild lime trees, where, in a scattering of raised barrel tombs, seven generations of Monroes dreamed away the decades in the long silver grass.

As Evie passed between the graves, she brushed one or two of them with her fingertips. When she reached the old poinciana tree at the far end, she glanced about her and gave a little nod, as if satisfied that the dead were resting quietly, and she could begin.

Taking her seat on the bench beneath the poinciana, she indicated that Belle should sit beside her.

Belle's apprehension grew. She wished she had the courage to walk away.

As she took her place beside Evie, something made her turn and glance south, past the emerald cane-pieces to the blue-grey line of the Cockpits. There, she thought, among those trees at the edge of the Cockpits, lies Eden. She repressed a surge of homesickness.

'So,' said Evie, following her gaze, 'you've not been spending much time at home these past few months.'

Belle turned back to her. 'Sophie's been talking to you.'

Evie smiled. 'Sophie tends to do that. Given that she's my friend.'

'I mean, about me.'

'Well, now. Some things I can see for myself, you know.' She leaned down and plucked a small purple flower, and turned it in her fingers. 'At Burntwood,' she said quietly, 'when you were standing on the steps. I saw your face.'

Belle's skin began to prickle.

'Cornelius Traherne,' said Evie, looking down at the flower. 'The way you looked at him. There's bad blood between you, I think.'

Belle did not reply.

Above her head, a flock of sugarquits descended on the poinciana tree, squabbling noisily. The rasp of the cicadas was loud in her ears. She smelt spicy red dust and the sharp green tang of the asparagus ferns among the graves. She felt trapped.

'He's a bad man, that Mr Traherne,' said Evie. 'A destroyful man, as my mother used to say. God rest her soul.'

Belle put her hands on either side of her. The bench felt sun-hot under her palms. 'I wonder,' she said as lightly as she could, 'who am I talking to at the moment? Mrs Isaac Walker, or four-eyed Evie McFarlane?'

'Which do you want to be talking to?'

Again Belle did not reply.

'You know,' Evie said calmly, 'I have my own reasons for wishing him ill. And before me, my mother had hers.'

Belle stared at her. He's done this before . . . He'll go on doing it . . . 'Tell me about it,' she said.

Evie shook her head. 'You don't need to know. What you do need to know is something my mother told me a long time ago. She said, "Evie, sometimes you can get vengeance for you own self. Other times, not. That man – he done lot, lotta bad things. And vengeance will come to him in the end, but not from me, and not from you either." ' Again she twirled the flower in her fingers. 'She made me swear on the grave of my great-grandmother never to try to confront him or face him down.'

'Why not?' said Belle.

Evie shook her head. 'No need for you to know,' she said again. 'The point is, vengeance will come. That's what my mother said.'

Belle felt herself becoming angry. 'But from whom? And when? He's rich. He's powerful. He's well-regarded. Who would ever believe me? I mean,' she corrected herself hastily, 'who would ever believe ill of him?'

Evie raised her shoulders in a shrug. 'That I don't know, Belle. But something's going to happen, and it's not far off. I've been feeling it on me for a while now.' She opened her hand and let the flower fall, and Belle saw with a shiver of unease that it was a sprig of Madam Fate.

Evie shaded her eyes with her hand, and with the other she pointed to the far side of the Burying-place. 'You see that tomb over there? The one with the crest carved on its side?'

Belle was puzzled. 'The Monroe arms. Of course. What about it?'

'Your mother's a Monroe,' Evie said thoughtfully. 'So is Sophie. And so, in part, are you.' She was silent for a moment. Then she said, 'A strange thing to put on a crest, I always thought. A crow carrying a snake in its claws.'

'I don't understand,' said Belle. 'What are you trying to say?'

Evie rose and dusted off her skirts. 'Only this,' she said. 'Maybe it's time for that crow to decide what to do about the snake.'

Belle turned her head away. 'Evie, it's not that simple.'

'Well, all right, then,' Evie said mildly. 'But think about this. Think about finding some way to give yourself power over him.'

Belle frowned.

'You don't have to use that power. But it would make you feel better if you had it. To know that if you wanted to, you could lance the boil.' Her lip curled. 'If you'll forgive so indelicate an expression.'

Belle's frown deepened. 'Evie, I don't know what you mean.'

Evie looked down at her, and in the glare of the sun her face was unreadable. 'Take time, Belle. Think about it. If it's meant to be, you'll find a way.'

After she'd gone, Belle sat on by the graves, listening to the surge and fall of the cicadas in the long grass, and the sugarquits squabbling overhead. The midday sun was harsh, and the glare off the graves was blinding. In the crow's claws, the serpent writhed.

As a child, Belle had been fascinated by that crest. What would the crow do next? she used to wonder. Would it tear the snake to pieces? Would it let go, so that the snake fell to its death? Or would it alight on a patch of grass and release it, so that it was free to slither away and do more harm?

She didn't want to think about that now. And she didn't want to think about little Margaret Cornwallis, who'd once been the family tearaway, and now spent her days rolling bandages by herself.

How could she, Belle Lawe, put an end to something that had been going on for so long?

And yet, how could she live with herself if she didn't?

She broke off a frond of asparagus fern and crushed it in her fingers, breathing in the sharp green tang.

Adam would know what to do, she thought suddenly.

Angrily she tossed the fern away. Why think of Adam now? What was the point? All that had ended months ago.

Return to sender. No reply.

CHAPTER THIRTY-SIX

'He just needs more time,' Dr Ruthven had told her, but Maud was beginning to have her doubts. These days Adam had time in abundance, but he wasn't getting better.

I simply want peace, he'd written at the end of March, before discharging himself from hospital against the doctors' advice. *So please, Maud,* don't *change your arrangements for me. Stay at the House with Max; he's settled with you now, it'd be bad for him to move again. I shall be perfectly happy on my own at the Hall. In fact, I should prefer it. I'm fine now, really. The arm is quite healed, I have scarcely a limp, and all that remains of the head wound is a scar down the left side of my face that wouldn't even frighten Max. Of course it's a bore not being able to talk, but I'm getting accustomed to that too.*

I know you think I should have listened to the doctors, but the truth is, I'm sick of hospitals. First it was Wimereux, now Farnborough. I just want to come home.

That had been four weeks ago. Since then, things had gone on perfectly well – on the surface. Adam visited them almost daily, and took Max for long walks on the beach. Often Felicity Ruthven joined them for the day. Twice they let Julia out, and watched in awe as she swept low over the beach, scattering terns and oystercatchers with imperious squawks.

But Maud was too honest to fool herself. Adam was not the

same. A light had gone out of his eyes. His smile seemed forced. He was playing a part.

She could see perfectly well what was going on, and it surprised her that he could not. Or perhaps, she told herself, he doesn't want to see.

Belle had written to her twice from Jamaica. To begin with, Maud had considered ignoring the letters. She was furious with the girl. She didn't deserve a reply.

But Belle was Belle, and her letters had been so frank, and so desperate to know if Adam was all right, that after much angry deliberation, Maud had relented.

She had not, however, told Adam about the correspondence. Nor had she told him that Belle had gone out to Jamaica. She simply hadn't mentioned the girl at all.

Unfortunately, Max was unaware of this. Which was why, one afternoon, as they sat at tea in Cairngowrie House, he proudly showed Adam an engraving of an emerald parakeet in his new bird book and said, 'And this one's Caribbean, so I expect Miss Lawe sees them all the time in Jamaica.'

There was a silence. Maud set down her teacup. Adam pretended to study the engraving with interest. Max, never slow to pick up an atmosphere, realized that he'd caused it, and looked at Maud in alarm.

I expect there are lots of parakeets in Miss Lawe's garden, Adam wrote on his notepad, in an attempt to reassure the boy.

But Max wasn't fooled, and neither was Maud. Soon afterwards, Adam made an excuse and left. Some time after that, Max quietly put on his outdoor things and went out to the beach to brood. Maud found him halfway to the Point, clambering solemnly onto a favourite rock, then jumping down onto the wet sand, to see how deep he could make his footprints.

It was a raw April day with only an hour of daylight left, and the wind roared across the beach, tugging at Maud's hat and reddening Max's cheeks.

'I upset Captain Palairet,' he said when she got within earshot.

'No you didn't,' she replied. 'Miss Lawe was the one who did that.'

'But *why* did she leave?' said Max for the hundredth time. He'd admired Belle enormously, and still talked wistfully about the zoo biscuit morning.

'I don't know,' said Maud. She took his hand and gave it a little shake. 'But we know why she had to go to Jamaica, don't we? Because her papa was hurt in an accident, and she had to be with him. Which is just as it should be.'

'Mm,' said Max doubtfully. He was too intelligent to be fobbed off with less than the whole story. 'But I thought Captain Palairet *liked* her.'

'He does.'

'Then why—'

'Max, that's enough. Now come along. It'll be dark soon. It's time we went inside.'

As they made their way back to the House, Maud thought about Adam up at the Hall: dressing for his solitary dinner, drinking his solitary whisky, then settling down to a solitary evening with a book, while doing his best not to think about what Max had let slip over tea.

She wondered if she ought to speak to him – try to persuade him to write to Belle, instead of just walking away like this. But then she remembered the postscript he'd added to his letter a month before.

In answer to your question, Maud: yes, I was aware that Belle was in Flanders, and no, I didn't see her. What would have been the point? It's over. I see no reason to rake it up.

Belle sat hunched on her bed in her room at Fever Hill, contemplating the sky-blue envelope lying on the counterpane.

It had taken her a week, but she'd finally managed to do what Evie had suggested. She'd found a way of gaining power over Cornelius Traherne.

And all because of little Margaret Cornwallis.

The day after the conversation with Evie at the Burying-place, she had sought out Margaret at the sanatorium.

As usual, the girl was alone, winding bandages. When she saw Belle, she gave a guilty start.

310

Belle hoisted herself onto a table and sat swinging her legs. Remembering her own confusion and guilt, she knew that she had to approach the younger girl with care – but not too obliquely. It might help to hint that she suspected what was going on. It might give Margaret a chance to talk.

Still swinging her legs, she said, 'I got a letter from Dodo.'

Margaret went on with her work. She was a smaller, prettier version of her sister, with limpid hazel eyes and a clear complexion, but the same imposing Cornwallis nose.

'She says,' Belle went on, 'that you've become friends with Mr Traherne.'

Margaret nearly dropped her bandages.

'It's all right,' Belle said quietly. 'I understand. I really do. I – *know*.'

Margaret did not reply. Ungainly red blotches were spreading up her neck and inflaming her cheeks.

'I also know,' said Belle, very deliberately, 'that it's not your fault.'

Margaret bit down hard on her lower lip. She had bony, boyish hands with badly chewed cuticles. Watching her struggling with emotions she was far too young to understand, Belle felt a surge of pure rage at Traherne. 'These drives,' she said, struggling to keep her voice steady. 'Where does he take you?'

Another silence. Belle could feel her own cheeks growing red. She was hating this as much as Margaret. Feeling the same guilt. The same sense of being dirtied for ever . . .

It had been painful for both of them – but it had been worth it. For now, several days later, the sky-blue envelope lay before her on the counterpane. Her proof. If she chose to use it, she could bring him down. If.

But Evie was wrong about one thing. Gaining power over Traherne didn't make her feel better. It made her feel worse. Because if she chose to use what lay before her, then she too would be found out. Mamma and Papa would know that she was not who they thought she was. They would know that she was someone else altogether.

On the counterpane, the envelope seemed to throb like a live thing. With the tip of her forefinger she touched its corner, then snatched back her hand. Damn Evie. Damn her for giving her the choice.

And after all, why *should* she do anything at all? There was no longer any need to worry about Margaret Cornwallis. Belle had lost no time in seeing to that, sending a cryptic wire to Dodo: *Mags coming home. Be patient. She will tell in time. I will write soon with more. Belle.* Then she'd arranged for the child to be sent back to Southampton with a motherly cousin of Mrs Herapath's, and resolved to have a last talk with her before she went, to try to start repairing the damage.

So, yes, Margaret was safe now, and would soon be home with her sister.

And yet – Belle knew perfectly well that this had never been about protecting Margaret Cornwallis; or not only about that. It was about telling Mamma and Papa.

'But I can't,' said Belle out loud. 'I just can't do that.'

Coward, she told herself silently. How can you simply do nothing? Margaret won't be the last. You can't fool yourself into thinking that any more. If you don't do something now, and it happens again, how will you live with yourself?

'Coward,' she whispered.

But the very thought of doing something made her feel sick.

Quickly she snatched up the envelope and ran to her chest of drawers and wrenched it open.

She'd opened her underwear drawer. How peculiarly appropriate to hide it in there.

Lifting a pile of crêpe-de-chine step-ins, she tucked the envelope underneath, then pushed the drawer shut with both hands.

There, now, she thought. Now you've got it under control.

CHAPTER THIRTY-SEVEN

Cairngowrie was at its best in May. The hills were ablaze with yellow gorse, the hedges laced with cow parsley and creamy drifts of hawthorn, the woods aglow with wild garlic and bluebells.

This May it had looked particularly beautiful, for the weather had turned warm, and the days were sunny and fine. The loch, thought Adam as he walked on the shore with Maud and Max and Felicity, looks so blue that it's almost Caribbean.

He was aware of all this, but the strange thing was that he couldn't really *feel* it. He was merely an observer. All he could feel – all he'd been able to feel since the explosion – was frustration and irritability, and a fiery mistrust. A desperate need to be on his own.

He watched Max racing over the dunes, pockets rattling with shells, skinny legs already lightly tanned as he tried in vain to surprise the rabbits before they made it back to their burrows. Max adored the rabbits, and he still couldn't quite believe that such beautiful creatures lived in *his* dunes, near *his* house – and could be seen whenever he liked, for free.

Adam watched him run, and tried to feel glad.

Over the months, Maud had wrought nothing short of a transformation in the boy. Gone was the sallow, frightened child whose shoulders used to rise up round his ears whenever anyone spoke

313

to him. He now spent much of his time outdoors, and was tentatively making friends with the Reverend's young son, Clovis. He'd lost all fear of the woods (despite an epic encounter with a patch of stinging nettles), and had recently announced plans for befriending the seals.

Maud, too, looked happier and more relaxed than Adam had seen her in years. Adam tried to feel glad about that, too.

He stooped for a pebble and sent it skimming over the water. Things are going as well as you could wish, he told himself. This is what you wanted. Peace. What does it matter if you can't speak? What does it matter if Belle—

'Cairngowrie is at its best in May,' said Felicity beside him. 'Don't you agree? The mayflowers, the bluebells, the gorse. It's all so lovely.'

Adam gave her the expected smile, while repressing a flicker of irritation. These days, Felicity never missed an opportunity to put things into words. Everything, however blindingly obvious, had to be noted and described. Perhaps she fancied that she was giving voice to his feelings, since he couldn't do so himself. Whatever the reason, it was becoming wearing.

'And the loch looks so *blue*,' she remarked. 'Almost tropical, wouldn't you say?'

Again Adam nodded. After all, he reminded himself, it isn't her fault if she has no imagination.

To his relief, her father was waiting at the House to drive her back to Kildrochet. After she'd taken her seat in the motor, she unwound the window and put out her head. 'We shall be seeing you next Thursday, shan't we? Oh, do say yes.' Her words were meant for all of them, but she was looking at Adam.

'Of course,' Maud said crisply. 'I've already replied to your invitation. Or had you forgot?'

Adam took out his notepad and wrote, *We're looking forward to it*. He didn't like doing it. Somehow, writing a lie felt worse than saying it.

At some stage, he thought as he watched them drive off, he was going to have to do something about Felicity. He'd been careful not to lead her on, but nevertheless her visits were becoming more frequent, and her father was starting to look upon them fondly.

After they'd gone, Max helped Maud bring the tea things out into the garden, and Adam forgot about Felicity and tried to lose himself in the sunshine on the loch and the terns wheeling and mewing above the Point.

'I had a letter this morning,' said Maud as she handed him his cup. She moved the plate of biscuits a fraction to her right. Then she said, 'It's from Belle.'

Adam threw her a glance, but she kept her eyes on the tea tray.

'Is Miss Lawe coming home soon?' said Max.

There was a small silence, and he darted a glance at Adam to see if he'd spoken out of turn.

'I'm afraid I don't think so,' said Maud, studiously addressing the boy instead of Adam.

'Oh,' said Max, disappointed. 'But I thought her papa was better.'

'He is,' said Maud. 'A great deal better, thank goodness.'

'Then why does she have to stay in Jamaica? It's not fair.'

'Well, Jamaica is her home,' said Maud. 'And you see, she is having such a nice time staying with her aunt and uncle, and helping out at a sanatorium for invalid officers.' Two spots of colour had appeared on her cheeks. She had the air of a general who has just successfully opened a campaign.

She's been planning this, thought Adam. He didn't know whether to be exasperated or amused.

'In fact,' Maud went on, still talking only to Max, 'she seems to be having *such* a nice time that I shouldn't wonder if she'll decide to stay in Jamaica for good.'

'Oh, *no!*' cried Max. 'But then we'll never see her again!'

'I know,' said Maud. 'And wouldn't that be the most terrible shame?'

At last she raised her eyes and met Adam's. 'I just thought,' she said calmly, 'that you ought to know.'

Adam stood at the library window watching the last blush of the sunset warming Beoch Hill. It was half past ten in the evening, and the day was fading in one of those endless northern twilights which imperceptibly turn the sky from oyster to aquamarine to deepest cobalt.

A perfect May evening at Cairngowrie. He wondered what Belle would say if she could see it.

In her first week here, she'd grumbled about the weather. *I hate Scotland. It's so appallingly grey.*

No it isn't, thought Adam.

And suddenly, as he stood there at the window, the last rays of the sun caught Beoch Hill, and the gorse blazed a fiery gold.

Adam caught his breath. In his chest, something shifted. Something rekindled. He felt a moment of pure, exhilarating joy. A moment of rejoicing . . .

His eyes began to sting.

Ah, Christ, Belle, I wish you were here to see this! I wish you could see the buttercups in the meadows, and the red campion by the burns, and the rhododendrons in the grounds, and the young ferns unfurling in the woods, and how very blue the loch looks in the sun . . .

An image of Belle came to him with startling vividness. Not Belle as she'd been when he'd last seen her, but as she'd been at the height of her illness, in the garret in East Street: huge-eyed and chalky-faced, spouting black blood all over him, while she clawed at his hands and raved about yellowsnakes.

Beautiful, strong, flawed, unpredictable, infuriating Belle.

He wanted her back.

But as hope came roaring back, so also did fear. He remembered Maud's little bombshell at teatime. *I shouldn't wonder if she'll decide to stay in Jamaica for good.*

My God, he thought, feeling suddenly cold. This is wrong. It's all wrong. You've got to get her back.

The doctor's surgery was spartan by comparison with Clive's comfortable book-lined lair, but somehow Adam found that reassuring. Dr Ayers was said to be the best in Glasgow. Clearly he didn't need to waste time in dressing up his rooms. Or, for that matter, in reassuring his patients.

'I'll be blunt with you, Captain Palairet,' he said as he put his elbows on his desk and fixed Adam with small, startlingly blue eyes. 'You should not have discharged yourself from Farnborough so soon. The fact that you did makes me question your wish to get better.'

I need to be able to talk again, Adam wrote in his notebook.

'You didn't seem to care about that before,' said Dr Ayers. 'So why now?'

Adam hesitated. *Before it wasn't important. Now it is. Just tell me what you can do.*

The doctor studied him for a moment. Then he nodded, as if satisfied. 'In cases like yours, there are a number of treatments I use. But I have to tell you, Captain Palairet, they all hurt. Some of them a great deal.'

I don't care, wrote Adam.

Again Dr Ayers fixed him with his blue gaze. Then he seemed to decide that Adam meant it, for he gave another nod. 'I'll start with bouts of faradism to the neck and throat,' he said briskly. 'That's electricity to you and me. If that doesn't work, hot plates to the back of the mouth. Then stronger pulses of electricity. And if all else fails,' he gave a grim smile, 'my personal favourite. A lighted cigarette to the tip of the tongue.'

Adam thought about that for a moment. Then he picked up his pen. *Try them all,* he wrote.

CHAPTER THIRTY-EIGHT

The day of the hurricane dawned windless and hot.

The tree frogs had been loud all night, and Evie's sleep had been troubled. Her mother had dreamed to her; and that hadn't happened since she'd been put in her grave.

Evie rolled onto her side and watched the steady rise and fall of her husband's chest. Then she slipped out of bed, tucked the mosquito net around him, and made her way out into the garden, pulling on her peignoir as she went. She didn't bother with slippers. When one of the dead came visiting, she preferred to feel the earth beneath her feet. It helped her to think.

Padding down the verandah steps, she went out into the garden. It was still getting light, and mist floated among the giant bamboo. Bluequits chattered in the banana palms. A lizard fled at her approach.

The rains had been late this year, arriving right at the end of May, but they'd been good, and the trees around the house had burst into flower: scarlet poinciana and mauve June rose; the pale greenish flowers of the wild almond. The air was heavy with the perfume of sweetwood and spider lilies. Evie took a deep breath, but still felt breathless.

Like most great houses in Trelawny, Arethusa faced north. From where Evie stood, the cane-pieces stretched away to the east, while the steamy darkness of Greendale Wood loomed to the west. Due north, following the course of the Martha Brae, ran the red slash of the Arethusa Road, and far in the distance lay the restless glitter of the sea. Evie sensed that the trouble would come from the north. But that could mean from the river, or Falmouth, or from the sea itself.

Which?

In the dream, her mother had walked soundlessly down the Fever Hill Road, her bare feet raising red plumes of dust. She'd been wearing her obeah things: her green print skirt hitched up to the knees to show her gleaming brown calves, her head tied about with the white kerchief she wore for spell-making. The necklace of parrot beaks had clinked softly at her breast.

As Evie watched, dream-still and silent, her mother had come to a halt, and turned to face her. She was standing at the point in the road where two side roads turn off: one winding north towards Parnassus and the sea, and the other leading south between the gatehouses that guard the Fever Hill estate.

With arms outstretched, Grace McFarlane had spanned the road, one long-fingered hand casting a shadow over the track to Parnassus, the other tracing the coils of the serpent on the Fever Hill gatehouse. Then a great wind had blown up from the sea. The blast had forced Evie to her knees, but Grace McFarlane had stood unmoving at the eye of the storm: the Mother of Darkness, her face as hard and smooth as carved mahogany.

What does it mean? thought Evie, as she went to sit on the verandah steps.

A ground dove alighted by her foot, and stared at her with a bright crimson eye. She waved her hand to chase it away. It fluttered off a few yards, only to waddle back again.

A duppy bird is not a good sign. Despite the heat, Evie drew her peignoir close about her.

Her mother had sent a warning. But for whom?

In her heart, Evie sensed that it must be for Belle. That brown hand caressing the Monroe crest . . .

And yet − spirits are trickified things. It's easy to get their message wrong-side, with terrible results. Evie knew that better than most.

The sun was growing hotter, sucking the breath from her lungs. She thought, but if it's Belle, then why today? What is special about today?

Then it came to her. Sophie had mentioned it over tea the other afternoon. 'Big day on Thursday,' she'd said, raising her eyebrows. 'Maddy's going over to Burntwood to inspect the plans for the new extension. I told you she's a trustee? That was my idea, to get her closer to Belle. Well, so far it hasn't exactly worked; they're still avoiding each other – or not really communicating, which amounts to the same thing. But this Thursday they won't be able to, as there's a luncheon. So let's cross our fingers and hope for the best.'

Burntwood, thought Evie.

Jumping to her feet, she ran up the stairs. Then she came to an abrupt halt.

Across the verandah, a line of red ants was winding its way towards the house. Evie's belly tightened. Her old uncle Eliphalet had taught her the weather signs before she could read, and now his voice echoed in her mind.

Red ants moving inna the house, it mean the big blow go come.

At Eden by mid-morning, a light breeze had sprung up: just enough to lift the pony's mane as Moses brought the dog cart round from the stables.

'You know, you could take the motor,' Cameron told his wife as she stood in the hall buttoning her dustcoat.

'I need some air,' she replied over her shoulder, 'and so do the twins. It'll do us good.' Putting her hands to her temples, she smoothed back her hair. Then she met his eyes in the looking-glass, and smiled. She was nervous. He wished he knew how to reassure her.

Following her out onto the steps, he glanced at the sky, where a flock of jabbering crows was speeding towards the hills. 'Looks like we could be in for some weather,' he murmured. 'You'd better let Moses drive.'

'I shall be fine,' said Madeleine. 'Besides, if you're concerned, you could always come with us and do the driving yourself.'

He sighed. 'I told you, I have some things to see to here first.'

'Nonsense,' she said as he helped her into the dog cart. 'You're staying behind to give me a chance to be alone with Belle.'

He laughed. 'Am I that transparent?'

She threw him one of her looks.

'Well, my darling, then so are you. You're only taking the twins along for moral support.'

'What's moral support?' said Lachlan.

'It's what you take with you when you're nervous,' said Cameron, scooping him up and tossing him into the dog cart.

'Like a teddy bear?' said Douglas, waiting for his turn.

'Or a lucky parrot claw,' said Lachlan as his brother tumbled in beside him.

As Madeleine gathered the reins, Cameron put his hand over hers. 'You'll be fine,' he told her. 'You love her, and she loves you. You just need to start talking to each other. It's that simple.'

'Men,' she said, shaking her head. 'I shall expect you there for luncheon. Punctually, one o'clock. *Promise* you won't think up some excuse not to come.'

Again he laughed. 'Come hell or high water, I shall be there. I promise.'

Belle was pacing the gallery at Burntwood when she heard the dog cart in the carriageway.

'They're here,' said Drum, who'd come up for the day to lend moral support. 'Oh, look,' he added with a grin. 'She's brought the boys. D'you want me to take them off your hands for a while?'

Belle nodded. 'But not just yet.'

It was ridiculous to feel nervous, but she'd scarcely seen her mother for weeks. Every time she went to Eden to visit Papa, Mamma was either out, or busy with the twins. The constraint between them hadn't lessened. It had grown.

Pressing her palms together, she was surprised to find them slippery with sweat. And this weather didn't help. It had been oppressively hot all morning, but now a norther had started to blow, and clouds were beginning to darken the noonday sky.

'Strong weather on the way,' one of the nurses had told Belle as she was making her way downstairs. 'Bees staying home, the rain go come. That true to the fact.'

Already the twins were jumping down from the dog cart.

Drum turned to Belle. 'Ready?'

She nodded. Her hand sought the satchel hanging by her side. Although she felt a little foolish about it, she'd done as Sophie had suggested, and brought along some of her portrait photographs. 'If things get sticky,' Sophie had said, 'just show her your pictures. She'd love to see them. You may not believe me, but she's awfully proud of you.'

The satchel contained something else, too. Something that nobody knew about but Belle.

For days, the sky-blue envelope had lain hidden in her chest of drawers. Only yesterday, after her farewell talk with Margaret Cornwallis, had she felt brave enough to take it out.

'Tell your sister everything,' she had urged Margaret as they walked in the ruins of the old slave village at Fever Hill. 'Dodo's the kindest person I know. She'll understand. Especially now that my letter has – prepared the ground.'

'I will,' said Margaret, staring at the ground. Then abruptly she'd raised her head and fixed Belle with a bright, intense stare. 'It helps so much that you know. That you . . .' she took a breath that turned into a gulp, 'that you don't mind.'

It had been all Belle could do not to break down. 'Of course I don't mind,' she said, putting her arm round the girl's shoulders and giving her a little shake. 'Why should I mind? None of this is your fault. Remember that, Margaret. It wasn't – it never was – your fault.'

Not your fault, she told herself now as she watched Drum helping her mother down from the dog cart. How strange that it had taken Margaret Cornwallis to make her truly understand that.

Her fingers tightened on the sky-blue envelope. Her proof. The means with which to bring down Cornelius Traherne.

Who knows, she thought. This might be the day on which I use it.

Sophie was annoyed to find that her hands were shaking as she pinned on her hat. If she didn't hurry, she'd be late for her appointment. And she still hadn't decided whether to tell Ben her news, or wait till afterwards, when she was sure.

She glanced at herself in the looking-glass, and decided against it. But as she ran down the steps to where Jericho was holding the door of the motor, she changed her mind.

To find Ben, they had to drive all the way down to the gates and then turn left, heading west up the Fever Hill Road to the fringes of Pinchgut Wood, where Ben had set up a schooling ground at the edge of the estate. He was in the paddock, school-ing his new grey mare, who seemed to be giving him an unusual amount of trouble.

When he saw Sophie getting out of the motor, he cantered over to her. But he did not dismount, and was clearly preoccupied with the mare.

'I can't work out what's got into her,' he told Sophie, putting his hand on the mare's shivering neck. 'Yesterday she was mild as milk, and today she nearly threw me—'

'Ben,' cut in Sophie impatiently, 'may I have a word?'

'Course you can,' he said. But he was looking at the horse.

'A proper word,' said Sophie.

'Right,' said Ben.

'Oh, never mind,' muttered Sophie. 'I'll tell you later.'

Turning on her heel, she stalked back to the motor. To her surprise she found herself blinking back tears. And it didn't help that the wind was getting up, and whipping the dust into her eyes.

It's just this wretched weather, she told herself as she asked Jericho to drive her into Town. I shouldn't be surprised if we're in for a storm.

'Now what's got into her?' murmured Ben as he watched his wife driving off. 'And what's got into you too, my beauty? Hm?' he said to the mare.

The mare sidestepped and tossed her head.

With a sigh, Ben jumped down and started walking her in

circles, talking to her softly under his breath. Usually horses listened to him, but today the mare would not be soothed. She kept chewing the bit and showing the whites of her eyes.

When a horse was upset, Ben paid attention. He wondered what the mare had sensed that he could not. Whatever it was, it wasn't good.

An old man in blue overalls was coming down Pinchgut Hill. When he saw Ben, he came over and leaned on the fence. 'Bad weather on the way, Master Ben,' he called.

Ben led the mare over to him. He knew old Eliphalet Tait from years back, when he'd holed up at his place in the Cockpits for a while. 'How bad will it get, Father?' he asked, using the proper form of address among country people.

Old Eliphalet sucked his teeth and watched a john crow flying towards the hills. 'Well I goin tell you a ting, Master Ben,' he began. 'Down at Salt Wash, the people, they coming inland, like the john crow.'

Ben thought about that. He wished now that he'd listened to whatever it was Sophie had wanted to tell him, instead of letting her go. For a moment he considered riding after her. But he'd never catch up with the motor. Besides, if Eliphalet was right, and a storm blew up – or God forbid, something worse – she would know to take shelter in Town, where she'd have a better chance than he would out here.

Swiftly he made a mental review of his workers and the servants up at the house. All of them were capable people, who'd need minimal direction to get things battened down. But the horses – *Christ*, the horses. That morning they'd been brought in from pasture for the monthly farrier's visit, and now they were all in the enclosure on the banks of Tom Spring. If a storm blew up, they might panic and trample each other. He had to get them into the stables, fast.

He turned back to Eliphalet. 'What about you, Father? You want a ride up to the house? Take shelter with the rest of us in the cellars?'

The old man bared his toothless gums in a grin. 'You don trouble bout me, Master Ben, from dis I can take care I self. But watch youself, sah. Don go losing that other eye.'

Ben returned his grin. 'Thanks, I'll bear that in mind.' Swinging up into the saddle, he squinted at the faraway great house. One of the irritating things about losing an eye is that distances are so hard to judge. It had to be three miles; and when he got there, a fair amount to do, seeing everyone safe . . .

He'd better get moving.

Two hours earlier

'You have chosen a singular time for a visit, Captain Palairet,' said Miss May Monroe as she rearranged her grey-gloved talons on the head of her cane. 'There is a hurricane on the way. Or did you not know?'

'A *hurricane*?' said Adam. 'I was told it was only a storm.'

'You were misinformed.'

Adam took that in silence. But he had no intention of being intimidated into leaving. He'd come for information, and, hurricane or no, he meant to get it. Even if it took all morning.

The old lady who sat before him on her hard mahogany chair had turned a hundred the previous month. She was so shrunken that it seemed inconceivable that there could be flesh and blood beneath the stiff folds of her pewter silk gown. She belonged to another time: a time when a lady never ventured out in daylight for fear of the tropical sun; a time when she never, ever, leaned back in her chair.

'A hurricane,' Miss Monroe said again, and there was a gleam of satisfaction in her inflamed blue eyes. 'It is to be depended upon, Captain Palairet. The signs are all there.' She paused for breath. 'Since yestereve,' she went on, 'a swell has battered the Monroe quays; the quays that my father built. And a long swell, Captain Palairet, a swell which is out of all proportion to the strength of the wind, is an early sign of a hurricane. You shall soon find out that I am correct.'

'I don't doubt it, Miss Monroe,' Adam replied.

And yet, sitting here in the dim, wood-panelled gallery, lit only by a glimmer of daylight seeping through the louvres, it seemed impossible. He could hardly even hear the sounds of the street below. A *hurricane* . . .

He thought of Max, whom he'd left chatting happily to Mrs Herapath in her little town house further down the street; Max whom he'd only brought to Jamaica at the last minute, when Maud had sprained her ankle.

'There is no need for concern,' said Miss Monroe with icy scorn. 'The townspeople will take shelter in the church, as they always do. St Peter's will see them through.'

'What about you, Miss Monroe?' said Adam. 'Shall I help you to the church?'

With her cane, the old lady rapped the parquet. 'I shall remain here, in my house, as I always have.'

'But—'

'Captain Palairet. I have seen more hurricanes than you have seen years. I intend to see one more.' She paused, and her narrow corseted chest rose as she sucked in another breath. 'Besides, it will not arrive for another few hours.'

Adam bit back a smile. 'You're remarkably well informed, Miss Monroe.'

'I make it my business to be, Captain Palairet. Now, no more talk of the weather,' she said, dismissing hurricanes as if they were April showers. 'You arrived on the Northside only last night, no doubt eager to see your – *beloved*,' she enunciated the word with disdain, and Adam felt himself reddening, 'and *yet*,' she went on, 'I am the first person on whom you call. I find that singular.'

Adam opened his mouth to reply, but she silenced him with a stare.

'Permit me to hazard a guess as to why, Captain Palairet. You seek information. You seek to know more about Cornelius Traherne.'

Adam was too astonished to reply. The old lady was right. On the steamer from Southampton he'd had plenty of time to think, and he'd realized that simply asking Belle to marry him wasn't going to solve anything. There was something about Traherne – something that was getting in the way, at least in her mind. He had to find out what. So who better to ask than the old lady who knew all that went on in Trelawny?

He asked Miss Monroe how she knew.

'That you wish to enquire about Traherne?' The thin lips tightened with contempt. 'Sir, you broadcast your intentions the moment you arrived, by asking after the whereabouts both of the gentleman in question, and of my great-great-grand-niece, Miss Isabelle Lawe. A singular enquiry, and one which put me in mind of a visit I received many years ago.' Again the grey-gloved talons rearranged themselves on the head of the cane. 'Miss Lawe was still a child at the time.' She paused, remembering, then brought herself back to the present. 'Such an evil man,' she said to the room at large.

Adam felt a flicker of unease. What did she mean?

'I have long known the worst of him,' she went on. 'But I have bided my time.' The chill blue gaze returned to him. 'So, Captain Palairet. We find ourselves in accord, do we not? For I, too, want something from you.'

Adam blinked. 'What can I do?' he said.

'I have lived for precisely one century,' began Miss Monroe, 'and this year will be my last.'

Protestations of regret would have been hypocritical, so Adam remained silent. That earned him a wintry gleam of approval.

'Before I die,' the old lady went on, 'I wish to attend to one final matter.' She paused. 'I had hoped to obtain assistance from my great-great-grand-niece, Miss Isabelle Lawe. She has not, however, seen fit to honour me with a visit.' Again she broke off, and Adam realized with a flash of compassion how much this interview was costing her. 'I have been – remiss,' she continued. 'I have left this almost too late. So your arrival, Captain Palairet, is fortunate. Except that I do not believe in chance.'

'Miss Monroe—'

'Do not interrupt.' Another laboured breath. 'You wish to marry my great-great-grand-niece. I wish to settle my matter. Our interests coincide. Cornelius Traherne must be brought down.'

Two hours later, Cornelius Traherne was sitting down to a solitary luncheon in the state dining room at Parnassus when a footman informed him that a parcel had arrived from Falmouth.

'A parcel?' said Traherne, glancing up from his saddle of mutton with a scowl. 'Why the devil are you bothering me now?'

He was not in the best of tempers. His meal had been interrupted once already, when a stiffening norther had forced him in from the verandah. Interruptions played the very devil with his digestion, and this constant wind wasn't helping in the least.

'It from Town, Master Cornelius,' said the footman, who was beginning to shake. 'From Miss May Monroe.'

Traherne blinked. In seventy-three years he'd never received so much as a visiting card from Miss May Monroe. What was this about?

Wiping his mouth with his napkin, he watched the footman bring in a flat, oblong parcel slightly larger than a book, neatly wrapped in brown paper and string. It looked ordinary enough, but the footman seemed glad to be rid of it. Something about it made Traherne feel cold.

'Out,' he told the servants.

They fled.

His heart was pounding unpleasantly as he cut the string. The brown paper seemed to fall away of its own accord. Inside was a plain, unadorned box of polished Jamaican mahogany, with an envelope of thick ivory card lying on top. For reasons he chose not to acknowledge to himself, Traherne refrained from lifting the lid of the box, and decided to read the note first.

It gave him an unpleasant little jolt to see that the name on the back of the envelope, scratched in spidery copperplate, was that of Miss Monroe herself.

'I wonder what the old witch wants with me,' he said out loud. His voice echoed in the enormous dining room. He didn't sound as calm as he would have wished.

The envelope contained a single sheet of ivory writing paper on which five lines had been carefully inscribed. There was no opening greeting. Perhaps for the first time in her life, Miss Monroe had departed from proper form.

For six generations, she wrote, *your family, sir, has been a stain on the parish of Trelawny. Of all of them, you have been by far the worst.*

Traherne felt the sweat starting out on his forehead. Of all the confounded . . .

I write to make you aware that you are about to be exposed for what you truly are. This will be unavoidable. It is therefore time for you to commit the first decent act in your reprehensibly long life, and bring it to an end. The note was signed *May Alice Falkirk Monroe.*

Traherne tried to laugh. Muttering 'Senile old fool', he tore the note into fragments. Then he tore the fragments into fragments, and scattered the pieces on the floor. His heart was racing. He could feel his face flaming.

It's that Lawe girl, he told himself as he got to his feet and began to pace the dining room. She's always been malicious. Tainted, like all the Durrants. You can see it in their eyes . . . Oh, yes. It's her. She's been biding her time, but now she's enlisted the help of that old witch to do me down.

But what does she imagine she can do? Who would ever believe her? If it wasn't so bizarre, it would be laughable.

You are about to be exposed . . . this will be unavoidable . . .

'Nothing is unavoidable,' said Traherne between his teeth.

He rang for the footman. 'Have the motor sent round directly,' he said when the man appeared. 'I need to go to Burntwood. At once.'

The footman swallowed and shook his head and tried to speak all at once. 'Motor car not working, Master Cornelius. The tyres—'

'Then saddle my horse,' snapped Traherne.

'But the wind, Master Cornelius,' hazarded the footman. 'There's a big blow getting up, and—'

'I *said*, saddle my horse.'

When the footman had gone, Traherne turned back to the box which lay in wait for him on the table. His heart was still racing unpleasantly, although whether with rage at Isabelle Lawe, or something else, he could not have said.

But he was not afraid. Oh, no, not in the slightest.

Wiping his damp hands on his napkin, he lifted the lid.

Inside, on a bed of faded blue velvet, lay a silver-handled duelling pistol.

'But he should have been here an hour ago!' cried Mamma, pushing the twins before her down the corridor.

'Mamma, he wouldn't have set out in this,' said Belle, raising her voice above the noise of the wind.

'Yes he would,' insisted Mamma. 'It wasn't as bad as this an hour ago.'

'And Papa did promise,' said Douglas and Lachlan in unison. They were keeping close together, now and then glancing up at their mother with big round eyes.

Burntwood was in a state of controlled uproar. Both the upper storeys had been evacuated, and the great inner shutters securely nailed shut. The men were preparing to take refuge in the cellars, while the female nurses – all nine of them – were feverishly laying in supplies of water and food in the cutwind, to make ready for a long, cramped stay.

Almost as soon as Mamma had arrived, the wind had strengthened alarmingly. The electricity had been the first to go. It was now so dark that they could hardly see to find their way along the corridors.

'He might have set out and then had an accident,' Mamma told Belle as she herded her children through the dining hall towards the west wing, where the door of the cutwind stood open. 'You stay in there with the twins, and I'll take the dog cart—'

'*No!*' cried Belle and Drum together.

'Mrs Lawe,' said Drum, pulling everyone out of the way of a large nurse hurrying past with a pile of blankets in her arms. 'You cannot drive alone in an open dog cart for eight miles through the backroads in a hurricane.'

'I'll get there before it hits,' said Mamma. 'But I've got to find my husband. He's still not up to his full strength, whatever he might think.'

At the other end of the dining hall, someone shouted for Drum, and he turned his head. 'I'll be back,' he told Belle. Then: 'Don't let her go anywhere.'

'Come along,' said Mamma. 'Into the cutwind with the lot of you. Quickly. The others are already inside.'

The great bulletwood door stood open on a shadowy interior that was dimly lit by a hurricane lamp hanging from the ceiling. A musty chill flowed from within. The twins eyed the entrance doubtfully.

'Do we have to?' said Lachlan.

'Yes,' snapped Mamma. 'Right now. And be quiet, and do everything your sister tells you.'

The twins edged unwillingly into the gloom, where the nurses welcomed them with gleaming white smiles.

'Mamma,' said Belle, 'I'm not letting you—'

'Oh yes you are,' said her mother. Her face was set, and in the stormy light Belle could see the effort she was making to keep her composure. 'He should have been here by now,' she muttered. 'If he's out there on the road – unconscious, or worse . . .' Her voice trailed off.

Over her mother's shoulder, Belle saw Drum reappear and start down the corridor towards them. He looked harried, but utterly capable. She thought quickly. 'You are not,' she told her mother, 'going out in that dog cart.'

'Belle, I told you—'

'No,' said Belle. Putting her hands on her mother's shoulders, she pushed her bodily into the cutwind. 'I'll go,' she said. 'You stay here with the twins.'

Her mother opened her mouth to protest, but Belle talked her down. 'No arguments.' Over her shoulder she spoke to Drum. 'That's everyone inside, help me shut the door. And don't let my mother out till it's over, whatever she says.'

Mamma clutched her hand. 'Belle—'

'I'll find him,' said Belle. 'I promise.'

In the final moment before the door slammed shut, she reached into her satchel and pulled out the sky-blue envelope. 'Here,' she said, pressing it into her mother's hands. 'If anything happens, open it. You'll understand.'

'*Belle*—'

Belle slammed the door shut.

Drum leaned against it. 'I won't let them out till it's over,' he said. 'I promise.'

Belle bit her lower lip hard. 'Thank you,' she said when she could speak.

She started for the main doors, but he held her back. 'Belle, you can't—'

'Yes I can,' she said fiercely. 'I'm not mad, Drum. I know what I'm doing. If I take your horse and go by the backroads, I can reach Eden before it hits.'

'But you don't know that. I can't let you—'

'You haven't got a choice!' she cried. 'Now stay here as you promised, and look after them! I've got to go and find my father.'

CHAPTER THIRTY-NINE

Lightning flickered out at sea as Belle urged her mount past the Maputah works. The wind screamed in her ears. Palm fronds whipped past her. The sky was as dark as dusk, and she knew that it wouldn't be long before the full force of the hurricane hit.

But as she bent low against the gelding's neck, a strange, fierce exultation surged through her. Whatever happened now, she was free. She'd given the envelope to Mamma. She'd lanced the boil.

'It helps so much that you know,' Margaret had said. 'That you don't mind.'

'Of course I don't mind,' Belle had told her. 'It wasn't your fault.'

It wasn't your fault. How simple. How true.

She felt as if a great weight had been lifted from her shoulders. She felt powerful and ready for anything . . .

Now she had to find Papa.

She clattered into the works yard and skittered to a halt. 'Papa!' she shouted.

No answer. Urging the big gelding forward, she checked the boiling-house and the distillery, the steam engine shed, the trash-house, and the carpenters' and coopers' sheds. Nothing. Good. That must mean they'd already taken cover.

But as she turned to go, a horseman appeared at the gates,

blocking her way. To her astonishment, she recognized Cornelius Traherne.

His face was chalky white, and beads of sweat stood out on his forehead. A palm frond flew past his face, but he didn't even flinch. His pale blue eyes were fixed on Belle.

She dug in her heels to ride past him, but he moved his mount sideways to block her.

'I won't let you do this,' he said. His voice was oddly flat, and hardly audible above the scream of the wind.

'What are you talking about?' she cried. 'Get out of my way. I have to—'

'You could never bring me down. I'm too strong for you. I'll always be too strong.'

'Have you gone mad?' cried Belle. 'We're in the middle of a hurricane! My father might be lying somewhere, injured in the road – and you're worrying about your reputation?'

'I won't let you bring me down,' he said again, still in that dead, toneless voice.

'I don't care about bringing you down!' shouted Belle, fighting to keep control of her mount. 'All I ever wanted was to be free of you!'

A furious gust of wind lifted a panel of zinc on the boiling-house roof, and Traherne's horse squealed. 'I'll crush you,' he said. 'I'll crush you like a cockroach.'

Belle reined in her mount. 'Cornelius,' she said, and the very act of speaking his name increased her sense of power. 'Can't you see that it's over? Can't you understand? It's no longer our "little secret". People know. I'm free. You don't matter any more.'

For the first time something flickered in the pale goat eyes.

And as Belle faced him, she saw him with startling clarity: no longer the monster of her nightmares, but a lonely, vicious old man with a festering darkness at his core.

'Now get out of my way,' she told him. She dug in her heels and put her mount forward.

Traherne moved to cut her off, but her gelding was too fast, and she shot through the gates. As she thundered down the road towards Eden, she heard a grinding roar behind her, and looked back to see a part of the boiling-house roof peel off and go crashing to the ground. The works yard, the gates, Traherne – all disappeared in a choking cloud of dust.

She dug in her heels and rode on.

But behind her, as the dust thinned, Traherne staggered out of the gates: limping, dust-covered, but still grasping his horse's reins. Yanking them savagely to bring the animal about, he reached into his saddlebag with his free hand and pulled out a revolver.

The giant bamboo was whipping about like grass as Adam urged his hired mount up the Eden Road.

Why had Belle left Burntwood and started for Eden? The telephone line had gone dead just as Drum was about to tell him, leaving him with nothing but an overpowering dread, and the conviction that he had to find her, hurricane or no, before – as Miss Monroe had chillingly put it – she did something foolish, and took the law into her own hands.

Precisely why Belle might 'do something foolish' to Cornelius Traherne was a revelation the old witch had thoroughly enjoyed making just as Adam was about to leave.

'Of course,' she had said, her voice dripping with distaste, 'in the case of my great-great-grand-niece, it is no more than conjecture. But conjecture based upon a lifetime's observation of the man himself, and upon the girl's visit to me many years ago . . .'

When she'd finished telling him, she'd sat very straight on her chair and watched him struggle to take it in.

Conjecture it might be, but he knew she was right.

Belle had been a child. A child of thirteen. And Traherne had done that . . .

In moments, everything fell into place. Her self-destructive streak. Her conviction that she belonged in the slums. Her fear of Traherne . . .

Miss Monroe had made him promise to bring down Traherne if she didn't live to do it herself: a promise, he'd told her, that he hardly needed to give, since he would do it with pleasure. 'Then be sure to act with despatch,' she had told him, the blue gaze glittering. 'I have not, as you know, been honoured with a visit from the girl herself, but from what I have gathered, I believe she may do something foolish. Perhaps even take the law into her own hands.'

What did she mean? Was she simply making more mischief, or did she know something, or think she knew something? Adam didn't intend to take any chances.

A telephone pole flew past him, and he ducked just in time. Keep your mind on what you're doing, you fool. The aim is to find Belle, not get yourself killed.

But as he urged on his flagging mount, he couldn't help thinking back to that day on the beach at Salt River, seven years before. The dark, unsmiling child walking towards him across the white sand. The silver-haired old gentleman strolling beside her, holding a parasol over her head. Claiming his own. As they'd drawn nearer, the child had raised her head and looked at Adam, and he'd caught something in her eyes: an appeal? Or was his memory coloured by what he'd just learned? It didn't matter. What he did vividly remember was that he'd just had an argument with Celia, and hadn't wanted company – that he'd turned on his heel and walked away.

Well not this time, he told himself grimly.

As he galloped down the iron-hard road, a rider cantered out from a cane-track, leading a struggling grey mare behind him. He was riding fast, without looking where he was going, and it was all Adam could do to avoid a collision.

'Watch where you're going!' the man yelled angrily.

'Same to you!' Adam flung back.

'Good God,' cried the rider, breaking into a wolfish grin. 'Is that you, Palairet?'

Adam took another look, and recognized Ben Kelly, whom he'd last bumped into two years before at battalion HQ. Kelly was in shirtsleeves and covered in red dust, but, bizarrely, he seemed to be enjoying himself. With his black eyepatch he looked like a buccaneer.

'I need to get to Eden,' said Adam. 'Please, Kelly, get out of my way.'

'You won't make Eden on that nag,' Kelly pointed out. 'She's knackered. Or hadn't you noticed?'

Before Adam could reply, Kelly had brought his horse alongside him. 'You any good at riding bareback?'

'What?'

'Take the grey, she's got plenty of go in her, which is why I've just had to chase her halfway across Trelawny to bring her home.'

No time to argue. Besides, he was right. Quickly, Adam slipped off his hired nag, untacked her, and sent her clattering off down the road to Town. While he did so, Ben Kelly somehow managed to keep his own seat, avoid flying branches, and maintain control of the grey mare until Adam had jumped on her back. 'So why Eden,' he said as he tossed Adam the reins.

'I need to find Belle.'

To his surprise, Kelly barked a laugh. 'In a hurricane? Bloody hell, Palairet, your timing's even worse than mine!'

Adam did not reply.

'Come to think of it,' said Kelly, turning thoughtful, 'you're not the first idiot I've met who's out for a ride. I ran into Cornelius Traherne a while back. He was heading for Eden too.'

'*Traherne?*' cried Adam, reining in his horse. 'When? When did you see him?'

'Half an hour? Why?'

The pieces were falling into place, and Adam didn't like the picture they made. Miss Monroe must have done something to tip off Traherne, and somehow he'd got wind that Belle had left Burntwood, and was heading for Eden . . .

'I think he's after Belle,' he said.

Kelly didn't waste time asking questions. 'Well come on then,' he said, yanking his mount's head round. 'What are we waiting for?'

Ben will have taken shelter in the cellars, Sophie told herself as she followed Mrs Herapath through the crowded church. She tried and failed to picture her husband sedately taking cover. It wouldn't be like Ben. He would take some stupid risk, and get himself—

A gust of wind rattled the windows, and further down the nave a woman cried out in alarm. She was instantly hushed. An old man chided her not to frighten, they all right in the house of the Lord. In other words, there might be a hurricane outside, but there was no need to panic.

It was so dark that the lamps were being lit, and soon the scent of kerosene was mingling with the sweet-onion smell of perspiration. But there was also a heartening aroma of coffee and spiced johnny cake. After all, people still had to eat.

St Peter's was packed, and Sophie had been one of the last to arrive. She'd been surprised at how shaken she felt, and how reassuring it was to see Mrs Herapath's formidable bulk bearing down on her.

'*So* nice that we chanced to meet,' said Mrs Herapath in her cut-glass tones as she sailed through the throng like a brightly coloured galleon with Sophie following in her wake. 'I've made myself a little encampment by the old Mordenner tomb, attracted *quite* a collection of waifs and strays. Here,' she told Sophie over her shoulder, 'you can look after Max.' She indicated a small red-haired boy who was sitting in the shadow of a large roll-top tomb, trying to read a book about parrots.

He seemed faintly familiar. With a jolt, Sophie recognized Sibella's little boy. 'Hello, Max,' she said, surprise momentarily elbowing out her worry over Ben. 'What are you doing in Jamaica?'

'We've only just arrived,' said Max shyly.

'His guardian left him with me for safekeeping,' said Mrs Herapath, as if Max was a library book.

'Adam Palairet?' exclaimed Sophie. 'He's here?'

'I didn't know you knew him,' said Mrs Herapath. Casting a wary glance at Max, she added in French, 'Extraordinary man. Said he had to "find someone", and simply *rode off*! In this!' She waved a plump hand at the storm-dark windows. 'It's always the quiet ones who surprise one, don't you agree? They never—'

She was interrupted by a crash and a splintering of glass, and the scream of the wind grew suddenly louder.

Craning their necks they saw, just below the transept, the branches of a tree poking through one of the upper windows of the church. The people underneath had been liberally showered with leaves and broken glass, and were now brushing themselves

338

off, shaking their heads regretfully at their spoiled food. Some glanced up at the branches in the window, and crossed themselves.

Clutching his book against him like a shield, Max looked from Mrs Herapath to Sophie, then back again.

Aware of his scrutiny, Mrs Herapath affected not to find anything amiss, and calmly started taking off her hat.

'What was that?' Max asked politely.

'Only a tree, dear,' said Mrs Herapath through a mouthful of hatpins. 'One of the duppy trees in the churchyard has fallen over, the poor thing. Happens all the time. Nothing to worry about. It'll simply let in a welcome breath of fresh air.'

Max studied her for a moment. Then, reassured, he went back to his book.

Mrs Herapath caught Sophie's glance and rolled her eyes. 'Incredible,' she said in French, 'how much faith they have in adults at that age.'

'Incredible,' echoed Sophie. She'd just been thinking how reassuring she, too, found Mrs Herapath's beribboned bulk.

A terrific flash of lightning and a peal of thunder – and rain began to hammer on the roof.

Sophie thought of Ben, and told herself firmly that he must have taken cover by now.

People began to pray in earnest. Mrs Herapath studied them curiously, for she herself had given up Christianity when her husband died, in favour of spiritualism. Raising her eyeglass to squint at the duppy tree in the window, she leaned over to Sophie and shouted in her ear, 'I can't help thinking that a spot of obeah might be rather more appropriate!'

Up at Arethusa, they'd finished closing the shutters, and everyone was already down in the cellars. Everyone except Evie.

At the cellar door, Isaac called to his wife to come *quickly*, but she said no, she had something to see to first. One look at her face, and he wisely decided not to argue.

So now here she was in the darkened house, like the last person left alive on a sinking ship, while outside the wind howled and the rain hammered on the roof.

Running to her room, she snatched her bankra and her obeah-stick from beneath the bed, and let herself out onto the back porch. A crazy thing to do: in seconds she was soaked to the skin, and it was all she could manage to stay standing in the onslaught. But she had to be outside to do obeah.

Curiously, though, she wasn't frightened at all. She was in a power to work her turning-spell. Not to take vengeance against Cornelius Traherne, oh no, she wasn't about to go breaking her promise to her mother; but to turn him away from doing harm to Belle.

A glare of lightning lit up the trees bent almost to the ground, and in the flashing light the serpent carved about her mother's obeah-stick writhed.

Squatting in the porch, Evie reached into her bankra and pulled out the handkerchief of Cornelius Traherne that she'd confiscated from Belle seven years before. Quickly she twisted it into a coil and tied it round the neck of the serpent; then she smeared it with the paste she'd prepared of grave-dirt and asafoetida mixed with lime juice, and a few other things, too besides.

Then, bracing herself against the wind, she held the obeah-stick high, and began to chant. Power surged through her like a lightning flash.

Lightning lit up the old guango tree that guarded the turn-off to Eden great house. In the glare, Belle saw that the wind had completely stripped it of its leaves.

The house was in darkness. Shingles were flying off the roof like arrows. 'Papa!' she shouted. '*Papa!*'

She couldn't get through to the front of the house. The path that led to the verandah steps was blocked by the remains of the bath-house roof. Digging in her heels, she put her horse at the wreckage. They sailed over. She cantered into the garden.

A flash of white by the verandah – and there he was, in his shirtsleeves and soaked to the skin, as she was, but unhurt, thank God.

When he saw her, he froze. '*Belle?* What are you doing here?'

'I had to find you!' she shouted above the scream of the wind.

Grabbing the bridle, her father pulled her out of the saddle and into his arms.

Suddenly she was shaking so hard that she could hardly stand. 'I had to find you,' she mumbled into his chest.

'I thought you were at Burntwood,' he said, holding her tight. 'I thought you were with Mamma and the twins.'

'I was – they are – they're in the cutwind – but I—'

A terrific gust of wind nearly blew them off their feet, and above their heads part of the verandah roof lifted and blew down, blocking the way to the cellars at the other side of the house.

The horse reared. Papa grasped the bridle with one hand, and put the other arm round Belle. 'Come on,' he shouted in her ear. 'No time to get to the cellars! I know where we can go.'

A gust of wind dashed what sounded like an entire tree against the outside of the cutwind. It didn't even shudder.

Inside there was an air of cramped and sweaty companionship. No-one was unduly alarmed. Some of the nurses were humming cheerful hymns, and several were also fingering little charm-bags at their necks, just for good measure. The twins were digging each other in the ribs and giggling. Everyone knew they would be safe in the cutwind. In the hundred and seventy years since it was built, it had weathered more hurricanes than anyone could remember – and protected the rest of the great house, too. Burntwood might have a reputation for being 'bad luckid', but no hurricane could bring it down.

A laundrywoman lifted the lid off a basket on her lap and started doling out squares of cornmeal pone and wangla nut brittle. She offered a piece of pone to Madeleine, who managed a tight smile, but shook her head.

It was just over an hour since Belle had pushed her into the cutwind. Had she reached Eden safely? Had she found Cameron? It seemed too much to hope that they would both survive. Madeleine shut her eyes and tried to picture them at Eden, safe and well. If she'd been a believer, she would have prayed.

In her lap, the blue envelope had become damp with sweat from her palms. She opened her eyes and stared down at it.

'If anything happens,' Belle had told her, 'open it. You'll understand.'

Another crash outside. Madeleine's hands tightened on the envelope.

Well, she thought, I think a hurricane counts as 'something happening'. I think it's time to find out what this is about.

The hurricane was on its way.

At Romilly, a tree across the road brought Adam and Ben to a precipitate halt.

'Any time now,' yelled Ben through the wind and the rain, 'and it's going to get dodgy!'

'We'd better take cover under the bridge!' shouted Adam.

'And hope to hell there isn't a flash flood!' cried Kelly, jumping off his horse and leading it down the streaming bank.

In the town house in Falmouth, Miss May Monroe rearranged her gloved talons on the head of her cane, and listened to the waves battering the quays that her father had built over a century before, and waited for the hurricane to strike.

In St Peter's, the inhabitants of Falmouth listened to the sea battering the quays, and redoubled their prayers. Max huddled in Mrs Herapath's lap and hid his face in her bosom, and resolved to describe this adventure *in detail* in his next letter to Julia and Miss McAllister. Sophie clasped her knees and prayed that Ben would make it through alive.

At Arethusa, Evie felt her husband's arms tighten around her as they crouched in the cellar. 'You're soaked,' he said against her temple. She nodded but did not reply. She was thinking of the obeah-stick she'd left planted in the ground, with Traherne's handkerchief wrapped about the serpent's coils.

In the cutwind at Burntwood, Madeleine sat staring at the photograph on her lap as the truth about her daughter crashed over her like a wave. The picture before her was over-exposed, and clearly taken in haste. It showed a young girl – her face in shadow, but recognizably Margaret Cornwallis – seated on a bench, while an old man sat close beside her. Every line of the girl's body was fraught with tension. Cornelius Traherne's liver-spotted hand was planted firmly on her breast.

The photograph was a recent one: Madeleine could still smell the chemicals from the darkroom. But on the back, Belle had written: *Juvenile Fancy Dress Ball, May 1912. Bamboo Walk, June 1912. I could never tell you. Sorry. Belle.*

The fancy dress ball, thought Madeleine. Memory flooded back. Belle dressed as a devil. Traherne . . .

In the undercroft at Eden, Belle huddled against her father while behind them in the gloom, Drum Paget's exhausted gelding munched a bag of oats.

'Where's everyone else?' said Belle, her teeth chattering.

'In the cellar,' said her father, 'where I would have been if you hadn't turned up when you did. I'd only come out for a last look round. Damned lucky I found you.'

Belle nodded, and pressed herself closer against him. His arm tightened round her like an iron bar. When she shut her eyes, she felt the beat of his heart against her cheek. 'Will we get through this?' she said.

'I should think so,' he replied. He sounded astonishingly calm. 'We might lose the roof, but the house and the undercroft should stand.'

'How can you be sure?'

'Bulletwood frame,' he said, stroking her hair. 'They call it bulletwood for a reason, Belle darling. Besides,' he added, and she heard the smile in his voice, 'we're in your mother's darkroom. No hurricane in its right mind would dare come in here. Although when this is over, we shall have some explaining to do about the horse.'

At the turn-off to Eden great house, Cornelius Traherne's horse skittered to a halt. She was in there somewhere, he knew it. He just had to find her. Then everything would be all right.

Above him the guango tree thrashed its leafless limbs. In the flaring lightning it looked oddly threatening, like some sort of skeletal guardian.

Shaking off the thought, Traherne drew his revolver and put his horse forward. 'I won't let you bring me down,' he told Isabelle Lawe under his breath.

Again the lightning flared. And now, beneath the leafless tree, a woman was standing, watching him.

Traherne cried out in alarm.

She was a black woman in a cheap print dress hitched up to her knees. Her head was tied about with a white kerchief, and she was standing completely still, quite unmoved by the chaos around her. Not a fold of her skirt stirred in the raging wind.

Traherne's throat closed. It couldn't be. It couldn't *be*. Grace McFarlane was dead . . .

His horse reared.

The guango tree creaked and groaned.

Then the hurricane hit.

CHAPTER FORTY

They'd been trapped in Mamma's darkroom for nearly twelve hours, and thirst was becoming a problem. A gap at the bottom of the door let in a sliver of light and a breath of air, but it wasn't enough to dispel the fug of sweat, mud and horse. And the door wouldn't budge. Something had fallen across it on the other side: something too heavy for Belle and Papa to shift.

After the endless assault of the hurricane, the stillness was deafening. At first all they could hear was the drip, drip of water, and the rustle of wind in the coconut palms. Then the whistling frogs started up; then the crac-cracs and the croaker lizards. Now the morning was alive with chirruping, twittering and cooing. Sugarbirds and bluequits; wild canaries and jabbering crows; and in the hills, the echoing hammer of a woodpecker.

'Someone will come soon,' said Papa. 'They're probably still digging themselves out of the cellar.'

Unless, thought Belle, they're trapped, like us. She knew her father had thought of that too, but didn't want to frighten her.

'Here.' He put the vacuum flask into her hands. It was the last of the coffee: cold and bitter and refreshing. Many times as they'd sat side by side in the gloom, they'd blessed Mamma's habit of keeping refreshments at hand when she was working.

Belle took a mouthful, then handed back the flask. 'You have some too.'

'Finish it,' said Papa.

She screwed the top on for later, and leaned back against the wall. From the other side of the darkroom, the horse whiffled and shifted his hooves.

'What will we do if no-one comes?' she said.

'Eat the horse,' said Papa.

She blinked. Then she felt him shaking with laughter. 'Darling Belle,' he chuckled, 'you've always had such a sense of the dramatic. Have faith. Someone will come. And if they don't, we'll find a way to get out.'

She heard him reaching into his pocket. Then a match flared. 'I think,' he said, getting stiffly to his feet, 'it's time we had some more light.'

Gratefully, Belle watched him light the kerosene lamp on Mamma's work table. He was making things better, just as he used to do when she was five years old, and had padded into his study after a nightmare.

Once the lamp was lit, he sat down again, and together they watched the steady glow illuminate the photographs pegged to the walls. The twins prowling through guinea grass, brandishing sugar-cane spears. Sophie seated on the folded roots of a silk-cotton tree, absorbed in a book. Ben leaning over a fence to talk to a mare. Papa down on one knee, frowning as he disentangled a mastiff puppy from its lead. And Belle herself, laughing with Mrs Herapath on the verandah.

Her throat tightened. She hadn't even known that Mamma had had her camera with her that day. 'She's very good, isn't she?' she said, to mask her emotion.

'So are you,' said Papa.

She turned to him in surprise.

'The other day, Sophie showed me some of your work. You've inherited your mother's talent. You both have a knack for revealing the truth.' His lip curled. 'That is, when it suits you.'

Belle clasped her hands about her knees. She felt a sense of enormous peace, and yet at the same time of utter exhaustion.

If they got out of this alive, Mamma would tell him about Cornelius Traherne. Belle tried to imagine how he would feel; what he would do. It was too huge. She couldn't manage it. Besides, what mattered was that now, as they sat here together, they understood each other.

Turning to him, she noticed suddenly how tired he was looking. The lines at the sides of his mouth were deeply etched, and when he moved, he did it awkwardly, as if his back was giving him pain.

She put her hand on his arm. 'Are you all right?'

He opened his mouth to reply, but then there was a knock at the door.

'Hello?' called a voice. 'Anyone in there?'

Belle leapt to her feet. 'Ben? *Ben!*'

'Belle? Are you all right? Is your father in there too?'

'Together with a very smelly horse,' called Papa.

A bark of laughter. 'Hang on. We'll soon have you out of there.'

His voice faded as he turned away to speak to someone else. Then they heard a grinding of wood and a scrape of stone. A horse squealed, eliciting a deafening answering whinny from the gelding. Then the slit of daylight widened and the door broke open to let in a blinding glare – and Ben.

He was covered in red mud, and his eyepatch was askew. 'Crikey,' he said. 'Look at you two.'

Belle threw herself into his arms.

'Made a bit of a mess of things in here, haven't you?' he said when she'd released him. 'Cameron, you're going to have some explaining to do to your wife.'

Papa made his way to the door and grasped Ben's hand. 'What about the others?' he said. 'Did you get to the cellars?'

'We're liberating them right now,' said Ben with a grin. 'All safe and sound, even the dogs. No need to worry.' Then the grin faded, and he touched Papa's arm. 'The house wasn't so lucky, I'm afraid.'

Papa met his eyes. 'How bad?'

Ben hesitated. 'It took the brunt. Although the stables and out-houses are untouched. That's hurricanes for you. The old guango

347

tree came down, too. Killed a horse, and—' He broke off, and Belle sensed that there was something else he wasn't telling them. 'Well,' he added, 'like I said, it killed a horse.'

Papa pushed past him and Belle followed him, blinking into the daylight.

They reeled back.

The entire upper floor of the house was gone. The beautiful high-ceilinged rooms with their golden panelling; the airy fretwork eaves; even the wide verandah with its flower-entangled balustrade. All had been carried away into the forest. What remained was the undercroft where they stood, the bulletwood skeleton of the upper floor – and the double sweep of the white marble steps, showing through a wreck of toppled tree-ferns and fallen sweetwoods.

Papa sat down heavily on a tree trunk, and his shoulders sagged. He rubbed his face, and Belle was alarmed to see how his hand shook.

She met Ben's eyes, then glanced quickly away.

Ben muttered something about the cellars, and took himself off.

Belle went to stand beside her father, and tentatively touched his shoulder. 'We'll rebuild,' she said shakily. 'It – it was a ruin before, when you found it. You made it beautiful. We'll do it again.'

He nodded and forced a smile, but she could tell that he was only doing it for her benefit. She wished Mamma was here. Mamma would know what to say.

At that moment, someone came round the side of the house, picking his way through the debris. As he emerged from the shadow of a fallen coconut palm, he saw her and came to a halt. 'Hello, Belle,' said Adam.

Belle sat down heavily beside her father.

Like Ben's, his clothes were caked in red mud. There was a cut on his hand that was bleeding freely, although he didn't seem to have noticed, and a ragged new scar that started at his left temple and disappeared into the dark stubble at his jaw. His eyes were red with fatigue, and he wasn't smiling – but she could tell that he wanted to smile.

'You,' she said numbly.

Adam hesitated. He glanced at Papa. Then he took a step forward and awkwardly held out his hand. 'Adam Palairet, sir,' he said, sounding bizarrely as if he was introducing himself at a cricket match. 'We met a few years ago? But I don't suppose you—'

'I know who you are,' Papa said stiffly. To Belle's astonishment, he ignored Adam's outstretched hand. 'My sister-in-law told me all about you. You're the young man who sent back my daughter's letter without a reply.'

Adam went very still.

Belle winced.

Papa did nothing to break the silence.

At last Adam spoke. 'There was, um, a reason for that.'

'Really,' said Papa, visibly unimpressed.

Belle knew that she ought to say something, but her mind had gone blank. She was exhausted and filthy, and she'd just lost her home. And now here was Adam – *Adam* – and Papa was bristling at him like a mastiff who's just scented an intruder. Suddenly all she wanted to do was burst into tears.

'I think,' she said, 'we need to go and find Mamma.'

CHAPTER FORTY-ONE

Only four people attended the funeral of Cornelius Traherne. His estate manager; his attorney; Adam Palairet (in his capacity as guardian to Cornelius's grandson); and Olivia Herapath – who reported the proceedings to everyone else.

Her account had very little to do with Traherne, whom she'd always cordially disliked, and everything to do with Parnassus. The estate had taken the full force of the hurricane, and as Traherne had diversified into coffee instead of keeping to the more storm-resistant cane, most of it now lay in ruins, including the great house itself.

'The question is,' said Mrs Herapath as she held court in her drawing-room the following morning, 'who will take it on? There's the elder son out in Australia, but Cornelius cut him off years ago; and poor Davina succumbed to the 'flu; besides, she only had daughters; which of course leaves little Max Clyne. As if the poor child didn't have too much money already! Do you know, I happened to bump into that extraordinary guardian of his this morning, and he told me that he's inclined to appoint a manager, and take him back to Scotland until he's of age. I must say, that seems sensible . . .'

If the Traherne funeral attracted only four mourners, it was a different matter the following Monday, when the whole of

Trelawny turned out as a mark of respect. Shops closed early, and landowners gave their workers a half-day off. On the roads from the Cockpits steady trickles of people made their way down from the hamlets of Disappointment and Turnaround.

By half past three, the Fever Hill Road from Falmouth to the gatehouses was lined with people waiting in silence to watch the hearse go by. Some were there out of respect, and many more out of a kind of superstitious dread; but afterwards all agreed that as they watched the black horses drawing the carriage through the red dust – and later as they thronged the slopes of Fever Hill to see the new tomb sealed at the Monroe Burying-place – they experienced something else, too. A sense that a part of old Trelawny had gone for ever, with the passing of Great-Aunt May.

As a child she had survived the Christmas Rebellion, when fifty-two great houses had gone up in flames. Afterwards she had sat beside her terrible old father and watched the appalling reprisals that he'd visited on his slaves. She'd witnessed the emancipation and the breaking up of many of the great estates. She'd lived through hurricanes, earthquakes, cane-fires, cholera and influenza.

She'd despised pleasure and enthusiasm, as well as the poor, the sick, and the less than beautiful. Her hatred of the Trahernes had corroded her soul. But she'd punished herself far more harshly than she'd ever managed to harm anyone else, and for all her faults, she had been a living link with the past.

Now she was gone, having died as she had lived: alone and undaunted in her shadowy drawing-room. It was said that when they found her, she was sitting bolt upright, supported by her corseting. In death, as in life, Great-Aunt May did not lean back in her chair.

Once her death became known, a rumour swiftly spread that she would make an unquiet ghost. Soon it was an open secret that Master Kelly had asked Evie Walker to do what was needed to stop the old lady from walking.

'But Great-Aunt May can't walk any more, can she?' Lachlan asked his mother after the funeral refreshments had been consumed and the crowds had finally dispersed.

'She is dead, isn't she?' asked Douglas doubtfully.

'It's just an expression,' said their mother, rolling her eyes at Belle. 'Now off you go and ask Hannah to draw you a bath.' The family was staying at Fever Hill for the time being, Ben's great house having narrowly escaped the worst of the hurricane. Mamma watched the twins race each other to the back verandah, then turned to Belle. 'Let's take a turn about the lawns,' she suggested.

Belle hesitated. 'I was going for a drive with Papa. There's something I want him to help me with.'

'I know,' said Mamma, 'but this won't take long.'

She sounded nervous, and Belle guessed what was coming. It was five days since the hurricane – five days since Mamma had opened the sky-blue envelope – and apart from a long look and a press of the hand, they hadn't acknowledged it at all.

There had been so much to do. Great swaths of Trelawny had been devastated – provision grounds swept away, the village of Salt Wash reduced to ruins – although, amazingly, there had been very little loss of life. The whole parish had been working from dawn till dusk to distribute emergency rations, and re-establish water and power.

A perfect excuse, thought Belle as she glanced at her mother, to avoid painful conversations. And she should know, for she'd been avoiding Adam. After that first appearance at Eden, he'd stayed in Falmouth with Max to help in the relief operation. But from the way he'd looked at her, she knew that he'd been told about Traherne. She couldn't face him. Not yet. It was still too raw.

Besides, she didn't even know what to feel about Traherne.

She knew that she ought to feel *something* now that he was dead. Relief, perhaps. Or a sense of vindication. But she could not. Perhaps, she reflected as she walked across the lawn, that was because the sense of release had come *before* his death, when she'd given the photograph to Mamma. By the time he'd died, he had become irrelevant.

'Moses is doing wonders at Eden,' said her mother, cutting across her thoughts. 'I do wish your father would go and see it. But he still finds every excuse not to.'

'I know,' said Belle.

'I'm worried about him. It's hit him harder than I would have expected. I've never seen him so disheartened.'

'Perhaps he just needs time.'

Her mother pressed her lips together and nodded. 'Ben's been marvellous. Forcing him to help with the relief effort. Dragging him along to see the plans for the new village. You know, until this happened, they were never really easy with one another, but now . . . And of course,' she added with a curl of her lip, 'Ben keeps asking him for advice. The other day, your father told him just to think of it as another foal on the way. Apparently that did nothing to reassure.'

Belle gave the expected smile, but inside she felt breathless and shaky.

Her mother picked a dead leaf from the grass and turned it in her fingers. 'How did you ever manage,' she said without meeting Belle's eyes, 'to take that photograph?'

For a moment, Belle was caught off balance. Then she squared her shoulders and told her mother everything: about keeping watch on Margaret Cornwallis, and following her to her next encounter with Traherne; and waiting for a gust of wind to mask the click of the camera; and making a sudden noise immediately afterwards, to startle him into leaving. And that final talk with Margaret before she left for London – although Belle didn't go into details about what was said.

'She was lucky to have you,' said Mamma. She sounded wistful. 'When it happened to you, you had no-one.'

'It wasn't that I couldn't talk to you,' Belle said carefully. 'It was that I felt – I deserved it. I know it sounds odd, but I felt – tainted. No, not exactly that. As if I'd always been tainted, and he had merely discovered what I was really like.'

Mamma walked on in silence. 'You know,' she said at last, 'when I was a child, and for a long time afterwards – well, until I met your father – I felt the same.'

Belle stared at her. 'You?' Her mother had always seemed so assured. So beautiful and accepted and loved.

'Things happened to me . . . Oh, some day I'll tell you, but not now. The point is, I know what it's like to feel dirty and worthless. It can take years to get over. But one does, Belle. One really does. You don't ever forget it, but in an odd way it becomes a part of you, and it makes you stronger.'

'I had no idea,' said Belle.

Her mother gave her a shaky smile. 'Well. Why would you?'

For a while they walked side by side. Then Mamma said, 'That good-looking Captain Palairet. Are you going to marry him?'

Belle swallowed. 'I don't know. He hasn't asked me.'

Mamma snorted. 'You've hardly put yourself in his way.'

'Well, no, but—'

'I just want to say,' said Mamma, 'that if he does, and you say yes, I should be delighted. And I think you ought seriously to consider living in Scotland.'

Belle's eyes filled. She'd been thinking about that a lot. The pull of Cairngowrie was strong. But to leave all this . . .

'You wouldn't really be leaving,' her mother said gently. 'Not now that we know each other so much better. Besides, I heartily approve of your living in Scotland.'

'Why?' said Belle.

'No malaria, no earthquakes, and no hurricanes. As a mother, one thinks of these things.' Before Belle could speak, she added quickly, 'Oh, look. There's your father with the dog cart.'

'Mamma—'

'We'll talk more later, Belle. I promise. Now hurry along. You don't want to keep him waiting.'

Belle put her hand on her shoulder and kissed her cheek.

Mamma blushed. 'What's that for?'

'For being my mother,' said Belle.

'So where would you like to go?' said Papa as he flicked the reins and told the pony to walk on.

'Down to the road and turn left,' said Belle.

'You sound very sure.'

'I know what I'm after,' she replied.

'And you're still not going to tell me.'

'Not yet.'

For a while they drove in silence beneath the royal palms. After the hurricane had savaged Parnassus and then Falmouth, it had veered south to strike Eden, but had left Fever Hill largely unscathed, apart from a swath of destruction across the eastern cane-pieces. But if Papa felt the disparity, he did not show it. He had money enough to rebuild. Money wasn't the problem. It was the will to go on.

'You ought to see what Moses has achieved with the house,' said Belle when the silence had gone on long enough.

Her father sighed. 'Is this some plot of your mother's?'

She smiled. 'No. It's some plot of mine.'

'Hm. Somehow I don't find that reassuring.' He caught her eye and returned her smile, and suddenly she knew that Mamma had told him about Traherne.

She turned back to the road. 'When did she tell you?' she said.

'Just before the funeral.'

Found out, found out. Her skin prickled. She couldn't breathe. 'I'm sorry,' she said. 'I mean, sorry that I couldn't tell you. I just—'

'Belle,' he said gently, 'there's nothing to be sorry about.' Taking the reins in one hand, he put the other arm round her and drew her close. 'It's all right,' he said. 'Everything's going to be all right.'

For a while they drove in silence, while the pony clip-clopped across the bridge over Tom Spring and past the old aqueduct and the ruined slave village, and Belle leaned against her father and struggled not to cry.

At last he said, 'What you must have gone through . . .' He shook his head. 'I always knew you'd inherited the best of your mother. And believe me, that's saying something.'

She sniffed. He handed her his handkerchief. 'But I have to say,' he added, and his voice hardened, 'that I'm not as civilized as either you or your mother. It's just as well the guango tree got him. If not, I'd have ripped his spine out.'

One look at his face told her that he meant it. His jaw was knotted, and his light grey eyes were glassy as he stared at the road.

He'll be all right, thought Belle. If I can just get him to Eden . . .

They passed between the gatehouses, and turned west into the Fever Hill Road, and after a few hundred yards Belle asked him to stop.

'Here?' he said in surprise. There was nothing around them except nursery cane-pieces and a few straggling trees at the edge of the road.

'Here,' Belle said firmly.

'Why?'

'You'll see.'

The day after the funeral, Adam put Max in a hired dog cart and drove them both up to Eden.

He'd paid his respects to old Miss Monroe at the church, but hadn't gone on to the reception at Fever Hill great house because he wanted to see Belle alone, after things had quietened down.

That evening, however, a note had arrived from her mother.

Dear Captain Palairet, I was sorry not to see you at Fever Hill this afternoon. What with all the clearing up, I haven't had a chance to thank you properly for rescuing my husband and daughter – which was a blatant untruth, as the day after the 'rescue' she'd sent a charming, deeply felt note of thanks with an invitation to dinner, which he'd politely declined – *but we shall all be up at Eden tomorrow afternoon,* she went on, *for a picnic and a look at the renovations – if that's the right word when one's practically starting from scratch. Belle will be there, of course. You ought to come. Say around five? Best wishes, Madeleine Lawe.*

No coyness, no beating about the bush. It made him want to know her better.

He and Max arrived as ordered around five, to find Mrs Lawe sitting with her sister on the verandah steps, with the remains of a picnic spread out beside them. The ruins of the garden had, with tropical vigour, already acquired a coating of thunbergia that masked the worst of the scars, and behind them the bones of the new house were just beginning to rise from the undercroft.

'I'm afraid you've just missed my husband,' Mrs Lawe told Adam with a glint of amusement. 'He's gone to the works at Maputah to inspect the repairs. But Belle is round by the stables. Why don't you go and find her?'

She offered to keep Max, but Adam decided to take him along for moral support. The last time he'd talked to Belle – really talked – had been at Stranraer. Since then, their only contact had been that stilted exchange after the hurricane, and the letter he'd sent back in Flanders without a reply.

He found her at the bottom of the slope leading down to the stables, kneeling in a patch of red earth that had been cleared of debris. She was planting a tree: a slender sapling with large green leaves that stood just a little taller than Max. The twins were standing by with spades and a watering can, looking solemn.

All three glanced up at their arrival, but nobody spoke. Then Belle turned back to her work.

Ah, thought Adam. So she isn't going to make this easy for me.

'You hold it upright,' she told one of the twins, 'and Douglas, stand back and tell me if it's straight.'

Douglas took a step backward and screwed up his eyes. 'It – yes, it's straight.'

Belle turned to Max. 'Do you agree?'

Max sucked in his lips. 'Um. Yes.'

She smiled at him. 'Thank you, Max.' Pointedly ignoring Adam.

'What kind of tree is it?' asked Max, emboldened by the attention.

'It's a silk–cotton,' said Lachlan.

'We also call them duppy trees,' put in Douglas.

Both were taller than Max by at least a head, and quite clearly sizing him up.

Daunted, he edged closer to Adam.

Belle came to his rescue. 'But *this* one,' she said, 'is actually a Tree of Life. That's what my grandmother used to call them. Her name was Rose, and she used to come to Eden when it was a ruin, and meet my grandfather in secret under the Tree of Life that grew on the hill over there.'

'Is it still there?' said Max.

'Not any more,' said Belle.

'Is that why you're planting another one?'

'Partly,' she said. 'But also because the hurricane blew down the old guango tree which used to guard the house from harm.' She paused, and Adam knew that she was thinking about Traherne. 'And a house,' she went on briskly, 'must always have a guardian tree. Which is why we've just planted a new one, and given it an offering of rum and lime juice to start it off.' She sat back on her heels. 'Lachlan, Douglas, you must promise to water it and talk to it every single day.'

'We promise,' they said.

'Can we give it a blood sacrifice?' said Lachlan.

'Not yet,' said Belle.

Adam decided that he'd been patient long enough. 'Douglas, Lachlan,' he said, 'I want you to show Max the river, so that I can be alone with your sister.'

Max looked shy, and the boys glanced at Belle for instructions. She was busy brushing the dirt off her hands, so they stayed where they were.

Adam reached into his pocket and brought out a handful of change. 'Five shillings each. Lachlan, Douglas, Max. Now off you go, at the double.'

They went.

As he watched them go, Adam felt a twinge of guilt at abandoning Max to the twins. But as they disappeared round the side of the house, he heard Max asking if the river had any seals; and when the twins admitted that it did not, and what was a seal, Max started to tell them. He seemed to be learning to hold his own.

After they'd gone, there was a silence which Belle made no attempt to fill. She got to her feet and pushed back her hair behind her ears, and wiped a smudge of dirt off her nose. She was wearing a loose red cotton frock with a square neck and no jewellery or make-up. Adam thought he had never seen her look so beautiful.

He said, 'It's taken a while to get to see you alone.'

'I've been busy,' she replied, crossing her arms.

He put his hands in his pockets. Then he took them out again. 'How is your papa?'

'Better, I think.' She nodded at the tree. 'He helped me find this, and cleared a space for it himself. It was a way of getting him up here to see the house. Yes, I think he'll be all right.'

'He still doesn't like me,' said Adam.

'Oh dear,' said Belle unfeelingly.

'It turns out,' said Adam, 'that one of my uncles officiated at his court martial.'

Belle laughed.

'It's not funny,' Adam said ruefully.

Again Belle laughed, and he saw that she was just as nervous as he.

'I know that I hurt you,' he said. 'I mean, when I sent back that letter.'

'Yes, you did.'

'Can you forgive me?'

'No.'

He threw her an uncertain look to see if she was joking, but her face gave nothing away. She'd definitely decided not to make this easy for him.

'But you know,' he said, 'you hurt me too.' He hesitated. 'Then afterwards, in hospital, I couldn't see anyone. I couldn't even speak. I didn't – I didn't want you to see me like that.'

'But you can speak now,' she said. 'What happened?'

Again he hesitated. 'I got better.'

She gave him a long look, and he could see that she knew there was more to it than that, and that she intended to find out. But not now.

He said, 'I know about Traherne.'

She caught her lower lip in her teeth, and the colour rose to her cheeks. 'I thought you might.'

'Is he the reason you've been avoiding me?'

'. . . I suppose.'

She was looking down at the duppy tree, struggling to keep her composure. He desperately wanted to take her in his arms.

'How did you find out?' she said, still without looking at him.

'Your Great-Aunt May told me.'

She stared at him. '*Great-Aunt May*?'

'It's a long story,' he said. 'The point is, it doesn't matter. None of it matters. You've got to believe that.'

She swallowed.

He crossed the distance between them and took her in his arms.

'Mind the duppy tree,' she said.

He kissed her.

After a moment's hesitation, she put her hand to the back of his neck and kissed him back.

She smelt of star jasmine and green growing things, and the red earth of Eden. 'God, I missed you,' he murmured into her neck. 'We're going to get married right away. This week. No arguments.'

Her lips curved in the wry smile that he loved. 'Why would you think I'd argue?'

'Because that's what you do.'

'Not this time,' she said.

Behind them a hummingbird hovered over the duppy tree, its wings flashing emerald in the sun. Then it flickered away over Eden.

THE END

The Serpent's Tooth is the third book of the Eden trilogy. The first book, *The Shadow Catcher*, is published in paperback by Corgi. The second book, *Fever Hill*, is published by Bantam Press.

To find out more about Michelle Paver and her novels, visit her website at www.michellepaver.com

ACKNOWLEDGEMENTS AND AUTHOR'S NOTE

As with *The Shadow Catcher* and *Fever Hill*, I must thank my aunt Martha Henderson for her help, particularly as regards hurricanes and the cutwind at Cinnamon Hill. I'd also like to thank Ellie Edmans for assistance with aspects of things Scottish. (Needless to say, however, any errors are of course my own.)

Concerning the story itself, I have taken some liberties with the area to the north of Stranraer, in order to accommodate the estate of Cairngowrie. Similarly, I've somewhat altered the geography around Falmouth, to make room for the fictional estates of Eden, Fever Hill, Burntwood, Arethusa and Parnassus.

As regards the *patois* of the Jamaican people, I haven't attempted to reproduce this precisely, but have instead tried to make it more accessible to the general reader, while retaining, I hope, at least some of its colour and richness.

Michelle Paver